I daydreamed about Brendan. I longed to know what it felt like to have one person eclipse everything bad in your life— be a place of pure joy.

"Why can't I get you out of my head?" I whispered to myself. "I wish I just knew what your deal was."

I leaned against a lamppost, trying to steady my breath and my thoughts. The light above me flickered, catching my attention. I looked straight up into the light. It burned very brightly for a moment—as if it were on a dimmer switch that was suddenly put on full blast. I heard a crackling noise, and nervously stepped away from the lamppost—just as the light inside burst, shards of glass clinking against the frosted glass case....

PRAISE FOR *SPELLBOUND*

"*Spellbound* by Cara Lynn Shultz is my kind of enchanted read. Magic ingredients for teen read perfection: a spunky Buffy-licious witch, a good dose of mayhem, *and* Brendan! When's the next one?"
—Nancy Holder, *New York Times* bestselling author of *Crusade* and the Wicked series

"With its magic ingredients of witty banter, a BFF-worthy heroine, Hot Boys and a super-spooky mystery, *Spellbound* held me in its thrall from beginning to end!"
—Rachel Hawkins, author of the Hex Hall series

"*Spellbound* by Cara Shultz is a rapturous story that adeptly marries the classic fairy tale with the modern experience of the Facebook world. Shultz's debut novel has the potential to do for witches what Stephenie Meyer did for vampires with her Twilight Saga series."
—Trent Vanegas, *Pink Is the New Blog*

Spellbound

CARA LYNN SHULTZ

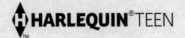

HARLEQUIN®TEEN

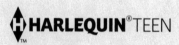HARLEQUIN®TEEN

ISBN-13: 978-0-373-21030-5

SPELLBOUND

Recycling programs for this product may not exist in your area.

For questions and comments about the quality of this book please contact us at Customer_eCare@Harlequin.ca.

www.HarlequinTEEN.com

Printed in U.S.A.

For Grandma. I love you.

Chapter 1

It's always embarrassing to have someone take you to school. Your dad, your mom, anyone with her hair in rollers.

But for my first day as a junior at my new school—a ridiculously expensive private school on New York's Upper East Side—I was being walked to school by my baby cousin. A *freshman*.

It really wasn't that terrible. Even though we grew up apart, Ashley and I were email buddies. She was a sweetheart, there was no doubt of that, but if my knowledge of the inner workings of my familiar old New Jersey public school, Keansburg High, meant anything, I knew that juniors did not hang out with the lower classes. It was like hanging out with a bunch of vegetarians and wearing a bacon necklace.

Talk about unwelcome.

But it was important to my aunt Christine that I got to school early and she was afraid I'd get lost. My great-aunt had taken me in over the summer, and I'd learned quickly that when she got an idea into her head, you were better off just going along with it. I didn't want to argue with her—I owed her everything. My life, really. She'd been asking me to live with her ever since my mom died a year and a half ago, leaving me with Henry, my stepfather whose blood–alcohol content hovered somewhere between "wasted" and "how is he even alive?" But after he nearly killed me last June with his particular style of driving (i.e., blasted), I stopped resisting Christine's offer.

Going from my aunt's place at Park and Sixty-eighth Street to the school at Park and Eighty-sixth Street is fairly basic: walk eighteen blocks left. But since she had been pretty cool about everything—stepping in, giving me a place to stay and leaving me with a "You'll talk to me if you need to" instead of hovering over me—I didn't press it.

Ashley was a bundle of excitement as soon as she stepped inside the door of Christine's three-bedroom co-op, her pink cheeks flushed, red curls pushed back by a black-ribbon headband. She's several inches shorter than me—I wouldn't put her past five feet. And that's giving a generous allowance to her curls.

"Hi Emma! Yay, first day! Are you excited? Do you like your uniform?" I smiled back. Her joy was infectious. You couldn't help but like Ashley—the girl never said a mean thing in all of her fourteen years. Then a black thought crept its way in: What if no one did like Ashley, and that was why she was so happy to have an ally? What kind of evil place was Vincent Academy, where someone could dislike a sweet little munchkin like Ashley? *Calm down, Emma, you're going to give yourself a panic attack.*

My smile got weaker, and I smoothed out my long-sleeved white Oxford shirt and black, blue and green Scotch plaid skirt that mirrored her outfit.

"You tell me, how do I look?" I asked her.

"You look fine," she chirped. "But why the long sleeves? It's soooo hot out. It's going to be like, seventy billion degrees today! Don't you have any short slee—"

Ashley looked at the ground and blushed, her red cheeks now matching her flame-colored hair.

"Sorry, I forgot about the scar."

The blazing scar from the car accident had made wearing short sleeves an impossibility. *Thanks, Henry. You're a champ.*

"It's okay. I'm okay," I reassured her. "Don't worry about it. *Really!*" I added when I saw the expression in her eyes.

She had always looked up to me, even though she lived in the city and I lived in the country, so to speak. Being two years older had its advantages.

And now the city mouse was taking the country mouse under its paw.

After Aunt Christine had slipped me a twenty-dollar bill "for emergencies" and sent us on our way, I drew in Ashley conspiratorially and asked, "So what's the real deal on this school? I know the basic stuff, like how practically everyone goes Ivy League after graduation. But what's this place *really* like?"

How I hoped, prayed, that it was like all those shows about rich, fashion-obsessed, drama-crazy New York teens who dressed like they were twenty-five. All the easier to stay in the background. I just wanted to get through the next two years and disappear to college. Preferably somewhere far away. Maybe Siberia.

"They like to say it's exclusive but that's just a nice word for it being expensive." Ashley giggled, toying with her oversize hoop earring. "It's the most expensive coed school in the city. There's a few girls-only or boys-only schools that cost more. So we're like our own little, I don't know, island, in the middle of it all. Everyone at Vince A more or less stays together."

"Oh." I tried to not sound disappointed.

In my head, I began rehearsing what I would say about the reason behind my move. Ashley didn't understand why I didn't just say I moved from Keansburg, but then I told her how my high school paper insisted on doing a story on the dangers of drinking and driving, pegged to the incident with Henry. The editor was hoping to use her hard-hitting story as her one-way ticket into the journalism program at Columbia. I figured it doubled as her ticket to Hell. Those who hadn't heard about Henry through the gossip mill read about it, front and center in the *Keansburg Mirror.*

Google me. Google Keansburg. Guess what your first hit is?

Alcohol Turns Home Life Tragic and Ride Home Dangerous for Sophomore Emma Connor.

So moving from Philly was the story.

Ashley gave me a cursory rundown of the school and some of the things I'd come to expect from high school. The principal wore horrible suits. The uniforms were itchy in warmer weather. The cafeteria food was comically terrible, but you were allowed out at lunchtime once you were a junior.

We crossed Eighty-fifth Street, racing against the yellow light and slowing our walk as we headed to the entrance.

"Here we are!" Ashley announced, throwing her arms open with a flourish.

I regarded the gray building in front of me. It was an old mansion that had been converted into a high school, and it sure looked the part, with cool stone walls and windows hugged by lavishly scrolled molding. Vincent Academy wasn't too tall— just five floors, no taller than the stately, old-fashioned brick-and-marble buildings on either side—but to me, it seemed massive and imposing, like it was some bully crushing his way through a crowd of old ladies.

I was suddenly very, very nervous. *Maybe the devil I knew was better than the devil I didn't know? Should I have stayed in Keansburg?*

We were early—frozen in an ornate entrance hall where, off to the right, was the office I was supposed to check into as a new student. There were a few kids around—students who looked like they were posing for the Vincent Academy brochure. Girls strewn about here and there, draped over high-backed chairs while they studied from thick textbooks. There were a few boys too, in dark pants, white shirts and mostly undone ties, lounging on a wooden staircase with a scrolled banister, or carrying a basketball and pushing open the double doors in the rear to what looked like a fairly large quad.

Vincent Academy was one of the only coed private schools in Manhattan, a fact, as I looked around, I wasn't sure if I was supposed to be happy about or terrified of. As I looked more closely at the girls, I saw that they matched their pristine uniforms with heels and expensive-looking boots. I looked down at my black tights and scuffed Mary Janes through my overgrown bangs—which were cursed with a cowlick—and grimaced. Big diamonds glittered in the ears of a long-haired, fake-tanned blonde, who was scrutinizing a calculus textbook and managing to look glamorous while doing so. In my ears? A row of three tiny imitation-silver hoops that I got at Hot Topic. On sale.

I decided to be happy. I wasn't looking for a boyfriend, since they tend to do pesky things like asking about your life and all that. I just wanted to be anonymous. And if this chick was any indication of what my classmates looked like, I was zero competition for any of these girls, who probably spent their morning putting on makeup and arriving at school in chauffeur-driven cars.

Ashley walked with me through the palatial hall to the office, her eyes eager to see a little bit of the hero she used to worship when we were kids. I smiled weakly and made a lame slit across my throat with my index finger. She laughed and I headed inside.

"You must be Miss Connor." The woman sitting behind the tall wood counter regarded me with iron-gray eyes. They matched her gray hair, pulled into a tight, no-nonsense bun at the nape of her neck. She was even wearing a gray cardigan. I glanced at the nameplate on her desk.

No. Way. Ms. Gray? I blinked and looked again. Mrs. Gary. Close enough! I bet she was wearing gray granny panties, too.

"Yes, um, yes," I stammered. "I'm Emma Connor." *How did she know who I was?* "How did—did you know that?"

She smiled, and a very faint hint of warmth crept into those steely eyes.

"You're the only student I don't know, and there's only one new student due today." She smiled. "Let me get your schedule for you."

I groaned internally. I had forgotten how small Vincent Academy was. Keansburg High had 650 students. How could I hide in a school that barely had 200?

"Here you are, dear," the gray lady said, handing me my schedule. "Your first class today is on the third floor."

But my locker, well, my locker was in the basement, in a row of old lockers so out of the way, they were always the last to be assigned, falling to latecomers like me and unlucky freshmen.

"Stay there and smile," the gray lady instructed as I stood in the same spot, scrutinizing my schedule. "Miss Connor," she snapped, her voice sharp.

"Huh?" I looked up, and she was standing behind some large beige contraption. Suddenly there was a flash. It surprised me—it was too bright, and I saw spots everywhere.

"You can pick up your ID after lunch. In the meantime,

please fill these out." *Oh, great, that's going to be an awesome picture. So sexy.*

The gray lady handed me several small yellow forms, telling me to give them to each teacher as I walked into the room. I realized there was no way I was going to avoid the awkward "Hey, kids, we have a new student here" nightmare.

Please, oh, please, don't make me have to introduce myself. Don't make me tell them something about myself.

Hi, I'm Emma. I'm basically an orphan and my life sounds like a Lifetime Original Movie. My dad left when I was six. My twin brother died when I was fourteen. My mom got sick soon after that, and died when I was fifteen. I lose everyone I love. And this past June, my stepfather wrapped a car around a telephone pole with us in it. So now, I live with my aunt, I have no friends except for my cousin anymore, thanks to my jerk stepfather, and I still keep a journal with all my hopes and fears in it. Also, my favorite color is purple and I think baby animals are cute.

I finished signing my forms and returned to my cousin, who snatched the schedule from my hands, scrutinizing my teachers.

"Your Monday through Wednesday schedule is almost the same. You have Mr. D for chemistry. He has people call him Mr. D because his name is so long. That's good. He's supposed to be fair," she mused. "Ugh, Mrs. Dell. She suuucks," Ashley said, drawing it out dramatically. "Sorry about that. But hey, we'll be in the same class!"

I looked to see which subject she was talking about. Latin. *Wait, Latin?*

I realized I had been put in freshman Latin.

I never really paid much attention to which classes I'd actually be taking. Christine was on the board at Vincent Academy and pulled some strings to allow me to take the placement exams late—which was why I was starting three weeks after the school year had already begun. I forgot that the Vincent Academy required students to take two years of Latin. All I knew about Latin was E Pluribus Unum.

I looked down at Ashley and tried to be optimistic about it. "Well, at least I have a friend in class!"

She smiled her billion-dollar smile and showed me to my locker, in a narrow hallway next to the chemistry lab and boiler room. I felt like some goblin, tucked away in the basement dungeon. I would not have been surprised if Freddy Krueger stored his books next to me.

"Okay, now I have to go to *my* locker." She smiled again, giving me an apologetic look. "It's on the second floor. I won't see you until Latin, which is the last class."

"After lunch," I replied woodenly. "Oh, crap!" I moaned.

"What?" Ashley looked alarmed.

I realized I couldn't tell her that I didn't want to go to lunch alone—and here, each grade took a separate lunch period because the cafeteria was kind of small.

"Nothing," I said, throwing on my brightest fake smile. "I thought I forgot to bring something."

"Oh. Okay, well, I'll see you in Latin. You'll hate it," she promised, then added, "but Mrs. Dell has a moustache so it's kind of funny to watch it move as she says anything that ends in '-ibus.' It truly…flutters in the breeze," she added dramatically.

I giggled, and gave her a hug.

"Thank you," I said into her mess of curls, and gave her a bigger squeeze so she knew how much I really did appreciate it.

She bounced back to the stairwell and turned back to face me, looking older than the fourteen years I knew her to be.

"You'll be fine." Ashley looked at me solemnly with her

giant blue eyes before skipping up the stairs, her overstuffed backpack bouncing up and down on her hip.

I eyed the emergency fire exit door and considered making a break for it.

"Don't be stupid, Emma," I whispered to myself. "Just two more years of high school. It can't be worse than living with Henry."

I shoved my notebooks into my locker and slammed the metal door defiantly.

Here we go.

Getting to school a little early was a good plan. My first class was still empty, so I was able to discreetly slip the form the gray lady gave me to my first teacher, Mrs. Urbealis, who greeted me warmly and said, "Sit anywhere."

She looked sharp and clever. I figured I could ask.

"Anywhere? Come on, where should I *really* sit?" Back in Keansburg, I always had the third seat in the second row. In every single class. Enough of a breeze if the window was open, and if it was cold out, the first row got the brunt of the chill. Great seat. Sonny, the funniest guy in class, always sat in the front…Cyndi, our class president sat behind him. I stared at the desks, knowing that they had been unofficially assigned since the first week of freshman year.

Mrs. Urbealis broke into a knowing smile.

"Okay, Emma. I would say, take that seat." She gestured to the last seat in the seventh row. The last seat in the classroom. If this were a chessboard, I'd just be a rook. Appropriate, since I felt like a rookie.

I smiled gratefully and sat down, pulling out my notebook and absentmindedly doodling on the green cover. I usually drew circles or loops…nothing meaningful. I got lost in my doodles, and started daydreaming. Maybe New York wouldn't be so bad. This is the city that people spend their entire lives trying to get to, right? There were enough distractions…it wouldn't be like home, where I knew everyone and was still so utterly alone.

I looked down at my green notebook cover and realized I'd just drawn a bunch of eyes. I shuddered at the ominous artwork and flipped the cover open, checking out the other students who had started to file in. They were all a little… glossy. I had wondered where everyone was right before the bell rang, then realized that all the girls must have been polishing their looks in the bathroom. Lips perfectly shiny. Hair brushed and freshly flat-ironed, or arranged in carefully messy curls. I self-consciously reached up to my cowlick, making sure it was behaving and staying in place, relieved to find it in line with the rest of my hair.

Good little soldier, I thought, patting my hair.

The bell rang, and Mrs. Urbealis called the class to attention.

"Okay guys, you know where we left off. Let's continue with Tammany Hall and the political machine. Please open your books to page 106."

I ran my hand over my history textbook, then turned the cover back. A large snap rang through the mostly quiet room as I broke the spine on my brand-new book. I could feel the eyes of every student in that room staring at me through my wall of hair, which was doing nothing to protect me.

"Class, we do have a new student. Miss Emma Connor." She paused.

Please, oh, please, do not make me come up there and tell you a little something about myself.

"Let's make her feel welcome, shall we? Show her the Vincent Academy way?"

She gave me a warm smile and I felt better, hoping, deep

down, that the Vincent Academy way would be a good thing.

It turned out that my next class, math, was in the same room, so I just sat in the same desk, as did the girl in front of me. She turned around with a big smile.

"Hi, I'm Jenn," she said with a big smile. "Jenn Hynes. How's your first day?" She seemed friendly enough, the kind of girl I would have hung out with back in Keansburg. All those friends ditched me because they either were afraid of Henry, or were afraid of how it looked to be friends with me, the poster child for tragedy. I stopped getting invited anywhere, since I wasn't considered fun at parties anymore. When I did bother to show up, I turned into the designated-driving police and was deemed a total buzzkill.

"Oh, it's okay so far." I tried to match her bright smile. "So far so good."

"Where are you from?"

"Philadelphia." I readied myself to churn out the performance of a lifetime. "My parents—well, my mom, actually—" *Why not make it my mom who got the job? Yay, female empowerment!* "—got a job transfer. They needed her in Tokyo, and I didn't want to go, so I moved to live with my aunt Christine."

Jenn seemed to believe my story, so I continued prattling on.

"Yeah, my family decided to move, but I don't speak Japanese, and sure, they have schools that are English-speaking, but I—I didn't really want to go...." I trailed off and realized that she was staring at my necklace.

"Hey, what's that?" she asked, pointing at the silver charm, which hung on a box-link silver necklace. Round and slightly tarnished, the charm was etched with a medieval-looking crest. It was a little larger than a quarter—a "statement piece," my aunt had called it once—but I loved it. My hands instinctively went up to the necklace.

"Oh, it's a charm my brother, Ethan, gave me years ago," I said, toying with the disc. "He said he thought it would bring me good luck. I just think it looks cool."

"It is cool," Jenn agreed. "Different." She brushed her pin-straight honey-brown hair back, and I noticed the Tiffany necklace glistening at her throat. *Of course.*

I took that as a cue to compliment *her* jewelry, which went over really well. Jenn seemed to decide I was acceptable enough, and asked if I wanted to sit with her friends at lunch.

The teacher, Mr. Agneta, called the class to attention, and called on me—a lot. I wasn't sure where all my aunt's tuition money was going, but it sure wasn't into the math program. A lot of this stuff just felt like I had covered it sophomore year. I got every answer right, and felt a little satisfied with myself. Maybe today wouldn't be so bad after all.

Jenn and I had the next class together—but she disappeared somewhere before I could find out where I was going. I flattened myself against a wall to avoid the crowd of students in the narrow hallway, scrutinizing my schedule and trying to figure out where to go.

"Hey, newbie, need help?" a deep voice to my left asked. I looked up…and up some more…into the blue eyes of an extremely tall blond guy.

"Um, yeah, thanks," I mumbled. "Do you know where room 201 is?"

"I'm headed there myself. I'll walk you." He smoothed out his red tie. "Anything for a beautiful damsel in distress."

"Uh, thanks?" I tried to keep the confusion out of my voice and failed miserably. *Who talks like that?* I fell in step beside him as we walked to the staircase.

"I'm Emma, by the way."

"It's *very* nice to meet you, Emma," he purred, a sly smile on his face. Blondo was attractive in that soap-opera way—tall, blond, definitely built—but something about the way he smiled reminded me of those National Geographic documentaries about animals in the African wild. He looked like a lion about to pounce. I felt very caribou-esque all of a sudden.

"And you are...?" I asked as we shuffled down the steps. It almost strained my neck to look up at him.

"Don't you know who I am?" Blondy McBlonderson snapped, the smile replaced with a smug smirk.

"Should I?" I asked blankly.

"I guess you're not from around here," he purred, putting his palm on the small of my back. I quickened my step and he dropped his hand.

"No, I'm from Philadelphia," I mumbled.

"That explains it. Because if you were from New York, you would make it your business to know who I am. And I would definitely have remembered you."

The slick smile was back on his face as James Blond spoke directly to my shirt's third button. Great. My first day and I attract the attention of the biggest manwhore I've ever met. I started thanking whatever lucky stars I had that we had reached the English classroom.

"Uh yeah, well, thanks for showing me to class," I muttered, eager to get away from him. This guy had more lines than loose-leaf.

"Oh, it was all my pleasure," Legally Bland said, leering at me. I'd always heard the phrase "mentally undressing someone with your eyes" but never had I actually seen it in action. This dude's eyes could perform a freakin' CAT scan, they were so thorough.

I spied Jenn and was thankful to see she had saved me a seat next to her, in the last row of the class. I practically ran over to her, and she introduced me to her friends Kristin Thorn, whom I'd recognized as the highlighted, tanned blonde I'd seen earlier, and Francisco Fernandez, a guy with a friendly smile whom I liked immediately.

Kristin looked me up and down as if I were dressed in a chicken suit, and not in the same exact outfit she was wearing.

"So, like, you're the new girl." It was an accusation, not a question. She tossed her long hair and glared at me.

"Yes, hi, I'm Emma." I flashed an awkward smile.

"So, like, why did you decide to leave…where is it you're from?" She sniffed, tossing her hair again and glaring at me like I had monkeys crawling out of my nostrils. I reached up and smoothed my cowlick, wondering if it was sticking out and flipping her off, based on the look on her face.

"Philadelphia," Jenn broke in, giving Kristin a wary look.

"So, like, did your family, like, throw you out?" she sneered, punctuating it with another toss of her white-streaked hair and crossing her red-soled shoes. Of course she wore Christian Louboutin heels. My cheeks got hot.

"So, like, do you have some kind of OCD that makes you toss your hair all the time?" I mimicked her, meeting her ice-blue glare. "Are you going to start counting things, and knocking on wood, too? I'm just concerned for you." I tried to make my voice sound sweet and convincing, like I really did have genuine worry over this glossy princess who had, for some reason, deemed me the enemy. But after my skeezy encounter with Blondo, my patience was wearing thin—and my sarcasm was evident.

I heard a snicker from the black-haired guy who'd just sat

down in front of me, and I knew that our conversation had been overheard.

Great. So much for staying anonymous. Is it too late to transfer again?

"No, I'm fine. Don't *you* even try to think about *me*." She bared a row of perfectly straight, bleached-white teeth that stood out in her fake-tanned face. White and orange, orange and white. This girl looked like a Creamsicle.

Kristin continued her nasty tirade. "I just think your arrival is…off. Why would you transfer out in the middle of September? Why not wait until the end of the semester? You don't make sense. Why are you here *now?*"

"Well, you see, my mom got a new job. In Tokyo. So I decided to stay in the States with my aunt Christine. Christine *Considine.*" I emphasized my aunt's last name—she had some serious pull at that school and if Blondo can pull the "Don't you know why I am?" move, why couldn't I?

A slight look of surprise replaced her scowl, but she kept up with her inquisition.

"So where are you actually from, though?" she asked me, Emma the cockroach.

"Philadelphia." *Did she not hear Jenn say it?*

"Hmm." She pursed her shiny lips. "My brother is at boarding school outside of Philadelphia. What school was it?"

"Oh, it wasn't a boarding school…you wouldn't know it." I stalled. *Crap. Crappity crap crap!* Why hadn't I decided to pick a fake alma mater? Knowing my luck, it would be her brother's high school. She would *own* the high school. It would have a wing named after her family. The Creamsicle Wing.

"Well, come on, Emma." The way she said my name was as if she was spitting out sour milk. "Was it Delbarton? Pingry? Which one?"

My mind raced, flipping through everything I knew of

Philadelphia. What was there? The Liberty Bell? The Phillies? Cream cheese? *Oh, yeah, Cream Cheese High School. Brilliant, Emma.*

Something from my fifth-grade studies popped into my head.

"Congress Academy," I heard myself saying, pulling the knowledge of the site of the first Continental Congress out of thin air.

Kristin wrinkled her nose, and the small diamond chip she had pierced on her left nostril sparkled. "I don't know it."

"Oh, it's really small. And exclusive," I added.

"Where is it?" she pressed.

"Downtown," I lied, hoping downtown was a good thing. For Keansburg's proximity to Philadelphia, I hadn't been since a school field trip in eighth grade.

"Downtown? I've never heard of any Congress Academy downtown. I'll have to ask my brother if he knows it," she continued. "If it's any good." She resumed looking at me with a satisfied look on her face. She might as well have said, "So there!"

"Hey, Kristin, why do you care?"

The smooth voice came from the row in front of us, from the black-haired guy who laughed at my dig earlier.

Throwing his left arm cavalierly over the back of his chair—so his arm was resting slightly on my desk—he turned around and faced Kristin, who turned beet-red and stammered, "I *don't* care. I was only—"

"You were only being a nasty little girl, as usual," he said, coolly. "Anyway, I know the school. We've played them."

He turned and looked at me for a brief second—and my pulse sped. I didn't expect my response. I'd been around good-looking guys before—but this guy looked like a rock star. Long black lashes framed his green eyes—twinkling green eyes that locked with mine.

"In fact," he added with a smirk. "At Congress Academy, they're *very* good."

I smiled back. *Is he flirting with me?*

His gaze dropped lower. For a split second I thought he was being Blondo 2.0 and staring at something else—okay, two something elses—on my chest, when I realized he was looking at my charm necklace. His eyes returned to mine and crinkled up at the corner with his smile. Then the boy with the rock-star eyes quickly turned around, returning to the exact same pose he was in before, which I now noticed was slouched in his chair, legs sprawled out, not caring in the least who might trip over them.

Chapter 2

Class was over, and it was time to go to lunch. I wasn't sure if my confrontation with Kristin would mean that I had lost my potential lunch partner in Jenn, or if I'd actually be lunch, with Kristin picking at my bones and my flesh.

Relief isn't the word for it when Francisco immediately said, "Hey, new girl, sit with us at lunch." He ignored the glare from Kristin and gave me a big smile.

Looking right at her, I replied, "Sure, thanks."

Three hours in, and there was no chance I would get to be invisible in this school. Anonymity I wanted, but it was clearly not an option, since I wouldn't be a doormat. I didn't take Henry's crap, why would I take it from some Upper East Side princess?

We strolled slowly to the cafeteria, Kristin racing down the stairs quickly with Jenn for what I could see was about to become a fully blown-out bitch session about me. Francisco hung back, peppering me with benign questions until Kristin and Jenn were far enough ahead. Then he threw in, "Don't let Kristin get to you."

"What's her deal?" I asked, exasperated. "I didn't do anything."

"There doesn't always have to be a reason," he stated plainly. "She was in these commercials for super-absorbent diapers when she was a toddler, so she thinks she's better than everyone. I still think she's just as full of crap as she was then. Some people are just rotten."

I burst out laughing, surprised by Francisco's candor.

"She has quite a history with Anthony—one of those on-and-off things—so I'm sure she's not thrilled that he was all over you in the doorway of the classroom," Francisco continued, giving me a sideways glance. "Way to make a splash on your first day, newbie."

"Was that his name? He seemed annoyed that I didn't know who he was," I said, then groaned internally. *Great, that's probably Francisco's best friend or something.*

To my relief, he just started laughing. "Yeah, I bet. His royal high-ass isn't used to that. So I take it you shot him down?"

"More or less," I mumbled, and he snorted with laughter. I breathed a sigh of relief—finally, *someone* that seemed normal.

"So, Francisco, who's the other guy, the guy who stood up to Kristin?" I had to find out a little more about the green-eyed mystery guy—who clearly knew I was lying about my hometown.

"Oh, just call me Cisco," he said, and I dropped the question, since we had arrived at the cafeteria, right behind Jenn and Kristin. I heard Kristin hiss, "So what, does he, like, know her already? I bet she transferred to stalk him or something."

Francisco just rolled his eyes and in a hushed tone, said, "She's a drama queen. Literally, too—she's *the* drama queen, so hope you're not planning on trying out for the school play," he added wryly.

"Who needs the school play? It looks like there's no way to avoid the drama at this place," I whispered back, and Cisco laughed as I followed him into the small cafeteria that was miles away from the industrial-style one I was used to in Keansburg. Instead of the scratched Formica I once knew, the tables were long, dark wood, looking like they'd be at home in any upscale dining room. Which, I realized, this was, since the school was in an old mansion and all. I suddenly was not very hungry. I grabbed a small prewrapped sandwich—no idea what kind—and an iced tea, and filed behind Cisco in line. I settled in at the table next to him, and gave a smile to Jenn, who was sitting across from me. To my relief, she smiled back.

"So, Emma, do you like Vince A so far?" The question came from a short, sandy-haired guy to my right—Austin, I think his name was. He was slightly freckled and smiling, and seemed nice enough.

"Yeah, it's cool. I mean, school's school. Right?"

"Well, do you think you'll be joining any of the clubs? We're looking for volunteers for Halloween Movie Night in a few weeks," he asked pointedly, playing with his tie which, I noticed, was dotted with a small pattern of the school's insignia.

"No, I don't think so," I said, smiling apologetically. "The only thing I really like to do is…run." Thanks to my aunt's location, I was close to Central Park, and could just get in there and run…and run. All my thoughts melted away, and I just focused on the pavement as it kissed my feet.

Austin seized on the opportunity. "We don't really have a track team. It's more like a club, but you should join anyway. The athletics at this school aren't one of the biggest priorities—that would be academics, of course—" He would have continued prattling on if something from across the cafeteria hadn't caught our attention—and the attention of everyone else in the room.

Amid the chatter in the room, two voices got discernibly louder, until one of the voices—belonging to the same black-haired guy that sat in front of me in English—stood up and flung his empty lunch tray across the table with enough force that it slid off and fell. He slammed his chair into the table, almost hitting the blond guy sitting next to him. The booming crack it made caused everyone to turn and stare. He grabbed a gray messenger bag and stomped out as the chair wobbled and fell to the floor with a loud clacking sound. The blond guy was seething as he turned around—and immediately locked eyes with me. It was Anthony, and he caught me staring at the confrontation. I blushed and looked down—not quite sure why I was embarrassed to be caught looking, since everyone else was staring too.

"So yeah, the athletics at this school, well, they're not that great, but they're getting better. I'm on the student council, and one of the things I'm trying to do—" Austin continued, unfazed.

"Wait!" I stammered. "What—what the hell was that all about?"

"What?" He looked dumbfounded.

"That!" I waved my left hand toward the source of the commotion.

"Oh, that. The basketball team," Austin said. "Dumb jocks, you know how they are. They might actually win a championship if some players didn't get kicked out so much for fighting. Especially that one. Him and his temper." He gestured toward where my mystery rock-star boy had stormed out.

"Who?"

"Brendan. Brendan Salinger." He pouted as he said the name.

"Oh." At least I had a name. Hot *and* a hothead. I returned to picking at my sandwich—*chicken salad, gross!*—when

I realized that our conversation had caught the attention of Kristin, who sneered under her breath, "So Emma's going after Anthony *and* Brendan? What a slut." I just rolled my eyes. I had zero interest in Anthony. But Brendan…he was intriguing.

"So Austin." I turned, putting on my brightest smile. "What's his deal? You don't seem to like him too much."

"He's okay. It's just annoying that Salinger gets away with everything. He never does anything for the school unless he's forced into it," Austin huffed, then changed the subject, trying to wrangle me into volunteering for the winter dance. I was still curious about Brendan, but was drawn into the chatter in the lunchroom and did my best to keep up. I didn't want to lose this lunch seat and have to sit alone or worse—go eat in the library like I had during those last painful weeks at Keansburg High, when I scarfed down peanut butter sand-wiches while standing in the dusty stacks in the Applied Sci-ence section, where no one ever went. It was less painful than answering questions from curious students masquerading as concerned friends. *Is your stepfather going to jail? Did he always drink? Why is your arm bandaged? Are you going to eat the rest of your fries?* It was better to put my headphones on and try to block it all out, alone.

After lunch, I picked up my ID, not even bothering to look at it as I raced to chemistry class. I walked in hesitantly, not sure what to do about a lab partner. I scanned the room of the basement lab, located conveniently next to my gremlin locker room, looking for anyone sitting alone. My eyes fell to a girl with pitch-black hair, blond roots and fuchsia tips, sitting alone and reading some printouts that she hid, badly, behind her textbook. She wore black tulle underneath her plaid skirt, which puffed it out like a tutu. I liked her right away.

She looked surprised that I approached her before regarding

me with serious, red-eyeliner-rimmed blue-gray eyes. "Your energy works for me," she said, raising her hand, her black-painted index fingernail extended as if she were trying to stir the air. I shrugged my shoulders and smiled, then noticed the pendants hanging around her neck and realized she was the school's resident witch. Every school had one.

Her eyes drifted to my necklace.

"Hey!" she exclaimed, smiling. "That's *really* cool. May I?" She reached out to touch the pendant, stroking the silver crest with her finger.

"Beautiful," she declared. "I've always loved this design. By the way, I'm Angelique Tedt," she said, her voice a little thick with dramatic emphasis. I was about to ask her where she'd seen the crest before when we were oh-so-rudely interrupted.

"Whatever, *Angela*," hissed a voice behind me. I turned around and saw Kristin, sitting at the lab table behind me. If Angelique could tell my fortune, she'd see lots of spitballs in my future.

"It's nice to meet you…*Angelique*," I said to my new lab partner, stressing her name. If she wanted me to call her Potato Chip, I would have.

Angelique smiled, and returned to her printouts, which I saw were spells printed out from some Wiccan website. As long as she didn't get me into trouble for stealing chemicals from the lab, I didn't care what she did.

I was counting the seconds to see Ashley in Latin. I had to find out what the story was with Brendan. *You just find him interesting, Emma. You are not allowed to be interested in him beyond that.*

I was barely in my seat before Ashley unleashed her questions.

"So, what do you think?" she asked, her eyes wide with

excitement. "Are the classes hard? Any cute guys? Do you like it so far? Any cute guys?"

"It's okay," I said cautiously. "A kind of funny thing happened though." I replayed how Brendan interjected to save me from Kristin's nasty inquisition and—darting a furtive glance to make sure that no one was listening—whispered, "He clearly knows I'm full of it with the whole Philly thing." Her eyes grew so big I thought they'd fall out of her head and roll down the hall.

"No way! And he defended you?" Ashley yelled, whacking me in the arm. I yelped, prompting the entire classroom to stare at me. I wished I could melt into the floor.

"Yes, now keep it down!" I hissed, casting a glance at Mrs. Dell. She didn't seem to have heard.

"*Dude!* He's hot. Super hot. He's got that total loner bad-boy vibe, too—I heard that he doesn't really hang out with anyone from school. He got suspended from the basketball team already this year for fighting, but he still plays in the pickup games after school, and he's *really* good."

Ashley continued rattling off facts as if she had been studying for A.P. Brendan Class. "He deejays, too. His mom's on the board with Aunt Christine so he ends up deejaying school dances. I heard his mom makes him do it as punishment any time he gets into trouble. Which I heard is *a lot*."

"How do you know so much about him?" I asked, amazed. "You've been in this school for three weeks."

"Well, after he got suspended from the team during the first game of the year, everyone was talking about him," she confessed. "It was a big deal. Some guy from the other team tripped him and tried to hit him and Brendan just knocked him out with one punch. Besides, he's so hot!

"Oh, and the best part? Kristin asked him out last year and he flat-out rejected her. He thinks she's the worst, the absolute worst," she cracked, laughing. "What I heard is that she asked him out, he laughed in her face and peaced out. Like, gave her the peace sign and walked away."

"Wow, that's cold!" The thought of that smug girl, my instant nemesis, getting shot down was pretty priceless. "I wish there was a photo of it." *It would be my screen saver.*

"Oh, come with me after school and watch them practice in the quad. There's a whole group of guys that play basketball. He's really good. It's fun to watch."

Watching cute guys after class? This was an extracurricular activity I could get into.

Finally, the bell rang, and I gave Ashley an eager look. Wow. One day and already I'm dorking out over some guy.

"Um, I don't mean to offend," Ashley said, eyeing me studiously, "but you need, like, some lipstick. Or something!" She giggled. "I mean, if Brendan Salinger singled you out on the first day…"

"He didn't single me out!" I cut in. I was down for looking—that's it. Window-shopping strictly. And besides, based on the girls I'd seen at this place, my boring self was hardly getting a second glance from someone who looked like *him*.

"I'm sure I'm just an excuse." I sighed. "He thinks Kristin sucks—with good reason—and just wanted to give the new girl a hand. That's fine, whatever. It's cool."

She just shook her head and pulled out a small bottle of some random pop star's signature perfume, spritzing me with the sickly-sweet smell.

"Oh, come on, Ash, that smells like a unicorn fart," I cried, recoiling at the overpowering, candylike smell. She just dragged me into the bathroom and pulled a pot of lip gloss out of her bag.

After about ten minutes of fussing over me in the bathroom—I borrowed some mascara and that was it—Ashley and I worked our way down to the quad, a large courtyard separating the main building of the school with an annex. They were playing basketball, but it might as well have been murderball. Guys were getting knocked down, players were getting kicked out of the game, then brought back in—and I noticed Kristin was in charge of keeping score.

"Eleven-eight," Kristin said smugly. She had rolled her uniform skirt up until it was practically a belt and gave a lusty look to one side of the court. I followed her gaze and saw Anthony and Brendan there—and instantly wanted to hit her with my backpack. My mind immediately went to what Cisco said. Some people really are just rotten.

Brendan spun around, dribbling the ball with one hand and brushing his black hair back with his other. He was fast, that's for sure. He had changed out of his uniform into a white T-shirt and gym shorts. Every time he aimed for the basket, his shirt hiked up, and I have to admit, it was hard not to notice just how very nice what was hiding under his shirt was. His black hair hung low on his forehead again, as he contemplated his next move, deciding to throw the ball to Anthony. Guess they'd made up.

And then he turned his striking green eyes on me.

Ashley was the first to notice. For all her exuberance, she kept her cool pretty impressively. For a minute.

"Oh. My. God. Brendan. Is. Staring. At. You." She tried her hardest not to move her lips, but failed miserably. *Wow, this girl has absolutely no future as a ventriloquist.*

"I know," I replied, trying to look cool as I met his eyes. He continued to stare at me, his gaze unbroken, with those bright emerald eyes peering at me from his messy black hair, until his teammate tossed him the ball. For someone not paying attention, he caught it easily, turning away to make the next basket. Brendan caught the ball as it swooshed through the hoop, holding it under his arm and turning around. He gave me a sly smile, tilting his chin up in a small greeting. I smiled back, taking note of an unfamiliar feeling in my stomach. *Holy crap, this must be what butterflies feel like.*

I broke his gaze, pretending to root around in my backpack for something.

"Ashley, let's go," I whispered.

"No way! Seriously, you should stay and talk to him." She grinned devilishly and wagged her eyebrows up and down.

I grabbed her arm. "No! Please!" I hissed, feeling panicky. "Let's go." Within seconds, we were out of the quad, walking home.

"Look, Emma…I don't pretend to know what you've been though…" Ashley started on the walk home. *Oh, no. Please. Don't make me talk about this.*

"Ashley, look," I began, a little harsher than I intended, and I instantly felt terrible. The truth was, today would not have been as easy as it had been without her.

"What?" She looked at me with wounded eyes.

"I don't…feel comfortable. At all. A lot of the time," I mumbled, picking at my dark nail polish and peeling the paint off nervously. "I don't think it's a good idea for me to start crushing on some guy who I have zero chances with. I don't even know how I'm going to do on the friend front. Kristin Thorn already hates me for some bananas reason. Don't you understand? It hasn't worked out all that well for me—being close to someone."

Ashley looked at me with more wisdom than I'd ever given her credit for. Suddenly, I felt stupid for denying her the knowledge of her fourteen years.

"Emma," she said, softly. "I get it. And it's okay if you want to feel a mess. But if you start to feel normal again, and if something makes you happy, it doesn't mean that you don't miss your mom or Ethan. It doesn't mean the last few years didn't suck. But remember, this is your chance to just be Emma. Not Emma with the wicked stepfather, Emma with the terrible home life, Emma the whole school is talking about. You're just Emma. Your mom would want you to be happy. So would your brother."

"I know, Ashley." I sighed, wincing as I always did anytime I thought of my mom and brother, Ethan, lost within a year of each other.

"Why on earth my mom decided to marry Henry when she knew she was sick, I'll never know." Henry had been asking my mom to marry her forever, and I never understood why a cancer diagnosis made her finally say yes.

"She wanted to make sure someone was around to take care of you," Ashley said quietly. "I get it. She didn't want you to be alone."

I am anyway. I pursed my lips, willing myself to keep a strong front as I shuffled along the concrete sidewalk.

"Emma, I'm serious," Ashley said, coming to a full stop. "Give yourself a break. If not for you, then for them."

I sighed. "I know, Ash, in my head. I'll work on convincing myself, you know, here." I pointed at my chest.

"In your boobs?" She hooted, giving me a devilish look, and I laughed, relishing the break in the somber mood. "Hey, you never showed me your ID. Lemme see," she said, pulling at my backpack. Glad for the change of subject, I reached in my backpack and pulled out the small white card.

"Jeez, Emma." Ashley let out a low whistle. "Seriously, this sucks."

"That bad?" I grabbed it back. "Let me see."

Oh, great.

I looked like the "before" picture on one of those makeover shows. I hadn't been paying attention to the gray lady, so she caught me looking up, startled, my mouth kind of open and slack-jawed. The too-bright flash had given my skin a tone that could only be described as yellow-gray. *Zombie girl, at your service.* Still, it was a nice picture of my necklace. It caught the light nicely—you could really see the crest on it.

"Sorry about the bad ID, Emma," Ashley said.

"*You're* a bad ID!" I said, laughing.

"Oh, you're still doing that?" she asked, rolling her eyes at my stupid little joke. Anytime I couldn't think of something clever to say, I just told the person they were whatever we were talking about. Ethan and I used to spend hours annoying our mom with it.

"It's dinnertime, kids," she would call from the kitchen. "Turn off the TV."

"*You're* a TV!" we'd call back in unison. Mom would just chuckle and shake her head, chalking it up to one of our random twin idiosyncrasies.

"Eh, it still makes me laugh." I shrugged, smiling at the memory.

"Yeah, you'll be fine," Ashley said dryly as we reached the front door of my aunt's building. "See you tomorrow!"

One day down. 168 to go.

Chapter 3

The next two and a half weeks kind of plodded on—although crossing them off in the back of my notebook as if I were serving a prison sentence sure didn't help the time fly. Jenn, I assumed, was afraid of losing favor with Kristin, since some days she was warm and friendly—and others, she just kept her head down and ignored me. Cisco and I were becoming fast friends, and at least, I always had someone who talked to me at lunch. (Well, Austin did, but he was just trying to get me on the winter dance committee.) Angelique, my chemistry partner, refused to eat in the cafeteria, so on sunny days we'd just grab something to go and walk around the neighborhood.

I could tell that my friendship with her was not going over well with some of my classmates, who were put off by her quirky ways. (Once, she blamed her missing homework on the moon.) Angelique was also on scholarship, so of course the snobs at the school treated her like she lived in a mental hospital, not in an apartment building on Tenth Avenue. I, personally, thought she was a trip. Besides, these were people who had yet to even say three words to me, and Angelique— one of the best students in the class—had generously offered me all her notes to copy. Finally, Angelique admitted to me one day that she did play up her beliefs to get a rise out of everyone.

"They don't understand anything that doesn't conform to what they believe, or what they think, so of course I do whatever I can to make them uncomfortable," she confessed to me over knishes on a bench in Central Park. "I, truly, *am* a witch. My mom's a witch, too.

"It's not like you see in the movies. Sure, there are some bad witches, those with evil intentions—my mom's met a few," Angelique whispered conspiratorially, flipping her jet-black hair back. "But not all are bad. And truly, I do see auras, and I really can see and sense people's energy. But I'd be lying if I said it wasn't the best feeling to make these look-alike sheep so uncomfortable. I make stuff up sometimes just to annoy them."

That afternoon, she expertly completed an experiment in acid/base properties, and loudly announced that the chemicals spoke to her, winking at me out of the corner of her eye.

Thanks to Angelique, I caught up on schoolwork pretty quickly. But things weren't necessarily hard at this new school…just competitive. Still, I threw myself into my studies, telling myself that I was trying to get on the Principal's List, to make my aunt happy. I hated to admit the truth: I was trying to distract myself from a growing, nagging interest in Brendan. (A regular name on the honor roll? Brendan Alexander Salinger. *So much for being a dumb jock.*)

He strode into English class on my second day, and all I could think was, "Damn." He put the hot in "hot mess." And the mess. His black hair was sticking out like it had exploded, his shirt was untucked and his tie barely knotted. But the disheveled look worked on him, like he had just rolled out of bed and onto the set of a jeans commercial.

Brendan turned his vibrant green eyes on my light brown

ones, and I took that as my cue to say, "Hi." He gave me a curt nod, then flopped down in his desk without so much as a polite "Hey" in response. I felt like I had been slapped. After that, when he came into class (always late, and always going un-scolded by the teacher), I would, invariably, look up at the wrong moment and catch his eye briefly. My eyes would dart back down to my Shakespeare text, reading the same line over and over again, toying with my necklace—a nervous habit that had gotten a lot worse. It was like a whole new level of Hell, one that Dante had forgotten about.

I didn't know why I was so drawn to him. But fortunately, apart from English class, it was easy to avoid Brendan. I begged off watching the pickup games in the quad after school, telling Ashley that I was thinking about joining the track team after all and needed to get my stamina up by jogging in the park.

"It's not a team. They don't compete," she drawled. "It's a *club*. The Running Club. Seriously. They just go to the park and, like, run around."

"Are you kidding me?" I asked, incredulous. I pictured the glossy girls at the school, teetering about the park in heels. *Okay girls, there's a Louis Vuitton bag in here somewhere. Go find it!* And they'd scatter, fluffy Pomeranians clutched in their arms, as their little club scurried around.

So I was a running club of one, leaving the school through the gym exit so I could avoid Brendan and his friends in the quad. Well, I was avoiding Brendan and Anthony, for different reasons. I was afraid I'd lose control: I'd throw myself on Brendan—or throw up on Anthony.

After two and a half weeks of "Lookin' good, newbie," and "When are you gonna give me your number?" Anthony finally cornered me in the doorway of English class.

"What's a hot piece like you doing hanging out with a freak like Angela?" Anthony's frosty blue eyes looked me up and down, and he rested his hand on the polished wooden frame of the doorway, blocking me in the hallway.

"Angelique," I corrected, recoiling at being called a "piece." "And she's not a freak."

"I know who your aunt is, Emily. You need to associate with people on your level," he purred.

"She *is* on my level," I snapped. "At least she knows my name."

"Come on, you're really not going to pass up a chance at all this, are you?" he asked, running his hand down his muscular chest before brushing my bangs out of my face. I smacked his meaty hand away.

Anthony's smile quickly turned into a sneer. "You better keep your hands to yourself if you know what's good for you. Just remember—*I'm* not the one whose parents dumped me at my aunt's house so they could go out of town. You should consider yourself lucky that I'm even talking to you."

Then—to my absolute shock and horror—Anthony winked at me. "Let me know when you've come to your senses."

Before I could even respond, he strode away and flopped into his seat—even his walk was arrogant.

I heard Mr. Emerson coming up the stairs behind me, so I ducked into the English classroom—catching Cisco's eye and trying to avoid Brendan's. *Great. The one time he actually shows up to class on time, he sees you get into a confrontation with his buddy.*

"What was that about?" Cisco asked. I leaned over to tell him, but Mr. Emerson shuffled in, coughing with the tenacious remains of a nasty cold. He attempted to read a few lines of Shakespeare before launching into a fit of hacking and wheezing. I felt bad for Mr. Emerson, but truthfully, it was kind of gross. Finally, he gave up, forcing the class to read aloud instead.

"You." He pointed at Austin before blowing his nose. "Read. Page seventy-three." (Although with his cold, it sounded like "Debendy-dwee.")

Austin beamed—anything for school spirit—and turned the pages to Shakespeare's Sonnet 2, taking his task seriously.

"When forty winters besiege thy brow..." he began, and I darted my eyes around. I locked eyes with Anthony—who licked his lips at me. *Oh, puke.* I quickly broke eye contact.

"Gross," I whispered to myself, staring down at my textbook. *Stare out the window, Emma. Yep, that's a safe place.* I twisted my head away from Anthony to face the eastern window, at the sun that was beaming in, and considered skipping my afternoon classes—I had to get out of that school. Besides, it was great running weather.

I sighed, losing myself in an extensive examination of my split ends. I was so overdue for a trim. My ends looked like tree branches. Why Anthony had any interest in me—I was hardly as polished as my classmates—I had no idea.

When Austin was done, Mr. Emerson asked for a volunteer to read the next sonnet, and Kristin raised her hand. *Shocker!* Eager to show off, her hand was raised so high that she only had one butt cheek left on her seat. Mr. Emerson flapped his hand in her direction, and she smiled primly.

Kristin stood up—Austin had stayed in his desk—and flipped her hair, overacting and putting a ridiculous amount of emotion behind every word. I sat there, bored, my head propped up by my hand, my eyes rolling so far back in my head I could practically see my own brain.

"*Shall* I compare *thee* to *a* summer's day?" She was emphasizing the wrong words. I smirked to myself, listening to her emote. Cisco pretended to shoot himself in the head and I stifled a giggle fit. Then I went back to my split ends. Wow, I really needed a haircut.

"Emma."

My head snapped to attention. Mr. Emerson was looking at me, and I'd been caught staring at my hair.

"Huh? I mean, what did you say, sir?"

"Please read Sonnet 29. And—" he broke into another coughing fit "—stand up."

I flipped to the sonnet—oh, great. No matter what it meant to Shakespeare, it was going to take on a whole new meaning for me. *Just try not to let your voice crack on the word* outcast, *Emma.*

I took a deep breath and stood, holding my textbook in front of me. I put my fist to my mouth and exaggeratedly cleared my throat, an icebreaker which elicited a few laughs from the room. I started reading, in a clear, strong voice:

"When, in disgrace with fortune and men's eyes,
I all alone beweep my outcast state
And trouble deaf heaven with my bootless cries
And look upon myself and curse my fate..."

I paused, looking up at Mr. Emerson, and saw Brendan shifting in his seat. He turned sideways, folding his arms on the back of his chair and resting his cheek on his crossed arms. He looked up through those long black lashes. I bet if I touched them, they'd be velvet-soft. As his eyes found mine, I glanced back down at the words in my hands, holding the textbook in front of me like armor. I could still feel his eyes on me, but all I allowed myself to see was the black-on-white text I was gripping in my palms as I continued to read.

Bravery—or stupidity, I couldn't tell which—prompted me to meet Brendan's eyes for the last two lines:

"For thy sweet love remember'd such wealth brings
That then I scorn to change my state with kings."

I smoothed my plaid skirt underneath me as I sat down, and Brendan was still turned around, looking at me. I kept my eyes on the sonnet, daring myself to meet his gaze and say, "What? What the hell do you want?"

Instead, wordlessly, I raised my eyes and, as if they were some kind of heat-seeking missiles, they locked with his. He slowly blinked—really, it was more like he'd closed his eyes for a full three seconds—then opened them again, still keeping my gaze. His face—frozen for the past two and a half weeks in still, unfeeling concrete whenever our eyes met—softened a bit, and I could have sworn I saw the corner of his mouth turn up in a smile.

Mr. Emerson finished his hacking cough, then called on another student. I broke the stare. Brendan turned away.

That afternoon in Central Park, Blink-182's "Carousel" was at the top of my playlist as I ran faster, letting the crisp fall air fill my lungs with the familiar scent of grass and dirt and the newly familiar scents of hot dogs and pretzels warming on the carts that lined the pathways in the park.

I sang along, racing faster and listening to the track on repeat. "Go to your happy place," I told myself, thinking of Cisco and Angelique—legitimate new friends, I considered them. And Jenn was cool enough to me, even though some days, she just didn't talk to anyone. I daydreamed about Kristin getting an allergic reaction to a tanning session. Maybe she'd actually turn into an orange.

I closed my eyes, thinking of English class, how I'd identified with that sonnet. Feeling like an outcast, a loser but comforted by a great love. I longed to know what it felt like to have one person eclipse everything bad in your life—be a place of pure joy.

I stopped short, pausing for breath, and surveyed my surroundings. I was all the way over by the Bethesda Fountain. It was one of my favorite areas of the park—gorgeous, palatial. And still, all I could see was his face, and those eyes—which didn't look like they hated me in spite of how he acted.

"Why can't I get you out of my head?" I whispered, stopping in my tracks. "Brendan, I wish I just knew what your deal was."

I leaned against a lamppost, trying to steady my breath and my thoughts. The light above me flickered, catching my attention. My back leaning against the post, I looked straight up into the light. It burned very brightly for a moment—as if it were on a dimmer switch that was suddenly put on full blast. I heard a crackling noise, and nervously stepped away from the lamppost—just as the light inside burst, shards of glass clinking against the frosted case. The smell of something bitter hit my nose, and I winced. It was suddenly very dark all around me—reminding me that it was getting too late—and I should go back home.

Chapter 4

"Hey, Emma, let me ask you about something."

Cisco's voice was low as he leaned forward the next day at lunchtime. I gave him a big smile. In spite of having just as much money as everyone else at school—his mom was a big-time doctor at Sloan-Kettering—he was above the whole stupid social caste system.

"Sure, what's up?" I asked, picking my turkey sandwich to pieces. "By the way, you'd think this cafeteria could get a sandwich right. Look at this lettuce. I'd be better off eating my napkin." I shuddered at the transparent, almost white leaf of romaine and pushed it away. Cisco leaned in closer.

"Come with me to the quad when you're done eating," he said. I looked at the sandwich, now strewn about my tray like doughy confetti.

"Uh, I think I'm done." I laughed, surveying the mess I'd made, and walked with him to the door. I noticed he got very quiet until we were in the quad with no one within earshot.

"What are you doing tomorrow night?" Cisco asked, keeping his voice low as he stuffed his hands into the pockets of his black pants. *Oh, no. No, no, no. Please don't tell me he's asking me on a date.*

"Friday? Nothing much," I said, trying to sound casual. "Probably just going to the movies with my cousin, maybe play some pool after. What's up?"

"Well." he leaned in closer and his voice got lower. He sounded nervous. "My boyfriend Gabe's band is playing at this bar farther up on the East Side, and I wanted to know if you wanted to come with us and hang out. I'm going with my cousin and some friends, and it could be fun."

"Oh, *that's* what you wanted to ask me?" I blurted out, relieved. It's not that Cisco wasn't cute—he was plenty cute, with thick chestnut hair and warm cocoa eyes. But, as much as I hated to admit it to myself, I'd lost interest in anyone who wasn't *him*.

"You look relieved," Cisco said, smiling at me.

"Honestly, I thought you were going to ask me out and I'm on, well, on a guy-cation. Like a vacation. But from guys," I babbled on. "That probably sounds arrogant, but you know, we get along, you asked me all secretively, making me come out here...."

"Sweetie, you're cute, but you're so not my type." He smirked, laughing. I pretended to be offended.

"I just don't want anyone knowing my business," Cisco continued, getting serious. "It's *my* business and if you're ever in the guys' locker room, it's 'that's so gay' this, and 'no homo' that. Not exactly the most welcome coming-out party."

"It's never fun to be the one people are staring at," I said, instantly understanding. I crossed my arms and looked down.

"Exactly."

"Let me check with my aunt and make sure it's not a problem. I don't think it will be."

"Cool." He smiled, reaching into his blue messenger bag and

pulling out a notebook. "Here's the address and my number. Meet me on the corner of Third Avenue and Ninety-first Street tomorrow night."

Walking home with Ashley that afternoon, I told her about my plans to hang out with Cisco and his friends. I was so afraid of hurting her feelings—the past two weeks, we'd had standing weekend dates—movies or billiards hall—when she didn't have plans with some of her classmates. Although she always invited me along, I usually passed. Her friends seemed so much younger than she was, and a little too gossipy for anything I could handle. To her credit, her face fell only a little bit before composing herself.

"No, it's cool," she said, smiling at me. "You should get out of the house," she added, giggling. "And hey, Francisco's cute."

"Oh, no," I stammered. "It's not like that."

"Why not?" Ashley pressed. "He's cute. You can tell, he *totally* works out. And he seems really nice."

"No, really. We're just friends." Even though I knew Ashley wouldn't care, I had to respect his privacy. It wasn't my story to tell.

"Anyway," I continued. "Do you think that Aunt Christine will mind if I go out?" I wasn't prepared for Ashley's response—breaking out in uncontrollable laughter.

"What's so funny?" I asked, but Ashley just continued laughing. She laughed so hard tears actually started rolling down her face, and she had to lean against a building for support. "*What* is so funny?"

"Are you kidding me?" she howled, her tears causing her eye shadow to leave iridescent streaks down her cheeks. "She's going to be happy that you're going out with someone other than me. Ooh, maybe you'll actually get to bed *after* 9:00 p.m. for once. Really, Emma. You're in the early-bird dinner crowd these days. Are you going to play bingo next? Are there hard candies in the bottom of your backpack?"

"Okay, Ashley, I get it." I rolled my eyes.

"I mean, I thought you were going to start stealing Splenda from diners...." She continued mocking me until we were at her parents' place on Sixty-second Street—and until I left around dinnertime.

That night after I was clearing the kitchen table—my aunt had ordered in some Indian food—I broached the subject. "So, Aunt Christine, a guy in my class invited me to hang out tomorrow night...."

"Which guy?" she asked without looking at me, scrutinizing her nighttime cocktail as she swirled it around in its glass. She and my uncle George used to toast each other every night with a dry martini, extra olives. After he died, she continued the tradition, making two martinis every night and drinking just the one.

"Cisco. I mean, Francisco Fernandez."

"Oh, yes, I know the family," Christine said, smoothing out her billowy cloud of dark brown curls. "His mother's lovely. His sister and cousin, I believe, also attended Vincent Academy. That's fine." She looked at me blankly. "Am—am I supposed to give you a curfew?"

I stood there and stared dumbly back.

"Um, I don't know." I shrugged. And the truth was, I didn't know. I was so young when my mom died—I wasn't exactly hitting the clubs in eighth grade. And Henry kept switching from no curfew to wanting me home right after school. I never paid attention to either rule.

We stared at each other blankly. Christine swirled her cocktail again and took a sip.

"How about, oh, let's just say when someone tells you what time they have to be home, you say, 'Me, too,'" she said.

"Wow, um, thanks Aunt Christine," I said, a little amazed.

"Well, you haven't done anything to make me not trust you, so don't make me lose that trust." She went back to sloshing her martini in its Waterford crystal glass. "I'll leave you some money on the counter. Buy yourself a new shirt or something."

I ran over and hugged her. "Thanks, Aunt Christine," I breathed into her neck, which smelled heavily of Estée Lauder's Beautiful.

The next day, I sat in Latin, staring at the clock tick slowly, slowly, slowly. 2:51. 2:52. 2:53. 2:52?

I rubbed my eyes and looked back at the fuzzy numbers on the clock, squinting. Is time actually going backward? No, no, it's 2:54. Just six more minutes. Ashley and I were going shopping after school. I was getting a new shirt—actually, a replacement shirt, since I'd left a lot of things in Keansburg. Once I'd decided to finally move in with Christine in late July, I'd moved *quickly*, and never went back for anything I'd left behind. I was sure that, by now, Henry had sold or trashed my stuff, with mementos from my life finding new homes in plastic garbage bags. Every now and then, I'd look for a shirt or hoodie and realize that I'd left them in the laundry bag, or hanging in the closet.

When the bell finally rang, I ran out of my seat and down the stairs to my locker. I had to be at Third Avenue promptly at 8:00 p.m. Since I didn't have a cell phone, I had no way of finding out if there were any changes in plans. I used to have a cell phone—a cute purple one at that, loaded to the hilt with my favorite ring tones, too—but I'd left it in Keansburg, in the charger on my nightstand. It was just as well: it had pretty much stopped ringing.

Shopping with Ashley was fun, even though she kept trying to talk me out of buying the plain black, long-sleeved boat-necked shirt I wanted. I figured that, with jeans, would be fine. It was the first time I'd see any of my friends out of uniform—and the first time they'd see me. I had to admit, I was a little nervous. I figured I'd play it safe with my outfit.

"Come on, this would look so pretty with your eyes!" she pleaded, holding up a shirt with a bright green design on the front. "It brings out the hazel, really!" she trilled in her high little voice.

"No thanks, kid. I like black."

We walked back to my aunt's house slowly, strolling down Madison Avenue and looking in the windows at all the high-end boutiques. For some reason, I thought about Brendan, and wondered what he did on Friday nights. He probably had a girlfriend. *Or girlfriends.* Ashley had said he was a deejay on the side. I'd bet he spent his nights spinning in the VIP section of some club so exclusive, there wasn't even a sign on the door, and model-like girls fell over each other to fawn all over him. I couldn't blame them if they did.

I *hated* this. It wasn't a crush so much; I didn't daydream about him asking me out, or think about twisting my fingers into his messy hair—not that much. I was just so curious about him. I wanted to *know* him. What bands he liked. What movies he liked. If his mind ever wandered to me, as mine often did to him—like now, since I'd been thinking about Brendan and ignoring my cousin.

I tuned in to Ashley, who was squealing about something. "He winked at me. Winked!" she shrieked, going on about some upperclassman who shared a free period with her. "And on Facebook, he keeps sending me kisses and stuff. I mean, who does that? It's so…cute."

By the time we were getting into the elevator in Aunt Christine's lobby, I had the full story. Her paramour was Blondo—and Ashley thought Anthony Caruso was the best thing since push-up bras.

"Ash, I don't mean to make you feel bad, but only yesterday, he hit on—" I paused. *No sense in making her feel like she's in my shadow, right?* "He hit on a girl in our class. I think he's trouble. He got really nasty with her when she turned him down."

"Oh, he's just a harmless flirt," she said dreamily, twirling as she stepped out of the elevator.

"I don't think so," I said, warily. "He's pretty shady."

Ashley turned and regarded me with serious, almost cold eyes. "I *like* him, okay? Just let me like him. Jeez, Emma, it's not the end of the world."

I knew that tone—that stubborn, "you can't change my mind" attitude. I had inherited it from my mom, and she had inherited it from her dad—my mom's brother, Dan. I sighed as I put the key in Aunt Christine's front door, resigned to be on the lookout for trouble between Ashley and Blondo.

"Ash, I just think you should be care—" I never got to finish my sentence. Ashley squealed, spying something. She pushed past me and ran to the kitchen table.

"Finally!" she yelled, picking up a small object next to the Waterford salt and pepper shakers.

"A cell phone?" I squeaked, running over. I picked up the small yellow note that had been slid underneath the salt shaker.

I figured you should have one. The guy at the store set it
up. Just please don't call China on it. Have fun tonight.
Love, Aunt Christine.

"Aw, she's the best," I murmured, stroking the shiny case of the phone.

"About time you had a phone!" Ashley exclaimed, grabbing the owner's manual and flipping through it. "Quick, call me so I have your number. And then you can text me tonight and let me know if anything happens with Cisco!" I started to explain for the thousandth time that it wasn't a date, but she pushed me toward my bedroom door. "Go, start getting ready!"

Two hours later, I had finished blowing my hair dry, flat-ironing it until it hung long and straight. My bangs, once merely in need of a trim, were now just long layers, hanging halfway down my face. At least it pulled my cowlick straight. I parted my hair on the left and tried to brush my bangs to the side. No wonder Ashley thought it was a date. I was acting like it was. I didn't know why; I just felt like I *had* to look nice tonight. I was probably just nervous about being accepted by Cisco's friends.

"You need less eyeliner," Ashley critiqued, hovering over me as I sat cross-legged on the floor at the end of my bed, my makeup scattered around me as I peered into the floor-length mirror on the back of my door. "You should do something with bright color, like a bright green or bright pink, and play up your eyes. Really, they're your best feature."

"Hardly," I griped, reaching for some more black eyeliner and applying it heavily before rubbing it in for a smoky look. "Everyone else in this family has blue eyes. Me, I get the brown eyes. The boring brown eyes."

"No, they're pretty," she said, her own crystal clear blue eyes twinkling. She then flung herself on my bed, kicking her legs in the air. "They're not brown. They're lighter. They're not hazel. I don't know, I'll come up with a name for it. Mink. Yeah. They're mink!" She started giggling and I rolled my "mink" eyes.

"*You're* a mink," I shouted gleefully, and Ashley just threw a pillow at me.

"Whoa, better hurry up," Ashley said abruptly, sitting upright and checking out the alarm clock on my nightstand. "It's seven-twenty, and it's going to take at least thirty-five minutes to walk up there." I trusted Ashley's New York sensibilities when it came to time. Since I knew I could walk everywhere, I estimated every destination to be about five minutes from Aunt Christine's home. I was often wrong. And late. And ended up running everywhere. I finally get my driver's license, and then move someplace where no one drives. Christine didn't even have a license.

I reached into one of my cardboard boxes, still packed in the closet, and grabbed my black boots, pulling them on over my jeans.

"So, what do you think?" I asked.

Ashley scrutinized me for a moment. "Take off your necklace," she ordered. "It interferes with the shirt's neckline."

I looked at myself in the mirror and saw the charm, hanging awkwardly over the straight boatneck of the shirt. She was right. But I never took off my charm necklace—it was one of the only things I still had from my brother. I pulled out the fabric and dropped the pendant between my skin and the shirt, so all you could see was the thin silver chain.

"Better?" I asked.

"Much. Now hold on." She reached into her backpack and pulled out a small bottle.

"Hell, no!" I yelled, recoiling as I remembered the sickeningly sweet stuff she sprayed on me last time. "That stuff smells like munchkin sweat."

"It's a different fragrance." She sighed, handing it over. I took a cautious whiff. *Okay, this is actually nice. Very light. Beachy, almost.*

I handed it back to her after spritzing it lightly around my shirt and hair.

"Now, you smell good," Ashley said, smugly. "You're no longer stinky."

I gave my smirking little cousin a hug and smoothed out the front of my shirt. "All right, I'd better get going."

Chapter 5

The air was brisk and I pulled my leather jacket more closely around me as I walked up Third Avenue, regretting not wearing a scarf or something warmer. I hadn't realized how wacky New York weather could be—cold one day, warm the next.

I got to Ninety-first Street and pulled out my new cell phone to check the time. I was eight minutes late. For me, that was early. I looked around and realized that I was standing in front of a sandwich shop.

For a split second, I wondered if it was all a joke on me. That Cisco was watching me from across the street, laughing as the loser girl stood there, waiting for friends to show up who would never come. *What a waste of a good flat-ironing job.*

"Hey, chica!" A few minutes later, I heard the call from down the block and looked up. Francisco was walking closer, flanked by three friends.

Relief colored my face. "Hey, look, new cell phone!" I waved the phone at him.

"Yeah, welcome to 1998." He laughed, taking my cell phone and calling his number so I'd have it. "This is my cousin, Samantha," he said, gesturing to a petite, older-looking girl to his right, "and her boyfriend Omar. They graduated last year. This is my friend Derek, he goes to St. Agnes."

"Hey, guys," I said, nodding to them. My breath came out like smoke against the cold.

"We're just waiting for one more person." Cisco elbowed me in the side. I cocked my head and stared at him quizzically. "In the meantime," he said, reaching into his pocket and pulling out a small card, "you'll need this." He pressed the card into my hand and I looked down.

"A learner's permit?"

"Correction, my sister's learner's permit. She got her license when she went to Michigan State. You look enough like her. For the rest of the night, you're Angie Marie Fernandez. I forgot to ask you if you had fake ID."

"Okay, I'm Angie Marie. And look, I'm still an Aquarius. That's nice," I said, smiling as I looked down at the card. Apart from the same dark hair, we looked absolutely nothing alike. I was mentally telling myself to get over my internal freak-out about going to a bar when I heard Cisco call to someone.

I looked up and saw a figure stroll over slowly from across the street. I really hoped my eyes didn't look like the Frisbees they felt like.

I was suddenly *very* happy that I'd spent so much time trying to look my best. At Vincent Academy, Brendan Salinger looked like the hottest guy in school. Outside of Vincent Academy, he looked like the hottest guy in Manhattan. Maybe the state. It didn't help my pathetic case that he was completely my type. I'd always liked dark hair. Brendan wore a dark T-shirt pulled over a long-sleeved gray one, and had some sort of leather cuff on his wrist. Of course, his hair was still messy. It was legitimately messy too, not that look-what-I-can-do-with-gel look. Total wash-and-go hair. I doubted he even owned any hair products. Brendan carried a black hoodie under his arm, and greeted Cisco with one of those one-handed, back-pump bro-hug things. *What* was *the deal with those things, anyway?*

Brendan bent down to kiss Samantha on the cheek and I was instantly jealous. I tried to remind myself that he likely just knew her from school—she graduated last year, after all.

Then, those green eyes were focused on me.

"Hey, Brendan," Cisco began. "Have you actually met Emma yet?"

His eyes stared into mine. "Not officially."

"Hey, what's—uh, what's up?" I tried to act nonchalant, but my voice cracked midgreeting.

Brendan's eyes were so serious, staring at me, but a smile played on his lips—those ridiculously soft-looking lips!—before forming a short, curt greeting. "Hey, Emma."

Cisco rounded us up and we walked down the block to a small dive bar, marked by a sputtering red neon sign reading Idle Hands in the window. The bouncer's eyes flitted to my face briefly when looking at the expired learner's permit. He rolled his eyes and waved me inside. No one else seemed to have any trouble either, so we headed into the slightly crowded, dark bar. An old Green Day song pumped out of the jukebox, and the crowd was a mix of underage kids downing pitchers of cheap beer and old men playing cards and drinking scotch. Peanut shells crunched on the floor under the heel of my boots, and I almost slipped on one, catching my balance just before I completely humiliated myself. I stopped to scrape the shell off as everyone else walked past me and filed in, one after another, at the bar along the wall on the left. Cisco was first, greeting a short, cute brunet whom I assumed was Gabe.

"Thanks so much for coming, you guys," Gabe said with an anxious laugh. "Just remember, we're really not that good.

But hey, we get a cut of whatever the bar makes tonight, so as long as we don't get booed off the stage we should be okay.

"And you must be Emma." Gabe smiled, looking at me warmly as I was still trying to scrape the peanut shell off my heel. "I've heard a lot of nice things about you."

"All lies," I said, grinning. "I paid Cisco off."

Gabe laughed, and said, "Well, hope you're not expecting much tonight. We're really not that good. So yeah, don't hate me."

I smiled back at him. After finally getting the shell off my boot, I looked around to hop on a bar stool and realized the only one left was between the wall and Brendan. *Gulp.*

"So, what do you do in the band?" I asked, stalling.

"Drums," Gabe said, raising his voice over the music. "The band is just for fun. For now anyway, since we really do suck. Okay, round of shots anyone? I need some liquid courage."

Everyone in the group agreed enthusiastically. Or should I say, everyone else. I stayed silent. Sure, I was no stranger to drinking. I'd had plenty of warm keg beer and Goldschläger at friends' parties. But since the accident, I hadn't done much other than nurse a light beer in a feeble attempt to show that I was still socially acceptable. And I had never been to a freakin' bar before! Keansburg was way too small for that. Before I could even think, the bartender was lining up shots at the bar. I stood at the empty spot, between Brendan and the wall, and lifted the shot glass. Giving a wary glance to everyone, I made sure they weren't looking and threw it over my shoulder.

I wiped my mouth and sucked on the lemon the way everyone else had, casting a look behind me to see if I'd hit anything—or anyone. The tequila had landed on the wall beside me—leaving a small swoosh on the pale plaster.

"All right, I gotta set up. See you guys in a bit," Gabe said, flashing a big grin. "And seriously, we do suck. So don't leave in the middle of it!"

"Do they really, or is he going to get up there and be the next Blink-182?" I asked, calling across to Cisco after Gabe was out of hearing range.

"Oh, they're not good. *He's* good," he emphasized proudly. "But the band isn't all that great."

"They're not *that* bad," Samantha disagreed, lightly slapping her cousin on the shoulder. Cisco gave her a pointed look, and Samantha conceded. "Okay, they *are* pretty bad. Gabe is the only bright spot. Some of it might make your ears bleed. Nails-on-a-chalkboard time."

She formed a claw with her hand and made a screeching sound and I winced, laughing. Brendan motioned for the bartender to come over and he threw down a black credit card.

"I got this round," he said to the bartender. If Brendan noticed that the bartender's jaw dropped a little when he got a good look at the card, he ignored it. "Round of tequila shots and whatever everyone else wants," Brendan said. He then regarded me over his right shoulder.

"So, Emma, what would you like?" *Um, how about you, shirtless?* The minute Brendan talked to me, my brain felt like it exploded. *What did he just ask me? Oh, yeah. Drinks.*

"Just a beer, whatever, thanks." I tried to sound casual as I absentmindedly dragged my necklace back and forth on its chain before tucking it back under my shirt.

"What's that?" Brendan asked, pointing to the base of his own throat.

"Oh, nothing, just a charm necklace," I said dismissively, smoothing out the neckline of the shirt. If I answered, then he'd ask about my brother…and my family…and he'd never want to talk to me again. He already knew I was lying about where I was from.

"You know," he said, his voice low as he leaned in more closely. I could smell Brendan's shampoo—it was a clean, fresh scent, like grass in the rain. "You don't *have* to drink. I don't care—I mean, no one cares if you don't."

Did Brendan see you throw the tequila over your shoulder? He doesn't sound judgmental.

The bartender arrived with the shots and Brendan took mine, placing it in front of him.

"No sense in wasting good liquor. Or, as is the case here, very cheap tequila." Brendan kept his eyes on me as he drained my shot, and I began to wonder if a beer wouldn't be a good idea, just to calm my nerves.

I met his gaze. "I'm good with a beer, thanks."

He shrugged and ordered my drink, which the bartender promptly brought over. Then Brendan casually leaned back against the bar, stretching his long legs in front of him.

I tried to think of some kind of conversation starter. "So, how do you know Cisco?" I asked, sitting on the bar stool next to Brendan.

"We go to the same school," Brendan replied, tilting his head toward me. "Maybe you've heard of it? Vincent Academy?" His voice was playful and teasing.

"*You're* a Vincent Academy!" I blurted out.

Brendan laughed—a big laugh—and shook his head at me, smiling.

"What the hell does that mean?" he asked.

"I, um, have no idea," I said, embarrassed. I couldn't believe I pulled that stupid joke in front of Brendan, of all people.

"So, is Gabe's band your kind of music?" Brendan said, still laughing.

"I don't even know what kind of music Gabe's band is. Other than bad, apparently. So I'd have to say no, it's not my

kind of music. I'm weird like that. I only like good things."
What am I babbling on about?

"You really weren't far off with the Blink-182 reference," Brendan said, brushing his hand through his hair, causing the black locks to fall haphazardly.

"Maybe I'll like them," I said. "I love Blink."

"Me, too. You ever listen to their old stuff?"

"You mean *Dude Ranch*, or you mean their *really* old stuff?"

His eyes twinkled at me. "Oh, you're a musicologist, are you now?"

"I don't know about that…I can't play an instrument to save my life, but *Buddha* is one of my favorite albums. I always go back to it and get obsessed with a different song."

"What's your current favorite?" Brendan asked.

"Well, lately it's been 'Carousel,'" I started…then realized I'd given up way too much info. Ten minutes into conversation, and I'm telling him about the song about unrequited love and loneliness that's jumped to the top of my iPod playlist. *Smooth, Emma. Why not pick "Pathetic" while you're at it?*

I took a quick swig of my beer and kept my eyes trained on his, keeping my voice level. "I just really, really like the chorus on that song."

Brendan opened his mouth as if he was about to say something, then just shut it. "Oh, hey, they're about to start."

We turned around, leaning against the bar as Gabe's singer and guitarist, a lanky guy with badly dyed cherry-red curls enthusiastically screamed into the mike, "Hey, we're Broken Echo, and are you ready to rock?"

Apart from our little group, no one cheered. Gabe just looked embarrassed—and his face burned as red as the singer's curls when he burst into an off-tune guitar riff. I wasn't sure if it was supposed to be *that* out of tune, or if it was a mistake, but judging from the crestfallen look on Gabe's face, I could tell their gig had started off badly.

Gabe, for his part, was actually talented, but unfortunately, the guitarist ruined most of their performance. Grandstanding poses, sticking his tongue out and throwing up the horns every chance he got... His schtick got old before the first song was over.

In the middle of the second song, a butchered version of a My Chemical Romance song, Brendan leaned in next to me, placing his left arm along the bar behind my back, and I felt my breath quicken.

"In chemistry today, Cisco told me that Gabe's dying to leave the band and start his own, but Kenny—that's Captain Clownhair over there—he started the band. So Gabe feels loyal, like he can't leave." I snickered at the joke about Kenny's hair, but could feel my cool slipping away as Brendan's breath tickled me, warm on my ear. So I just nodded in agreement. His arm lingered along my back, and I realized I was holding myself stiffly against the bar, afraid to lean into him.

I extended out my arms in front of me and pretended to stretch, resting more of my weight against the bar. Brendan's arm stayed against my back. I acted like I didn't notice and focused on the band, peeling the label off my now-empty beer bottle. Summoning some more courage, I leaned back into Brendan some more.

Brendan removed his arm—only to turn around and order something else from the bartender. Wordlessly, he handed me a new beer. *Was he paying that much attention to me that he noticed I needed a refill?* I mouthed, "Thanks," and put it to my lips.

After getting his drink, Brendan lounged against the bar and stretched his arm along its very welcome spot along my back. I cast a sideways glance at him, and internally imploded when I saw he was looking at me, too. I smiled, a little shyly, and he leaned in more closely until he fully had his arm around me. *Aaand, my guy-cation is officially over.*

Two songs later, Brendan started drumming his fingers on my side in time to the music. I felt like my heart was keeping time with the ramming bass line. Every time he'd bend in to ask me something, or laugh at something I said, the bass line in my chest turned into a hardcore song.

The band was winding down their final song—which ended with an earsplitting two-minute solo guitar riff from Kenny. I squirmed uncomfortably on my bar stool, and Brendan covered my ears with his hands, laughing with me the entire time. He only kept his hands there a few seconds, but they felt warm against the side of my face. The pounding bass line in my chest was now speed metal.

When the set was over, we all cheered, enthusiastically yelling Gabe's name—much to Kenny's dismay. The jukebox came back on, and Brendan and I turned to face the rest of our crew.

"So, what are we doing now?" Samantha asked over the music, tapping her glossy pale nails on the bar. "Let's go to the Met. I wouldn't mind seeing who's there. Come on, Omar, it'll be fun," she pleaded when he made a gagging sound.

"I never went when I actually was a student at Vince A, and I'm not going to start now," he snorted.

"Let's go," Cisco said, looking at the time. "Gabe has to load up their equipment and bring his drums home—I won't be meeting up with him until later."

"Um, what's the Met?" I asked.

"You know, the Met? The Met!" Derek exclaimed, looking at me like I was a confused fourth grader. "The Metropolitan Museum of Art!"

"You guys hang out there?" I looked at my phone. It was 10:30. "Is it even open?"

"We hang out *next* to it," Cisco explained, shaking his head at my cluelessness. "There's a big glass wall, and you can see in, see the Egyptian temples and stuff. It's cool."

"Okay…I'm in," I said, a little bewildered. At Keansburg High, we hung out behind the gym. At Vince A, they hung out behind priceless works of art. *Riiight. And I bet the school play is directed by Martin Scorsese.*

We started walking toward the museum, and Cisco fell in line with me while Brendan and the others walked on ahead. I heard Brendan asking Samantha about Columbia, which is where she was studying business. I pulled my leather jacket around me and tried not to shiver against the cold.

"So, what's going on, Miss Connor? Makin' some new friends?" Cisco asked, shooting me a big grin.

"Nothing's going on," I mumbled, embarrassed. "I'm just making friends, like you said. So," I started, turning my head to him, "Why is this the first time I'm hearing that you two are friends?"

"He's not my best friend or anything—he keeps to himself, if you haven't noticed—but we're cool. We had every class together in freshman year. He's actually the first person at school who found out I was gay."

"Really? How'd that happen? I've never seen you guys together," I said, wrapping my arms around my thin jacket as another cold blast of wind shot through me.

"You don't have chemistry with me—we're lab partners. But last year, Brendan saw me with Gabe at Warped Tour. I asked him to keep it to himself. He did and told me he didn't see what the big deal was anyway. Nothing changed."

"Wow. Decent guy."

"Yeah, he is. And," Cisco said, getting a teasing tone in his voice, "he asked me about you. *You're* why he's here tonight.

You know, you're the only girl at school that hasn't tried to kick it to him at one time or another."

"He's here because of *me?*" I squeaked, then lightly punched Cisco on the arm. "Why didn't you tell me he was coming? What exactly did he say?"

He just chuckled. "You had no cell phone! Besides, he only just asked about you this afternoon in chem. I told him you were coming tonight, and he should come and find out for himself. I mean, damn, Emma, you stare at the guy enough, I had to do *something.*"

"Oh, no," I moaned, covering my face with my hands. "Am I that obvious?" I anxiously peeked at him through my chilly fingers.

"Nah, it's not too bad. I just sit next to you so I noticed. It's not like you're going to cut a piece of his hair off and build an altar to it," Cisco said, putting his hands together and bowing. "Oh, Brendan, you're my hero! You're ever so dreamy!" he whispered in a high-pitched imitation of a girl's voice. "I wuv you *so* much! I want to have a trillion bajillion of your babies."

I whacked him in the arm again.

"So, how'd it go with him?" Cisco continued, elbowing me in the side with a knowing look. "You two sure looked *comfy* at the end of the bar."

I tried to figure out how to phrase it. When I didn't think about what he looked like, lounging at the bar next to me, I felt like I was talking to someone I'd known for years. And then I'd get a look into those twinkling green eyes, and realize how we just didn't match.

"I feel really…comfortable with him. Which is weird, cause, well, look at him."

"You *do* look, all the time," Cisco teased, then lowered his voice. "Heads up, he's coming this way."

"Hey, I'll meet you guys at the Met. I'm going to stop for a water and some beer," Brendan said, the wind whipping his hair in a billion different directions.

"Emma, do you want anything?"

"I'll just take an iced tea, thanks." I'd had a few beers and the last thing I needed to do to Aunt Christine was show up on her door hammered, after everything that'd happened and all she'd done for me.

Brendan regarded me for a minute standing there with my arms wrapped around my jacket.

"Take this," he ordered, shrugging out of his black hoodie.

"Won't you get cold?" I asked, hesitantly taking the black sweatshirt from him with frozen fingers.

"No, I'm good," Brendan said dismissively. *Hell yeah, you are.*

I pulled the oversize—well, oversize on me—hoodie around my jacket and instantly felt better. The sleeves hung low, several inches from my balled-up fists.

"I'll see you guys in a minute," Brendan said, turning to walk away. With his hands in his pockets, Brendan walked that same slow, deliberate walk to a deli on the corner.

About fifteen minutes later, we made our way across Fifth Avenue and crossed into Central Park. The Met stood there, silent and imposing, and I could hear some noise coming from the right side of the building.

Cisco and I followed Omar, Derek and Samantha, climbing up the rolling green lawn to the right of the massive white building. I recognized the shadowy forms in the distance as some of the people from my class—including Jenn, who staggered over with her arms open. I spotted a two-liter bottle of lemon-lime soda in her hand.

"Emma! You never come out," she slurred, her low-cut

white sweater stained with droplets from whatever she was drinking. Jenn shoved the soda toward me and offered me a drink. The sugary citrus-and-cranberry-vodka smell was heavy and sweet as it wafted up from the bottle.

"Oh, no thanks," I said, recoiling at the smell. It reminded me of the perfume Ashley loved. "Beer before liquor, you know."

She looked confused, then stumbled back to the group of people near the trees. I squinted my eyes, trying to make out who was there when I noticed Kristin actually smiling in my direction. I stared, stunned, as she waved to me, beaming a bright smile. I raised my hand up to wave and stopped halfway when I realized she was waving *behind* me—not actually *at* me. Kristin hadn't noticed me standing there, until the person she had targeted in her gaze was right behind me and Cisco. And then her gaze turned ice-cold.

Brendan poked his head between us, throwing his arms around me and Cisco. He had an iced tea in his left hand, and started tapping it against my cheek. The coldness of the glass, coupled with another chilly wind, forced me to shiver again.

"Oh, thanks," I said, hastily grabbing the drink. "How much do I owe you?"

"You're kidding, right?" Brendan asked incredulously, dropping his arms and reaching into the white plastic bag at his feet, pulling out a bottle of water.

"Cheers," he said, tapping his plastic bottle against my still-unopened iced tea. Brendan handed Cisco the bag of beers and Cisco walked away, giving me a thumbs-up as he left. I hoped Brendan didn't notice.

"No beer for you?" I asked, gesturing to his bottle of water.

"No beer for you, either," he pointed out, tapping my glass again with the top of his water bottle.

"Yeah, I just didn't want to—I mean, not get wasted," I stammered, trying to explain myself. "Um, why aren't you drinking?"

"It's not a big deal." Brendan shrugged. "I didn't want you to feel weird, like you were the only one not drinking."

"Oh," I murmured, in shock and half in love with him for squashing one of my biggest social insecurities with a bottle of Poland Spring. "Um, thanks," I said shyly. "That's really nice of you." *I can't believe he's curbing partying...for me of all people.*

"No problem," Brendan said, playfully taking the hood on his sweatshirt and flicking it up over my head. "So Emma, are you feeling a little warmer?"

"A lot warmer, thanks." I laughed as the oversize hood fell over my face, covering my eyes.

"So," I began, peeking out from underneath the hood, "what's that Halloween movie thing next week at school all about?" I tried to sound nonchalant, but I already knew all about the event at school: Austin had been gabbing in my ear for a week about Vince A showing scary movies for Halloween. I had to find out if Brendan was going. Then it might be worth *me* going.

But he didn't get a chance to answer, since our attention was grabbed by a series of high-pitched squeals across the grass. We turned our heads to Kristin, who giggled loudly and deliberately looked over at Brendan as she let Anthony lick tequila salt off her neck.

"The bar's open!" she called, holding out a shot and patting more salt on her collarbone—and a little lower. Kristin's invitation was clearly meant for one specific person. The possessive way she stared at Brendan infuriated me.

"Less than fifty feet from priceless art, surrounded by a ton of people and oh, Kristin's doing a body shot," I snorted, then feared I sounded way, way too bitchy. To my relief, Brendan just laughed.

"She sucks," he said, waving his hand dismissively. "So Emma, back home, where did you guys hang out?" he asked, suddenly serious as he turned away from Kristin to stare intensely at me. "The Liberty Bell?"

"What do you mean, the Lib... Oh." My guard was completely down around Brendan. I exhaled nervously, reminded that he knew the truth. "You know, it's a landmark and all, so that was impossible."

"So, you hung out at school, right? At that magical high school on the corner of Made-Up Street and Fiction Avenue?" Brendan smirked a knowing smile. More significant than him standing up for me that first day was the fact that he knew my story was faker than pro wrestling.

I tried to think of an excuse, a good story to tell, when he took another gulp of his water and said, "You don't have to tell me anything right now. But I'd appreciate you telling me eventually."

"Why does it matter?" I asked, annoyed. He ignores me, and now I owe him my life story?

"Why wouldn't you want to tell me?" Brendan asked. "Don't you trust me?"

I opened my mouth to reply, but I had no idea what to say. For someone with major trust issues, I already did trust him. And that just felt unnatural. Fortunately, I didn't have to answer—Cisco called us over to the sloped glass wall of the Met, where he was standing over a very passed-out Austin.

"I think we need to get him in a cab," Cisco said, chuckling slightly at the slumbering Austin. Here he was, the student council rep, who had spent every lunch period since we first met trying to convince me to join *any* club, looking like he

was the poster child for our chapter of SADD. Which, ironi-
cally, was the club Austin had tried to get me to join at lunch
that very afternoon.

"I'll help you," Brendan said, lifting up Austin effortlessly.
It surprised me, since after the way Austin had talked about
Brendan on my first day at school, I was under the impression
that they weren't exactly friends. Brendan and Cisco were
about the same height, so they balanced the shorter guy between them easily. Austin woke up, stammering, "What? Ma?
Time for school?"

"Yeah, buddy, it's time for school," Cisco said, grinning,
then added to me, "Emma, we'll be right back."

They were gone for merely seconds when Jenn came bound-
ing over again, her bottle almost empty.

"What were you guys… Who left?" She drained the rest of
her beverage and looked around, dismayed when she noticed
Austin was missing.

"Aw, he left me his drink," she giggled, waving the now-
empty two-liter at me. "So sweet. I'll give it back to him
tomorrow," she whispered loudly. "We're going skating at
Wollman Rink!" She meant for her voice to be low, her statement confidential, but her drunken confession spilled out all
over the lawn.

I put an arm around Jenn to steady her and advised, "You
should throw that bottle out, you know. I'm sure he doesn't
need it back. But that's cool about the skating." I didn't expect
either one of them to be out of bed before 2:00 p.m.

"Let's go hang out over by the—oh, no. Wait." Jenn was
gesturing at the cluster of trees where Kristin was holding
court, until she realized that Kristin had her usual "Death to
Emma" glare trained on me. Closer to us, Anthony and a short
guy I recognized from math class were arguing. It looked like
the conversation was getting heated.

"I think Anthony's gonna beat Frank up," Jenn whispered conspiratorially. "They've been fighting all night. Too bad. Frank's kinda cute."

I looked around anxiously for Cisco and Brendan, my friends—I could count Brendan as my friend now, right?

"What time do you need to be home, Jenn?" I asked, looking again at my phone. Even though I didn't have a real curfew, I didn't want to push my luck.

She shrugged, then ran down the green, yelling, "Cisco!" Jenn jumped on him, knocking him down. At the same time, Anthony shouted something I couldn't quite make out at the other guy—Frank Carney—and my feet started twitching to run in the other direction. Henry was quick with his hands when he was drinking, and his alcohol-fueled rages had taught me at least one thing—I had an uncanny ability to know when things were about to get physical. Even though it had healed, my scar began to throb.

I jogged over to Cisco and helped him off the ground.

"Hey, you're meeting Gabe soon, right?" I asked, darting my eyes to where Anthony and Frank were getting more agitated. Anthony menacingly shouted something in Frank's face. Kristin and her posse had moved away from the guys, but she pulled out her cell phone and started recording them, snickering as she clearly enjoyed watching someone else's misery.

"Yeah, I'm meeting him downtown. What's up?"

"I just— I want to get out of here before that—" I gestured to the fight "—becomes something else."

"I wouldn't be surprised if it did. Anthony's always starting trouble," Cisco said.

I knew it. There is no way Ashley is allowed near him.

"Where's Brendan?" I twisted my head around, searching for him.

Cisco smiled. "We couldn't get a cab. He sent me back here to make sure you were okay."

I blushed a little, almost forgetting where I was. That was sweet. *Really* sweet. *First he stops drinking, now this...he's probably just a nice guy.* Then a shout broke through my thoughts.

With his lips curled back over his teeth, Anthony snarled several choice swear words at Frank before pushing him into a tree. Frank crumbled on the ground, then pulled himself back to his feet, charging at Anthony to shove him in his chest. Anthony barely budged—Blondo towered over the smaller guy. Anthony threw the first punch, hitting Frank forcefully in the stomach. Frank doubled over, gasping as he clutched his midsection. Anthony took advantage of Frank's vulnerability, kicking him again in the stomach with his heavy boot and knocking him down on the grass. Once the smaller guy was down, Anthony—stumbling a little in his drunken state—hurled himself on top of Frank, throwing a hard punch in his face. It connected with a sickening thud. I wasn't sure what to do—call someone? Why wasn't anyone stopping this? Fortunately, someone did, as a third figure ran past me and jumped in.

I realized it was Brendan, breaking up the fight. In one quick movement, he pulled Anthony off Frank.

"Stop it! What the hell is wrong with you?" Brendan spit out, steadying Anthony by holding a fistful of his collar. Frank sat upright, wiping away the thick smear of blood coming from his nose. His eye already looked red.

"Stay out of it," Anthony growled, trying to stand upright. He couldn't quite coordinate all his limbs in his drunken state and fell on his rear.

Brendan leaned forward and helped Frank up, leaving Anthony on the ground. "Get up, dummy," he said to Anthony, sounding annoyed. He turned to Frank. "You good?"

"Yeah, I'm fine." Frank brushed some leaves off his brown jacket, glaring at Anthony. "We'll continue this later."

"Oh, shut up, no you won't," Brendan snapped, sounding more and more like a ticked-off kindergarten teacher. "Enough of this crap. Stop being such friggin' babies."

Frank stalked away, while Anthony scowled at his back. Brendan leaned in and said some hushed things to Anthony, his hands gesturing wildly—it looked like he was reading him the riot act. Loudly, Anthony told Brendan where he could stick his head and walked—or should I say, stumbled—toward a concerned-looking Kristin.

The whole scene made me very, *very* uneasy. This was the real Anthony, I figured—not the charming sweetheart that my cousin thought he was. I turned to Cisco and said, "I'm out of here. Tell everyone I said bye, okay?"

"Tell everyone? Or tell him?" Cisco replied, with smart-alecky emphasis on the "him." Before I could answer, Cisco said, "Actually, tell him yourself." I looked up and saw Brendan walking over, a little faster than I was used to seeing him move.

"Hey, guys—Anthony and Frank had a fight at practice and clearly are taking things home with them. Anthony said something about Frank's mother. Anthony's an idiot. He's not going to start anything else tonight, though," he explained, looking back and forth between both of us. Brendan then stopped and turned those emerald eyes back on me.

"You're leaving." It wasn't a question.

"Yeeeah." I drew it out slowly. "I'm— I've got to get home. Curfew, you know," I lied, hastily draining the rest of my iced tea, then shuddering from the cold drink.

Brendan just nodded. "I'll walk you to a cab," he said quietly. He stayed silent, walking toward Fifth Avenue with his hands stuffed in his jeans pockets until we were back in front of the museum, looking down the street for an available taxi.

"That was nice of you to get Austin a cab," I said a little formally, leaning against a lamppost. I wasn't sure what to say to him all of a sudden.

"Least I could do. He's your friend, right?" Brendan said matter-of-factly.

"I guess."

"He sits right next to you at lunch every day," Brendan pointed out. *Wait, did he get Austin a cab for* me? *Does he think I'm dating Austin?*

Before I could clear up my relationship with Austin, Brendan spoke. "Did Anthony scare you?" he asked, his eyes searching mine.

"No," I fibbed, then looked down. "Well, I wouldn't say *scared*…." I mumbled, hiding my embarrassment by picking at some chipped paint on the lamppost.

"I wouldn't let him hurt you," Brendan said, his voice almost a whisper. I was taken aback by how seriously he said it. I tore my eyes away from the flaking paint to face Brendan, and was surprised at how close he was to me. His face was mere inches from mine. I took a deep breath, getting lost in those eyes as the lamppost above me flickered on and off. I could see the light dancing in the flecks of gold in his eyes, as he stayed close to me. The light fizzled out with a thin hiss, but I could still see the intensity in his eyes in the shadows. Brendan rested his palm on the iron street lamp behind me. He leaned in more closely, and I let my fingers brush against his side, skimming along his dark shirt. I felt that familiar fluttering in my stomach again, hoping, praying that he was going to kiss me. Brendan was so close I could smell his shampoo again, which overpowered the sulfuric smell from the burned-out light above.

But Brendan stopped short—pulling back and flagging the lone available cab cruising down Fifth. I straightened up awkwardly. If I wasn't already red from the cold, I would have blushed a thousand shades of crimson.

"Thanks," I mumbled weakly. "And yeah—thanks for this," I said, pulling the hoodie off.

"Keep it, it's cold out," Brendan said, his tone businesslike as he opened the taxi door for me. He gave me another smile, then, slamming the door shut once I was inside, he turned on his heel.

Chapter 6

I woke up late on Saturday morning, feeling oddly exhausted for having slept so long. I'd had the most vivid, disturbing dreams. They didn't make any sense—at first, all I saw were images of *me*. I was wearing my charm necklace—but I was wearing different outfits. They were costumes, almost—it looked like I was flipping through some kind of scrapbook that spanned centuries.

The scrapbook stopped short at one photo; in it, I was dressed in a heavy-looking gown, tending to beautiful roses that climbed up the stone face of a picturesque cottage.

The photo came alive and suddenly I was in the scene, feeling the weight of the heavy gold dress. I removed dead petals from a perfect red rose, which had just started to wilt, when I sliced open my finger on a razor-sharp thorn. I felt it rip through my flesh, shredding my skin. I pulled away my finger, gripping it tightly to stop the bleeding. But it wouldn't stop. Blood poured down my hand, pooling in the grass as I felt something warm on my chest. I looked down, and blood seeped across the front of my bodice, soaking the front of the gold dress with deep crimson.

I pawed at my chest but couldn't find the wound, my fingers frantic as I searched my bloody skin for an injury.

A familiar voice called me from behind. I whipped around, and my brother Ethan was standing among the roses. Even though I was dressed in this heavy medieval-looking gown, my twin looked the way I remembered him, in jeans, ratty Converse sneakers and a Ramones T-shirt.

"Emma, it's starting," Ethan said, his voice sad. "Stay away from him."

I bolted upright in bed as if I had been shocked by a Taser. It felt like Ethan was right next to me, his voice as real as the ambulance siren I heard wailing in the street four floors below me.

I hadn't dreamed about Ethan in some time. I tried to shake the weird dream off, but it was too unsettling. I chalked it up to my subconscious going haywire. I'd avoided telling Brendan about him last night, after all. That had to be the cause of the weird dream.

Right?

I stretched out in the bed and rubbed my eyes, looking over at my pile of clothing on the floor—my boots strewn about, my jeans crumpled up with my socks still in the legs. The previous night came flooding back to me when my eyes flickered over to the white-painted desk chair, where I'd carefully laid Brendan's hoodie. I covered my face and giggled, then frowned when I looked at my grimy hands.

Ugh, I'd forgotten to wash my face when I came in last night! I'd walked to my room in a daze—thanks to Brendan's near-kiss—and started writing in my diary. I jumped out of bed and padded into the bathroom, trying to remove the now-smeared dark mascara that had taken up residence all over my face. I stopped and looked at my reflection—cowlick sticking up straight, hair knotted, raccoon eyes—and giggled again. I looked like a goth model. I sucked in my cheeks and attempted a serious, model-like pose.

"What's up, Zoolander?" I said aloud, splashing water on my face. I was in too good of a mood this morning.

My attempts to wash my face just ended up in streaking mascara all over the place, so I hopped into the shower, turned on the pink plastic shower radio and sang along to a Paramore song, scrubbing my face.

Slipping into my worn plaid bathrobe, I pulled my wet hair back with a large clip, and opened the door to find a giddy Ashley standing there. I was not expecting to see anything but the short hallway back to my room—so I screamed.

She screamed back.

"What the— You can't just do that to people!" I huffed, leaning against the door frame.

"Sorry! I forgot that you had a cell phone now and I could just call you! I was afraid Christine would give me the third degree about you and Cisco if I called the apartment."

"Ashley, for the last time, me and Cisco are not—"

"Whatever," she interrupted, "I had to tell you the good news in person anyway." She was a little waterfall, overflowing with good cheer. Ashley practically skipped back to my room, her high red ponytail bouncing on the top of her head like a genie. I saw my aunt, savoring her morning coffee in the kitchen. "Hold on a second," I told Ashley.

"Aunt Christine, thank you so much for the cell phone," I said, giving her a big hug. She hugged me back, a little more tightly than she usually did, then returned to her usual stiff demeanor.

"Well, I couldn't have you be the only one running around town without one," she sniffed.

"I love it. Thanks."

"Well, you're welcome. Did you have fun?"

"Yes," I said, beaming.

"Good. I'm glad. Now go see what your cousin wants. That child is persistent when she wants something!" Aunt Christine laughed.

I trotted in to see Ashley, my slippers making a soft "swish, swish" sound on the floor.

"Okay, so I totally want to hear about your night, but first—oh, my God." She giggled. "Remember how we were talking about Anthony?"

Before I could scream in protest, Ashley continued, "Well, he messaged me on Facebook again and asked for my number!"

I noticed she was tightly clutching her cell phone in her hand. Waiting to answer the second he called, no doubt.

Anthony? I braced myself to cut her daydreams off at the knees.

"Ash, I have to tell you something." I sat down on the bed and looked at her. Well, I looked at her sneaker-clad feet. All along, she'd been so excited for me, and so supportive of me, and here I was, about to crush her new crush.

I quickly—and as kindly as I could—relayed what I observed the night before. Her jaw dropped so far, I thought it might fall in her lap.

"He's not a good guy," I said gently. "I don't think you should talk to him anymore."

"Maybe it's a different Anthony," Ashley mumbled.

"It's a small school," I reasoned. "How many guys in the junior class are blond basketball players named Anthony?"

"Maybe Frank started it," she suggested hopefully, biting her lip.

"Not from where I was standing," I said softly. "Regardless, it seemed like Anthony's a little quick with his hands. I think he might be trying to play you, Ash. I'm sorry."

"Well, I don't agree." Ashley raised her chin defiantly. "Are you sure you're not just overreacting, because of…well, you know. What you went through?"

I considered the Henry effect for a second. Sure, Anthony was arrogant and ready to punch a guy out at a moment's notice, but did I really want to put him in the same category as a raging drunk who had no problem backhanding me when I mouthed off?

"I can see where you think I'm overreacting," I conceded warily. "But just understand that I also have some experience in this area. I think you should be extremely careful around him," I warned.

"Okay, whatever," she said, sticking out her bottom lip in a pout. I felt awful. To her, he was so hot, one of the best athletes at the school and definitely one of the "cool" guys at Vince A, whatever that meant. And he had singled her out, a freshman, for attention. And I had to come and rip her little wonderland to shreds.

"Well, tell me about your night." Ashley sighed, resigned. She flopped into my desk chair and longingly stroked my sticker-covered laptop—a present from Aunt Christine. She probably wanted to open it and log on to Facebook, I realized.

"Did *you* get to make a love connection with Cisco?" she asked petulantly.

"We're just friends, Ashley," I began. "But, that hoodie you're leaning against—" I paused dramatically "—it's Brendan Salinger's."

That snapped her out of her glum mood.

"What?"

I bit my lip and grinned. She pulled herself upright and laid the sweatshirt against her. It fell below her knees.

"What is this, his car cover?" she snickered. "He's a giant."

"No, you're just a shrimp." I laughed, and Ashley threw the hoodie at me. She then leaned forward and said, "So, tell me *everything!*"

The rest of the weekend seemed like a never-ending ocean of time—all I wanted to do was get to school and see Brendan again. I distracted myself with homework for most of Saturday—even emailing Mrs. Urbealis a pretty big history paper about a week before it was due. My lack of a social life was turning out to be great for my grades. But thanks to Aunt Christine, I didn't have to worry about filling the rest of the hours with distractions. I padded into the kitchen where Aunt Christine was sitting at the table, perusing takeout menus and working on Uncle George's martini. (She drank both cocktails on Saturdays.)

"You need a haircut," she surmised, swishing her martini around. "You're starting to look like that girl from that movie you made me watch."

I looked at her confused, then my eyes widened in horror. *"The Ring?"* I asked incredulously, touching my hair. It had gotten long and my ends were screaming out for a trim. But really, *that* bad?

"Yes, that's it, dear. You look like the girl from *The Ring.* And not the blonde one," she said, pointing a manicured pink fingernail at me. "The wet one. You need a haircut. Hand me the phone, dear. I'm going to see if I can sweet-talk Melissa into seeing you tomorrow afternoon. She sometimes takes special appointments on Sundays and with the amount of clients I've sent her way, I think she'll squeeze you in. You can't go around looking like you're about to climb out of my television set."

I chalked that last comment up to the martinis, pleased that when I did see Brendan, I'd have a nice new 'do. And it was a few more hours of diversion—where I didn't have to think about how his shampoo smelled, or how he felt pressed up against me.

Monday morning, I carefully hung his hoodie in my locker, since it wouldn't fit into my overstuffed backpack. It still smelled like that fresh, clean-rain scent, now mixed with the light beachy perfume my cousin had sprayed on me. I touched the sleeve and sighed—then stifled a giggle. What must I have looked like, standing near my musty basement locker like a gremlin? "My precious," I snickered in an awestruck, strangulated Gollum-like way.

My thoughts continued to be unfocused throughout the morning. Absentmindedly, in math class, I was tap-tap-tapping my pen on the coils of my spiral notebook, not really paying attention to anything Mr. Agneta said, until Jenn whipped around and slammed her hand on top of my pen. I was taken aback.

"Too…loud," she hissed in a raspy voice, and I noticed her eyes were bloodshot.

"You okay?" I whispered.

"Long night." She grimaced, then paused. "Did I… I saw you this weekend, didn't I?"

"Yeah, Jenn, by the Met, on Friday."

She looked dumbfounded. "Oh. I don't really remember." She turned back to her notebook, then whipped back around at me. "Wait, did I do anything stupid?"

"I wasn't there that long," I said, realizing this wasn't what she wanted to hear. "I mean, while I was there, you were fine." I considered my statement and amended it. "Well, fine-ish. You were having fun. It's okay. Most people were drunk."

"Well, that's a relief. I remember nothing." She paused again. "Hey, haircut!" Jenn exclaimed. "It looks nice."

"Girls, is there something you'd like to share with the class?" Mr. Agneta interjected, staring at us and tapping the large chalk protractor against the board.

"No sir," we both replied.

"Well, since you're already done with your work, Miss Connor, perhaps you can tell me the answer to this equation?" Mr. Agneta glared at me.

I looked at the jumble of x's and y's on the board and tried to bluff my way out of this.

"Uh…pi?" I asked, hopefully.

He grimaced, his mouth set in an angry line. "It would be nice if you paid attention, Miss Connor." All discussion was clearly on hold until later.

I slid into my desk in English, where Cisco greeted me warmly. Jenn, for her part, was looking greener by the second. Suddenly, all those times when she kept her head down and didn't talk to me made total sense: she was completely hungover. Often.

"You guys, I really gotta get out of here," Jenn said, rubbing her temples. "Let's go outside for lunch. Okay? I need air."

Before I could answer her, Brendan sauntered in, his black hair messy as usual, his white button-down shirt untucked and his black tie undone. I felt that familiar fluttering—only it was stronger now, spreading through my body like a dull ache. Seeing him again confirmed it for me: I really, really liked Brendan. And it scared me, because the word *like* didn't seem strong enough to describe how I felt. I craved him in a way I wasn't used to. It was a little—okay, *a lot*—more intense than a crush. My feelings for him could kick a crush's butt.

I never found out about Halloween Movie Night, I realized.

Is he going this Friday? Could we go together? And there's a winter formal coming up....

My toe tapped a little impatiently. I couldn't wait to talk to him. Brendan sauntered over to his desk and I leaned forward, opening my mouth to say hi.

Without even casting so much as a glance in my direction, Brendan sat down in his desk and slouched low, stretching those long legs in front of him like he was lounging at home in front of the television, not sitting at attention in class.

I sat back and closed my mouth, and cast a furtive glance to Cisco, who just shrugged. Jenn, for her part, looked like she was too busy holding on to her breakfast to notice, but I caught a smug glance coming off of Kristin to her left.

Damn it, I thought, and whipped open my notebook with such fury that I ripped one of my pages.

The next hour was torture. I would rather have been waterboarded, suffocated, forced to lick the subway floor—anything!—to get out of that classroom. I found myself studying the back of Brendan's head as if it would give me any answers. Every scratch of his messy hair, every time he leaned forward, every twist he gave the small silver hoop pierced in his cartilage, I just wanted to throw my pen at him. I envisioned it ricocheting off the back of his head.

The bell rang and he reached for his bag. I found myself leaning forward and the words were tumbling out of my mouth before I could stop them.

"Hey, Brendan?" I asked hesitantly. My voice sounded thin and insecure, and I cringed. He paused in his chair and leaned back, turning his left ear in my direction but he didn't look at me. "I have your hoodie. It's in my locker. I would have brought it to class but it didn't fit in my bag. So it's in my locker. So, yeah. Just um, let me know what you want me to do with that, 'cause it's in my locker." *Shut up, shut up, shut up.* The words tumbled out like an avalanche of dorkiness.

He tilted his face in my general direction, but his green eyes barely focused on me. "Oh, yeah. I forgot about that. My locker's open, just leave it in there if you can. It's number 445. Thanks."

With that, he slung his bag over his shoulder and walked out.

He forgot about that? I felt my face getting red, redder still when I overheard Kristin walk by, mimicking me to Amanda and Kendall, her like-minded minions. "It's in my locker," she mimicked in a high-pitched voice, darting an evil glare my way as Amanda cackled.

Cisco gave me a mournful little smile, while Jenn looked dumbfounded. "Why do you have his hoodie?" she asked. "Did I see him on Friday?"

Happy for a change of subject, I leaned over and said, "You cannot still be drunk from Friday."

"No!" Jenn seemed insulted. "I went out for brunch on Sunday with my sister and we ended up pub crawling. We have *awesome* fake ID."

"With Austin, too?" I asked.

She looked at me, lost.

"You told me you and Austin were going to Wollman Rink this weekend."

Jenn turned a little greener. "So that's why he left me a weird message." Jenn paused, then clutched her stomach. "I need to get out of here. Are we going out for lunch or what?"

I agreed to go. The last thing I wanted to do was be in that cafeteria with *him.* I felt so stupid for thinking there was some kind of connection. I was probably something like a starving person, I surmised. A starving person will eat a rancid slice of pizza and think it's a gourmet meal, because they're so hungry for food. Well, I was starving, only I was starving for normalcy, starving for acceptance, and all Brendan had offered me was a month-old slice of pepperoni.

I rationalized in my head all the way to McDonald's, which Cisco suggested to calm Jenn's raging hangover. She ran into the bathroom as soon as we sat down—and Cisco immediately leaned forward.

"So Miss Connor, do you think he got the point that his hoodie is in your locker?" His brown eyes twinkled at me.

"Shut up." I frowned, balling up my napkin and throwing it at him. Cisco deftly blocked it, laughing.

"Seriously, though, what the hell was that about? You went on and on and on. And on some more."

"I don't know," I wailed, dropping my head into my hands. My face made a smacking sound when it hit my palms. "I am so embarrassed! I went to say hi to him and he just ignored me. Jerk."

"Okay, he wasn't a jerk, per se," Cisco began, "but I did think he'd be, I don't know, warmer to you. Or something. You guys really got along on Friday."

"He almost kissed me on Friday." I sighed, then mumbled, "I probably just imagined it." Cisco gave me a sympathetic look, and mouthed the word "Sorry."

"Em, I got the vibe that he was into you," Cisco continued, trying to make me feel better. "I thought he liked you. He doesn't really hang out with anyone from school, except when he deejays at dances and stuff. The only reason Brendan came out on Friday was for *you*. Maybe he's just having a bad day."

I just shrugged and tore my French fries into little pieces, drowning them in barbecue sauce. Talking about it made my head hurt as much as Jenn's probably did.

"We should get Jenn and head back," I said glumly. "She's been in there awhile." And truly, I was starting to get worried. She'd spent almost the entire lunch break in the bathroom.

Once back at school, I tried to put Brendan giving me the cold shoulder out of my mind. I got to Latin class late so I wouldn't have to face Ashley's line of questioning, and after class I raced down to the dungeon so I could get his stupid hoodie and put it in his stupid locker, all the way up on the stupid fourth floor.

"Stupid, stupid, stupid," I muttered to myself, stomping to my locker in the very pit of the building. I flipped the combination lock and saw his hoodie hanging there. Mocking me. Great, someone had slipped a flyer for Halloween Movie Night in there. *Oh, hi, paper cut, meet lemon juice.*

"Scenes & Screams! This Friday, hold on tightly to your favorite person for our night of zombie movies!" the orange slip of paper shouted at me. I crumpled up the flyer and threw it in the wastebasket, then turned my scornful eyes on his hoodie. I flicked the sleeve with my finger, giving it a dirty look before grabbing it and running back up the flights of stairs until I got to the fourth floor. I walked along the hallway until I saw locker number 445. The lock dangled there, open, so I removed it and slammed the door open with such force, it bounced off the locker next to it and slammed shut again.

I hung my head back, exhaling loudly. I opened the stupid door again, this time more slowly, and reached in to hang the sweatshirt on the hook. I thought for a moment about leaving a note—*Thanks for letting me borrow this. Here's your stupid sweatshirt, you moron. I totally wish I'd spilled nail polish on this. By the way, do you have an evil twin?*—when I figured I should say, "Thanks." At least *my* behavior would be beyond reproach. I pulled a small notebook out of my bag and hastily wrote, "Thanks for the loan—Emma" on a scrap of paper.

Casting a quick glance around me and making sure no one was watching, I checked out the photos taped to his locker door. There was a picture of Brendan and some guy I didn't know deejaying, and some group shot of a bunch of people in Central Park. No pictures of him with girls, at least—a small consolation. A small paper sketch of a medallion, taped in the bottom right corner, caught my eye.

"No. Freakin'. Way," I said aloud. I reached around my neck and unclasped my necklace, holding my medallion up against the drawing. Yep. Of course Brendan's medallion looked familiar. I've seen it every day—around my own neck.

I'd tried to find out what the crest meant hundreds of times before, but an internet search for "medieval-looking crest" only brought up pages and pages of similar designs and "make your own crest" websites.

"I have no idea what it means, Ladybug." My twin brother Ethan had smiled at me, using the nickname he'd given me when we were eleven, and both covered in spots from the chicken pox. (Except then, he called me Ladybug-Face and I called him Spot.) Ethan gave me the necklace after finding it at a garage sale, just a few weeks before he died. He went looking for vintage video games and came home with this instead.

"It just seemed like you. I hope it brings you good luck, Ladybug."

I had always thought it was something special—I fancied it to be a one-of-a-kind, rare design, something only shared between me and my brother, my hero. And now that stupid idiot Brendan had to go and ruin it. He probably saw it at the mall.

I stared at my beloved necklace, my only tie left to my brother, until tears pricked at my eyes, blurring my vision. I slammed Brendan's locker door shut and grabbed my bag, running as fast as I could away from his locker, away from the school—away from all reminders of him. I needed to get out of there.

Chapter 7

It would soon be too cold to go jogging in the park, but I needed one last day before hanging up my sneakers for the winter. I had to clear my head.

There was a chill in the air, thanks to a morning rain that had dampened my walk to school. It chapped my cheeks, still wet from tears that sporadically burst forth. I tried to keep them at bay, running as fast as I could through the leaves. *Just work it out, one more time in your head.*

Could I have been imagining a connection with Brendan? I thought about the way he'd put his arm around me at the bar. The way we'd talked. The way he said he wouldn't let anyone hurt me. The way he leaned into me, saying goodbye. I'd always read about seeing emotions in someone's eyes, but it had never felt real to me before. I know I'd seen something *real* in his emerald eyes. And losing that connection today made me feel so alone—more alone than I did during those last few weeks at Keansburg High.

I ran for about an hour, slowing to a quick walk as I neared the Eighty-sixth Street exit to the park. It was the same exit for the Met, and I turned to the imposing white structure and defiantly gave it the finger.

Seeing the Met set off a new series of emotions, so I decided to keep going. I was racing faster than I ever had, so there was plenty of time for me to get back to my aunt's for dinner. I headed across town, aiming for the pathway that ran along the East River. Once the shimmering black water came into view, I slowed to a walk and pulled my foot up on the metal base of a streetlight to retie my loose laces. Suddenly it was dark.

"What the hell…?" I said aloud, looking up. The streetlight was soot-black, as if it had exploded from the inside—just like the lamppost at the Bethesda Fountain a week ago. And the one that burned out when Brendan hailed me a cab. *Again? What's the shelf life of these bulbs?*

My eyes adjusted and I finished tying my shoelace.

I pulled my earbuds out and walked along the sparkling water, listening to the wind skipping along the waves. I wrapped my earphones around my purple iPod cover and stuck the player in my pocket.

I kept my ears peeled for footsteps, looking behind me sporadically as Aunt Christine had drilled into my head, to make sure I was not being followed. There was nothing behind me but a dark expanse of pathway, garishly lit by the yellow streetlights. All I could hear was the soft squishing of my own feet on the wet leaves as my sneakers pressed them into the concrete.

And then I heard it: a low, hissing, popping sound that made my bones jump. It was similar to the sound of a balloon exploding, only deeper. I whirled around, seeing nothing but the river, and the still, silent pathway spreading out behind me. A bitter, almost sulfuric smell burned my nose. I looked up, and saw that another street lamp had gone out. *That's… also weird.*

I picked up my pace, breaking into another jog. *Hiss. Hiss.*

Pop. POP! I stopped short, as if I had run into an invisible wall. I was frozen in my tracks, afraid to look behind me. I slowly turned around, dimly aware that I had started shaking. Four street lamps were extinguished, the lights dead and black from within. The pathway was velvet dark, the only illumination coming from Queens, across the river. I placed my left foot behind me, carefully, as if I were walking the plank. My eyes were still riveted on the dead street lamps as I backed away from them cautiously, the way someone would step away from a wild animal.

I heard another popping sound behind me. It started off low—almost guttural. I spun around. The streetlight in front of me was smoking, black plumes streaming out as if it were on fire. I heard a sharp sizzling, crackling sound and instinctively crouched down, covering my head with my hands. I screamed as the frosted glass light exploded, a flash of flames shooting glass and filaments into a halo on the ground below. The burning embers extinguished as they fell on the wet leaves, sending off a sinister, snakelike hiss as the heat died out.

The next thing I heard was choked-up breathing—mine. I took off, ignoring the burning in my chest as I sprinted down the pathway. I tried singing to myself, to distract myself from the sounds that I knew I could not be hearing. But the crackling, the hissing demanded to be heard, getting louder as it chased me, reaching out to grab me with unseen claws as I raced along the river. Every light I passed ruptured and died. Every streetlight blew out as I passed it, like I was the wind extinguishing a row of lit matches.

I ran off the pathway and across the street, ignoring the blaring horns of a taxi as it stopped short in front of me. Getting hit by a car would be preferable to letting the blackness catch up with me, I knew it. I had to get out of there before I was in total darkness.

I stumbled forward, my palms falling onto the yellow hood of the cab. For a short moment, the driver's eyes and mine met—he flinched when he saw my face.

I pushed myself off the taxi's hood and stumbled onto the curb, gasping for breath. Grabbing hold of the building on the corner, I whipped myself down the side street, my back against the cool stone of the building. Sweat dripped down my forehead as I peered around at the sinister-looking stretch of the East River, a smoking dark tunnel that threatened to entomb me. It was a black pit of nothingness.

Slowly, all the lights flickered and came back on. It looked like any other night, a postcard-perfect view of the East River.

If I'd been looking for something to take my attention away from Brendan, this did it. I didn't even notice him—well, not much—in English class the next day. I was pretty much useless in all of my classes. I lied to Cisco and Jenn at lunch, when they asked me why I was so quiet.

"I think I'm catching Mr. Emerson's cold," I fibbed, my voice clear as a bell. "I just don't feel well."

I was too freaked out when I'd gotten home the night before, but I planned to spend the rest of this evening on Google. There had to be some explanation. Maybe the street-lights were not up to code? Maybe they were overdue for maintenance? Maybe I really was going crazy, and imagining a bond with Brendan was the first symptom?

In chemistry class, I slumped in my seat, giving Angelique a weak smile as she walked in. She halted in her tracks when she saw me, a terrified look on her face. I glanced over my shoulder, wondering what Kristin was doing to provoke such a reaction. Spitballs, most likely. That girl had remarkable aim. Then I realized Angelique was horrified because she was staring at *me*.

She grabbed at one of her necklaces and mumbled something to herself, then slowly slid next to me.

"Hey," I said, trying to be casual.

She ripped a page out of her notebook and wrote down three words.

Call me tonight.

Angelique then took off one of her rings, a silver band engraved with some unidentifiable symbols inside and outside, and handed it to me.

Wear it.

The serious look on her face told me to do what she said. I hastily slid the ring on my finger.

It was almost 5:00 p.m. when I was able to give Angelique a call, since Ashley (who was still in full infatuation mode with Anthony) stayed over for a while, giggling about her flirtatious emails with Anthony and ignoring my protests. She wanted me to come over to her house for dinner but I begged off, using the same cold excuse that seemed to work earlier in the day.

I sat on my bed and dialed Angelique, who answered on the first ring.

"Hello—Angelique? It's Emma."

"Yeah, I know."

"Wow, are you psychic, too?" I asked in awe.

"No, I have caller ID." *Oh, yeah. Duh.*

"So," Angelique continued. "What happened to you?"

"What do you mean?" I stalled, knowing full well what she meant.

"When I came to chemistry class, you weren't *there*." She

paused. "It was like there was a black hole where you were supposed to be. You were in the dark."

I bit my lip, fighting back the sick, creepy feeling that spread up through my stomach and gripped my heart.

"Funny you would say that," I began. "I kind of was." I told her about the streetlights—how it felt like I'd triggered the explosions.

"Well, it was right of me to give you my ring then," she said, sounding relieved. "Are you wearing it?"

"Yes," I said, turning the ring over on my index finger.

"It's been blessed," Angelique continued. "It should protect you. It's just a precaution, though. Even though you saw the lights exploding above your head, you likely weren't ever in any real danger."

"Well, except from the exploding shards of glass," I corrected her.

"Not really," she explained. "They might not have really exploded. It's possible that you only *saw* them explode. How can I put this so you'll understand?" She paused. "What happened was the spirit world's way of saying, 'I'm not touching you,' then sticking their fingers in your face. Like a little kid would do, only much, much scarier."

"If the spirit world wants to annoy me, couldn't it just give me a wedgie or something?"

"It doesn't work like that," Angelique said, ignoring my lame joke. "And besides, even though spirits are technically not more active around Halloween, people are more aware of them, so they have a bigger reach to the mortal realm, so to speak."

"But I don't believe in ghosts," I protested.

"Eh, that really doesn't make much of a difference," Angelique replied, cavalierly. "And it's not necessarily ghosts, mind you. There are energies, spirits, forces in the world no one really understands." She paused again. "You didn't deface any sacred grounds, did you, Emma?"

"Like what, Bergdorf's? I'm on the Upper East Side, Angelique. The most sinister thing I could do is wear white after Labor Day."

"Or last season's nail polish," she agreed, laughing. "Still, I don't understand why you would be marked by the spirit world like this."

"Marked?" I squeaked. "Marked by what? *For* what?"

"It could be any number of things," Angelique explained. "Maybe you're a channel. Maybe someone's trying to warn you. Maybe this is a sign."

"I like my explanation better." I sighed. "That the street lamps were in dire need of repair. I mean, I've seen lights go out over my head before."

Angelique was suddenly silent. "What did you say?" she asked, her voice chillingly low.

"It's happened before," I said dismissively. "Just a few times—but it's been kind of the same thing—the lights burn out, then I smell the bitter, sulfury smell."

"The sulfur smell generally indicates something negative, so it sounds to me like you're being warned about something— something pretty bad. And whoever is reaching out to you had to make a big show to get your attention since you clearly were ignoring the warning signs."

"I don't like the sound of that." I twisted my purple comforter into knots.

"Well, don't get freaked out just yet. I'll do a spell of protection for you this Friday—Halloween is this weekend, after all. If this spirit is malevolent, the spell should protect you. But if it's not—if someone is warning you—well, I think you'll want those warnings. Just bring me something personal. And let me know if anything else happens. This is exciting!"

"Exciting for you," I pointed out. "I don't want to end up possessed, or trapped in some third dimension."

"Oh, don't be silly," she said, as if the phrase "marked by the spirit world" was any more believable than "trapped in a third dimension."

"Look," she continued. "The way I interpret this, I'd say a spirit, or some force, is reaching out to you. I know it seems like it was malevolent, but spirits are dramatic, so there's no certainty that there was any ill intent. That said, I would still be careful. Wear the ring.

"And," she continued, her voice sounding confused, "I'm surprised you don't believe in ghosts—or anything spiritual at all. I thought you were into this."

"No, not really," I said. "Why did you think that?"

"Well, your necklace, for starters," Angelique explained.

"My necklace? It's something my brother gave me," I said, remembering how I saw the same thing in Brendan's locker. "It's just some common design."

"No, it's not," Angelique said emphatically. "It's completely and totally not. It's quite significant. I've seen it in a few spell books—but I never bothered to read the spells, since I don't believe in love spells. So I couldn't say what exactly it symbolizes. But I also recognize it from one of my mother's textbooks—she teaches Medieval Studies at Fordham. I've also seen it on some websites—dark magic sites, actually."

Angelique stopped, then took a breath. "It means *something.*"

"I don't know what it means, but if you have any books about it lying around, I'd love to borrow them." I toyed with the necklace as I spoke. "The necklace…it's pretty sentimental. I'd like to know what the story is."

"Of course, Emma. I'll look for some books. But—" She paused, then sounded sheepish. "You've been so *nice* to me. I thought it was because you were sympathetic to the witch's plight."

"*You're* the one who's been nice to me from day one," I reminded her. "And I don't really care what your religion is, although I have to admit, it's coming in handy for me right now." She laughed. We kept talking for a while—and she reminded me to bring in a personal item for the protection spell.

"Just jog on a treadmill from now on," she advised.

I was relieved when, over the next two days, I walked to school with Ashley and no locusts clustered at my feet, no frogs rained down from the sky, and when I turned on the faucet in the girls' bathroom, the tap ran clear with good ol' water—not blood. I was even slightly comforted when Brendan continued to keep me on his pay-no-mind list. Any change in his behavior and I would have thought the spirit world was *really* screwing with me.

In chemistry, I handed Angelique the key to the home I had shared with my mom and Ethan, pre-Henry. I kept it on a purple ribbon and used it as a bookmark in my journal. She had asked me to bring something personal—the more personal, the better.

"It's really sentimental, so it won't get ruined in the spell, right?" I asked, concerned.

"Not at all," she assured me. "Truthfully, that necklace might be the best, but we'll work with this and go in for the big guns if we have to."

Angelique then leaned over and ripped out a few strands of hair. I clapped my hands over my mouth to stop from yelping.

"Sorry," she apologized. "I should have warned you. I forgot. I'm just excited."

"I could have pulled them out for you myself." I pouted, rubbing my scalp. "I think you got some skin there."

She stuck my hair in an envelope for safekeeping, and promised me that, by midnight tomorrow, I would be protected—and if not totally protected, at least I'd likely stop seeing lampposts explode. I had to admit, even though I wasn't really sold on the whole supernatural thing, I appreciated her concern.

After school, I walked home with Ashley, and figured she'd get a kick out of my supernatural adventures.

"That *is* creepy," she agreed. "I've definitely had lights go out above my head, but not a whole row of them. But maybe they were on the same power grid or something, and short-circuited."

I liked her explanation. We were talking about the complexities of electrical engineering—we may as well have been talking about how to build a spaceship, since neither one of us knew a thing about it—when I realized she was rubbing her palms together, which she did when she was nervous about something.

"Ashley, what's going on?" I demanded, putting my hands over her fidgety fingers as they mashed together.

"You'll be mad," she said mournfully.

"I might be *going* mad," I conceded, "but I'm sure I won't *be* mad. Tell me."

"Okay," she said hesitantly, then it all tumbled out, her words tripping over themselves in her exuberance. "I'm seeing Anthony tonight! I know I told you that we were still talking on Facebook and stuff, but he also started talking to me in the library during free period, and he asked me out earlier this week. I didn't want to tell you 'cause you hate him but he's really nice and so cute, so don't hate me."

She paused, but only because she was out of breath.

"Ashley, everything I've seen of Anthony tells me he's not a good guy," I pleaded. "He's not worth your time."

"Oh, I asked him about the fight in Central Park, and he said Frank insulted his mother," Ashley said smugly. "He was just defending his mother's honor."

"That's not the way I heard it went down, and even if it was, he didn't have to beat on the guy the way he did," I argued.

"Emma, I'm happy. Can't you be happy for me?" Ashley gazed at me with her best puppy-dog eyes.

"I don't trust him, Ashley," I maintained. "I wish you'd think about this."

"I did," she said, her voice less wheedling, more assertive. "I like him, I'm going to hang out with him tonight, so you can either be happy for me and hear all about it, or not."

"Do Uncle Dan and Aunt Jess know?" I asked protectively. If her mom and dad okayed it, it had to be all right. "I mean, he's a lot older than you are."

"It's only two years, Em. And I told them I was going out with some friends, which is kind of true. He asked me to come over to his house, since he was having a party after the school Halloween movie thing. A whole bunch of people from your class are going to be there. So I might even see you at his party anyway."

"I wasn't invited," I muttered, and Ashley blushed.

"I'm sorry, Em."

I sighed. "Really, it's okay." I flinched at the thought of Brendan, partying it up at Anthony's house with all the "cool" kids while I sat at home like a loser. That night with Brendan seemed like another lifetime ago, not just last weekend. I winced at the memory, surprised that I felt physically pained at the thought of how cold Brendan had been to me this week. It was like a thousand little needles were stabbing me in the chest.

I pulled myself out of my misery to focus on my baby cousin. "Are you going to be okay? He just comes across like such a player."

"Emma," she said, rolling her eyes, "I've been to parties before. I'll be fine. I'm just going to go and hang out with him a bit. Nothing's going to happen!"

"Famous last words," I said dryly.

A little after midnight that night, I was sitting up in Aunt Christine's floral recliner after she had gone to bed. Angelique had called me to assure me that the protection spell was completed and I might even feel the change in my energy. I thanked her, and though I had decided that the lampposts most likely just needed maintenance, I was still secretly relieved when she told me to keep the ring.

What an exciting Friday night, I thought, cringing when I compared it to last Friday, which I spent with *him.* I placated myself with the thoughts that it's not every day you get a bona fide witch doing spells in your honor on Halloween weekend. I eyed my cell phone, resting on the cushion next to me, warily. I had asked Ashley to call when she got to the party, so she could let me know that she was okay—and she definitely should have phoned me by now. I just couldn't shake my uneasy feelings about Anthony. He was the reason I'd split last weekend, and left Brendan's side. Which was, apparently, the only chance ever I'd have to be by it.

I was half working on my term paper on *A Midsummer Night's Dream* and half watching a classic Knicks game on some random sports network—Christine had the deluxe cable package and had hundreds of channels. Ever since I'd met Brendan, I suddenly had an interest in basketball. *I'm such a loser.*

I was typing the quote, "The course of true love never

did run smooth," from Act 1, when there was a knock at the door.

I paused. Maybe they have the wrong door?

The knocking turned to pounding, and I heard a timid voice call my name.

"Emma? I hear the TV...are you there?" The voice sounded tearful.

I tossed my laptop on the floral couch next to me, flew to the door and saw my little cousin standing there, fat tears rolling down her cheeks. Her lips trembled, and I grabbed her into my arms.

"What happened? Are you okay? What's going on?" I pulled Ashley into the living room and plopped her on the couch. She just sat there, sobbing so hard she triggered a coughing fit. I ran to get her a glass of water, and quickly sat back down next to her on the floral couch.

"Drink this," I commanded, shoving the cold glass into Ashley's hands.

She gulped down half the glass, then put it on the coffee table.

"I feel like such an idiot," she whimpered, her eyes shimmering with tears, which overflowed again.

"What happened?"

She opened her mouth to speak, and instead started sobbing again—big, heartbreaking sobs.

"Ashley, you have to talk," I said frantically. "I'm going crazy here! What happened?"

"Well, I showed up at Anthony's apartment, right when he told me to," she began, nervously biting her lip to keep the tears at bay. "And I thought I was early, because there was no loud music or talking or anything. It was supposed to be a party, right?

"When he opened the door, it was just him, and he looked

me up and down and said, 'Yeah, welcome to the party.' And then he grabbed my wrist and pulled me inside. I asked him where everyone else was and he just laughed and handed me a vodka and orange juice and it was like, *all* vodka, too." Her words came tumbling out. She took a big, sobbing gulp of air, then continued.

"I waited for a second and asked him about the basketball team, like, when are they playing again and all the stuff we talked about on Facebook, and he was kind of giving me one-word answers and stuff, and then he sat down next to me and I asked him again, "Where is everyone?"

Ashley's voice broke, and I handed her a tissue from the fuzzy pink box Christine always kept on the end table.

"His family's place is *huge* and there was definitely no one else there. Anthony started rubbing my neck so I asked him *again*."

I tried to keep my voice even. "And then what?" I asked.

"He says, 'Don't be stupid, you know you're the party.'" She spit it out bitterly, wincing at the recollection. "I mean, what a lame line, right? And then, he starts laughing, and rubs my thigh. So I push him away and I tell him to leave me alone, and he keeps telling me, 'Come on, you're so hot, you know I could get any girl I want,' blah, blah, blah, and that I should be so flattered. I didn't even have my coat off."

She looked down, her already-crimson cheeks turning even redder. When she looked back up at me, her tear-streaked face was contorted with anger.

"He kept trying to get me to open my legs," she choked out hoarsely. "He kept wedging his hand between my knees, so I slapped him. Then I reached for the drink and poured it in his lap."

I was torn between rage at Anthony and pride in my cousin. "Good for you," I said through clenched teeth.

"Not really, because then he got mad."

My eyes widened. "Did he…hurt you?"

"No, it was nothing like that," Ashley hastily said, seeing where I thought this conversation was going. But then she started in on the tears again.

"But he started yelling at me, 'You're nothing but a tease. You're ugly anyway. You're gonna pay for this couch.' And he yanked me off the couch, and took my purse and threw it, and me, out the door." She looked down, mournfully, at her black Betsey Johnson bag, her favorite accessory now a woeful reminder, then turned her bloodshot blue eyes back at me.

"I'm really sorry, Emma," Ashley whispered.

"What?" I was incredulous. "Why are you apologizing to *me?*"

"Because you were right. I should have listened to you."

"Look, there was no way to know what you were walking into," I said, putting my arm around my cousin and rubbing her shoulder. "I only thought you were going to a party that was going to get out of hand. And that was only because I hung out with those guys once and I felt like *I* was in over *my* head. I had no idea he was capable of this…."

I continued what I felt were feeble attempts at comforting Ashley, who just shrugged glumly. My heart sank. I realized this was *the* moment for her, the moment your innocence—not your physical innocence, but your emotional one—was lost. After that, you looked at the world more harshly and your heart was harder.

"It'll be okay," I said, softly. "Really. You'll feel better in the morning." I tried my best to convince her but it was difficult because I didn't really have any faith myself.

I called her parents and convinced them to let her stay the night. I said she had a fight with one of her girlfriends at the party and was upset, so after leaving a note on the kitchen table for Aunt Christine explaining our overnight guest, Ashley and I tucked into my bed. Our plans for Anthony's destruction were sporadically interrupted by me consoling her and telling her she really wasn't stupid, this really wasn't her fault, she really was pretty and, no, not all guys are evil. I told her if I really did have some supernatural force after me, I would sic it on Anthony. For a moment, I truly hoped I did have a bitter spirit in my arsenal. If so, I had work for it to do.

Chapter 8

We walked to school on Monday, having passed the weekend helping Ashley's parents give out candy to the trick-or-treaters in their building. Ashley didn't want to leave home, and I didn't want to leave her alone. As we crossed the street to Vincent Academy, I reminded Ashley again that she likely wouldn't even see Anthony. They didn't have any classes together—just a free period—which she could spend in an empty classroom, doing homework.

For me, it wasn't so easy. In the cafeteria, I spent most of my time glaring at Anthony from across the room. He didn't even notice me—I wasn't on his radar anymore; there were younger girls to be preyed upon, after all. I was seething—angry at him, angry at myself. I knew I should have stopped her, but she was so determined to go her own way. *No, no excuses, Emma. You should have looked out for her better. But you were too caught up in Brendan ignoring you to take care of Ashley.*

As we were walking out of the cafeteria and heading to our next class, I turned to Cisco.

"Okay, I have to get this off my chest," I said, my eyes narrowing.

"Emma, I'd be pissed at Anthony, too. I saw you giving

him the stink eye," Cisco admitted, giving me a sympathetic look.

"He's a such piece of— Wait, how do you know why I'm mad at him?" I asked suspiciously. I felt an angry pit beginning to form in my stomach and began walking more slowly.

Cisco slowed his walk as well, keeping in step with me. He leaned in and whispered in a low voice, "Well, if my baby cousin slept with a creeper like Anthony and then he told the entire school, I wouldn't be thrilled, either."

I could feel my blood boiling. The pit in my stomach sprouted, and the anger took over all my senses.

"That's *not* what happened," I hissed, my hands clenched into fists. "*Here's* what really went down." I quickly relayed the events of Friday night—how my traumatized cousin had come over, a fountain of tears.

Cisco sighed and paused on the staircase. "You know, he's always bragging about this girl and that girl." Cisco adopted Anthony's swaggering pose and mimicked his voice. "'I banged this chick from Dominican Academy…I totally hooked up with that piece from Dalton.' He probably either coerced them or just straight-up lied."

"Well, this time, he's lying," I seethed.

"How's Ashley?" Cisco asked, concern in his voice.

"Last time I saw her, she didn't know Anthony was saying all this about her. I'll see Ash at the end of the day in Latin. I swear I'll kill him," I fumed, turning to head downstairs to chemistry.

"If you hear anyone say anything…" I began.

"Don't worry, I'll tell them he's lying," he assured me.

At first, Angelique thought her spell had gone sour. "There's such anger and rage around you," she fretted. "I need to do the spell again." She reached into my hair to yank out more strands when I stopped her, explaining what was happening.

"He said *that* about your little cousin?" Her eyes darted around the room. "I can't do anything *to* Anthony, you see. Whatever I put into the universe comes back at me threefold. But maybe there is something we could do that isn't *too* bad...." She started scanning the printouts that were tucked into the back of her notebook.

"It's okay." I smiled. "But thank you. You're a good friend." Angelique grinned, and we both grimaced when we heard Kristin make kissing noises behind us.

"Get a room, freaks," she sneered. I just rolled my eyes and flipped her off. She was the least of my worries.

The seconds ticked by slowly, slowly, until it was time to walk into freshman Latin. I scanned the room for Ashley's face but couldn't see her anywhere. I wanted to give her a hug, a kind word, a dartboard with Anthony's face on it when I noticed her friends glancing at me uncomfortably.

I slid over to her gaggle of girlfriends who were, for once, silent.

"Spill it, where is she?" I asked bluntly.

Catharine, a pretty brunette, mumbled, "She went home sick." Her fingers made air quotes around the word sick. "She was really embarrassed."

My eyes narrowed. "What Anthony's saying about her isn't true. You guys know that, right?"

"I know, I know," she said emphatically. "But try telling her that. The entire freshman class thinks she's easy. Three guys asked her out today—and this one guy told his friends it's 'cause he heard she was a good time."

I felt it again, my blood boiling. Cotton stuffed my ears, and all I could hear was my own pulse, throbbing in my head.

"Not everyone believes it!" Catharine was quick to say. "But—" she looked down "—a lot of people do."

Vanessa, Ashley's fellow redhead, leaned in and said, "He said she was easier to get into than public school." *Wow, arrogant* and *cruel, what a combo.*

I didn't hear much after that. Not Mrs. Dell, the Latin teacher. Not the chalk as it scratched on the blackboard. I was only aware of the sound of the large clock hanging above the blackboard as it ticked down the seconds, and the throbbing I felt in my own head. When the bell finally rang, it sounded like a scream. I grabbed my backpack and flung it over my shoulder.

"Are you going to Ashley's house? Will you tell her to call me?" Catharine asked, concerned. Gossipy or not, at least these girls genuinely cared about my cousin, I realized.

"Not quite yet," I muttered. My feet couldn't move fast enough as I sped down the flights of stairs, past the gym and through the double doors that opened onto the quad. I shoved them open with a forceful push. I glared at the end of the quad where Anthony, Frank and the rest of that crew were starting up their usual after-school basketball game. Somewhere in my head, it registered that Brendan wasn't there.

I dropped my bag—threw it, actually, under a bench to my right—and walked right into the middle of the game, pulling my long hair back into a ponytail with the black elastic band I had on my wrist as I marched forward.

I strode in front of Frank, cutting him off. "Yo, we're playing here," he said curtly.

I ignored him, heading straight for Anthony.

He had his back to me. He was huge, and built like a linebacker. Anthony had to be at least six-four, the alarmed thought went off in the back of my mind.

"Anthony." My voice was low and angry, but steady.

He ignored me, still dribbling the orange ball.

"Anthony Caruso!" I yelled.

Startled, he stepped forward and lost his handle on the ball. It sputtered on the floor, then rolled away. Anthony straightened up, turned around and faced me.

"What do *you* want?"

Justice? Was that a good answer?

"I want you to tell the truth about my cousin," I said, my voice loud but calm.

"And just who the hell is your cousin?" Anthony snapped. He wasn't so calm.

"Ashley? The girl you're lying about? Saying you slept with? Does it ring a bell?" I shouted back. There went my calm. A small, interested crowd of about ten people started to form.

He laughed and adjusted his shirt. "Sure, I'll say that." He leaned in and, loudly enough so everyone could hear, sneered, "It's not like I'm proud of it. She wasn't any good."

Anthony laughed—an evil little cackle that seemed to spread across my skin like flames—and spun away from me to return to his game.

"Don't you dare turn away from me, you liar," I screamed at his back, my face feeling hot. "Or do you only harass freshmen and girls a foot and a half shorter than you? Because that makes you a *real* man, right?"

I heard snickers coming from the guys gathered around us, and Anthony turned back to face me.

"You wouldn't know what a real man is, but your cousin sure does," he said, grinning menacingly. "Let me know if she wants another go."

Henry's face appeared in front of me. They were so alike— they only preyed on those who were weaker, smaller, powerless, those with no one to stand up for them. Not this time.

"You're lying!" I yelled, my hands clenched into fists. "She rejected you, and you know it. But tell me another story, Mother Goose. You seem *full* of fairy tales."

Anthony glared at me, stepping closer. I only came up to his chest, but I stared straight up, meeting his cold blue eyes. He was just a few inches from me.

"Who do you think you are, you little freak?" He shoved me, both hands hitting my shoulders hard. I definitely wasn't expecting that. I stumbled when he made contact, losing my footing and almost falling backward. I took a few steps and maintained my balance, staring back at the monster.

"You need to watch your mouth, little girl," Anthony snarled, his voice low and menacing as he crouched low in front of me, meeting my eyes. "You won't like what happens to you."

"I'm not afraid of you," I snapped. "Tell the truth about my cousin. Admit that you didn't sleep with Ashley."

His eyes narrowed, and I knew he was going to shove me again. I expected it this time. Like I had with Henry so many times before, I jumped back before he could make contact. He stumbled forward, and I heard the guys in the crowd laugh and jeer at Anthony, getting shown up by a *girl*. I didn't think this was a good thing—with his ego, it would only make him madder, I assumed. I hadn't been looking for a brawl in the schoolyard; all I wanted was for him to admit the truth about my cousin. I realized too late that I should have approached this with some kind of strategy.

I warily glanced at the growing crowd to see who was watching. *Oh, everyone.* Past them, I saw Brendan pushing open the main doors to the quad. He had his headphones on and was looking down at his cell phone, completely oblivious to the spectacle before him.

Anthony had regained his footing and was advancing, his hulking form filling most of my view. I whirled my head around for an exit strategy and spied the nearest door. *If things get* really *ugly, I can just make a run for it.*

"If I slept with your skanky cousin that's none of your business, Emma," Anthony yelled in my face. I was surprised that he remembered my name. "What's your problem, huh? You want a piece? Sorry, you're not my type."

"Right, 'cause *I'm* not afraid of you, remember?" I glared back.

I heard someone yell at Anthony to calm down.

"Back off, man, she's a girl," Frank called timidly. He had a black eye and bruised nose from his last encounter with Anthony. But the monster just ignored him.

"You're going to regret this," Anthony fumed, pure hate in his eyes. I knew that look—things were definitely about to get ugly. I took a few quick steps back—right into the side door, ready to make a run for it. My hands fumbled behind me on the doorknob, frantically twisting it to no avail. Anthony's chest was practically touching me. I'd cornered myself.

"No one makes me look stupid and gets away with it," he hissed.

I couldn't let him see that I was scared—especially now that I was trapped. People like him fed off other people's fear.

"Move," I demanded. I heard someone else yell for him to back off.

"No, you got what you wanted," he snarled. "Well, you have my attention now."

"Move, I said!" I screamed, and pressed my palms to his huge chest, trying to push him back.

"I told you, keep your hands to yourself, skank," Anthony hissed, his eyes narrow.

"Oh, what are you gonna do if I don't?" I asked—and then I regretted my question immediately.

I got an answer pretty quickly. Anthony pulled his meaty right hand back. It was clenched into a grapefruit-size fist.

I was frozen against the door. I didn't flinch. I'd taken a hit from Henry before. In my mind, all I could think was, *Go ahead. Hit me, and then you'll get expelled.*

He never had the chance. Within seconds, Brendan had pinned him on the ground, his knee pressed into Anthony's chest as his fingers gripped him by the throat, forcing him onto the cold concrete.

"Don't touch her." Brendan's voice was almost a growl as it shook with rage. "Don't you ever touch her." His green eyes flashed as if they were filled with flames.

Dazed, Anthony lay on the ground. Realization dawned on him, and Anthony saw that he was no longer standing and facing off with me, but pinned down by his teammate.

"What do you think you're doing, Brendan?" Anthony shouted, clawing at the hand around his throat. Brendan's other hand was clenched tightly into a fist, cocked back and ready. He dug his knee farther into Anthony's chest, and the blond gasped for air as his legs kicked out, trying to find some purchase against Brendan's iron grasp.

"You don't touch her. You don't talk to her. You don't look at her. *Ever,*" Brendan ordered again, keeping his green eyes locked on Anthony's face.

"What's your problem, bro? She started with me!" Anthony yelled, whipping his head sideways to glare at me.

"Oh, really? Something Emma did deserves you trying to punch her?" Brendan's voice was calmer this time, which made it startlingly more threatening.

"I wasn't gonna punch her, bro," Anthony whined, still kicking. "She started with me!"

"It seems to me that you started everything, as usual," Brendan said. "You running your fat mouth again?"

"Whatever, man, get off me." Anthony squirmed, his efforts useless against the viselike grip Brendan had on him. Anthony was bulkier than Brendan but it was obvious that Brendan was much stronger. I saw the tendons in his forearm flex as he held Anthony immobile.

"Nope." Brendan's voice was almost playful underneath the malice. "Can't do that, buddy. If what you've been saying about her cousin isn't true, admit it. Or—" Brendan lowered his face closer to Anthony's, his voice frighteningly cruel "—*you'll* regret it. I promise you that, Ant."

I stood there in shock. I scanned the crowd and saw Kristin, eyes narrowed, filming the whole thing with her cell phone. Clearly, this would be available on YouTube later.

"Fine, whatever, I didn't bang Ashley." Anthony darted his eyes in my direction. He wasn't just shooting out daggers—his eyes were shooting out missiles, bullets, weapons of mass destruction. "But I could have hit it if I wanted to."

"That's *not* what I want to hear," Brendan growled, tightening his grip on Anthony's neck as he pressed his knee farther into his chest.

"Fine, fine, what she said!" Anthony cried, wheezing. "Just get off me."

Brendan shook his head, a bitter look on his face. He got off Anthony, shifting his grasp to grab him by his collar. He deftly pulled Anthony off the concrete, but kept a steel grip on him.

"Get out of here," Brendan said plainly, shoving him back with both hands. Stunned, Anthony stumbled backward. He paused to smooth out the front of his shirt and pop his collar—then Anthony's eyes locked on mine. They narrowed, and he took a step toward me. Brendan mirrored his movements, blocking Anthony's view of me.

"You try to hurt another girl again—and if you so much as *think* Emma's name—you're done."

"Oh, is that another promise, Brendan?" Anthony scoffed.

"It's a guarantee," Brendan answered, his fists clenched so tightly his knuckles were straining against his skin.

"This ain't over, Brendan. You picked the wrong guy to mess with, bro," Anthony sneered, gesturing wildly. Anthony stormed away, kicking my backpack on his way out of the quad. Thankfully, there was nothing breakable in it. Unlike my reputation, which looked very fragile at the moment.

After the door slammed behind Anthony, Brendan turned to me, still immobile and shocked in the same spot against the door. My jaw had literally dropped. Brendan leaned down so he was eye-level with me. He tucked the tips of his fingers under my chin and shut my agape mouth, his eyes searching my face.

"Emma, are you all right?"

I nodded, then reached up and touched the back of his hand with just the tips of my fingers.

We stood there for what could only have been a second, but the warm feel of his hand under mine burned its way into my memory. He slowly slid his hand along the side of my face, cupping my jaw, and my hand tightened around his.

"Thank you," I whispered, staring up into his eyes as his thumb stroked my cheek. I heard someone yell, "Yo, I think they're gonna do it!" The sound of laughter made its way through my pounding head.

Suddenly aware of his audience, Brendan straightened up and we both dropped our hands.

"No problem," he said, cocking his head to the side. He surveyed the crowd the altercation had attracted and scratched his black hair, making it even messier.

He dropped back down to my eye level, crossing his arms. "Are you going home now?" he asked me softly.

"I'm going to my cousin's," I said. "I should at least tell Ash that her good name has been restored. And that she literally gets guys fighting over her."

He smiled, then turned those intense green eyes on me. "I wasn't fighting for *her*."

I just stared back, confused and thrilled by what Brendan had just said.

Then a look I couldn't quite identify flickered across his face. Slowly, he reached out his hand and picked up my charm, turning it over.

Brendan dropped it suddenly and, nodding curtly at me, whirled around on his heel and headed back inside the school.

Everyone in the quad was whispering and staring at me—the only one of the three left. I grabbed my backpack from under the bench and raced out of the quad, onto Park Avenue, and I didn't stop until I made it to Ashley's house.

She had already heard the news. Catharine and Vanessa were also in the quad, filming the whole thing and texting a play-by-play to my cousin. Between exuberant hugs that were wet with tears—this time, of joy—she kept returning to her laptop, where she was replaying one of several videos which had already been uploaded to Facebook.

"You have to watch this!" Ashley giggled, her eyes, puffy from crying, crinkled up in the corners.

"No thanks," I said, not able to relive it; if I saw how close I came to having my face smashed in, I might lose all composure.

"I cannot believe you did that!" she marveled, shaking her head at me. I picked, absentmindedly, at the hem of my plaid skirt.

"I'm just tired of people like him," I said, suddenly exhausted. "People who take advantage. I wanted the right person to win. For once."

She grinned and I added, "At least your reputation is restored."

The status of *my* reputation, on the other hand, was debatable. I was the girl who hung out with witches and picked fights with boys. I didn't care so much about what everyone at school thought of me. I only cared about what Brendan thought…and I couldn't wait to get to school the next day, in spite of the certainty that I would be the number one topic of conversation.

"I'm nervous," Ashley confessed, looking at me cautiously as we walked the final stretch of blocks to school the next day. I knew how she felt—she didn't want to be the subject of discussion, the focus of hundreds of eyes. Why is it always when someone is wronged, they're suddenly more interesting?

"You'll be fine," I said, trying my best to reassure her. "*You're* not the one who picks fights after school."

"What are you going to do if you see Anthony?" she asked, worried.

"I'm avoiding him," I said sheepishly. "Angelique already agreed to go outside for lunch with me indefinitely—as long as the weather cooperates." I figured if I was out of the lunchroom—and left school through the annex—I could avoid any unnecessary Anthony encounters.

We crossed the street, and I noticed a familiar-looking figure leaning against the mailbox a few feet from the front entrance of the school. At first I didn't recognize Brendan, since he had his mop of hair tucked under a wool cap.

Ashley gave me a big grin. At that moment, a classmate ran up to her, squealing.

"Oh, my God, Anthony totally had his butt handed to him! I can't believe that cutie Brendan defended you!" Her giddy friend giggled, and I knew Ashley would be okay. She'd be the center of some good attention, for once. She gave me the thumbs-up, ran to the door—then whirled around and yelled, practically at the top of her lungs, "See you after school, Emma!"

Brendan heard my name and turned in my direction, lifting his chin in a nod as he had that first day in the quad. Nervously, I played with my necklace, dragging the charm back and forth on the chain. Finally I decided to take the first step.

I walked calmly toward him, feeling those green eyes pulling me in. I couldn't figure out the expression on his face. He looked relieved—happy, even. But he also looked troubled. No, troubled isn't quite right. *Melancholic?* I figured I should say thanks, again, for stepping in.

"I wanted to thank you again," I said, staring up into his eyes, for once unobstructed by his dark locks, which were pulled back under his wool cap. Brendan's eyebrows were black, with just enough arch that they were dramatic. His green eyes were like glittering emeralds, fringed by those enviable black lashes. His cheeks were slightly flushed from the chilly weather, two spots of color in his otherwise pale face.

"You don't have to thank me again, Emma," he said, shaking his head with that same puzzling expression on his face.

"Well, I want to." I don't know how you could have described the expression on my face. *Hopeful? Pathetic? Falling in...something?*

"I'm just glad I was there. I wish I had gotten there sooner." I suddenly felt very shy, breaking his gaze to stare at my black

Mary Janes. He tucked his finger under my chin and lifted my face so we were eye to eye again.

"Emma, is there *anything* else you want to tell me?"

His tone wasn't nasty or rude, but I still felt like I'd been punched. "Should there be?" I asked, confused.

"I guess not." Brendan sighed, shaking his head. "I'm just glad you're okay." Turning away from me, he pulled open the door to the school and walked inside. I stood there dumb-founded. Wasn't *he* the one who had been ignoring *me* for the past week and a half?

I followed him into the building—but of course, I had to go to my dungeon, to the row of lockers reserved for unlucky freshmen and transfer students. And bridge trolls, which is what I felt like at this moment.

I was heading to class when I heard someone running behind me, furiously and quickly. I whipped around, fists up instinctively. Not that I had any idea what to do with them, but what if it was Anthony, coming for retribution?

"Emma, you didn't call me! I have to see it on Facebook? What the hell, dude?" It was Cisco, looking worried and happy and excited all at once.

"I'm sorry—I'm a terrible friend." I gave him a weak little frown.

"But a great older cousin. Holy crap, that was amazing. I can't believe that you just went up there to him and called him out like that," he said, breaking out in a short round of applause.

"Thank you." I bowed, giving a toothy grin. "But I had help."

"I know," he replied, giving me a suspicious smile. "What *was* that whole Brendan thing about? Is there something going on that you haven't told me?"

"Cisco, until that moment, he hadn't spoken to me in a week and a half," I said, raising my right hand. "I swear."

"I don't know if I believe you," he replied, continuing to walk up the stairs to class. "That boy flew across the yard. Flew! And knocked Anthony straight down. That's not just chivalry."

I shrugged, thankful that I had to leave and go into history. I waited in the hallway until about a second before the bell rang, racing to my seat behind Jenn. She turned around and mouthed to me, "Oh. My. God. We. Have. To. Talk."

I just nodded and put my head down on my desk. I didn't want to talk about the fight. I couldn't even think about something so...inconsequential. What was all that about this morning? What did Brendan want me to say? What did I do wrong?

Jenn peppered me with a barrage of questions as we walked to English class.

"Were you scared?"

"No, I wasn't thinking, I just reacted. I was angry."

"Did you tell Brendan what you were going to do?"

"No, I just reacted, Jenn."

"Anthony admitted he was lying! I can't believe it. How did you know you could get him to admit it?"

"I didn't know. I just reacted." I sounded a little exasperated on that last one.

"Oh," Jenn said, it finally sinking in that I didn't have some master plan cooked up. "So, you and Brendan, huh?" She gave me a thumbs-up and raised her eyebrows up and down.

I sighed. I wished there was a "me and Brendan." I even liked the sound of our names together. Brendan and Emma. Emma and Brendan. If we were a celebrity couple, we'd be Bremma. Or Emden. No, Bremma. That sounded better. Too bad it was impossible since I'd apparently offended him this morning.

"No, Jenn. There's no me and Brendan." I tried to hide my mopey tone.

Once at my seat in English, I dropped my backpack and rifled through it for my notebook, trying to keep my eyes from staying glued to the door for when Brendan walked in.

He sauntered in a few minutes later. My eyes followed him, and they weren't alone. The entire class followed his movements, eager to see what our interaction would be. They hadn't seen our little tête-à-tête in front of the school. My classmates needed hobbies. Jeez, learn to knit or bowl or something.

He walked to his desk and faced it, his eyes down. Brendan dropped his backpack and slid into his seat, sitting sideways. I could feel such a pull to him, and unconsciously, my hand slid up across my desk, closer to him, where I brushed the back of his chair with my fingertips.

Brendan turned to me, taking note of the attentive audience of juniors. *Seriously, people, CityVille, even!*

"Look, Emma," he started, his voice full of the same soft tone he had used in front of the school.

"Class, class, let's get started," Mr. Emerson cut in, clapping his hands and walking in. I actually jumped a few inches in my seat, and then forced my eyes to stare at my textbook. At the end of class, Brendan bolted out of the room.

I desperately wished I had my iPod with me so I could muffle the voices of my gossipy classmates as I walked down the halls. Thankfully Angelique could care less about the fight—all she could talk about during lunch was that her mom had just returned from giving a lecture at Georgetown and promised to bring me some books on ancient medieval symbols that she was borrowing from a colleague. Angelique had talked to her mom, and Dr. Evelyn Tedt was positive that my necklace somehow factored into the whole supernatural shebang. Like I could even focus on exploding streetlights. How could I worry about spirits when I couldn't even seem to manage to get along on this normal plane?

Wednesday morning arrived—and I was a tired mess. My eyes didn't just have bags—they had five-piece luggage sets. I tossed and turned all night. I dreamed I was walking through New York, the way I had seen it in movies about the early 1900s. I swished through the dirty streets in a shirtwaist dress, my hair neatly pulled back under a wide brimmed, feathered hat. Oddly, my hair was blond. I was in a wrap-style wool coat, lavishly trimmed with braid, and I carried a large dress box. The twine on the package caught on the oversize silver brooch pinned to my coat, ripping the pin from the fabric. I tried to chase the brooch as it rolled down the street, but I was weighed down by the large box. I didn't know what exactly was in it—I just knew it was precious and I couldn't put it down.

In a flash, I found myself in front of a grand white house. The Hudson River was reflected in the home's spacious front windows—windows which crackled and buckled as orange-and-red flames danced behind the glass. The windows shattered—the force of the explosion blowing my hat off as molten shards danced around my feet. I didn't flinch at the blazing heat, keeping my vigil in front of the inferno.

"It's not safe with him. Can you stay away?" I whirled around and saw my brother Ethan standing there. He grabbed my left hand and tried to whisk me away, gripping my hand so tightly, it hurt—and I realized I was wearing a diamond ring. The stone pressed painfully into my skin as he clutched my hand in both of his.

"I have to go," I yelled, running into the house and feeling the heat from the fire assault my skin as the flames ravaged the home, charring everything in its path. The flames licked at my skirt, clawing their way up my white dress, setting my coat on fire. And then the fire crawled into my hair.

I woke up, screaming and scratching at my own face.

Suffice to say, it was not a good dream, with images of it playing in my head as I walked to school. Why the hell I would run into a burning building in my dreams, I had no idea. Once I arrived at Vincent Academy, I was dealt another crushing blow. There was no Brendan in English class. For a brief moment, I hoped that maybe he was home sick, and then felt like the worst person in the world. *Really, Emma, you're wishing illness on him now? Shame on you!*

My mood perked up in chemistry, when Angelique told me to meet her by her locker—330, on the sunlit third floor, that lucky witch—after school. My eyes bugged out when she produced a leather tote bag stuffed with two thick, antique-looking books and one brand-new one.

"I don't have to tell you, be very careful with these," she said, going through them. "Here's *Ancient Symbols and Myths*, and *Hadrian's Medieval Legends.* That one is super old. It's missing pages, so be careful. The binding is cracked. And this one—" she pointed to the shiny red paperback "—is *Spells for the New Witch*. You know, in case you're interested."

I thanked her a thousand times for the books, and staggered home with them, wishing Ashley hadn't made plans after school. I could have used some help with the heavy tomes. Once home, I made myself some coffee and took the mug to my room, telling Aunt Christine that I had a ton of homework and needed to focus.

Sitting cross-legged on my bed, I laid out the three books in front of me. I started with *Ancient Symbols and Myths,* which looked like an old, dusty college textbook. I opened it and, unsure where to start, just began turning pages. I took off my necklace and placed it on the purple comforter next to the book, looking back and forth between the symbols on the worn pages and the charm I'd had for so long. I'd think I found it, then look more closely and see some kind of difference. My crest was a simple shield, with a faint outline of a unicorn in the center. A sword and a rose were crossed behind the shield, and the bloom was wilted, a detail I'd never noticed before. A petal fell from the rose—it looked like the flower was crying. Under the sword, a crescent moon with a small star appeared where the petal was on the opposite side of the medallion. The back of the crest was plain, save for three large scratches and a few nicks and dings that came with age. I lovingly stroked the face of the pendant. How could I think this was from a mall?

I turned the pages painstakingly, and then, I felt my breath stop. There, on page 307, was an artist's rendering of my necklace.

The Crest of Aglaeon

My hands were surprisingly steady as I read through the basic description of the crest. Yep, a crossed sword and wilting rose behind a unicorn. That was my necklace.

The Crest of Aglaeon dates back to the 12th century— approximately 1150, and belonged to Lord Archer, Earl of Aglaeon. An update to the original family crest of two swords crossed behind a unicorn, Lord Archer him- self designed the revised crest, following the murder of his wife, Lady Gloriana. The wilting rose, beautiful in its fragility, was added to honor his late wife. As Lord

Archer himself wrote after her death (translated from the original Middle English):

"And whilst my beloved has left me alone
She is still as fair as the loveliest rose
Tears may fall, but they are not alone
Every rose will weep petals as she goes."

I was moved by the unrestrained beauty of Lord Archer's words; even flowers would cry at her loss. At least I knew what my necklace meant: it symbolized love—a true love— lost brutally.

I continued reading.

The change to the family crest was not well received— and Lord Archer's father, Lord Alistair, the Earl of Aglaeon, refused to accept the revised crest, as Archer had married a peasant instead of proceeding with the marriage his father had arranged to secure their lands.

There was no more information on my crest in the book, so I carefully placed it back in the leather tote bag and, after a mug of fresh coffee, turned to the *Hadrian's Medieval Legends* book, curious if there was anything on the sad tale of Lord Archer and Lady Gloriana.

I ran my hand over the ancient leather cover, which was peeling with age. It was still beautiful, though, with embossed scrollwork that ran along one side. The threadbare binding cracked and flaked under my fingertips, and many pages were loose or starting to slip. Lacking a table of contents, I turned the pages of the tome gingerly as the sun started to fade out- side of my window. The prose was lovely—if a bit flowery at times—and I found myself getting lost in the romantic legends of dragons, demons and sorcery. Sometimes I'd get drawn into a story, only to find that the last few pages were missing, having fallen out from the fragile binding. I got quite lost in a story about witches using the blood of lovers in a sinister spell, only to find the next few pages were gone. Finally, at page 502, I saw it. I took a nervous sip of coffee and began reading.

Chapter 9

The Legend of Lord Archer, Earl of Aglaeon, and his Peasant Wife

Lord Archer of Aglaeon was envied by all. Those who didn't covet his great wealth, craved his strength, his artistic skills with a brush or his fair face. And Archer was aware of the rampant adoration that surrounded him. Pride swelled his chest and his head. Yet it was pride that was his only flaw. A fair and just man, Archer treated the peasants who toiled on his lands with kindness and respect. He perceived them less as slaves—an attitude adopted by most lords—and more as workers in his employ.

Archer's youth was spent in the pursuit of less-than-noble endeavors. He loved hunting with fellow lords on his seemingly endless lands, sampling wine and finely prepared meals and engaging the eager young women at court.

But as Archer grew from a rakish youth into a man, his father, Lord Alistair, was eager for his restless son to find a wife and produce an heir. Yet Archer was bored with the women at court, finding them distasteful and silly. Their conversation was studied and careful. Their greatest talents were musical—one could play the harpsichord, another could sing—yet they all seemed to possess the same level of talent, as if they cultivated just enough bait to snare a husband.

Archer's boredom with the women at court grew to disgust, and he believed he would never find a woman who was his equal, who could engage him the way he desired. To appease his father, Archer agreed to an arranged marriage with Lady Eleanor, daughter of Lord Charles, Earl of Keane. Although beautiful, Archer found Eleanor silly and foolish. His dislike for Eleanor grew after he saw her berate a servant, slapping the girl for clearing Eleanor's empty plate from the table.

"I had not yet finished my meal!" Eleanor shouted, striking the girl across the face.

Weeks before the wedding, Archer was riding in his fields alone, not wishing to share his miseries with anyone when he came upon a small, yet meticulously cared-for cottage. A young woman was outside, tending to roses that climbed the cottage's facade.

She looked up and blushed, hastily bowing.

Archer was taken by the woman's beauty. It was not powdered and pressed the way the women at the court were. She was natural, almost wild, with black hair that fell to her waist. He dismounted and asked to speak to her.

He found that, although she wasn't highly educated, she was smart. She was clever, yet kind.

Turning to her roses, she pulled something small off the petals and cupped it in her palm. "I'm holding the loveliest thing your eyes will ever behold," she told him, and Archer begged to see.

With that, she showed him the tiny ladybug nestled in her palm. When Archer scoffed, she explained, "You cannot find beauty in this small creature? It can fly—we cannot. Its jacket is bright red and spotted. We are simply plain. If you cannot see the glory in the palm of my hand, what chance have you to see beauty anywhere else?"

Archer asked the peasant what her name was, and when her father would be home. Gloriana was stunned when he told her, "Tell your father Lord Archer will return tonight to speak with him." Although his fine robes told her Archer was a man of great import, she didn't know he was her family's own lord. Gloriana apologized, fearful that she had angered the lord. He promised her all would be explained when he spoke to her father.

That evening, he asked Gloriana's father, John, for her hand in marriage. Her father feared for retribution from the powerful lord, yet didn't want to sentence his daughter to a lifetime of misery. The only joy afforded peasants was the chance to marry for love.

John told Archer he must ask Gloriana for the pleasure of her hand. Surprised, but intrigued, Archer proposed to Gloriana.

"Might you court me first?" she asked. "Afford me the same respect you would a maiden a thousand times my stature."

Archer, already in love with Gloriana, agreed. But when he told his father he wished to cancel his wedding, Alistair feared for the life of his son. Snubbing Lady Eleanor and her powerful family—for a peasant!—was tantamount to treason.

Still, Archer persisted in his courtship of Gloriana, even after learning that the young maiden practiced pagan rituals. Those in court scoffed at the satchel of herbs he wore around his neck for protection—a gift from his beloved.

Members of society whispered that Archer had lost his

mind, leaving a fine woman like Eleanor for a heretic peasant. But Archer would not be stirred; the bolder and more independent Gloriana was, the more deeply he fell in love. Finally, she accepted his marriage proposal. The two were wed in a small ceremony, with just her family and his father in attendance. Society had refused them.

Archer didn't trouble himself with the court's chatter. After all, he and Gloriana shared a true love. He offered her all the jewels and servants she could want, yet all she desired was an education. So Archer employed scholars to give his bride the knowledge she craved. Soon, she was writing love poetry that rivaled the epic poems Archer himself wrote to his beloved.

Their seemingly infinite joy grew when Gloriana gave birth to a son. But their happiness was tainted when the Cardinal refused to see the child and baptize him. The reason given was that Archer had insulted Lady Eleanor, whose family was great friends with the Cardinal. Archer suspected that the rumors of Gloriana's heresy had reached the Cardinal, influencing his decision. So Archer made plans to travel to the Cardinal and petition him personally to christen the child. He planned to explain that Gloriana was filled with goodness and light, and didn't practice the dark arts of evil witches.

Although it pained him greatly to leave Gloriana's side, Archer felt compelled to, as he worried for the child's soul. Gloriana's labor had been difficult, and both she and the child, Alexander, had struggled with fevers. For a moment, Archer fervently hoped his wife really was a witch, so she could simply take away their pain with a spell, but Gloriana gently explained that it was not quite as simple as that. Should the child die before getting baptized, Archer feared Alexander would spend his eternity in Purgatory.

Archer kissed his beloved, and his sweet son, promising them that he would soon return to their side.

"My eyes are not worthy to look upon your face," Archer told Gloriana. "Yet they will not rest until they see you again."

"Nor will mine," she promised. "For I belong with you."

But she never saw her husband again.

When word reached Lord Charles that Archer and Gloriana had produced an heir, fury gripped the bitter man's heart. His own daughter, scorned by Archer for a peasant—and a witch, at that!—was too ashamed to show her face at court. She was forced to live as a spinster—no proud man would accept a woman who was rejected for some moon-worshipping commoner.

As Archer petitioned the Cardinal, Lord Charles hired mercenaries, who crept into Archer's manor under the cover of night, to kill Archer's beloved.

Gloriana, still sick with fever, was awoken by a young servant girl, Mary. "They're coming for you! You must flee!" Gloriana gave the servant her infant son, Alexander, begging her to make sure he was safe. Weak and frail, Gloriana knew she couldn't run as swiftly as the young maiden. She directed Mary to her cottage, empty and dark since her family now resided in the manor. "Tell my family to escape to our dear cousins' home. Do not wait for me. I will meet you at the cottage," Gloriana instructed the girl. With one last kiss to Alexander's head, Gloriana handed over her son. Mary fled.

Struggling against fever and weakness, Gloriana clutched her final poem to Archer in her hand and stumbled through the manor's hallways. Shoving open the heavy door to the manor's grounds, Gloriana stepped into the cool blackness of night. Her steps faltered as she retreated through her cherished garden, where she was discovered by Lord Charles's mercenaries. They descended upon the frail maiden, and stabbed Gloriana in the heart. She died among the roses, staring up at the crescent moon.

Archer returned the next morning. There, he found his manor in shambles. Rooms had been burned, tapestries torn and shredded, valuables stolen. He raced through the rooms, seeking his wife and fearing the worst.

Archer dashed out of his manor—never looking at the backyard garden—and galloped through his lands, calling out Gloriana's name. Archer challenged his steed to run faster, hoping that he would find Gloriana at her parents' cottage.

Once there, he found the servant girl. Weeping, Mary told Archer that Gloriana had begged her to escape with wee Alexander, and that she had never arrived at the cottage as promised.

"Please stay with my son," Archer pleaded with the girl. "Thank you for saving his life. I shall return with my love."

Archer raced again to the manor, calling Gloriana's name throughout the burned, razed home. As if his heart was pulling him toward the site of its own destruction, he turned toward the garden.

There, amid the roses, was his beloved. Archer knelt by Gloriana, putting his head to her still heart.

"My Gloriana, my rose." He wept, cradling her in his arms and caressing her cold face with his hand. Needing to feel her touch one more time, he reached for her hand and pulled it to his face. A small scrap of bloodied parchment fluttered to the ground. Archer picked it up and found Gloriana's last love poem, still unfinished.

Like a fortress I feared I would harden
But upon a bright summer glare
Amidst the roses in my garden
I met my future there
My purpose, my life and my soul
I would give to free the worry from your brow
Ah! So they are yours, to keep and to hold
My soul, my love, I give to you now

Gloriana never had the chance to finish her poem. Cradling his wife in his arms, the despondent Archer left his steed and walked to his wife's childhood home. There he met the servant Mary, who helped him bury Gloriana in her family garden, underneath the roses where they first met. Mary stayed with Archer, aiding him in caring for Alexander, who still battled with illness, and gave Archer and his son safe refuge in her family's home.

Still grieving too much to contact his father, Archer spent weeks with the servant girl's family. Apart from weeping for his beloved and cherishing Alexander, the only thing that occupied Archer's anguished mind was his family crest. He was obsessed with designing a new crest to memorialize his lost love. He melted his dagger into a small disc, agonizing over the new design.

Seeing the true anguish in Archer's eyes, Mary's father Gregory—an opportunistic, manipulative man—tasted an opportunity for gain. He promised Archer that he could reunite him with his bride, for a price.

Desperate, Archer promised the man everything—land, wealth, women of ill repute—if it meant he could meet with his cherished Gloriana again. "You will have to pay me handsomely," Gregory said. "But remember, another price *you* pay may be even greater."

Archer was willing to suffer any cost to see his true love again. Knowing a woman as good and honorable as Gloriana would surely be in Heaven was no comfort to Archer. Gregory led him to a small stone cottage in the middle of a dark wood. He stood yards away with the nervous horses, which bucked and reared at the sight of the home. Gregory told Archer that if anyone could reunite him with his love, it was the woman who lived there.

So this is the home of the dark witchcraft feared by so many, thought Archer, as he knocked three times on the door. A small, withered old hag answered, a dirty, dark cloak wrapped around her hunched shoulders. Soft, fine hair dotted her chin, and her right eye was milky white.

"Archer, yes, I've been expecting you." The hag cackled. "It's love you seek, yes? A fine woman?"

"I don't seek a fine woman. I seek *the* woman, the fairest and finest."

"Ah, the one you seek, she's got the magick in her, yes?" The hag rubbed her papery hands together as she regarded the distraught man.

"She is well-versed in some spells…" he began, but the witch cut him off.

"Is?" she spat out. "She *is* not anymore. She is no longer of the mortal realm," the hag replied. "Still, I can help you. Have you anything personal of Gloriana's?"

Archer was surprised to hear that the hag knew his beloved's name, but in his desperation, he continued his quest.

In his vest, Archer carried Gloriana's final poem, her

last profession of love. He handed it to the hag, whose one black eye sparkled and gleamed when she read it.

"You own her soul!" the hag bleated. Gloriana's poetic words did, indeed, dedicate her heart, her life—and her soul—to her husband.

The hag started cackling again, and, placing her veiny claw on his arm, drew Archer close.

"I believe I can help you," she said, explaining what she could offer the heartbroken lord.

She would not raise Gloriana from the dead. "They always come back wrong," she hissed mysteriously. But the hag said when death comes to an innocent early, the soul may linger—and she believed Gloriana, a magickal soul troubled over her son's health, had not yet moved on. The hag said she could keep her soul earthbound until Archer's own mortal shell had perished. Then, Archer's soul would be reborn, as would Gloriana's. Reincarnated, they would be destined to reunite, a lifetime away.

"It is your soul that aches," said the hag, licking her chapped lips. "So what care you if you see her in this lifetime? You'll reunite in the next."

Archer agreed to the contract, believing it to mean that, reborn in new lives, he and the dearest Gloriana would reunite and enjoy the marriage of which they were robbed— and eventually, old and ailing, die. Their final reunion would come in Heaven, where they would spend eternity in each other's cherished embrace. He fervently wished for death now, so his next lifetime—a span of years with Gloriana by his side—would come.

"But how will I know my soul's mate?" Archer asked the hag.

She said signs would be put in place, signs that would suffice for a clever man and maiden. These signs would be no match for their attraction, which would be a great force on its own.

But Archer desired something definite—that could not be disputed. He had to know the woman he held was, indeed, Gloriana. The hag agreed to mark Archer's mate with a symbol—his family's crest—as it appeared now, with a weeping rose to honor his fallen, murdered love.

"Happy are you now?" she croaked. "You can not dispute the attraction when she's wearing this mark. Even a fool would recognize his soul's mate."

Pride still colored Archer's demands, so he demanded of the hag that his soul find rest in a descendant—one from his own proud bloodline. He should have a brilliant mind, the strength of ten men and be more handsome than any lord, with enviable wealth. For Gloriana, he begged speed, knowing his clever bride would have escaped the mercenaries had she been of fair health.

"Are these all your conditions?" The hag cackled. "Nothing more?"

Archer agreed to the contract, and the hag went to work. The simmering cauldron in the fireplace suddenly burst forth with blue flames, and the sinister black liquid inside started to bubble.

She held Gloriana's love poem in her withered, leathery hand.

"Of this contract we do speak
Written with a hand that now lies cold
Of the dark lord we do seek
Lost true love's tender hold."

Archer watched as the fragile parchment in the hag's hand crumbled to ash, blue flames shooting from her palm. She threw the ash into the cauldron, and it boiled angrily.

The hag withdrew a dagger and, taking the medallion from Archer, scraped the blade three times across the back of the medallion. She collected the scraps of metal and tossed them into her cauldron, which hissed and smoked.

Grabbing Archer's hand, the hag cackled again, holding the dagger high before dragging the jagged blade across Archer's palm, squeezing his hand to force the blood out. It spilled into the cauldron, and the liquid swirled and bubbled. Using a spoon carved from bone, the hag scooped the blue-black serum into a curved gray-white bowl. Archer reeled at the sight, fearing the bowl had been carved from a skull. The hag handed the potion to Archer, instructing him to drink the bitter, vile liquid. As he choked down the thick serum, the witch began chanting:

"Keep their souls on earth bound
Finding their way with this crest's face
And whence each other they have found
Death comes after their destined embrace."

"Death? What magick is this? A lifetime is what I require!" Archer shouted. The hag cackled, and her wrinkled face began to smooth. The hair on her chin withered, and her milky eye turned clear as both eyes began to glow yellow. The hag stood up straight, and transformed into a young man. His catlike beauty peered out from the cloak, which began to shimmer as if it were on fire. Archer realized the witch was, indeed, a true agent of the devil.

"You might have thought of that before damning your true love's soul from entering Heaven," the feline man said, grinning and baring a row of sharp, fanglike teeth. "Perhaps her soul should have been of more concern than your own beauty or wealth. But don't worry, you selfish fool, you'll reunite with her again. And again. She'll always be wearing your precious crest. And you'll know the fresh pain of her loss for all eternity."

"No! I pray of thee, say lifetime. Give us a lifetime together!" Archer screamed, falling to his knees. The man laughed at Archer's torment, as Archer begged him to change or undo the spell. But it was too late. He had damned his and Gloriana's souls to an eternity of pain, a never-ending cycle of reunion, romance and then tragedy, as their love would be cut short by her death. They would reunite in another life, only to repeat the same doomed cycle.

If, on your true love a crest is worn
Be cautious, from you that love will be torn
You'll be spellbound, enraptured until her last heartbeat
Which is numbered the moment your eyes meet
If freedom from the curse is your goal
Be warned, it takes a selfless soul.

Chapter 10

The next three pages were missing. I shut the book and, very carefully, placed it in the leather bag. I looked for my cell phone to call Angelique, but saw the time—1:10 a.m. *Damn.* I had been reading for almost nine hours straight. I didn't know if it was coffee or adrenaline, but I didn't feel the slightest bit tired.

Moving my neck from side to side, I became aware of a sharp strain from sitting still, in the same position, for so long. I heard my neck crack and stood up to stretch out.

It was a good story, nothing more. Right? How many fairy tales had caught my attention in that book before I found one that revealed the origin of my crest? Before getting lost in the tale of Lord Archer of Aglaeon, I read epic fables of evil witches and sorcerers and knights who rescued fair maidens from dragons. And come on, there's no such thing as dragons, right? *Right?*

I reasoned with myself. My necklace has to be an antique or something. My brother Ethan just picked it out because he thought it was cool. And Ethan happened upon a legitimate antique at a yard sale. Isn't that the ultimate dream of everyone who watches *Antiques Roadshow?* That some hand-me-down was, truly, a valuable antique? What are the odds that my medallion, through some dark magic, found me to mark me as someone's true love? My charm was merely a bauble worn around the neck of a society woman. Or a brooch, pinned to her coat. Just like in the dream I had, where it fell off my coat, and rolled away from me before I died. The three scratches on the back of the crest couldn't be from a witch in the woods, right? *Right?*

I paced my room, gripping my mug. *Okay, let's run with this a minute. What else do I have to lose?* Let's say that the crest is a sign. That I'm wearing the legendary Crest of Aglaeon, which marks me as someone's true love. That this medallion has found its way to me, its doomed, but rightful, owner. The fable—and it was just a fable, right?—had mentioned other signs, signs that a clever lord and lady would pick up on. And am I supposed to believe that Brendan is my destiny when the only thing he's shown me is indecision?

I laughed out loud, thinking of Archer showing up at Gloriana's door, one day full of praise and adoration, and ignoring her the next day when she tried to show him the beauty in another ladybug.

Ladybug.

"I hope it brings you good luck, Ladybug." The words my brother said to me when he gave me the necklace.

My mouth was suddenly dry, and I put the coffee to my lips with shaking hands—promptly spilling it down my shirt.

I put the mug on my nightstand and ran to the bathroom, wetting a hand towel and dabbing at the spots on my blue tank top. I regarded my agitated reflection in the mirror.

Did I look like the reincarnated soul of a tragic fabled peasant? My life was no fairy tale. Sure, once upon a time, I was happy. Then my twin brother, my best friend, died of meningitis. Then my mother got sick—and married her loser boyfriend so I wouldn't be alone after she was gone. But I would have been better off alone—my wicked stepfather practically killed me driving drunk and now I'm stuck dealing with a bunch of rich princesses on the Upper East Side, living with my aunt Christine…who was my godmother. And had been like a fairy godmother to me. I stared at my reflection.

Do I look like a freakin' fairy-tale princess to you?

"Actually, would that be an earl-ette, since Gloriana married the earl?" I asked myself, then realized, wow, I really was going bonkers.

I splashed water on my face, trying to stop my heart from beating right out of my chest. The story says there were other signs. What other sign was there, other than my unnaturally strong attraction to Brendan? I'd had crushes before. And my freshman year boyfriend, Matt, was pretty cute. But even my biggest crush didn't compare to the pull I felt to Brendan.

Brendan, who's smart. Very smart. Just like Archer was supposed to be, when he was reincarnated.

The signs flashed through my head, coming at me faster now, like a meteor shower.

His name was Brendan Alexander Salinger. Alexander was Gloriana and Archer's son. And, come to think of it, I *was* pretty speedy, just like Gloriana was supposed to be when she was reincarnated.

Brendan was strong, too—he knocked down Anthony like he was flicking over a domino. And Brendan was definitely more handsome than any lord—I mean, he was certainly the best-looking guy at school. His family was probably loaded, too. Most people at that school were.

And then there was the biggest sign of all: the crest in his locker. What could that mean to him? What could it mean that I was wearing it? I braced my palms against the marble sink in the bathroom. Was he into witchcraft? Had he seen the design in a textbook, as I just did? Or was it…his family crest?

"Could the street lamps flickering really have been a warning, like Angelique said?" I asked myself.

I stared at my reflection—dark bangs, freckle underneath my right eye, nothing special—until the bathroom light started to dim. My heart pounding, I ran back to my room, throwing myself facedown on the bed, refusing to glance back through the open door to see if some supernatural force had triggered yet another light to burn out as a warning.

Cautiously, I raised my head and peered through the doorway, where the bathroom light shone brightly.

"You're losing it, Emma. You are seriously losing your mind," I croaked, my voice hoarse. "Your poor aunt is going to have to have you committed, and locked in a little padded room. You're seeing streetlights explode and you're believing in legends and that bulbs burning out are some ominous sign that you're destined to have a doomed fairy-tale romance."

And now you're talking to yourself?

I pulled the covers over my head, telling myself that I was just tired, that I hadn't been sleeping well—thanks to dreams where I lived in another time. Where, in a medieval gown, I tended to a rose garden and was covered in blood. Where my brother warned me to stay away from *him*. Where I died.

I hugged my pillow to my chest, squeezing my eyes shut, but I was hyperaware of every sound. The traffic four stories below me. The rolling sound of an approaching storm. The raspy wheezing of my overexcited breathing. There was no way I was getting to sleep tonight.

Throwing my covers back, I got up and defiantly turned off the bathroom light. When I got back to my room, I grabbed my laptop and pressed the power button, anxiously peeling off my nail polish as I waited for it to turn on. In the search engine, my fingers shook as I typed in "Reincarnation dreams."

More than a million hits. I clicked on the first one that looked halfway legit and didn't have a web address like "MagikSoulTime.com." I skimmed the site.

"Past lives and past memories can manifest in your subconscious dream state. Although it's more likely that what you're seeing are images from movies, television and film…

"Ultimately, no one except the dreamer will know if the dream is, in fact, a past life reaching out, or if it's merely the product of a mind overexposed to mass media…

"…if it is a past life, the dreamer should consider what message is being conveyed, as most adherents to the tenets of reincarnation believe that the soul returns to learn lessons and atone for sins committed in a previous life. Once when the soul reaches true enlightenment, it may exist in Heaven…"

I clicked on a few more sites, but saw nothing about a witch's curse forcing my soul to be earthbound forever. My eyes were starting to get heavy, and the web pages blurred in front of me. I shut down the computer and rested my head on my pillow, staring at my nightstand. The lights on the alarm clock read 5:46. Great. School began in less than three hours.

I huddled under the comforter, which provided little comfort to me this night. Part of me wanted to sleep—to stop my mind from twisting itself into a frenzy.

And then there was the other part of me, the part that was so terrified of what I might see in my dreams, it shook me into consciousness when I'd start to slip into slumber.

After dozing off in fitful ten-minute intervals, around the time the view outside my window turned from a dark shadow of the building across the street to a hazy fog, I finally fell asleep.

My eyes felt like they were pried open by crowbars when my alarm went off, the sound piercing into my brain. I stared at the foggy weather through the raindrop-stained window.

Oh, today's just going to be great.

"Holy sh—sugar, Em," Ashley said when she saw me, censoring herself as my aunt sat in the floral recliner in her pink bathrobe, sipping a steaming mug of coffee.

"Hey, Ashley," I croaked. She had come upstairs to get me since she didn't feel like waiting in the drizzling rain.

"I didn't really sleep well last night." *Or sleep at all.* I figured I had ninety minutes, total, of sleep. And that's a generous estimation.

I felt guilty as my aunt soothed me with a cup of warm tea, clucking about how hard I had been hitting the books lately. Well, I had been hitting the books, they were just antique volumes filled with supernatural tales, not my Latin books. Christine took pity on us and even though the rain had halted to a fine mist, handed over a crisp twenty-dollar bill for a taxi to school.

"I feel bad for you, dear, lugging all those schoolbooks around," she said, gesturing to the tote bag filled with Angelique's books. I had covered the telltale antiques with an old sweater, and I never felt guiltier in my life—especially since I should be focusing on Latin, not doomed medieval romance.

In the cab, Ashley rummaged through her bag and shoved some concealer in my hands.

"Seriously, you look like you just went ten rounds in the ring." I surveyed the destruction in her mirror and stared, dismayed, at the dark rings under my eyes. I had more bags than Louis Vuitton. I brushed my hair hastily with the tiny plastic brush that Ashley kept in her backpack—seriously, that girl's bag had more beauty products than books. I couldn't get rid of the tangles so I just gave up, slipping an old baseball cap on and pulling my damp hair back into a loose braid. I tried covering up my eye bags, but the makeup looked chalky on my skin, and drew even more attention to the shadows. Resigned, I handed Ashley back her mirror.

"You really look like hell," she said, then made an embarrassed face. "Sorry."

"It's okay, I feel like hell," I replied. "At least it's Thursday. Just one more day of this." She raised an eyebrow at me.

"You stayed up all night *studying?* Really?" Ashley sounded unconvinced.

"Yep, I just took on this project," I lied. "It's an independent study." *Well, it's kind of the truth.*

The cab went too far and dropped us off a block past the school. We walked back the rest of the way, but Ashley may as well have been carrying me as my tired feet—laden with Angelique's books—plodded forward slowly.

As we approached the school, my heart leapt—then fell.

Brendan was back. The hood on his North Face jacket was up, shielding him from the misty weather as he leaned against the damp mailbox, looking in the direction I normally walked from. My cousin rolled her eyes at me and ran ahead, yelling, "Emma, see you later."

He turned around, his face brightening when he saw me—then his features fell when he got a good look at me. I self-consciously smoothed my messy braid and suddenly was so thankful for my cap. I pulled the brim lower as I approached.

"Emma, hey," Brendan said, flicking his hood back and

brushing his damp hair off his forehead. "Are you feeling okay?"

"Yeah, I was just up late…reading?" It sounded like a question.

"Oh, reading? Is that what you kids are calling it these days?" And suddenly, the easy, breezy familiarity was back. Lord Archer would never play games with Gloriana like this. I stuck my tongue out at him. I couldn't summon a mature reaction. I was too tired.

"Well, Emma, I was waiting for you to ask you something, but you've made me late for class. Always a troublemaker, huh? I'll see you in English," he said, a smile playing on his lips as he swiftly went to the door and opened it for me. I stood in the entranceway, dumbfounded—until I realized I had about three minutes to get to my basement locker, then back up to my third-floor class before getting a tardy slip. I raced away, barely beating Mrs. Urbealis to history class.

I was useless again in my classes, and told Jenn that I just didn't feel well. At least this time, I looked the part. I was tired yet somehow full of a single-minded energy…I had to get to English, my only class with Brendan. The one thought raced through my mind: What did he have to ask me? *Can I copy your English notes? Want to catch a movie with me? Want to start a fairy-tale romance with me? BTW, it might be doomed, k?*

Finally, in English class, I felt like I could relax, because I knew my eyes would find that familiar face coming toward me, those eyes twinkling at me, that smile hiding more than it let on.

Brendan walked in late, of course, but still managed to beat Mr. Emerson. With just a nod and a smile in my direction, he slid into his desk and faced forward. *Is that a snub? Another snub?* I was furious. What did he want to ask me? And who does

Brendan think he is, toying with me like this? I was too tired to think it through anymore, so my body reacted for me.

I kicked the back of his desk. The rubber bottom of my shoe didn't make enough of a noise for anyone to notice, but his desk pitched forward a few inches. Brendan threw his left arm behind his seat, twisting around in his chair and staring at me with those green eyes, which I saw were sparkling, if a little stunned.

My eyes narrowed and I pursed my lips, giving him a dirty look.

Wordlessly, Brendan bit his bottom lip and a mischievous look crossed his handsome features. He quickly reached out his hand and grabbed my kneecap, pinching it between his thumb and forefinger.

"Hey!" I yelled. I wasn't hurt—just surprised. I flicked my pen at him. It bounced off his shoulder and he laughed.

"Tsk, tsk, Emma," Brendan admonished, wagging a finger at me. "Starting another fight. Has anyone ever told you that you're an instigator?"

Before I could reply, he leaned in and in a low voice, said, "By the way, I'm out tomorrow, and leaving school right at lunch, so please try to not provoke any wars or attempt to take on the entire junior class."

"I was just going to fight a few freshmen," I retorted. "I can take them. They're little and weak."

"Okay then, just the freshmen," he added, grinning. The entire front half of the classroom was listening to our back and forth verbal volleyball.

"Anyway, Emma, listen—" Brendan added, brushing his hair back off his forehead and giving a frustrated look at Mr. Emerson, who just walked in. "Damn it," he said in a low voice. "Listen, I *do* want to talk to you, okay? It just would have been nice to do it without an audience. What's your locker number?"

"Eight," I groaned. "Lucky me, it's in the basement."

"Ouch." Brendan laughed. "That sucks."

I nodded my head in agreement, a little confused. Wow. Violence worked. I wonder if I kicked Mrs. Dell's desk, I'd get an A in Latin.

Mr. Emerson started his lecture, and I fidgeted in my chair, feeling the weight of every single person's eyes on me. Jenn poked me and I looked at her hesitantly. She pointed down to her notebook, where she wrote:

U better not try 2 tell me that U guys are not some secret couple. How could u not tell me?

I looked around for my pen, which I realized had rolled several feet away after it bounced off of Brendan's shoulder. Jenn huffed exasperatedly, and handed me a spare pen.

I took it and wrote a hasty, *We're not!!!!!* in reply to her note, underlining it for emphasis.

Well ur not so "secret" anymore.

I shrugged and Jenn gave me a look that clearly signaled, "This conversation isn't over." I sighed and turned my attention to the lecture. Brendan shot out the door after class, and after waiting around my locker for the first ten minutes of lunch with him a no-show, I realized I would spend another weekend with him foremost in my thoughts, now wondering what he had wanted to ask me.

If the rain had to keep my body stuck in the cafeteria, at least my head was in the clouds—in fairy tales and stories of ill-fated love. I hadn't been going to the cafeteria this week, so I didn't know that Kristin had defected to the crowded corner table of "cool" kids—where Anthony had also apparently moved after his fight with Brendan. I had successfully avoided all contact with Anthony since the fight Monday, but stuck here in this small cafeteria, my eyes locked with his briefly. Glaring at me, he mouthed the word *whore*. I scowled back in response, giving him the finger. We continued our staring battle until I overheard Anthony's name mentioned at my table, and I tuned in to the conversation.

Apparently, my confrontation—and Anthony's confession that he was lying about my cousin—had triggered a butterfly effect. All my classmates were going over the list of conquests Anthony had claimed over the past two years and revisiting the validity of his claims. I overheard Kristin's name and was surprised that she kept going back to him after he shared—or should I say, overshared—just how far she was willing to go.

"What's the deal with Anthony and Kristin anyway?" I asked Cisco, keeping my voice low as I took a swig of my energy drink. Hey, I needed to stay awake.

"She threw herself at him freshman year, right when school first started. It was obvious she was into him. And she's *still* into him. He picks her up every now and then, then drops her. And she goes for it every time."

Cisco shook his head, disgusted. "The Thorns are loaded and big-time 'old money' people in New York." He made air quotes around the words. "She's got it into her head that only certain people are worth her time. His dad's a big famous lawyer and all that."

"The way Anthony treats her, you'd think she realizes it makes her look bad," I mused.

"Instead you'd think she shot diamonds out of her butt, the way she acts," Cisco snorted. "I've only ever seen her lose her cool over one other guy like that. I'll give you a guess on who that is."

I rolled my eyes. "Oh, great. Does his name rhyme with Schmendan?"

"Bingo," he said. "But he wasn't into it—at all—and that really made her mad."

"So, are Kristin and Anthony back on?" I asked, confused.

"More or less. From what I heard, Kristin and Anthony reunited over a mutual enemy." He gave me a pointed look and I just buried my face in my hands. Maybe I didn't have to worry about a curse. I'd be lucky to make it out of junior year alive.

In chemistry, Angelique's eyes predictably bugged out when she saw me staggering toward the table.

"Your books are in my locker," I explained. "I read them all night long. Which explains—" I circled my face with my hand "—this sexy mess that you see before you."

"You found something. I can see *something* has changed." Yep, you really couldn't pull the wool over Angelique's eyes. I still wasn't so sure about the whole reincarnated-maiden thing, but I had plenty of faith in Angelique's uncanny abilities.

"I *think* so." I sighed. "I discovered what my crest means. And honestly, I'm not sure how to handle it. On the one hand, it explains a lot of things that have been going on…but on the other hand, if I believe it, then that's likely the first sign of dementia. The pieces are falling into place, but the puzzle… it's a very *unrealistic* puzzle. But the pieces fit."

"I get it." Angelique pursed her crimson lips thoughtfully. "Imagine putting together a jigsaw puzzle without having the benefit of the picture on the box." I nodded along, getting her analogy.

"It would be difficult, right? And you would go through a billion different ideas of what the final picture is. But as more pieces fall into place, you start to see the picture. That final picture is not the picture you thought it would be from the start."

"Right, but, Angelique, I thought I was putting together a still life of a bowl of fruit, and instead, it's a medieval battle scene."

She furrowed her brows, confused.

"I'll bookmark the pages," I said. "If you can, I'd love for you to take a look."

I paused as Mr. D walked into the classroom, then faced her again.

"Oh, and that whole 'marked by the spirit world' thing?" I whispered. "I'm pretty sure someone's trying to warn me or tell me something in other ways." I thought of the flickering bathroom light and felt my stomach flip.

Angelique's jaw dropped. "I *knew* it!" Then she stopped and put her head on her chin, her dark-painted lips turned into a frown. "I wish a spirit would make contact with me," she whined.

"Um, nope. You really don't," I muttered. "You absolutely don't."

"I'll read them tonight," Angelique promised. "Just leave your locker open and I'll grab them during my free period."

After chem, I returned to my dungeon to remove the lock—and I spied something sticking out of my locker. A note.

Emma
I'll be back on Saturday. I'd like to see you, if that's okay. I feel like we should talk—someplace where the entire school isn't eavesdropping.
Brendan
P.S.—Please don't beat anyone up until then.

I snickered. Brendan went on to leave his number. I carefully folded the note and tucked it away in my backpack. I wondered how long I was supposed to wait to call him. Right after school? Tomorrow? My questions were answered for me when I got home and stretched out on my bed, my schoolwork spread out in front of me. I was passed out, nose in my Latin book, by 4:00 p.m.

Chapter 11

I woke up at 8:00 p.m. and freaked out when I saw the time. Jumping out of bed, I frantically dug through my backpack for my cell phone. When I couldn't find it, I turned the whole thing upside down, emptying pens, loose-leaf and computer CDs all over the floor.

No cell phone. "Son of a…" I said out loud, looking up… and seeing it on my nightstand.

I smoothed out his note and dialed the numbers, trying to calm my somewhat frazzled breathing. *Great, voice mail.*

"Hey, Brendan, it's Emma. I'm free all day Saturday, so let's get together. I agree, we should…talk. Um, talk to you later. Yeah. Okay. Bye."

After I left the (completely awkward) message, I freaked out. What if he deliberately sent me to voice mail? What if he regrets giving me his number? I decided to calm my raw nerves with a shower—which is where I was when he called back. The voice mail was filled with static, but hearing his deep voice rumbling through my phone still sent shivers down my spine.

"Emma, it's Brendan. My cell reception sucks where I am. Meet me at the corner of Seventy-ninth and Fifth on Saturday.

I'll be there at six. Text me back if that's cool with you. See you Saturday."

I decided to keep our meeting—I didn't feel comfortable calling it a date—a secret from my friends. Besides, Angelique and I had business to attend to.

On Friday afternoon, she and I sat in Cosmo's Pizza. There were two pizzerias near school, and I opted for the one with the worse pizza—we knew it wouldn't be crowded with Vince A students—and I didn't want anyone overhearing our conversation.

"I read the tale of Aglaeon," Angelique began hesitantly. "How can I put this? Do you feel like you're Gloriana?"

"I *feel* like I'm eating crazy sandwiches," I said, nodding.

"But Gloriana was a peasant, and the impression I got is that Archer didn't want Gloriana coming back as some rich chick. He really, really hated those society ladies, or whatever you call them." Angelique paused, taking off one of her stacked silver bangles and spinning it on the table. "I don't mean this in a bad way, but your aunt is on the board at school and she's kind of rich. And your mom is at some fancy job in Tokyo. You're hardly what I'd call peasant material."

I took a deep breath. I figured if she didn't think I was crazy about this fairy tale, she'd forgive my earlier fables. I had told Cisco the truth, but so far, he was the only one who knew my real story, the very *un*fairy-tale start to my life.

"Yeah, about that…." I began. "There's no mom in Tokyo. I moved here after having an 'issue' at home." As I said the word *issue,* I rolled up my sleeve and showed her my scar. Her eyes widened a bit, but she steadied herself. Without going into too much gory detail, I explained about how I ended up with Henry, whose drunkenness finally brought me to live with my aunt.

"Well, it's understandable why you'd lie. But you're here for good, right?" She seemed worried that I was temporary.

"As far as I know, I'm here until graduation. If I don't get kicked out for failing Latin."

"Okay." Angelique smiled, then frowned. "Oof. So that means the peasant requirement—sorry to use those words—is actually kind of met in this case, doesn't it?"

I gave her a weak half smile. "Emma the plebian, at your service," I said, bowing my head.

"Let's run with the assumption that you are a reincarnated soul," she said, spinning her bangle on the table again. "I don't know a ton about reincarnation, but I have heard that you're supposed to have déjà vu a lot."

"I've heard about that, and I've never had it," I said, relieved.

"What about weird dreams—you know, where you're in another time and stuff like that?"

"That," I said, "I have had." I told her about the dream where I was burned in a white house, and the very first dream, where I was in a medieval-looking gown, and her brow furrowed.

"It's a beautiful, tragic story," Angelique mused. "And most likely, you're just wearing an antique—even though that one dream does sound suspiciously like you dreamed you were Gloriana."

I considered that—the dream where I was bloodied, among the roses—and shuddered.

"Let's hedge our bets here," Angelique continued. "Take off the damn necklace and Archer2000 won't be able to find you. You'll meet another guy. They're all the same anyway. Give me the thing and I'll use it in a spell." She held out her hand and beckoned to it with black-painted fingernails.

I rubbed the pendant between my fingers, pursed my lips and shook my head.

"Come on, Emma," she persisted. "I know it's a sentimental necklace, but there's no sense in tempting fate."

"But can you really fight it?" I asked, still holding on to the necklace.

She gave me a disapproving look, then dropped her jaw as if a thought just occurred to her.

"Your brother—was he really protective of you?"

I thought about Ethan; the time I fell on my bike and he put his headphones on me to distract me from the pain in my fractured ankle. How he beat up his friend Ted who used to lock me in the hall closet and turn off the lights when we were little.

"You could say that."

"I wonder if he's the one warning you...all these weird things happening to you, like the lights turning out above your head. I wonder if he's trying to get your attention, to get a message to you—and I basically gagged him with that protection spell, since nothing really big has happened since."

I thought about that for a moment, and suddenly, I felt like I had weights tied to my limbs. It made sense.

"I saw him, and I heard his voice," I said, my voice small. "Ethan was there, in those dreams."

"What did he say?" Angelique asked insistently.

"He said, 'It's starting.'"

"And?" Angelique prompted me.

"And...nothing! That was it. I woke up after that."

"Why didn't you bring this up before?" she cried, slamming her hands down on the table, her rings making a clacking sound as they hit the white Formica. "Ugh, this explains so much. *He's* the one warning you. I just know it."

I opened my mouth to protest, but nothing came out. Sure, it sounded absolutely mental. But it also felt right.

Tears started to prick at my eyes. "Do you really think my brother is warning me?" I whispered, feeling that familiar, dull ache of loss in my chest. His concern for me was enough for him to reach across spiritual planes? I ran my fingers across the face of my medallion, a few tears spilling out no matter how hard I tried to blink them back.

"I know it's hard, but you have to focus, Emma," Angelique said, tempering her stern tone with a sympathetic look. "'It's starting,'" Angelique repeated. "When did this happen?"

I thought back to that first dream—which I had the night Brendan and I hung out, at the Met. When he'd given me his sweatshirt. When we clicked like we'd known each other for years. And when I dreamed I was bleeding from a stab wound to my heart. But I couldn't face telling Angelique that just yet. Sure, I could tell her I thought I might be a reincarnated medieval maiden, and that lights exploded over my head and I heard my brother in my dreams. But could I tell her I was actually considering the theory that Brendan Salinger of all people was my soul's destined mate? Now *that* was some crazy talk right there.

"I don't remember," I lied. She didn't look convinced.

"This has to do with Brendan Salinger, doesn't it?" Angelique asked, punctuating her question with another spin of her bangle. "And that's why he just *had* to jump to your defense on Monday even though he barely knows you."

I evaded her question. "But if Ethan's trying to warn me, that means whatever tragedy is supposed to happen could be avoidable, right? If it was inevitable, what's the point?"

Angelique took a deep breath. "It seems that way. I just wish we could zero in on why, after generations of cursed Emmas, *you* are the one who might be able to break the curse?"

"'Cause I'm due for some happiness?" I said hopefully. Angelique just snorted.

"I don't know. There just seems to be a lot of supernatural stuff happening around you—the dreams, the warning signs. Hell, even meeting me and being able to find out about the curse. It's like on the one side there's the curse, and then there's something else battling it."

"I don't know why," I mumbled, picking the burnt eggplant slices off my pizza. "I'm just some girl."

"If you were part witch it would make more sense," Angelique mused. "Witches can't really curse other witches, from what I know. The spells are never that effective."

"But like I told you, I'm not really into all that stuff. I don't even believe in ghosts!" I amended my statement. "Well, I didn't *used* to believe in them. I don't know what I believe anymore."

Angelique paused. "Maybe you're a born witch? I mean, yes, you have to study the craft to hone your skills, but you could also have inherited certain—how shall I put this?—special talents. Especially since with reincarnation, sometimes some traits can stick with the person in their next life. You could have gotten Gloriana's mojo."

"I doubt it," I said, rolling my eyes. If I'd learned anything from my life, it was that I was hardly someone special.

"Oh, *now* you're going to be cynical?" Angelique huffed. "Just ask your aunt."

"I can't just stroll up to her and ask, 'Hey, Aunt Christine, I know I have my mother's smile. Was she also secretly a witch and did I get that from her, too? Or can I blame my past life for my witch skills?'"

"Well, if you're part witch, that could be why you have a shot at fighting this," Angelique reasoned. "It would be a nice bit of ammo in our corner." I realized that she said "our corner"—and felt bad for my cynicism. Angelique was in this with me.

"Have you ever known something before it was going to happen?" she asked. "That's one of the biggest marks of being a natural witch. It usually manifests when you're a little kid— all innocence, not jaded by the world."

"If I did, I would have tried to use it on winning the lotto," I joked lamely.

"It doesn't work like that, Em. It could be something small, like knowing what someone's going to say, or—"

"But even if I'm not, hey— There were pages missing in that book," I interrupted, trying to change the subject away from my alleged witchy ways. "The last words in the Lord Archer legend said something about breaking the curse and it requiring a selfless soul or something."

Angelique nodded. "If freedom from the curse is your goal, be warned, it takes a selfless soul."

"Wow." I was impressed. "Good memory."

Angelique tapped her forehead and said, "Photographic memory, actually. It's why my grades are so good." I gave her a jealous look.

"But you're right," she continued. "There seems to be some kind of way to break the curse. 'It takes a selfless soul'? There has to be some kind of sacrifice involved."

Seeing my face, Angelique corrected herself. "I doubt it's a *human* sacrifice, Em. I wonder… Hmm. I'll ask my mom about getting another copy of the book. One that's in better shape.

"Oh, and, Emma, it's so obvious that it's Brendan, but I guess I'll just wait for you to admit that to yourself before you admit it to me," Angelique said matter-of-factly, rolling her eyes as she said his name with a dramatically exasperated tone. I just pretended to be preoccupied with my cell phone and showed her the time. We had to hustle back to school, barely making it in time for chemistry. On the way back, I was silent, mulling over Ethan's other warning.

It's not safe with him. Can you stay away?

I knew the answer.

No, I could not.

Of course, I was running late on Saturday. I raced through my homework on Friday night, getting it done so I wouldn't have to deal with it for the rest of the weekend—and I even spent a little extra time on Latin, my subjectus terriblus. But mostly, I was trying to distract myself from obsessing over my impending time alone with Brendan.

I vacillated between going through with the date—I mean, meeting—and chickening out, but ultimately decided that canceling would be rude. After all, I reasoned, even though he had the same medallion in his locker, that didn't mean that he was my destined true love. And all we were going to do was talk, right?

Still, once I'd finally decided to go through with it, I'd had all day to get ready. At the last minute, I changed from a pair of cords into jeans. I paired a lightweight black sweater first with a pair of boots, then with my gray Vans sneakers, then the boots again, and finally, going with the Vans. My indecision had cost me: I had to run to make it there on time, and the unseasonably balmy temperatures told me my eyeliner would pay the price.

As each foot hit the pavement, my internal monologue spoke out matching rhythmic lyrics.

Oh. My. God. This. Is. Real.

I slowed my jog at Seventy-ninth Street and pulled out my cell phone to check the time, realizing that I was already eighteen minutes late. I spied Brendan, lounging against the stone entrance to the park. Seriously, did he ever stand upright?

He was holding a plastic bag filled with what looked like takeout.

"Hey," I said, a little breathless.

"I was starting to think you weren't going to come," he said dryly, his smile not quite matching his tone.

"Sorry about that. I have a problem with being on time," I said sheepishly, running my fingers through my hair—and feeling my face turn red when my hand got caught in a knot that had formed during the run over.

"You don't like to be on time?" Brendan asked, bewildered.

"No, no, it's not like that. I'd like to be on time. In fact, I'd love it," I said, fidgeting a little as I tried to explain my rudeness. "I just can't seem to make it happen. I'm always misjudging how long it takes to get somewhere. I think everything takes five minutes and it always takes so much longer."

He smiled, looking amused by my mini-rant, and pushed himself off the stone wall.

"Okay, let's go," he said.

"Where are we going?"

"Into the park. There's someplace I think you'd like."

I looked around confused, which Brendan interpreted as a sign of concern.

"Central Park is totally safe. You're with me. Didn't you see me with Anthony?" he bragged, puffing his chest out a bit as we started walking into the park. "I'm no joke."

"That's one way of putting it," I muttered. We walked wordlessly along the leaf-covered pathways until a tall, looming structure appeared, perched high on a bed of rocks.

"That's one of my favorite places to go. Belvedere Castle," Brendan said, leaning into me and pointing. I looked up at the stone structure, rising out of the rocks proudly as the sun started to set behind it.

"It's where we're going for dinner," he said, holding up the takeout bag.

We hiked up the pathway to the castle, finding ourselves in an open-air stone plaza at the summit of the rocks. Belvedere Castle sat on the second highest point in Central Park, overlooking a theater immediately below and to the left. After giving me a moment to admire the view, Brendan ushered me down a series of steps into a small, fenced-in area of smooth rock. Several yards beyond the fence, the rock jutted out into a jagged cliff, which overlooked a shimmering pond.

"That's an observatory." Brendan gestured to a building to our right.

"And that's where they do Shakespeare in the Park," he pointed out, following my gaze to the theater. "I thought you'd like this, based on...English class. You seemed into Shakespeare. You know, when you read the, um, poem. I mean, sonnet," Brendan stammered, and I was surprised that, for the first time, he didn't seem so sure of himself. He composed himself, dropping the bag of takeout on the other side of the fence, only to hop over the wall in one flawless, athletic move.

"I don't think you're supposed to do that." I looked around nervously. "I mean, that's why the fence is there."

"There's no security here until much later. Come on, the view's better over here," Brendan wheedled, motioning for me to join him. I tried to brace myself between where the stone wall framing the steps ended and the fence began, swinging my leg over the wall very *un*gracefully and missing.

"May I?" Brendan chuckled, ducking his head under my arm and lifting me over with ease. He held me in his arms longer than necessary before setting me gently on the rocks—and I tried not to notice how strong his hands felt. I silently congratulated myself for opting to wear my trusty Vans, which gripped the uneven surface as I made my way to the cliff's edge. If I had worn my boots, I'd go sliding off these rocks as easily as if I were wearing Rollerblades. I peered off the rocks uneasily at the drop to the Turtle Pond below.

"So I guess the only way out of here is over the fence again?"

"Nah, you can go around the castle," Brendan said, lounging on the cliff as he gestured to a narrow strip of rocks that jutted out around the observatory. I eyed the treacherous-looking strip of rock as I sat down cross-legged next to him. For a moment, we wordlessly overlooked the pond, shimmering with the lights of the New York skyline and the colors of the fading sun.

"This is really beautiful," I said, breaking the silence. "I didn't know this was here. I go running in the park all the time. I guess I never looked up." I looked around me in amazement. Brendan reached into the bag and pulled out a small wax-paper sack. "Egg roll?" he asked, holding it out to me.

"Thanks," I said, grabbing the crispy roll and taking a bite. I chewed it slowly, waiting to see if he'd start the conversation.

"I'm glad it's not cold out tonight," Brendan said, shrugging out of his hoodie, this time a black Bouncing Souls one, revealing a long-sleeved green T-shirt that almost exactly matched his eyes.

"I was afraid the rocks would be wet. Good thing it's so nice out," he continued, leaning back on his elbows as he continued to be a human thermometer. I rolled my eyes at him.

"What?" He gave me a surprised look. "It's *not* cold! Winter break is little more than a month away. You'd think it would be freezing out."

"So, this is what you wanted to talk about, without an audience?" I asked Brendan more than a little sarcastically. "The weather?"

He laughed, and stretched his long legs in front of him. "Okay, Emma, then how about we talk about how you're not The Rock?" he said, flashing that irresistible smile at me. "Really, what were you thinking? You've seen Anthony's temper before. I was there, remember? He had you practically running out of the park."

I raised my hands, palms out. "I— You don't understand. I was so mad." I dropped my hands into my lap. "I wasn't thinking."

"No, no, you weren't, you're right about that," Brendan agreed. "But it was pretty admirable how you stood up for your little cousin."

He paused for a moment, then looked at me with a slight smile. "Did you really call Anthony 'Mother Goose'?"

"I don't know. Maybe. It's all a blur, really," I answered honestly. "But I think I may have said that."

"You're adorable." He chuckled, rolling onto his back and staring up at the darkening sky, crossing his arms behind his head. "Even though you went after that big goon when you're only an inch taller than your cousin."

"I'm five-five," I said defensively, still reeling over the fact that he'd just called me "adorable."

"Yeah, maybe when you're standing on Ashley's shoulders," he said, smirking.

"Ha ha, very funny," I snorted, giving him a withering look. Tall people always have such egos about their height.

"But seriously, Emma." Brendan rolled over onto his side again, propping himself up on his right arm. "What the hell were you thinking? If I had gotten there a minute later…" His green eyes narrowed.

I opened my mouth to say something, then I shut it. "I don't know," I said softly. "It was my fault. I tried to stop her from even going out with him, but she didn't listen. I had to do something to make it right. I should have done something from the start."

"Emma, are you seriously blaming yourself?" he asked, pulling himself into an upright position. "You're kidding me, right?"

I shook my head. Brendan sighed and faced me, mirroring me by crossing his legs as I had. He grabbed my hands from where they were twisting together in my lap. "The only one to blame is Anthony."

"But I should have—"

"You should have *nothing*. You did nothing wrong," he assured, continuing to hold my hands, squeezing them gently. "You took down one of the biggest bullies I've ever known."

"Well, it was worth it, for her. She's the sweetest, and, well, she's young for her age. I don't mean that she's immature," I clarified. "Because she's not. Ash's really smart and mature about so much, but she's also just so damn *innocent*. She thinks people are good." I laughed a hollow laugh.

"And you don't?"

"I don't think people are either way. I think we have both in us, and you choose one way or another. I've known good people, and I've known—" I stopped short. "Let's just say I've known the opposite."

Brendan seemed to contemplate that for a minute. With a final squeeze to my hands, he looked down at the smooth rock between us and began tracing a crack with his finger.

"You know, Emma, I didn't see him shove you," he said quietly, "if I had seen him lay a hand on you, he wouldn't be breathing right now." Brendan lifted his eyes to meet mine, and the intensity in them made my breath catch. "I heard about it later that day. He's still going to answer to me for it."

"Don't go to any— I mean, why? I mean, thank you, but…I don't think…" I stuttered. Not sure of what to say, I looked back at the rock he seemed to find so interesting, tracing the same crack. Brendan took a deep breath and sat upright, rifling in the white plastic bag for the rest of the food. He laid it out—vegetable egg foo young, General Tso's chicken—and handed me a fork and an iced tea.

"Dig in," Brendan said.

"Thanks, I love iced tea. Not much of a soda drinker."

"Yeah, I know," he said slyly.

"How?" I asked, a little confused.

"You asked me to get you one—that night we went to see Gabe's band?"

"Brendan, about that night." I shook the iced tea bottle and smacked the bottom of the glass, distracting myself with the popping sound the lid made as I tried to work up my nerve. "The way you are now, is the way you were when we were at the Met and at the bar. But at school…"

"Yes?"

"You ignored me." I sounded more like a pouting little girl than I'd have liked.

"I know," Brendan admitted, his eyes downcast. "Look, I'm not proud of how I acted, honestly. I'd rather not get into it right now."

"It's just that…" I tried to compose my thoughts. One night

of hanging out two weeks ago and I felt like I had some claim on him? So what if I thought we had some kind of magical, supernatural bond? There was no way to explain myself without sounding like I was a sure bet for the gold medal at the Stalker Olympics. "It was unexpected."

Brendan nodded. "I get it. Look, Emma, I don't really like a lot of the girls at school—even just as friends."

"Well, we have that in common." I grinned a toothy grin and he smiled back before his face got serious again.

"I wasn't expecting *you*." His words just hung there, but he kept those green eyes on me.

I don't know if "uncomfortable silence" is the phrase I'd use for the wordless thirty seconds that passed, but then Brendan broke our unspoken moment.

"I *did* wait for you outside of school," Brendan softly reminded me. I nodded, smiling a little bit at the memory of how my stomach fluttered the two times I saw him lounging against the mailbox, clearly looking for me. The U.S. Postal Service should hire him for an ad campaign. If he were at the mailbox every time you sent a letter, no one would use email ever again.

"Did you mind?" he asked, cocking his head to the side. "I mean…I didn't mind waiting for you." I hoped I was reading the double meaning correctly.

"I didn't mind. I liked seeing you." Brendan started smiling his rakish grin back at me—then suddenly stopped.

"Then why won't you tell me?" he demanded.

"Tell you what?" I knew I sounded exasperated, but what was it that he wanted to know so badly?

"Why won't you tell me the truth? What's your real story?" I couldn't believe it, but Brendan actually sounded hurt. "You're not from Philadelphia. You're lying about *everything*. Whatever it is, you can tell me." So the real story of my shattered home life is what he wanted me to tell him, on that first day when he met me outside of school. I felt myself getting defensive.

"This is the most you've talked to me in two weeks, do you realize that? I don't even know where *you're* from. Where *you* live. Who *your* parents are," I spit out, my ripped-open wounds evident in my tone, much to my dismay. "At least *I'm* consistent with you. You treat me differently from one day to the next. You talk to me when no one's looking, like you're embarrassed to be associated with me or something. Maybe on Monday you'll go back to treating me like the social leper the rest of the snobs at that school seem to think I am." He cringed at that.

"I'm not going to do that, Emma."

"I'll believe it when I see it, Brendan," I retorted, crossing my arms defiantly.

He reached over and grabbed my hand, pulling my defensive pose apart. "Emma, I promise you, I won't ignore you like that again," he said, holding my hand in both of his. "And you're right. It's not fair of me to expect you to tell me *anything* when you don't really know me. You don't owe me anything. Especially after how I've been acting. Which, Emma, I really am sorry for."

Brendan's eyes searched mine as he slipped his fingers around my palm and pulled my hand up to his mouth, pressing his lips to the back of my hand. His kiss was featherlight, but I felt the imprint of his lips as they scorched my skin.

"And I promise you, I am not, in any way, embarrassed to be seen with you. I'm really, really sorry you think that."

He dropped my hand from his mouth, but still kept a gentle hold on it, looking down at the way our fingers intertwined. "I can't believe I made you think that," he whispered, more to himself than to me.

"Brendan—" I started, but he cut me off.

"I want to make it right. So, I'll make you a deal," Brendan said, the confidence returning to his voice as his gaze met mine. "Let's just enjoy dinner, and then I'll walk you home, like a good boy. After you've had fun tonight, and after I've had fun tonight, I'll ask you out properly. For tomorrow. Come over to my place. My parents are out of town, we'll have the place to ourselves."

I cocked an eyebrow, causing Brendan to amend his statement. "Aw, come on, Emma, I don't mean like *that*. We'll just be able to spend some time together. And you can ask me anything you want. You'll see where I live. You can even go through my stuff, rifle through my drawers and all that. Flip my mattress over, I don't care. And you'll say yes, like a good girl."

"You're pretty sure of yourself," I observed, popping a piece of chicken into my mouth.

"How so?"

"Well," I said after I had swallowed, "you said, '*After* you've had fun, and *after* I've had fun.' You're *so* sure I'm having fun and that I'll agree to see you tomorrow," I replied, trying to spear a piece of broccoli with my left hand, since my right was otherwise occupied. Brendan grinned at me and knocked my fork out of the way, stabbing the piece with his fork. I gave him a dirty look and he laughed.

"You're having fun right now," Brendan declared. "So, we're not going to talk about your alma mater, Imagination High. And we're *definitely* not going to talk about my behavior the past two weeks, so tell me this, at least. Yes or no question time. Are you really sixteen?"

I smiled at that one. "Yes."

"Okay, now we're getting somewhere," he said, grinning. "I'm seventeen. I started late.

"Is your name really Emma Connor?"

"Yep."

"Do you have any pets?" Brendan asked. I was aware that he was still holding my hand.

"I had a cat when I was little, but no pets now," I said, leaving out the part where Henry wouldn't allow pets.

"Ah, I had a dog," Brendan said, shaking his head. "I'm a dog person, you're a cat person. What am I doing with you?" I matched his smile, while my internal monologue screamed that Brendan just said he was "with me."

Brendan then let go of my hand, reaching out to my charm. *Oh, right. That.*

"Where did you get this?" he asked, his voice low as he turned it over in his hands.

"My brother gave it to me." I felt like I could tell him this truth, at least.

"Where did he get it?" Brendan's eyes were still glued to the medallion.

"At a garage sale. He said he hoped it would bring me good luck." I started to suspect that Brendan knew what the crest signified, but lost my train of thought as he dropped the charm and slowly slid his hand over my collarbone, up along my throat, and finally rested on the side of my jaw, where his thumb stroked my cheek.

"Emma," he said, his voice barely a whisper, still cradling my face in his hand. "I hope your brother's right." Brendan's face was as close as it had been the night of the Met, when I'd thought he'd kiss me. He searched my face with eyes that looked as deep and green as the pond shining below us.

Brendan dropped his hand into his lap, and seemed lost in his own thoughts for a moment. Then he cracked open a can of soda with a pop-and-fizz. Brendan broke the mood—again, I might add—so I took a swig of my iced tea, trying to not pick myself apart wondering what it was about me that made him so averse to kissing me.

"Is your brother back home in—" Brendan paused, cocking an eyebrow at me "—Philly?"

I shook my head, hoping Brendan would be satisfied with a minimum of information. I really didn't want to go there at this moment.

"I lost my brother a couple of years ago," I murmured, not meeting his eyes.

"Oh, Emma. I had no idea," Brendan said softly, reaching out to tenderly touch my cheek. "I'm so sorry, I didn't mean to—"

"It's—um, it's fine. So, basketball," I interrupted awkwardly. "Has there been any fallout from the Anthony situation? At practice or anything?"

Brendan paused for a second, tilting his head as if he understood that I needed a change of subject—immediately. "Not really. I'm already suspended from the team—one more fight and I'm off—so he takes it out on me at practice, trying to trip me and get me to throw the first punch or whatever, but—" Brendan smirked at me "—I don't really care. It gave me the opportunity to knock him into some folding chairs. Accidentally, of course." He smiled smugly.

"But of course," I agreed, glad for the new direction of the conversation. "Thanks again, for the whole stopping-me-from-being-a-stain-on-the-concrete thing," I said, looking back at that oh-so-fascinating crack in the rock.

"Stop thanking me. Besides, I doubt you'd go down without a fight," Brendan said.

"Still, I'm sorry if I broke up your friendship." To my surprise, Brendan laughed.

"He's not my friend. I just have to deal with him because we're on the same team and our parents travel in the same ridiculous social circles. I've known him since grammar school, and let me tell you, it was my absolute pleasure to knock him to the ground. Only next time—" he paused "—when you plan on stepping up to guys twice your size, give me a heads-up."

"I think I'm done street fighting for a bit," I said and he smiled at me.

"Good."

"So, why were you out of school this week?" I asked, peeling the label off my iced tea. This time Brendan was the one who looked uncomfortable, and changed the subject.

"What did you think of last week's chem test?"

I noticed that he steered the conversation to teachers we liked, teachers we disliked, teachers we *really* disliked, upcoming midterm exams—all safe topics.

"I aced Latin freshman year," he said after I confessed that Latin was my Achilles' heel, so to speak. "I can tutor you if you need help. Mrs. Dell hasn't changed her midterm in years. I still have it somewhere, so if you want, I'll help you study."

"Thanks." I grinned, more thrilled at the prospect of time with Brendan than the promise of pulling my grades up. "It's the only subject I'm having trouble in."

"I'm happy to help," Brendan said, then smiled a naughty smile. "Too bad you don't need tutoring in French."

"I'm quite good at French, thank you very much." I threw a little attitude into my reply, and Brendan grinned devilishly. But if it made him want to find out if I was bluffing, he didn't act on it. *Maybe he just likes me as a friend? A very touchy-feely, stroke-my-face friend?*

"Hey, kids, off the rocks," a security guard called, breaking our mood as he flashed a light at us from between the bars of the fence.

Brendan and I tried to hide our guilty laughter as we

wrapped up the empty food containers while the annoyed-looking guard stood there, tapping his foot.

After Brendan helped me over the stone wall, the guard gave him a dirty look.

"The fence is there for a reason, kids. That's a 130-foot drop."

"Sorry," we both mumbled around our smiles, as we headed back down from the castle.

"Hey, what time is it?" Brendan asked as we shuffled along the path. I checked my cell phone.

"Nine thirty-six," I said. Wow. We'd been together for almost four hours. I was glad I'd only drank the one small iced tea or else I'd had to have found a bathroom somewhere in the park. *Like that wouldn't have been awkward.*

"I need to get you out of here at a respectable hour if you're going to agree to see me tomorrow."

"So what is the plan for tomorrow, anyway?" I asked, tossing a peppermint Mentos into my mouth in an obvious hint.

"Wait for me to ask you like a good boy," he retorted playfully, grabbing the roll of candy and taking one, leaving me hoping that he picked up on my obvious hint.

"You just got me in trouble with security." I jokingly pouted. "Some good boy you are."

We slowly ambled through the dark park, listening to the crunch underneath our feet as we shuffled through the fallen leaves. Brendan, after dropping the Chinese food containers in a wastebasket as we exited the park, reached out and took my left hand. *Finally!*

"Where does your aunt live?" he asked, his hand warm against my slightly chilly palm.

"Sixty-eighth, right off Park," I replied. "Are you near there?"

"No, I live downtown. I just needed to know where to walk you home. I *have* to walk you home, you see. All part of being a good boy now," he teased, giving my hand a squeeze. I grinned back, and Brendan started walking even more slowly. I got the feeling he was trying to delay our goodbye.

Wordlessly, we strolled, the only communication being Brendan squeezing my hand every now and then. Every squeeze jolted me, triggering emotions stronger than any I'd ever known.

"Is this it?" he asked after we had crossed Madison, the wind whipping his black locks around.

"Almost," I said, still walking. "It's the next building." I started to take another step but he had stopped in his tracks, still holding my hand. Brendan pulled me back, tucking me into the darkened service entrance of the building next door.

My breath quickened as he drew me closer to him, releasing my hand and winding his right arm around my waist. "So Emma," he murmured, brushing my bangs off my forehead with the fingers on his left hand. "I've had fun tonight, as I hope you have."

I nodded—a little breathlessly, I might add—and he pulled me nearer still, holding me tightly against his body. I looked up at his playful smile, yearning for his lips to do something other than smile at me.

Brendan kept playing with my hair, and finally said, "I'd like to know what you're doing tomorrow."

"Oh, I'm busy," I said flippantly, trying to calm my own nerves with stupid jokes. Brendan just gave me a squeeze around my waist and raised one dark eyebrow.

"I mean, I'm busy…with you," I said softly, feeling a little shy all of a sudden.

"See, Emma," Brendan whispered, "I told you I could be a

good boy." He ran his hand through my hair, drawing me in more tightly as he lowered his face. The moment his mouth touched mine, warmth spread from my lips, through my limbs and settled in my chest, where my heart fluttered almost painfully. Brendan kissed me tenderly at first, cradling my face with his hand the way he had on the rocks earlier. I slid my hands up his strong chest and clasped them around his neck, pulling him closer to me. With that, Brendan's kiss became more urgent.

I tilted my head, parting my lips and allowing him to kiss me more deeply. I'd daydreamed about kissing Brendan plenty of times, but nothing could have prepared me for the overwhelming intensity of this embrace. It was unlike any kiss I'd ever had before. The way his mouth moved against mine, the way his right arm stayed wrapped around me, holding me against him while he raked his other hand through my hair… it overloaded my senses and felt natural at the same time—like this was where I was supposed to be. When Brendan eventually pulled himself away, he looked more reluctant than I was to end the moment. I was thrilled to see that he seemed just as dazed as I was.

He put his forehead against mine, and we both just breathed in for a second. I could smell that same clean-laundry scent. Brendan pulled his lips up and tenderly kissed me on the forehead. My fingers, still intertwined around his neck, toyed with the ink-black hair at the nape of his neck; it was as soft as I'd imagined.

"That feels amazing," Brendan breathed, bending his head to my neck, where he kissed my jaw softly before whispering in my ear, "I'll see you tomorrow—I'll text you my address. Come over as early as you can."

With a final playful nibble under my earlobe, Brendan ducked out of the doorway. I smiled and mouthed, "Bye," before walking—or should I say, floating—the few feet to the awning of my aunt's building. I ignored the doorman's knowing look and glanced back at Brendan, who was standing nearby to make sure I had made it into the building safely. I smiled again at Brendan—and scowled at the doorman—and went upstairs.

I'd seen movies where a girl shuts her front door and leans against it, grinning from the fresh imprint of a great first kiss. I always thought it was some standard movie schlock. I never thought I'd actually do it.

I shut my aunt's door and leaned against it, squeezing my eyes closed and grinning. I even sighed happily.

"Good night?" My aunt padded into the living room from the kitchen, in her pink chenille robe and matching slippers.

"Yes, Aunt Christine." I grinned.

"I assume, a boy?"

"Yes, Aunt Christine," I said again, smiling.

"He must be some boy," she mused, sitting down on the couch with a dog-eared *Ellery Queen* paperback. "I looked like that the first time your uncle George kissed me." My hand flew to my mouth and I realized my lip gloss was a little smeared. She pursed her lips as if she were about to lecture me, but then I saw her eyes flicker to the photo of her and Uncle George on vacation in Dublin, their last trip before he died.

"It was opening night, at the party afterward," she said of their first meeting, when she was a dancer on Broadway and he was a big-time producer. "We were inseparable and married six months later."

"Uncle George was really something," I said, looking at the photo.

"Yes, he was," Christine said. She sounded happy, not

mournful. "I am a very lucky woman, to have had that kind of love. So, is this boy from school?"

"Yes." I started nervously picking at my cuticles. "Brendan Salinger." I trembled a little as I said his name out loud.

Christine's eyes widened at the name. "The Salinger boy?" she asked, surprised.

"Yes…is that bad?"

"Oh, no, it's not *bad,* dear. His family's quite…prominent, though. I know his mother from the school board and some of her charity work."

Prominent? Before I could ask her what she meant by that, she asked if I was seeing him again.

"I'm going to see him tomorrow, if that's okay."

"Sure, dear. Ashley's family invited us over for dinner but I'm sure they'll understand. Just nothing too late, it's a school night." I gave her a big hug.

"Thank you, Aunt Christine!" I hugged her more tightly, and whispered, "Thank you."

As soon as I curled up underneath my purple comforter, thoughts of curses and witches and magical crests began assaulting my thoughts. I didn't understand how I let all of my concerns dance out of my head when Brendan was around—it was like each touch of his hand caused my IQ to drop a few points. *It's not just his hands…it's those hypnotic eyes…and those lips…and his hands… Okay, concentrate, Emma!*

I resolved to keep my focus better tomorrow—to look for some tangible signs that Brendan really was my soul mate— before I started worrying about what doom that could bring for me. After all, he kissed me tonight and nothing bad happened, right? Content with my plan, I snuggled under the soft fleece comforter and shut my eyes, letting sleep take over my senses.

★ ★ ★

When I opened my eyes again, I expected to see my open bedroom door and the short hallway to the bathroom. Instead, I saw heavy velvet drapes and an unfamiliar, musty room. I sat up, swinging my legs off the bed, and stared down. I was wearing a long white nightshirt that looked hand-sewn—not my familiar blue plaid pajama bottoms. Disoriented, I stood up, and the stone floor was cold and clammy underneath my bare feet. Each step brought on a new wave of nausea, and all I could think about was getting outside. Suddenly, getting outside was imperative.

I found a narrow staircase, and eased myself down the steps. My brittle fingernails split as I dug them into gaps in the hard stone walls, dragging myself forward. Each footstep made me sicker, and my feet were clumsy as I staggered on. A series of spastic chills shook my body. I rested my forehead against the wall, feeling sweat trickle down my face as I tried to stabilize myself. My body was wracked with spasms. I tackled the steps slowly, and finally reached the ground floor. Using what little strength I had left, I heaved myself off the staircase toward a heavy wooden door. I knew I had to get through it—salvation was on the other side. I shoved it open, expending all my strength on opening the bulky, thick door.

I was outside. The smell of roses hung heavily in the air, mixed with the chilly scent of grass and trees at night. Shaken and spent, I surveyed the manicured grounds, looking for a sign of danger before slowly stepping into the garden. Each footstep equaled pain as I faltered toward the roses.

I heard a guttural shout and whipped around. A group of large, hulking men approached from the clearing on the left. I couldn't make out distinct forms—they were just a pulsating, terrifying mass. I heard my brother Ethan's voice yell to me, "Run!"

I began running to the right, through the fragrant roses, but three men met me in the garden. I heard shouts behind me. I was surrounded. My eyes spun around wildly, my hands formed into claws as I feebly held them up defensively.

The mass of men closed in, surrounding me. My ears felt like they were plugged shut—I could only hear my own pulse as it sped and throbbed in my head. I couldn't make sense of what they were saying; I could only see their angry, mottled faces and stained beards as they shoved me back and forth, jeering at me, spitting on me, tearing my clothes as they lashed out. One thrust a wood club into my stomach, and I collapsed onto the soft, dewy lawn. Clutching the ground, I looked up through the wall of dirty garments at the crescent moon shimmering in the black sky. The sky disappeared. Then pain—a searing pain ripped through my chest.

I screamed, sitting upright in bed. My hands clutched at my chest. I could still feel it—the dreadful, burning pain that scalded my heart. Frantically, I clawed at my chest, and my finger slipped through the fabric of my tank top. There was a small hole over the spot where my heart was pounding.

The hole hadn't been there when I went to sleep.

I slipped my finger through the fabric and felt my heart thudding. I knew what I had seen: I had dreamed Gloriana's last moments. *My* last moments. Terrified, tragic moments.

What was I doing? Could I really face a fate that terrible? How could I do this to my family—to my aunt? To *myself*? A dizzying panic began to whirl around me, and I felt like I needed to lie down—even though I was already in bed.

I glanced at the time—it was too late to call Angelique, so I texted her.

Please call me back asap. Urgent development.

I sat up, waiting for her to call back. I had been promising myself to keep a better eye out for signs that the curse was real, I told myself. My fears were just manifesting in my dreams.

Oh, Emma, who the hell are you kidding? You wanted a sign, and you got it.

Now what was I going to do with it?

Chapter 13

I woke up Sunday morning, stiffly curled up in a ball with my cell in my hand. Angelique hadn't called back, so I called her immediately. My first voice mail was pretty calm. "Hey, Angelique, it's Emma. Can you give me a call?"

I tried her again after showering. My second voice mail was a little more agitated. "Angelique, it's Emma. Please call me back. There are new developments and only you can help me."

My third voice mail sounded like I called her from inside of an insane asylum. "Angelique! I dreamed Gloriana's last moments! And I'm supposed to hang out with Brendan today. Yeah, it's Brendan. He's the guy. Shocker, I know. Do I go? What's going on? Please, please call me back!"

I was desperately trying to get a hold of her before my meeting—oh, who was I kidding, date—with Brendan. Everything, as crazy as it sounded, pointed to one thing: we were cursed soul mates—and still, I couldn't stay away.

"If Angelique calls me back, I won't go," I decided, and plugged my phone back into its charger.

But she didn't call back—and all my calls eventually went

to voice mail. And I reasoned, I couldn't cancel on Brendan. *More like* wouldn't *cancel on him, Emma.*

And the more I thought about him—and how I felt when he kissed me—the more I knew I wasn't going to stand him up. But mostly, when I was with him—I was happy. The happiest I had been in years. And whether that was from a curse or just from my emotional wounds finally healing, I'd be crazy to let go of him.

So I decided to stuff all of my newfound knowledge into the back of my head, and go downtown to Brendan's house. But all that information refused to go unrecognized; it kept me frozen on the sidewalk as I regarded the four-floor, classically Manhattan brownstone. A scrolled, wrought-iron banister wound its way down the stoop, and the matching eight-foot-tall fence stuck out in comparison to the more modern structures lining the street, which faced a park with striking views of the Hudson River.

I checked the gilded numbers on the gate again. I was pretty sure I was on the right street. Brendan hadn't told me an apartment number, which meant the entire thing was his family's.

Now, what Christine had said made sense. When she called his family "prominent," she meant "rich." Very rich. Completely, totally, vacationing-in-Dubai rich. Well, Archer wanted to be reincarnated into someone wealthy, and it looked like he got his wish.

A tinny voice shook me from my thoughts, barking at me from the small, white security box on the fence.

"Are you going to stare at my house, or are you going to come in?" Even through the crackling security speaker, I'd recognize Brendan's voice anywhere.

I heard a buzzing sound, and realized he had unlocked the gate. I pushed it open, and the heaviness of the gate brought me back to my horrific dream, reminding me of how I struggled to open the door to the garden. My stomach began churning.

I was going to Brendan's house, and we were going to be *alone*. Just me, Brendan and the knowledge that he was most likely my soul mate. Come to think of it, it was going to get awfully crowded in there.

I was still walking up the steps when Brendan pulled open the heavy front door, dressed casually in jeans, socks and a black hoodie, worn open over a white T-shirt. I, on the other hand, had opted for gray corduroys, a scoop-neck black shirt and my fiercest heeled boots.

"Hey, Emma," he said, snaking one arm around me while he held the door open with the other. Still keeping a tight hold on me, Brendan whirled me around and kicked the door shut. Any anxiety I felt melted away the instant he pressed his lips to mine for a sweet, short kiss.

"You didn't run here from your aunt's house, did you?" Brendan smiled, breaking away from the kiss to help me out of my worn wool jacket, which he hung up on an antique-looking rack in the foyer.

"No, I took the subway," I mumbled, leaving out the part about how I got off on the wrong stop.

Brendan paused, looking down at my high shoes. "Not that I don't appreciate the look, but my mom has this stupid 'no shoes in the house' rule. Do you mind?"

"Nope," I replied, bracing myself against his shoulder as I used the tip of my right boot to pry the left one off. I was happy to remove them—they were already pinching—and happier still that I'd opted to wear cute polka-dotted socks.

Brendan grabbed my hand and offered to give me the grand tour. And holy crap, it was grand! He led me past a formal living room, decorated with jewel-toned, brocade-covered couches, to a cherry wood staircase. The stairs terminated in an impressively modern kitchen. It looked like it didn't belong in the same house as the old-fashioned room downstairs—let alone the same century. The kitchen resembled something from a Martha Stewart set. Airy and impeccably decorated, a double-door, stainless-steel fridge was the centerpiece. Brendan stopped at the fridge, rooting around in there while I surveyed the room. A white ceramic bowl filed with oranges sat on the stainless steel countertop and orange linen curtains hung in the nearby window. There was a modern-looking white table to the left, surrounded by citrus-colored chairs, and I realized the bowl of oranges was merely decorative. Who knew there was such a thing as fashionable fruit? Were bananas passé this season?

"This is your favorite, right?" Brendan asked, handing me a lemonade iced tea.

"Yeah, I love it. You too?" I asked. As I took the bottle from him, I noticed a case of the stuff chilling in the fridge.

"Nah, but I asked Dina to pick some up for you," he said, grabbing a Pepsi for himself.

"Dina? Is that your sister?"

"No, she's our housekeeper," he said nonchalantly. "Want to see the other living room?"

I nodded numbly, letting Brendan lead me into a large room behind the kitchen. Housekeepers? Four-story mansions in Manhattan? The *other* living room? Why would you even need a spare living room? If the first one is unable to fulfill its living room duties, the runner-up gets to step in?

But when I stepped into the spare living room, I realized that this "other" living room would be the centerpiece in anyone else's home. There was a giant TV and a complicated-looking stereo protected by a glass cabinet—which looked like it held nearly every movie and video game ever made. My toes sank into the thick, plush burgundy carpet. The room opened out into a balcony, which overlooked a meticulously cared-for garden.

I took a sharp breath, turning over in my mind the fact that this was, without a doubt, the most expensive home I'd ever been in. Or heard about. Or seen on television.

"Prominent" was the understatement of the decade. Possibly the millennium. All my thoughts about Brendan and I being "destined" suddenly seemed foolish. My dream was just that: a dream. How the heck could I ever think I belonged with someone this rich, this "prominent"?

"I know it's a little showy," Brendan said, curling his lips in an annoyed-looking grimace. "The kitchen alone...you'd think someone in this family actually cooked. My floor is way more low-key."

"Your *floor?*" I croaked. He might as well have said, "My island. You know, it's just a little place I keep, for fun." My stomach twisted in knots. Destined soul mate, my rosy peasant butt. There was no way this perfect guy, with this kind of life, was going to settle for me.

Brendan pulled me back to the staircase again, and we passed the third floor. "My parents' floor—their bedroom, and my dad's office, some other crap," he said dismissively as we continued climbing. Finally, we arrived at the fourth floor.

"You're in the penthouse?" I squeaked, meaning for it to come out teasing. Instead, it came out insecure. If Brendan noticed, he ignored it.

He pushed open the door, which was the same dark wood as the stairway. I braced myself, expecting to see a four-poster bed, or oh, raw uncut diamonds just scattered about, glittering on the floor. Maybe his walls would be solid gold. I stepped in and was happily surprised.

Pushed against the exposed-brick left wall was a bed, messily covered by a dark blue comforter. There was no majestic, fit-for-a-king headboard or frame—although it was a pretty big mattress—and a TV hung on the opposite wall, which was cool white plaster. His computer desk looked like it was from IKEA—simple and functional. Perched on it was a pricy-looking laptop, and several expensive-looking speakers snaked out from behind it. Aside from his deejay equipment pushed into a corner, there was some other modest furniture—a couple of dressers, a dark couch, a nightstand—but, like the computer desk, they all looked simple. The only adornments on the snow-white walls were a corkboard above his desk and some framed posters of musicians—from classic rock like The Who to deejays I'd never even heard of.

I was aware of Brendan's eyes watching me as I walked along the perimeter of his room, examining his well-stocked collection of vintage vinyl, and stopping to look at the Han Solo figurine perched on top of his speakers.

"Oh, hey, wait," Brendan said, racing over and pulling something off the corkboard above his desk.

"What, is that an ex-girlfriend's photo?" I asked lightly, trying to keep the jealousy out of my voice.

"No, it's nothing," he said, stuffing it into his pocket.

"C'mon, let me see," I wheedled, tugging at his shirt. "You said no secrets."

Brendan grabbed me around the waist. "Maybe later," he murmured into my ear, kissing my neck. I felt my knees go a little weak and was glad that he was holding me—I could have collapsed at that moment.

"I'm really glad you came over, Emma," he whispered, his voice tickling my ear before he resumed kissing my neck. I leaned into his chest, happily, perfectly content—until a voice in the back of my head told me I *should* be uncomfortable in this situation. *You're reading fairy tales and all of a sudden, you go*

*to some strange guy's house? Alone? Way to put yourself in a bad
situation. What's next, taking apples from strangers? Is this just a
big seduction ploy?*

I disentangled myself from his embrace—without any grace
at all, I basically just bolted from his arms. I hoped I hadn't
hurt his feelings, but I'd felt too comfortable, too content—all
too quickly—in his arms.

"Did I do some—" Brendan started, but I wouldn't let him
finish.

"I just— I mean, I still don't— Um, I'm sorry," I stammered, feeling foolish. *I daydream for a month about kissing
him, now I flee when he does?*

Brendan seemed to understand, and just grabbed his laptop
and sat on his couch.

"Hey, want to see something?" he asked, sitting cross-
legged on the worn-looking black leather.

"Check these out. My grandfather gave me a bunch of
old family photos. I scanned them in. There's some great
pictures of old New York in here." I figured he was looking
for a less seductive way to pass the time—and pictures of the
family were a surefire way to kill the mood. I appreciated the
effort.

As I joined him on the couch, Brendan twisted his head to
face me.

"As you reminded me, you know nothing about me or my
family, right?" He looked at me pointedly.

"Right," I mumbled. *If only you knew what I thought I
knew….*

"Maybe knowing a little more about me will make you
more…comfortable," he said. I sat down next to him, leaning back on my arms as Brendan clicked through some faded
photographs.

"This is my mom, when she was sixteen," he said, pulling

up what looked like a teenage model's headshot from the 1970s.

"She was a model in the '70s," he explained. *Of course.* Blonde and fresh-faced, she looked nothing like her rakishly handsome son—except for the green eyes that stared doe-eyed and glamorously out of the monitor.

Brendan continued to click through the pictures, showing me old shots of family members from the '60s and '70s, often at some gala event. I definitely recognized some celebrities in those pictures.

"My grandfather gave me this one picture that's *so* old," he said, clicking on JPEGs and then shutting them. "What did I name this JPEG?" he asked himself. "Emma, it's almost 100 years old, this shot. It's of the house that used to be on this site."

"This house is new?" I asked.

"Not really *new*. My great-great-grandfather bought this land and had a house built here. That was the early 1900s. This house, the one we're in now, my great-grandfather had built, right before the Depression. Oh, here it is!" he exclaimed, and double-clicked on the icon.

Even though the scan was grainy and creased, withered with age, I recognized the house. I'd recognize it anywhere. The image that filled the screen had filled my nightmares. It was the burning white house.

"No," I whispered, squeezing my eyes shut and turning away. My gaze landed on the view outside the window, where the Hudson River sparkled in the distance, and I knew I'd seen it from this vantage point before. Something flashed through my head—a feeling, a fleeting memory—*something*, that made me think I'd seen this view before. I tried to grab the memory, but it was gone. A sickening sensation washed over me, and even though I had never had it before, I knew what to call the feeling.

Déjà vu.

"Emma? Are you okay? You're looking a little pale." Brendan was staring at me, concerned, as I sat there, refusing to face him.

"Emma?" he asked again, sounding worried. "Emma, you're shaking."

The words were out of my mouth before I could stop them.

"I dreamed of that house." As soon as the words were spoken, whispered with a trembling voice, I regretted it. I returned to face him, to see the "uh-oh, she's crazy" look on his face. But Brendan wasn't looking at me like I was insane.

"You dreamed of this house—the one in the picture?"

I nodded.

"What did you dream, exactly?" he asked me quietly, staring back at the grainy scan of the black-and-white photo.

"I dreamed that I was *in* this house," I said, tracing the front door to the house with my finger.

Brendan still stared at the picture, but his voice was anxious. "Take a good look at it. Are you sure?"

I would know that house anywhere. "I dreamed it burned down," I said, my voice shaking.

He sighed, closing his eyes almost painfully. Then, shutting the laptop and placing it gently on the floor, he faced me.

"You know how I was out of school a few days this week?" Brendan asked, leaning in so his face was eye-level with mine. I nodded.

"I went to Ardsley. It's in Westchester," he added. "I was visiting my grandfather. I had to ask him about something, as the oldest member of our family.

"There's always been a joke of sorts among the Salingers," Brendan continued, reaching out and taking my hands in his. "That we have a—and I can't believe I'm saying this—curse on us. I always thought it was just a silly story that's been passed down from generation to generation, because—" he waved at the posh home around him "—clearly, we've been very lucky.

"Emma, you're going to think I'm deranged."

My heart caught in my throat. "I promise you, Brendan, I will not think you are deranged," I said, my eyes burning into his. "I swear it to you."

He eyed me warily, but took a deep breath and started speaking. "This curse was just an anecdote told at weddings and family reunions. Supposedly, every couple of generations, one of the Salingers is supposed to have this incredible romance—a straight-up, fairy-tale, true-love kind of thing. Only, it would end up an epic failure. Any time one of my cousins got dumped or shot down by a girl, we'd joke about the curse killing our game. *No one* took it seriously. I sure didn't."

Brendan's eyes flickered to me, gauging my reaction. I hadn't flinched yet.

"The curse is tied to a crest that's been in my family for ages—nearly a thousand years, I believe. As the story goes, if one of the Salingers met someone wearing the crest, they were supposed to be your...true love." Brendan's tone was gentle over those words.

"My grandfather has a pretty massive library at his house, with all these old family documents, books, photos and such. I figured I should research the crest a little more, because—" he paused, picking up my necklace "—you're wearing it."

He dropped the pendant, and I was positive that it was on fire, the way it was stinging my skin. I wanted to open my mouth, to tell Brendan that I knew what he was talking about, but I couldn't speak. A very small part of me had believed that the curse was just fantasy, my pathetic way of manufacturing a bond with Brendan. But as he spoke, the reality of the situation rushed at me, trapping my voice in my throat as I listened to Brendan talk about how he discovered the very thing I stumbled upon in *Hadrian's Medieval Legends.* The very thing my brother's spirit was warning me against.

"I found some old books, but they just repeated the same information that I already knew," Brendan explained. "It was an old family seal, belonging to some lord from forever ago, who redesigned it in honor of his wife.

"So I talked to my grandfather. And he told me about the house that used to be here."

Brendan leaned back, dropping my hands and rubbing his eyes. "I'm making no sense."

"Actually, you are." I leaned forward and, clutching his hands a little desperately into mine, begged, "Please tell me about the house that used to be here."

Brendan took a deep breath and began. "My great-great-grandfather Robert lived here—in the house you dreamed of. When he was on his deathbed, he warned his grandson—my grandfather—that he thought the curse might actually be real. Robert said when he was a young man, he fell head-over-heels for a factory worker named Constance. He called her his golden angel, because she was a blonde or whatever. It was love at first sight, of course. They had planned to elope, but she was killed the day before their wedding.

"The thing is, they thought they'd cheated death. She had worked at the Triangle Shirtwaist Factory, and she said she had a bad feeling about the place and wanted to quit. She'd been having horrible nightmares about being trapped in a fire. But she didn't want to look like she was out for Robert's money. He told her to quit—and she did, just a week before there was a huge fire that killed most of the workers. But it was like death was coming for her," Brendan said bitterly.

"Was she in this house when it burned down?" I asked quietly.

Brendan didn't reply, which was answer enough for me. "It was an electrical fire. The fuses were overloaded. Robert thought he had fixed the problem, but I guess he didn't do such a great job."

Brendan paused. "Back then, pennies were made of copper. So Robert stuck coins in the fuse box. An employee of his explained how to do it. Robert was so proud of himself for being industrious."

"Does that even work?" I asked.

"It does, but it's hardly what I'd call safe. When you do something like that, there's no way to regulate the electrical current. And Constance hated staying in the house alone—it was too huge and dark."

"So she turned on all the lights," I said, knowing too well what happened next. Brendan just nodded, grimly.

"Robert didn't have time to wait for the electrician. It was easier for *him* to just stick the copper penny where the fuse should have gone. Robert always blamed himself for her death—if he hadn't been so selfish, so impatient…" Brendan trailed off.

"The curse, as I said, has always been something of a joke in my family. Let's face it, when bad things happen, well, isn't that just life? Don't bad things happen?" My mind flipped through everything that had taken me to this moment and nodded.

"Was Constance wearing the crest?" I asked.

Brendan looked at me, his green eyes mournful. "Yes. She

wore it as a brooch." *Just like in my dream. Where I had golden hair....*

"I'd imagine it's not always as glaringly obvious as yours, with the crest practically a big neon sign on your chest," he continued. "But based on everything Robert told him, my grandfather believes that, yes, the curse is very, very real."

"So the story of Lord Archer really is true," I murmured to myself, and Brendan's hands tightened around mine.

"You know the name?" Brendan inhaled sharply. "How?"

"I did some research of my own," I admitted. "I always wanted to know what my necklace meant—but I could never find anything out. But then— Do you know Angelique?"

"The witchy chick, right?"

"Right. She's my friend, and her mom is some big expert in medieval stuff. Angelique recognized my necklace as having some significance. She lent me a few antique books about medieval crests and legends, and I found the story there."

"Why didn't you tell me?" Brendan demanded, and my jaw dropped.

"You're kidding, right?" I asked, incredulous. "What would you have thought of me? Besides, I read about this in a book that also had stories about dragons and curses and witches and unicorns! Like I could just roll up to you in the cafeteria, 'Hey, Brendan, guess what I think my necklace means?'"

He smiled ruefully at me. "All right, I see your point. But Emma, I don't know *how* the crest came to have that meaning. I only know what was passed down from generation to generation—that if someone wore the crest, they were destined for some terrible fate, just by knowing one of us."

"It's not *every* generation, Brendan. At least, not according to what I read," I said, hesitantly. "The book was pretty fragile. Some of the pages were missing. But I read most of the legend, how this crest came to have that meaning."

Brendan ran his hands through his ink-black hair and looked at me intensely. "Can you tell me the full story, Emma?" His voice was soft and pleading. I took a deep breath and began the sorrowful tale of Lord Archer, who had doomed himself and his beloved to an eternity of loss. I explained, as best I could, that the crest was to be worn by Archer's reincarnated love.

I didn't think I had to spell out for him what I took away from the story, although it was pretty obvious: we were soul mates. We'd spent a thousand years looking for each other. And we were probably cursed.

Chapter 14

Brendan hung his head in his hands, quiet, and I was afraid to move. Finally, I reached out to him and touched his arm. He suddenly grabbed my hand tightly and I jumped.

"I'm sorry," he said, dropping my hand as if he'd just grabbed a handful of broken glass. "And I'm sorry if I hurt your feelings by ignoring you. I just knew I was so attracted... No, attracted is not the right word. I need a stronger word." He stopped, and chewed his lip thoughtfully. Suddenly, Brendan exclaimed, "Spellbound! I was spellbound by you, and, to be honest, it took me a little off guard."

"Your choice of words is interesting," I said dryly, and he laughed a short, bitter laugh.

"Your first day at school," Brendan began, "I was so impressed by how you stood up to Kristin. And I hadn't even *seen* you yet.

"I turned around to give the new girl a hand, because Kristin was clearly harassing you. And then I saw your face." Brendan's voice was no more than a tender whisper, as he brushed my cheek with the back of his hand.

"And *then* I noticed your necklace," he continued. "I mean, it's a pretty big pendant, Emma. But, I didn't get a really good look at the actual design of it. I just thought it was cool that you would wear something so different."

Color touched Brendan's cheeks, and he put his head down, stealing a glance at me. "All I could think about was you. I felt like I had been missing *you* all this time. It didn't make any sense to me," he said, reaching out and touching the pendant. He was half-affectionately stroking the charm, and half resenting it.

"I couldn't understand why I was so drawn to you. I knew nothing about you, other than, well, you weren't a pushover, and you were kind of a liar." Brendan saw my insulted expression and was instantly contrite. "I'm sorry, Emma, but you kind of are. Congress Academy? I'm sure you have your reasons, but still."

The words continued pouring out of him. "Anyway, I sort of prided myself on my disinterest in girls at school. Really, one's worse than the next, so the last thing I wanted was to fall for some snob. And one with something to hide. For all I knew you were kicked out of your last school for setting the damn place on fire.

"That first day at lunch, Anthony made some comments about you. You were new. He had already cornered you before English class, I saw it. He thought you were an easy target."

I remembered that first day—Brendan had slammed his chair into the table and stormed out of the lunchroom.

"You guys got into a fight in the cafeteria," I said, awe-struck.

"You noticed me," he said, sounding slightly smug.

"You practically threw a chair," I pointed out. "*Everyone* noticed you."

He smiled at me and squeezed my hand. "The thing is, Emma, I shouldn't have cared what Anthony said. I didn't understand why it made me crazy. I told him to stay away from you. And let's just say when I walked into the quad that afternoon, and found out *you* were involved in all the commotion—I just *had* to get to you, to make sure you were okay. I pushed my way through the crowd, and saw him towering over you— I thought I was going to kill him. If I got there a second later, I might have." Brendan shook his head as if he were remembering the sight of Anthony terrorizing me. "I restrained myself as much as I did because I didn't want to scare you. After that night at the Met, I thought you'd be freaked out by violence. So I didn't do what I would have liked to do to Anthony. And afterward, when we spoke—"

"You noticed what I was wearing," I interrupted, remembering how he'd held my charm.

"I hadn't gotten a good look at your necklace before that. When I went back to my locker, I compared the two designs and started putting things together. I hadn't even thought about the Salinger family curse until that moment."

"Then what about before?" I asked. "Why did you ask Cisco about me and come out with us that night to see Gabe's band?" I was surprised, but Brendan looked a little embarrassed.

"Well, I thought I was doing a pretty good job of pretending I wasn't so into you—"

"You were," I interjected, thinking of how many times I'd pined for him to even sneeze my way.

"But then you read that sonnet." He scratched his hair again, nervously. "I felt like you were speaking to me."

I remembered how I stood up, speaking those words of love. "I kind of was," I admitted shyly.

"I hoped that was the case," Brendan mumbled. "I was so stupid to hope so, but it felt like it. And I was so... I guess the word is *intrigued* by you. You are so different from anyone I've ever met. So I asked Cisco about you, because you two were becoming best friends pretty quickly. And I knew I could trust him to not run around and tell everyone that I was asking about you."

I tried to tell myself that he wasn't embarrassed to be attracted to me, but the blush that colored my cheeks gave me away.

"Oh, Emma, it's not that—it's not what you think." Brendan's voice was soothing as he tucked my hair behind my ear. "Why do you keep thinking I would be ashamed? I didn't want everyone to know because I wanted to protect *you*. I didn't want people running their mouths about you."

"I know," I fibbed, not meeting his eyes. "Sure. So, go on, what were you saying…?"

"Emma, I really hate that you think I'm ashamed to be seen with you. That night, everything about you was so carefree…I didn't expect how easy it would be to be around you. I didn't expect to like it so much, so quickly. I didn't trust it. So I stopped talking to you and ignored you." He looked sheepish and glanced down at the gray rug. I was a little surprised at the normal answer. It stuck out amid all the talk of curses and witches. Standard guy behavior, no magic required.

"Couldn't you have just pulled my pigtails? It would have been so much easier," I joked lamely. Brendan gave my hair a gentle tug.

"Is that better?" he asked, ruefully smiling at me.

"Much." I grinned back at him. "So I wasn't imagining it," I said, feeling a little vindicated. "You wanted to kiss me that night, didn't you?"

"Oh, hell yeah," he admitted. "It took all my self-control to stop myself." But his smiling was fading—fast.

"Emma, I already care about you so much—too much," Brendan said, regarding me with somber eyes. "Do you really believe that there's something bigger than us going here?"

"It sounds crazy to say yes," I admitted. "But it's the only thing that makes sense and explains the crest and the dreams and the warnings and everything."

"Right, that's what— Wait." Brendan paused. "What warnings?"

"Um, do you promise to not think me crazy?"

"Oh, like those cards aren't already on the table for both of us," he retorted.

"Good point," I mumbled. I summoned my resolve and dove in, telling him about the streetlights, and Angelique's theory that I was being warned by my brother. If we're going to talk about curses, then my crazy visions couldn't be that much harder to believe.

"I've seen my brother, and I've heard him, in my dreams. If some tragedy was inevitable, why bother warning me?"

"Emma, he's telling you to stay away from me and you'll be okay," Brendan argued. "I'll transfer if I have to. I'm not going to be responsible for you getting hurt."

"No, Brendan," I cried. I attempted to plead my case. "Some of the pages were missing from the book, remember? The story was cut short." I racked my brain, trying to remember the final lines from the story. Where were Angelique and her photographic memory now?

"The last words were about breaking the curse. If freedom from the curse is what you seek, it takes a selfless soul to… something that rhymes with 'eek.' Or something like that. I don't remember. It rhymed in the book." I slammed my fist into the faded leather cushion, frustrated. "It sounded like the book was about to go into instructions on how to break the curse. Which means there's a way to do it! And besides, Angelique is positive that we have a chance—simply because we've identified it."

I smiled confidently, believing I had just laid out an unassailable defense. Brendan just frowned and shook his head.

"Emma, maybe the reason we can be the ones to break this curse is because we know to avoid each other." He leaned forward, resting his forearms on his knees.

"No." I remained adamant. "That can't be it."

"If it's this hard to walk away after two days, I can't imagine what it'll be like to walk away after two weeks." Brendan's voice was despondent.

Finally, I realized that there was only one way I was going to let him know how badly I wanted—no, *needed*—this. I took a deep breath.

"Would you believe me if I told you that these past two days are the happiest I've been since I can remember?"

Brendan looked up. "Things were tough in—" he paused over the next word "—Philly?"

"Keansburg, actually," I said, hoping my voice wasn't really trembling as much as I thought it was. "Keansburg, New Jersey."

This story was harder to tell than Lord Archer's tale. I told Brendan everything: about my father abandoning us. About Ethan dying unexpectedly at fourteen. About my mom, marrying a man she thought would look after me after she was gone, which she knew would be soon. About initially refusing Christine's offer to live with her—because everyone I ever loved left me. Because I didn't want to be a burden. Brendan kept quiet and let me talk, reaching out only once to place his hand over mine, when I told him about my mother dying, and speaking only once, to tell me he understood when I said this would probably be the last time I talked about that time in my life. I just couldn't handle revisiting those feelings.

Brendan kept his face composed, but his green eyes narrowed when I told him about Henry's liberal use of corporal punishment, how the tension at home was thick like a fog, how it filled your lungs until you thought you would suffocate.

Finally, I told him about the accident—how Henry showed up at school wasted. How I didn't even think about him being too drunk to drive when I got into the passenger seat of his tiny Honda—I was just trying to get away from the scene he was causing on the front lawn at my school. How I just wanted to start over and be anonymous in New York.

We sat in silence for a few minutes. Destiny or not, I wondered if my sordid home situation with Henry was a deal breaker. It had been for so many back home.

Then Brendan finally spoke. "And after surviving all that, you want to be doomed by me?"

"If I didn't see you again, that would feel like I was doomed."

"Don't be dramatic, Emma. I'm not all that great," Brendan said disdainfully.

"You've been the brightest spot in my life this past year," I confessed. "Do you want to take that away from me?"

"I don't want to take *anything* away from you. But that's what *this*—" he picked up my charm, then dropped it "—means. Don't you get it?"

My heart felt raw, exposed. It was irrational to hurt this much, I knew, after two dates. But I couldn't help it—all my old wounds ripped open. *Everyone you care about leaves you, Emma.*

"So I guess you want me to leave now?" I stayed in my spot on the leather sofa, not moving, hoping he would tell me to stay.

"I don't *want* you to leave, Emma." He reached into his pocket and pulled out a crumpled-up wad of paper—the item he had pulled off his corkboard.

"I saved this," Brendan confessed, gently shoving the paper in my hands. I stared in amazement at my own handwriting— the note I had left thanking him for the sweatshirt.

"Why?"

"It was a connection to you," Brendan explained plainly. "I can't imagine those feelings are going to go away the *more* time we spend together."

"It's the same for me," I admitted. "But, if you want me to leave…" I took the chance and pushed myself off the couch.

"I don't think I *can* let you leave, Emma," Brendan said, grabbing my hand and pulling me into his lap, holding me close to his chest. "The way I feel about you…I didn't know it was possible."

"I know," I said quietly.

"Aren't you afraid, though, of what could happen?"

"Not enough to leave," I whispered, toying with the zipper on his sweatshirt.

"That shouldn't make me as happy as it does." Brendan sighed, tightening his grip around me.

I stayed curled up in his arms for some time, letting the weight of what we believed to be true sink in. Finally, Brendan spoke.

"By the way, Emma, thank you for telling me the truth. I know that was hard for you," he said, intertwining his fingers with mine. "Honestly, it's nowhere near as bad as I was imagining. But I understand why you didn't tell anyone. Makes sense why you're the only person I know not on Facebook. Smart move."

He paused. "Then again, you're a smart girl, even if you're flunking Latin."

"Don't remind me." I laughed—a welcome release from the weighty mood in the room.

"You're no good to me if you get kicked out of school," Brendan said, that playful, flip tone creeping back into his voice. "So, first tutoring lesson begins now. You're a *puella pulcherrima.*"

"*Puella*'s a girl, so…what, a failing girl?" I asked, and he laughed.

"No, I'd have to think about how to say that. What I said was you are a very beautiful girl." I think I might have blushed. Being called "beautiful" would take some getting used to.

"And this," Brendan said, continuing his lesson, "is a *basium*." With that, he pulled my face close to his for the kiss I needed. His lips touched mine, and a thousand years of longing coursed through me, flooding into this one embrace. His hands were strong as they moved up my back and clutched a fistful of hair as I pressed myself closer to him. The kiss was deeper, almost demanding, and when he broke away with a low moan to kiss my neck, the only other sound I could hear was my own breathing.

I fell back on the couch, Brendan's mouth back on mine as he balanced his weight above me. It felt like he had sparks shooting out of his fingers as they ran down my arm, along my side and finally rested at my hip, where he hooked his thumb into my belt loop, pulling my hip closer. I tugged at his hoodie, pulling it off his shoulder and ran my hand along his arm, feeling the muscles move underneath his T-shirt. This time, I didn't feel uncomfortable—being with Brendan felt right. I had no intentions of stopping this embrace. But Brendan had other ideas: suddenly, he pulled back, his black locks falling over his eyebrows as he held himself over me. I felt a little lost as he looked at me through those black-fringed eyes.

He pressed his lips against mine softly—but with less passion than before. Then, taking a deep, almost resigned, breath, Brendan pulled himself upright into a sitting position on the leather couch.

"Is something wrong?" I continued lying there, staring at

the side of his face, a little puzzled at the halt in what had been the most phenomenal make-out session of my life.

"No, nothing's wrong," Brendan replied. He paused, then took my hand, pulling me upright.

"I should, however, behave and get us some dinner. It's getting late." I must have still looked confused at the sudden break in our embrace, because Brendan leaned over and kissed me very gently on the cheek.

"Just because you're my soul mate doesn't mean I should rush things with you," he whispered in my ear, softly kissing the spot under my earlobe. *Keep going, rush things!* my body screamed, but my head nodded in agreement as I tried to pull myself out of his kiss-induced haze. Somewhere in my mind, I knew he was right.

"Actually, *because* you're my soul mate, I shouldn't rush things with you." His lips tickled my skin as he spoke. "No matter how badly I want to."

"So," he continued, pulling his laptop over and opening a food-delivery website. "What are you hungry for?"

What I was hungry for was sitting nonchalantly next to me on the couch. The sudden break in our mood was still sinking in. I generally liked roller coasters, but any more ups and downs tonight, and I'd probably lose whatever dinner we were about to have.

"I should probably call my aunt and make sure she isn't expecting me," I said, looking for my cell phone and remembering it was in my purse, all the way downstairs. Brendan handed me his phone—a sleek, expensive-looking one—and I called Aunt Christine. Even though she was well into dinner at Ashley's family's house, I owed her the courtesy.

"I'm cool to stay," I said after talking to her. "I should get home soon after, though. I don't want to be on the subway too late."

Brendan rolled his eyes at me. "You're not taking the subway. I'll take you home in a car."

"No!" I exclaimed, embarrassed. "Nothing is going to happen to me on the way to Sixty-eighth Street. I don't need a sitter."

"I'm not your sitter," he said, winding his arms around me and kissing my neck so persuasively, he made my toes curl. "I'm your boyfriend. So get used to the princess treatment."

I wasn't exactly a stranger to feeling like a princess—if you meant the princess in the first half of the fairy tale. Cinderella as a scullery maid. Snow White with the wicked stepmother. But I wasn't used to what life was like *after* you meet the prince, after the slipper fits, after the kiss wakes you from your slumber. It would take some getting used to.

Which explains why I was floating, again, when I shut Christine's apartment door, still a little breathless from Brendan's good-night kiss in the back of the dark car. His family had a car service on call. Of course. They probably had a private jet on call, too. Still, I managed to collect myself when I heard Christine puttering around in the kitchen.

"Aunt Christine, I'm home," I called, letting my keys drop into the angel-shaped dish she kept on the coffee table and walking toward the kitchen.

"Did you have a good time, dear?" Christine asked, splashing some vermouth into the martini she held in her hand.

"Yep," I said, smiling a little too widely.

"So funny, you and the Salinger boy," Christine murmured, taking a critical sip of her martini and frowning.

"Why is it so funny?" I asked. *Of course it's funny. It's hilarious that a guy like Brendan would be interested in me, right? Even Christine sees it.*

"Not funny ha-ha, Emma." Aunt Christine sighed, taking

out a bottle of vodka and scrutinizing it as she poured it into her glass. "Just funny interesting."

"You've lost me, Aunt Christine." I dropped my purse and settled into the floral-covered kitchen chairs as she took another sip of her martini and frowned again, splashing more vermouth in it before pouring the entire glass down the drain.

"I could never make a martini as well as your uncle George," she said, and began making a fresh martini from scratch. "Well, dear, where were we? Oh, yes—you probably don't remember this, but when you were very young, your parents would take you into the city to stay the weekend with me anytime they went away."

"I remember," I said, thinking back to those happier times. They were times of seeing matinees of the *Christmas Spectacular* at Radio City Music Hall and making fortresses out of Christine's couch cushions with Ethan, all before my father decided to play absentee dad.

"Well, one weekend, we went to the playground in Central Park in the West Sixties. You were pretty adamant about going there instead of somewhere closer. I remembered the Salingers being there because his mother and I were working together on some charity thing for the school and she was being a bit of a pill about it. And you and Brendan played together that afternoon." Christine punctuated her bombshell with a rather large gulp of her new martini.

"No way!" My jaw dropped and I clutched the seat of the chair, my nails scraping against the fabric. "How old could I have been?"

"Oh, dear, this was before your idiot father left," she said, using the "pet name" she called my father any time he came up in conversation, which wasn't too often. "You couldn't have been more than three or four." Christine took another swallow of her martini.

"So we played together," I said nervously. "Well, I guess that's not *too* weird. I mean, I knew Matt in kindergarten and we dated freshman year."

"Oh, dear, that's not the interesting part." Christine chuckled. "When it was time to leave, you let out such a scream. You said that you knew Brendan would be there, and that's why you wanted to go to that park. Both of you threw such tantrums about leaving each other." She laughed, lost in the memory—and I was glad it was dark in the kitchen. There was no way she could see my face, which I would bet was drained of all color.

"Oh, well, I guess we liked each other at an early age," I said, laughing nervously.

"You sure did." She chuckled. "Your idiot father didn't appreciate it, though, when I told him the story."

"What do you mean?" Although part of me wanted to run into my room and hide to process all this new information, a bigger part of me realized I might never get Christine on a talking tear like this again. I wondered how many martinis she had sampled while trying to make the perfect drink.

"He never appreciated all your quirks," Christine said with a dismissive wave of her hand.

"What quirks?"

"Emma, dear, you know those little twin things you and your brother would do, speak in your own language and things like that."

"I remember him yelling at us to speak English." I thought back to him scolding us in the middle of Kmart for babbling in what we were later told was our twin-speak, which sounded normal to me.

"Yes, and when you'd guess who was calling before he

answered the phone, he hated that. Your mother used to do it, too."

I felt my blood run cold. "What did you say I used to do?"

"Oh, you know, dear. Someone would call the house, and you'd announce, 'It's Uncle Dan!' before anyone answered the phone. Your idiot father swore you and your mother had a caller-ID box hidden somewhere and were ganging up on him."

I was suddenly aware that I had been clenching my hands into fists, leaving little half-moon marks in my palms from where my nails were digging in. I tried to count to ten, then to five, to steady myself from the thoughts that were coming together in my head.

"Well, dear, it's late and I've got to get to sleep," Christine said, draining the last of her martini. "Have a good night." She kissed me on the top of the head and shuffled off to bed, leaving me flabbergasted in the floral chair.

Brendan and I had a connection when we were toddlers?

I was able to "predict" things when I was a kid?

I apparently inherited that ability from my mom?

Two words from Angelique popped into my head: *born witch*. I raced for my purse to check my phone, which I'd ignored since going to Brendan's house. Still no reply from Angelique. *Damn it!* I had fourteen texts from Ashley asking how my date with Brendan went, and nothing from Angelique. I had a lot to discuss with this girl. *Where was that absentee little witch?*

The next morning, I had my answer to Angelique's whereabouts before I even left the apartment for school. Angelique's mom had used the school's emergency contact sheet to call Aunt Christine and ask if I could bring Angelique's books home that night. Seems even witches can fall prey to the flu.

I had lied to Ashley the night before, saying I had to get to school early to hand in a late assignment. I hated fibbing to her, but I couldn't handle her constant stream of questions this morning. I had a lot to mull over.

After putting my headphones on, I stuffed my gloveless hands into the pockets of my wool coat as I walked down Park Avenue. First, stripping away anything supernatural about our romance, Brendan was my boyfriend. And whenever I was with him, I conveniently forgot anything but what it felt like to be in his arms—whether that was part of being "cursed," I didn't know. But when I was with him, I didn't care about little things like my soul being at risk.

And then there was the whole born-witch thing. I stared down at my hands, flexing my palms as if I expected to feel some kind of new strength emanating from them. Instead, they just felt chilly. I stuffed them back into my pockets and continued walking.

I had never thought I'd be the kind of person to give up everything—hell, anything—for a guy. I had seen my mother make all the wrong decisions to keep Henry around. But, I reasoned, Brendan wasn't just some guy. And I didn't feel like I was giving anything up. I felt like I was getting so much more.

With each step toward the school, I knew I was coming closer to my destiny—with Brendan. All that remained now was how to figure out how to keep that destiny—and me—safe.

Chapter 15

I arrived at school a full hour early, so I pulled out my books and slid into the empty history classroom, trying to distract my fuzzy thoughts with Latin's first declension. Jenn only greeted me with a grunted hello, and after catching a look at her red-rimmed eyes, I realized she was in too much pain to ask me how my weekend was. I was relieved; truth was, I had no idea what to answer. *Did some homework, watched* Anchorman *again, and I more or less spent the weekend with my soul mate—but you know him as Brendan.*

I survived through history and math class, but as Jenn and I made a silent, slow stroll to English, I started internally freaking out. *What do I do about lunch? Angelique isn't here...do I sit with Jenn and Cisco, or is there any chance Brendan will want to sit with me?*

Of course, Brendan wasn't in his seat when we got to English. *How should I say hello? Is this too much of a statement to make?* I didn't know what to do, remembering how I embarrassed myself the Monday after we had hung out together at the Met. Only this time, his rebuttal would absolutely flatten me.

I kept my eyes on the door, trying to hear who was coming

in above the chattering in the classroom—and feeling extremely disappointed when Mr. Emerson hurried in with a sour look on his face. A minute afterward, Brendan sauntered into the room in his signature state of hot disarray. His tie was barely knotted, and his hair was tousled, of course. I bet he didn't even own a hairbrush. Our eyes immediately met, and this scenario felt all too familiar to me. Only this time, his soft lips curled into a deliciously naughty smile that made my heart skip.

"Hey, beautiful." Brendan's voice was a low rumble as he slid into his seat and turned to face Mr. Emerson. I took a deep breath, trying to wipe the cartoonishly wide grin from my face. I glanced around and noticed that Brendan's sly little greeting hadn't gone unnoticed by one particular classmate. But instead of Kristin's usual bullets-from-the-eyeballs glare that she seemed to reserve just for me, she had a weirdly smug, satisfied look on her face.

I rested my head on my chin, listening to Mr. Emerson explain points he thought the class had gotten wrong in our *Midsummer Night's Dream* papers as I stared at the back of Brendan's head, thinking how, just a few hours before, I had been running my fingers through that unruly mop of hair.

As English ended, Brendan turned to face me, throwing his left arm cavalierly over my desk. "So Emma, want to get out of here for lunch?"

"Absolutely," I said, relieved, and started shoving my notebook into my backpack.

"Awesome, there's this great little restaurant just a few— Oh, hi, Mr. Emerson." Brendan's tone changed from flirty to formal, and I looked up to see our English teacher standing over Brendan with a disapproving look.

"Miss Connor, Mr. Salinger, you're wanted in Principal Casey's office. *Now,*" he said, his voice stern.

Brendan took a deep breath and stood up, casting a reassuring glance my way. "Mr. Emerson, if this is about the prank the basketball team *allegedly* pulled on Regis High School, I can assure you, Emma had nothing to do with—"

"Save it, Salinger. Just get yourself down to Principal Casey's office, now!" Mr. Emerson boomed, his ruddy face turning nearly purple from the exertion. Brendan looked at me and shrugged, holding out his hand for me to take. I cautiously grabbed it, hoping my palms weren't sweaty.

I had daydreamed about walking down the hallways of Vince A with Brendan Salinger holding my hand plenty of times. Only in my fantasies, we were never walking to the principal's office.

Brendan kept his grip on me as he led me down the flights of stairs to the first floor, where Principal Casey's office was, off to the right of where Gray Lady Gary held court. If he noticed the stares and whispers from our classmates, he ignored them. I, on the other hand, wasn't able to block out the voices even though I followed his lead and looked straight ahead.

"Holy crap, Salinger is holding that new girl's hand! Isn't she a witch or something?"

"Salinger and Emily Conrad? Where did that come from?"

"Brendan finally dates someone and it's *her?* I'm like, way prettier than she is," clucked a high-pitched voice to my left.

"Stupid skank. She had no idea who she was messing with." On that last comment, I turned to see who said it—and my eyes met the cold glare of Kristin Thorn.

I never thought I would be so relieved to reach the principal's office in my entire life.

But to my surprise, we weren't the only people there. Aunt Christine sat in one of the cracked leather chairs, and a stunning blonde woman—with piercing green eyes—sat on the opposite side of the room. And in the center sat Anthony— and an equally menacing, older version of Anthony, whom I could only assume was his father. His very angry, very large father.

"Please sit down, Mr. Salinger, Miss Connor," Principal Casey said, a steely smile on her tangerine-lipsticked lips.

I sat in a folding chair next to my aunt while Brendan sat next to his mother, rolling his eyes. I darted my own eyes toward Anthony, who stared straight ahead with an almost beatific smile on his face. I expected him to slap a halo on his head, his angel act was so good. It didn't take a genius to see where this was going.

"So, Mr. Salinger." Principal Casey's voice was steel as she typed something into her laptop. "What do you want to tell me about last Monday?"

She spun the laptop around, and there was an internet video of…me. On this grainy—and from what I could recall of the fight, heavily edited—short video of the encounter, I stood against the door in the quad, and Anthony had his back to me. You couldn't see that he was about to deck me from this angle.

Then Brendan, so fast he seemed blurry, came into frame. He grabbed Anthony in a choke hold and flipped him over his shoulder, dropping the blond on his back. In spite of the tense situation, I couldn't help but be impressed by his strength. The video ended abruptly, and Principal Casey played the ten-second clip again before slamming her hand on the desk.

"You can imagine my shock when I was emailed this link this morning. Unprovoked attacks, at my school? Brendan, what do you have to say for your behavior?"

"Clearly, Brendan attacked my son." Mr. Caruso jumped in, showing all the finesse of the shark lawyer I'd heard he was. "The proof is right there on video. It disappoints me, as I've known the Salingers for years.

"I'm sorry, Laura." Mr. Caruso's voice was greasy-smooth as he addressed Brendan's mother. "But there's only so much we can do as parents. What more proof do we need, especially with your son's history?"

"So it would have been better if I did nothing?" Brendan asked angrily. "I should have stood there and let your son beat up a girl? There's no way in hell you can tell me I'm in trouble for that."

"If that's the case, you should have gotten a teacher, Brendan," his mother said, smoothing her proper tweed Chanel suit.

"Oh, yeah, like Dr. Ouilette could have stopped Anthony," Brendan said, picking the name of the petite physics teacher who maybe weighed a hundred pounds—if he was soaking wet and holding a fifty-pound weight.

"Regardless, Brendan, we do not condone violence at Vincent Academy," Principal Casey began. Brendan cut her off.

"I don't condone it either. I stopped it. So we're on the same team here," he said winningly. Principal Casey looked at me pointedly.

"What's your role in this, Miss Connor?"

"Um…" I began, looking at my aunt nervously, trying to decide if she looked mad enough to ship me back to Keansburg. I didn't want to bring up Ashley and throw her into this mess, as well. To my relief, Christine just looked annoyed—not angry.

"Does it matter?" Brendan cut in. "She didn't lift her hand to anyone—she didn't break any rules. Emma doesn't need to be in trouble."

"It would help if we knew why she caused this, Brendan," his mother said, her manicured hand on his arm.

I felt like I had been slapped. I hadn't tried to cause any problems—for anyone. I was only trying to help Ashley. I was only trying to do the right thing.

"From what my son has told me, it was a lover's quarrel," said Mr. Caruso, turning to Brendan's mother. "I'm sorry, Laura, but my son and this girl were once involved, and Brendan was jealous, so he attacked him."

"Lover's quarrel? Ew, no way!" I blurted out, unable to help myself. I saw Brendan's mother give me an icy glare, while her son just tried to hide a smile.

"Well, right now, we can't see much from this video other than Brendan clearly attacking Anthony," Principal Casey said.

"This has gone on way too long," Aunt Christine said curtly. "Have you watched the whole video? If not, I suggest you log in to Facebook—there's several versions there, uploaded by most of the students who were in the yard that day and not this superb Thelma Schoonmaker–quality editing job."

"Yo, screw that," Anthony yelled, breaking his silence as his father's smug smile faded to a thin grimace. "It's right there! Kick Brendan and that slut out of school. She doesn't belong here anyway."

Principal Casey gave Anthony a hard look, then invited Aunt Christine to her side of her desk, where she logged in to Facebook. I was amazed. I had to teach Christine how to use her DVR, yet she's savvy enough to have a fake Facebook account?

Christine did a quick search, and within moments, the entire—unedited—fight replayed on the monitor, including the part when Anthony shoved me and nearly knocked me over. You couldn't hear what the fight was about over the colorful commentary in the crowd, but you didn't need sound to know what was going on. I had no idea how terrified I looked as I tried to flatten myself against the door in the quad. And here I thought I'd looked tough.

Principal Casey pursed her orange lips and folded her hands in her lap. "Well, clearly, this changes things," she said. "Mrs. Salinger, Mrs. Considine, can you please take your children outside for a moment."

Christine put her arm around me and guided me out of the room, but I turned around. I was already in trouble, but I had to ask.

"Principal Casey, who emailed you the video, if you can say?"

"Not that it changes things much, but it was anonymous, Miss Connor," was Principal Casey's curt reply, which confirmed my suspicions: we were set up. My eyes met Anthony's as I continued walking out with Christine—and the words he mouthed at me would have made a porn star blush. I didn't dare cast another glance Anthony's way—but I didn't have to. I heard him hiss several choice words at me as I left the room.

Aunt Christine and I sat on one side of the large waiting room, Brendan and his mother on the other side. Gray Lady Gary must have been at lunch, because the only sign of her was a heather-gray cardigan slung over the back of her chair.

After casting a glance at the Salingers—and noticing that Brendan's mother was too wrapped up in scolding her son to pay attention to us—I began apologizing. "Aunt Christine, I'm so sorry, I wish—" I began. She shushed me.

"I had been hoping you would come and talk to me about this situation, Emma," she said, her voice stern but kind. "You don't have to handle everything yourself."

"I know. I'm sorry. I didn't want to be a pain," I mumbled, embarrassed. I tried to catch Brendan's eye but he was slouched in his chair, staring at the ceiling with his arms crossed as his mother whispered a tirade against him. I heard the words, "How do you think this makes me look?" and it seemed like he was trying not to laugh.

"Well, Emma, I don't know what to do here." Christine was wringing her hands, and I was a bit taken aback; I'd never seen my aunt look less than confident before. "What you did doesn't feel punishable. Some guy was harassing you. Your beau stepped in. Let's just hope the school feels the same way."

"How did you know about Facebook?" I asked.

"Oh, dear, I've had a fake Facebook profile forever," she said with a laugh. "I'm on the board, how else do you think I know what's really happening at this school? It helps with the simplest things, like which teachers need reevaluating, and sometimes strange things—like getting my niece and her beau out of trouble."

My jaw dropped, and Christine just continued. "Anyway, I do hope you don't get punished too severely. It doesn't seem like I should really ground you or—"

Christine was cut off by a loud metallic banging against the wall directly behind our heads. On the other side of that wall? Probably a dent, because it sounded like someone had just thrown a folding chair in Principal Casey's office. We all stood up, unsure of what to do.

"I said, out now!" Principal Casey's voice was shrill in the next room. The door to her office swung open, and Mr. Caruso, dragging his red-faced son by the arm, swaggered out. His father stopped in front of me and shook Anthony by the back of the neck. I saw Brendan tense, ready to jump on Anthony at the first sign of attack.

"Apologize, Anthony," his father demanded. Anthony spoke, but it wasn't exactly an act of contrition.

"I said apologize," his father growled menacingly. I could

see where Anthony inherited his temper. The angry apple didn't fall far from the tree monster.

"I'm *so* sorry, Emma," Anthony sneered mockingly. Then his eyes narrowed. "No, I'm not. And I'm not sorry for what I'm going to do to you." Anthony lunged at me, but Mr. Caruso had his son in a wrestling hold before he could inflict any damage.

Brendan jumped forward but with one meaty hand, Mr. Caruso pushed him back, hitting him square in the chest. "Watch it, Salinger, this is my job," Mr. Caruso warned him before grabbing Anthony by the collar and dragging him out. We overheard his unflappable lawyer's voice on the way out. "We'll go clean out your locker and that's it, Anthony, this is the last straw. I've done all I can to help you. You'll have a nice vacation at home before we decide on boarding schools for the second semester."

I slumped back into the chair. *Last* straw? What else has he done that we didn't even know about?

Principal Casey called us back into her office, and shaken, I followed the Salingers and Aunt Christine into the room, where there was, indeed, a large dent in the wall. Likely from the now-broken folding chair, which was stowed away in the corner.

Principal Casey was brief: Brendan and I were not officially "suspended"—just asked to leave school grounds for the rest of the day, until the gossip died down. Yeah, fat chance. It would just mean people could gossip without having to worry if we heard them.

I got off with a warning. Because he was already in trouble for fighting on the basketball court, Brendan was put on probation—and Anthony was expelled, effective immediately.

After Christine and Mrs. Laura Salinger exchanged awkward goodbyes—and Brendan mouthed, "I'll call you later"—I was at Angelique's locker, stuffing her books into the spare tote bag she had crammed into the back of her locker. Christine had asked me to be home by dinner so we could discuss the day's events, but since she was already late for some theater charity group she was heading, she left me at school. She had already promised Dr. Tedt that I'd bring Angelique's books home, so I needed to complete that mission.

So much for a romantic first day as boyfriend and girl-friend.

Chapter 16

I arrived at Angelique's apartment on the West Side of Manhattan about an hour later. Angelique lived in a standard New York City high-rise on the corner of Tenth Avenue and Fifty-first Street. It looked like any number of skyscrapers that began littering the New York skyline in the '70s. I don't know why I was half-expecting an ancient stone corridor, dimly lit by flaming torches; instead, fluorescent lights buzzed overhead as I walked through the beige hallway until I reached a red-painted metal apartment door.

Angelique answered the door in black sweatpants and an oversize tie-dyed T-shirt that screamed "I Love It in Florida!" in glittery orange lettering.

"So, you love it in Florida?" I asked dryly, eyeing the bright shirt.

"Shut up. It's comfy," she pouted in a stuffy voice, holding open the door so I could enter the living room. It was bright and airy, filled with sand-colored fabric couches and a pale wood entertainment center. Only on closer inspection did I notice the tiny telltale signs that this was a witch's lair, so to speak—crystals scattered throughout the apartment, and antique books that resembled *Hadrian's Medieval Legends* crowding the bookshelves. I dropped Angelique's books on a cornflower-blue recliner and followed her into the adjoining eat-in kitchen.

"Sorry I've been MIA," Angelique said, pouring herself a glass of orange juice and sitting on the counter. "I only checked my voice mail today—I've been in bed since Friday night."

"Blame Mr. Emerson," I suggested.

"I do! He never takes sick days. Anyway, sorry I was out of commission," she said again, then added, "It sounds like you could have used my expertise."

"That's okay. Are you feeling better?" I leaned against the windowsill, trying to act nonchalant as I nervously started picking at my freshly painted nail polish. *Where to even begin?*

"Forget about me," Angelique said, taking a big gulp of orange juice. "It's the flu. Big deal. I want to hear about what I missed."

"Well, it's been an interesting couple of days." I slid into one of the white kitchen chairs and launched into my date with Brendan—and the revelations that came with it. She was pretty quiet until I got to the whole born-witch thing when she raised her hands in victory and let out a high-pitched cheer—only to end up in a coughing fit.

"I knew it!" Angelique coughed again and slid off the kitchen counter. "I knew I was right about you. There always seemed to be *something* about you—I knew it the moment I met you! But after we figured out the curse, I thought that might have been what I was sensing."

"Well, I think maybe you were on to something." I sighed, drumming my fingers on the blue place mat. Angelique chuckled.

"And just a few short weeks ago, you didn't believe in any of this stuff. Now you think you're a witch."

I just shrugged. "Next week I'm probably going to get a pet unicorn. What can I say, the craziest explanations make the most sense these days. Oh—speaking of crazy, I didn't even tell you what happened today!"

"There's more?" Angelique asked, grabbing two bottles of water out of the fridge and handing me one before sitting at the table.

"You aren't wondering why I'm at your house in the middle of the day?"

"Oh, yeah—that is weird."

"You're usually way more perceptive," I observed. "This flu is messing with your head."

"So, what happened now? Did you meet Frankenstein? I'd believe it, the way things are going."

"Not quite," I said, telling her about the packed drama of the day.

"Wow, I picked the wrong time to get the flu," Angelique said when I was done. "So who do you think emailed the link to the edited video? I mean, it's so obvious that you and Brendan were set up. Someone is trying to get you into trouble."

"Most definitely," I agreed. "Only it backfired. It had to be Anthony or—" I stopped short, remembering how self-satisfied Kristin had looked in English, and what she said—or rather, hissed—in the hall.

"Kristin," I nearly shouted. "Whoa, that girl has it out for me."

Angelique nodded in agreement. "Yeah, I mean, she's usually pretty nasty, but she's gone overboard on you."

"I have no idea how to handle it," I muttered. "The more I try to stand up for what's right, the worse things get."

"Just ignore her," Angelique advised, getting up and refilling her orange juice. "It's what I've done ever since the second week of freshman year."

"There's no way this could be the 'danger' I'm being warned about, right?" I asked, making finger quotes around the word.

"Nah, I doubt it. But you know, on that topic, I do have an idea," Angelique said conspiratorially. She stood up and grabbed her water and OJ. "Come back to my room. We're going to do a spell."

I raised my eyebrows as I slid the chair back. "For what? Spells are what got me into this mess—well, not *me,* but my past life me—oh, you know what I mean."

"This is different." Angelique led me down a sunny, yellow-painted hallway to her room—which looked much more like what I was expecting from a witch. The walls were dark purple, with glow-in-the-dark stars stuck all over them and a sun, moon and stars-printed tapestry hanging over her bed. Candles dripping with wax and dog-eared books lined the messy shelves of her desk, and an ornate bowl filled with dried rose petals sat next to her bed.

"So what's the spell?" I asked, kicking off my shoes and sitting cross-legged on her black velvet comforter while she rooted around in her desk drawer. Angelique pulled out a notebook and began scribbling some notes with an oversize blue pen.

"We're going to amplify your powers—or more to the point, unlock them," Angelique explained, tapping the pen on her desk for emphasis. "That way, whatever danger is on its way, you'll have a fighting chance at beating it."

"How so?"

"I don't know, it's not an exact science," she mused, taking a wooden box off her desk and pulling out some crystals. "We know you're safe right now, but I'm hoping this will at least give you some extra ammo to fight whatever the threat is."

"How do you know I'm safe right now?"

"You're still wearing your necklace," Angelique said. "Remember, in your dream, you lost the medallion before the fire? It snapped off your coat and rolled away?"

"How on earth do you remember that?" I asked, incredulous. "It was *my* dream and I forgot all about—"

She gave me a smug look and tapped her forehead.

"Right, your amazing memory," I grunted, still jealous. Angelique pulled out some white candles and set them in a circle on the floor, lighting them one by one. When she lit the last candle, she let loose such a powerful sneeze that she blew the candle out.

"Are you sure you feel up to this?" I eyed her critically, but she rolled her eyes at me.

"I'm fine," she insisted, and gestured for me to join her on the floor, where we sat among the flickering flames. Then she pressed a small stone into my hand. I looked down at the glittering, tiny blue rock. It was the half the size of a Tic Tac.

"Sapphire," she explained. "It amplifies a witch's powers. Now hold it, and focus."

"On what?"

"Just try to get in touch with your inner witch," Angelique instructed. "Think about it like you've got this inner treasure chest that you're trying to unlock."

I squeezed my eyes shut and tried to feel out whatever witchiness was in me as Angelique started chanting.

> "I call upon the Goddess to free this witch's mind
> In this day and in this hour
> To protect against impending evil, blessed be
> Give this witch her born power."

I opened my eyes and Angelique was handing me the notebook.

"Here, now you say it," she told me.

I looked down at the scrawled ink in the book and expected that I would feel foolish, casting a spell—but it felt right. I clutched the stone in my hand and began the spell.

> "I call upon the Goddess to free my mind
> In this day and in this hour
> To protect against impending evil, blessed be
> Give me my born power."

I was hoping to feel a rush of warmth, or hear a thunderclap—*something,* to show me that the spell was a success. But there was nothing, just the sound of my own breathing and Angelique's sniffles. I sat there for a moment, gripping the stone in my fist.

"Let me know this worked," I muttered. "Come on, give me a sign!"

And then I felt it. The room was filled with a swirling breeze—it seemed to start at the floor and spiral upward. I opened my eyes and gasped. It looked like we were sitting at the bottom of a whirlwind. The dried rose petals had blown out of their bowl and were floating on the breeze, surrounding us with the heady floral scent. Some papers on Angelique's desk blew around us in circles. Our hair whipped into our faces. And then, with one final burst of a stronger wind, the wind extinguished the candles. Lights out.

Then everything dropped to the floor with a slight rustling sound.

"Whoa." Angelique exhaled, brushing her hair out of her face. "Your first spell."

"There's no way your window is open, right?" I croaked,

already knowing the answer. Still, as she shook her head no, I dropped the sapphire. It hit the floor with a minute clacking sound. "Now, I'm a little scared," I admitted, looking at the petals and papers scattered around the floor.

"Don't be!" Angelique's voice was filled with excitement. "You wanted a sign, hey, you got it! And that wasn't even a proper spell—Emma, you have so much untapped potential. I'm so relieved I was right about you. I just knew it—I knew there was something about you!"

She wagged her finger in my face smugly. "I'm also going to undo the protection spell I did on you, by the way. I've been thinking about it and I totally gagged your brother with that. We want him to be able to warn you."

I just stared at where the sapphire sparkled on the floor. Three weeks ago, if you asked me to cosign on these plans, I'd have laughed and told you that you were crazy. Now, I wondered where I'd house that pet unicorn.

"So, what, now I'm a witch?" I asked, bewildered and a little thrilled by the events that had just unfolded.

"You always *were* a witch," Angelique said. "Now, you just know you are one."

She launched into another coughing fit—and was starting to look a little pale—so I took that as my cue to leave and let her get some rest, even though I desperately wanted to stay and soak up as much witch information as I could. It felt like one mystical thing after another was hitting me.

By the time I got home, school was out, and my voice mail was full of urgent calls from Ashley, Jenn and Cisco. I'd barely changed out of my uniform into a T-shirt and track pants when the phone rang again.

"Phone, now," I demanded, opening my palm and trying to summon it from my nightstand. Shocker—it didn't move an inch.

"You're a witch, not a Jedi, Emma," I chastised myself, picking my phone off the bed. I checked the caller ID—it was Cisco.

"I saw Anthony cleaning out his locker," Cisco said after I'd relayed the events that unfolded in Principal Casey's office. "He was *pissed*. I expected steam to come out of his ears, like he was a cartoon character or something."

"Well, at least I don't have to see him anymore," I said, relieved. "I just get to deal with all the gossip every day. Oh, joy."

"Okay, Emma, I don't know if I should tell you this but, well, I feel obligated to."

"Oh, great, what now?"

"Do you want to know the rumor that's going around school?" Cisco's voice was apprehensive.

"Sure, why not," I said dryly. *These days, only the supernatural can faze me.*

"It's so obvious that Kristin's behind this, because the stories are that you slept with Brendan *and* Anthony, that Brendan's embarrassed to be seen with you, and that Brendan's only using you. And all kinds of variations on the same story."

"Ew, so gross." I sighed.

"I know. But speaking of Brendan…" Cisco trailed off pointedly.

"That happened kind of suddenly," I admitted a little guiltily. Cisco thought I was keeping secrets. "We pretty much hung out all weekend, and now we're dating." Dating seemed to be a weak word for what we were, but it was all I had to work with.

"I knew it!" he shouted, and I had to hold the phone away from my ear. "You sneak! You were holding out on me!"

"No, I wasn't—trust me," I assured him. "As of Friday, we weren't together. It happened fast."

"You can say that again."

"It happened fast," I repeated, and Cisco laughed.

"Well, tomorrow should be interesting." I sighed.

"Emma, since you've started going to Vince A, things have been nothing but interesting," Cisco said. I just groaned. I wanted to see Brendan—but another day of going to school where I would no doubt be the topic of conversation…I was beginning to see a trend here. If it weren't for Brendan, I might have been tempted to long for the lonely days back in Keansburg.

I thought about having a home-cooked meal ready when Aunt Christine, the perennial queen of takeout, came home. I figured it was a way to start making things up to her. I thought of how she plucked me out of Henry's loveless house, and all the favors she pulled to get me admitted to Vince A, and felt shame color my face. My behavior was not exactly a shining example of how the niece of someone on the board should act. But a quick survey of the kitchen told me the only ingredients were French bread, a large slice of brie, some fruit and more tea than there was in the Lipton factory. And, of course, the makings for multiple martinis, but I doubted finding me with a vodka bottle would improve my standing with Christine.

I decided to go with a safer activity: catching up on what-ever schoolwork I missed that day to look slightly more like a model student. I was several pages into my history book when Christine came in an hour later.

"Let's order dinner, then talk about what happened today," she said, her voice brisk as she leaned against the door frame to my room. I gulped, expecting the worst. But after we'd ordered some chicken Caesar salads from the local diner, Christine's tone softened.

"Emma, as I told you earlier, I wish you had come to me,

especially if you were having a fight with a boy at school. How long has he been harassing you?"

"He wasn't really harassing me at first," I admitted glumly, picking at the hem of my blue top. "I kind of picked the fight. He was spreading some pretty vicious things about Ashley."

Christine's eyes widened until they seemed twice the size of her bifocals, and she didn't speak for a minute. When she did, her voice was cold. "What did he say?"

I squirmed, embarrassed. "Don't bring it up to Uncle Dan and Aunt Jess, please! She'd be so humiliated!"

"Emma…" Christine's tone warned me to spill it.

"Anthony was really mean to Ash. And then he said that he—well, you know—with her."

Christine just looked at me confused. "Use your words, Emma," she chastised.

"Fine. He said he slept with her. And it was a lie. So I confronted him. That's what was caught on tape—me trying to get him to admit the truth."

"And how did the two boys end up fighting?"

"Well, Anthony started getting pretty, um, aggressive with me—as you saw on the video—so Brendan stepped in."

Christine drummed her hands deliberately on the table. "Well, Emma, as I said, I was really hoping you would come and talk to me. I know you felt like you had no support system back home. I'd like you to realize that I'm here for you." Christine's voice wavered just once—but it was enough to let me know that she was hurt that I hadn't come to her.

"I'm really sorry," I whispered. "I know you had to pull some strings to get me into the school and this looks kind of bad—"

"Oh, please, Emma, I don't care about appearances that much," Christine scoffed. "Your boyfriend's mother, well, that's quite a different story, dear."

"I noticed," I mumbled, dreading all future interactions with frosty Laura Salinger.

"But I am really sorry. And I promise you, I won't keep secrets like that again." I got up from the table to hug Aunt Christine, but as I did, I was ashamed. Wasn't I already keeping a big secret?

After dinner—and a marathon phone call with Ashley—I climbed into bed with my laptop, alternating between watching *Family Guy* on Hulu and trying to move things around the apartment with my newfound witch powers. The most I succeeded in doing was accidentally knocking the power cord out of my laptop and having to restart it. I was mostly killing time, waiting for Brendan to call. But around nine-thirty, the last three days caught up with me—and I didn't even realize that I had fallen asleep until I opened my eyes and my alarm clock blinked that it was after 4:00 a.m. I shut off my laptop and noticed my phone's status light was blinking.

I grabbed it and saw a text message from Brendan at around 10:00 p.m.

Can u talk?

I furiously typed back that I had fallen asleep and I would see him in the morning, then guiltily added, I hope you're not in a lot of trouble!

I took a deep breath, thinking about Laura Salinger. She was so cold, she probably farted ice cubes. That was a situation that didn't seem like it was going to be an easy one to deal with. *Focus on the supernatural problems first, Emma. Then you can worry about how to win over your boyfriend's mother.* Even though I longed for my biggest problem to be that my boyfriend's mother hated me.

As I curled up back underneath my comforter, a rough plan started to form in my head. I would check the local news station, NY1, every day—and stay away from any areas of high crime. I'd avoid the park at night. If there was going to be bad weather, I'd fake the flu. Take whatever precautions I could to make sure I stayed safe. Curses, schmurses.

I drifted off to sleep, proud of my plan.

Chapter 17

Even though I'd told her everything on the phone the night before, Ashley had a few remaining questions for me on the walk to school. Well, it was really just the one question, asked over and over again.

"So he's really an amazing kisser?" Ash giggled, beaming up at me with bright eyes. And every time she asked me, I would blush and smile. Because every time she asked, I would think about his soft lips, and his strong, warm hands as they held me against him. *Every. Single. Time.* I didn't mind the questions—they kept my mind off my fear about going to school and dealing with being the object of stares and rumors and gossip. *Again.*

"Okay, how do I look?" I asked, smoothing my hair when we were about a block from school—where I knew Brendan would be out front waiting for me. It wasn't my newfound witch skills at work though—he'd texted me early in the morning.

"Ridiculously happy," Ashley said, digging in her backpack for one of the thousand or so lip glosses that lined the bottom of her bag, then attacking me with the tube even though I protested that I never wore makeup to school.

"That's not for you, that's for Brendan," she smirked. "It's lemon-flavored Fresh lip balm. If you're going to keep making out with him, you need to make sure you don't get chapped lips. Those are just so, so gross."

"Jeez, Ash, way to be subtle," I groaned, smacking my lips together.

Soon enough, Brendan came into view. He wasn't leaning against the mailbox this morning, but against the cool stone of Vince A, with his headphones on and his hands stuffed into the pockets of his North Face jacket. His eyes were closed and his head was back, bouncing slightly in time to whatever he was listening to. As if he'd heard us approaching, Brendan turned toward us and opened his eyes—giving me a warm, inviting smile.

Ashley let out a low whistle. "Damn, Emma. You better find out if he's got a cousin my age."

I burst out laughing as we approached.

"What's so funny?" Brendan asked, taking his expensive-looking headphones off. I could hear a burst of loud singing before he turned off his iPod.

"Just my cousin," I said, laughing. "Brendan, this is Ashley. Ash, meet Brendan."

"Um, nice to meet you," Ashley mumbled, before casting an excited glance my way. "Find out about the cousins!" she squealed before running into the school.

"The cousins?" Brendan asked, furrowing his jet-black eyebrows.

"I'll tell you later." I smiled.

"So are you going to give me a proper hello or what?" Brendan asked, feigning anger. With that, I got on my tiptoes to clasp my hands around his neck and pulled him down to my height for a kiss. Brendan teasingly nibbled on my lower lip before pulling away—but kept his hands on my hips, holding me close.

"Is that flavored?" he asked, licking his lips, and I nodded.

"Now that's the kind of hello I'm talking about!" Brendan exclaimed.

"I'm going to leave and come back so we can say hello again," I said, a little breathlessly, and he laughed before a serious look crossed his face.

"So, are you in a ton of trouble with your aunt?"

"Not really." I sighed.

"You don't sound happy about that," he observed.

"I'm not! I just feel so guilty," I cried. "I wish she'd grounded me, or something." But Brendan just laughed.

"I'll trade with you," he offered. "My mom's pissed. The last time she was this mad I was fourteen."

"What did you do?"

"Oh, we were spending the weekend at our ski house and I got caught breaking into a community pool to skateboard with some friends. The cops took me home." He shrugged, like he'd just admitted that he forgot to take out the trash or do the dishes.

"You did what?" I squeaked.

"Not a big deal, I got off with a warning," he said, shrugging. "But this involves public appearances, so of course my mother is acting like I set fire to the gym."

"I'm so sorry I got you into this," I moaned, continuing my apology tour.

"Emma, stop. Don't even think about it." Brendan's voice was adamant as he pulled me closer and kissed me on the tip of my nose. "Look, it's over now. I think deep down, she gets that what I did was right. I'm not really grounded, either. We made a deal. I just have to—ugh, get this—deejay the stupid winter dance next week."

"Why? That doesn't sound so bad." *Dances as punishment? Do you get a car for getting a D in chemistry?*

"It is. It's a competition for who spent the most money or had the hottest date. It's lame. My mom knows I hate it, but it makes her look good. It's that whole 'I'm on the board so it's good for appearances that *you* get involved in the school' thing."

"Sorry," I said again, feeling more and more guilty.

"Emma, stop apologizing. Please." Brendan sighed. "Listen, let's get out of here at lunch, okay? Let's just go straight from English class."

"Okay," I agreed, relieved for whatever break I would get from the sure-to-hear rumors at the school.

Brendan opened the door to the school for me and we headed inside, parting ways so I could go to my dungeon basement locker first.

I spun the combination on my lock and opened the door, rummaging through the books I'd need for my morning classes. And that's when I saw it.

The folded-up piece of paper wedged in the slot in the locker. I grabbed it, smiling. *Brendan must have snuck down here before waiting outside for me.*

When I opened the note, though, it was clear that it wasn't from Brendan.

It contained one word: *Slut.*

I took a deep breath, and tried to steady my shaking hands as I refolded the note. It was written in block letters so there was no way to even try to match the handwriting. Not that I had any doubts as to who had left this in my locker. And even if Kristin hadn't put it there herself, she'd probably told one of her little followers to do it.

Several ideas ran though my head. I'd go up to Kristin and hand her the note, saying, "Someone put this in my locker but it was clearly meant for you." No, I'd just slip it in her locker. No, I'd hold on to it as evidence.

But then I realized if I did anything, she would just come after me with even more energy and vengeance than she already had. I shook my head. *All this over Anthony, of all people. It's like starting a world war over a parking ticket.*

I crumpled up the note and stomped up the stairs to my classroom, first ducking into the ladies' room to throw the note in the garbage.

And that's when I heard the voice in the stall.

"I'd be surprised if Emma even showed her stupid face in this school again," came the nasal voice. I whirled around and recognized the red-soled Christian Louboutin heels under the stall door. Only one girl ever wore Louboutins to school. Kristin.

I heard a toilet flush and scurried to the last stall in the row, shutting the door as softly as I could. I was afraid they could hear my heart beating, it was pounding so fast. I stepped back as far as I could so they couldn't see my shoes.

"She'll show up," came another voice over the sound of a stall door opening. Amanda, I think it was. One of Kristin's minions with a lot of money that made up for an unfortunate skin problem. "That girl has no shame."

"That's for sure," came Kristin's cackle. "I mean, Anthony hit it right away, and she has the nerve to get all mad at him over her stupid cousin."

I breathed in sharply. It was one thing to be told what she was saying about me; it was entirely another to hear it firsthand.

"I can't believe she tattled on Anthony for that stupid fight in the quad," a third voice chimed in. Kendall, I think it was.

"She has some nerve getting him kicked out of school." *So the story is that I went to Principal Casey about the fight.*

"I can't believe Brendan fell for her nice girl act," Kristin sneered. "She's probably given him, like, a thousand STDs already." The other two girls laughed.

"Such a shame," purred Kendall, over the sound of a faucet running. "He's so hot. Remember when I hooked up with him at your Hamptons house in the summer?" Even though I knew it made no sense, I felt a stab of pain. I'd heard Brendan was no angel before I'd met him, but still—it hurt to hear it. I thought of Kendall—long strawberry-blond hair, legs that would have gone on forever if her shoes didn't stop them—and winced.

"He's totally dating down." Amanda cackled. "I mean, Emma isn't even that pretty."

"She's kind of cute," Kendall disagreed, then added very quickly, "but nothing special."

"Kendall, he'll be yours by Christmas break," Kristin promised.

"He better be," Kendall squealed. "I'll just need to wash him off first. I'd love to get him in the shower." The other girls laughed.

"Trust me, she's a nobody and he'll get tired of her soon," Kristin spat out, and I could hear the hatred bubbling over in her voice. "Unless she gets knocked up. I heard that's why she left her last school—she got pregnant and had no idea who the father was."

I pressed my forehead against the cool white tiles on the wall and tried to blink back the tears. The laughter faded as they left the bathroom. When I was sure the coast was clear, I slowly exited the stall. I splashed some water on my face, hoping the cool water would extinguish the red-hot embarrassment that colored my face.

I walked to class, forcing myself to hold my head up high

even though I wanted to stare at my shoes, letting my hair fall in my face to shield me from my classmates. I'd dealt with worse in my life. I wouldn't let them get to me. Or at least, see that they were getting to me. I just hoped that my brave act would hold until English class, when I'd finally be with Brendan—my oasis in the nearly friendless desert Vince A had become. Through some miracle, I managed to avoid being called on in my first two classes. If I had to speak aloud, I was sure my voice would crack and crumble.

"Hey, Emma, just so you know, I don't believe any of the rumors," Jenn said quietly as we walked to English.

"Thanks," I replied, flashing her a grateful smile. "And thanks for, well, I guess for being seen with me," I said with a hard laugh.

"Kristin and I used to be close," she whispered, glancing around to make sure no one heard. "She's changed a lot—she used to be a really fun person. She's just gotten so mean. And she's like, obsessive about Anthony. I think he was her first or something.

"Anyway," Jenn continued. "Try not to let it get to you. Most people know she's full of it because they've been the subject of one of her rumors at one point or another."

"Why is she so popular, then, if she's been mean to everyone?" I asked, frustrated.

"She throws these crazy parties and people want to be invited, her family is really powerful, and she's just one of those people," Jenn explained. "And I think everyone is happy she has a new target—and that it's not them."

I made a face. "I hate to say it, but it makes sense."

We got to English and instead of feeling excited or relieved to see Brendan, I just felt exhausted. I slid into my desk and fought the urge to put my head down, opening my notebook and pretending to review my notes instead. For the first time since I'd started at Vince A, my head didn't automatically turn when he came into the room—and I didn't realize he had entered the classroom until he was sitting in front of me.

"Hey, Emma, are you okay?" Brendan folded his arms on the back of his seat, his green eyes full of worry. "You look… bothered."

"It's nothing. Long morning," I mumbled unconvincingly. Brendan just pursed his lips.

"We'll talk at lunch," he said, then turned around since Mr. Emerson had shuffled into the classroom, loudly blowing his nose. Seriously, this guy needed vitamin C, or a vacation, because it was now plain gross.

We were barely out of the school before Brendan asked what was wrong.

"It's just…there's a lot of rumors flying around about me. And you. And Anthony," I admitted, not wanting to go into specifics. "It's frustrating to hear it. And to have people staring and talking about me. *Again*."

"You did nothing wrong. What could anyone possibly be saying about you?" Brendan asked. He kept his voice calm but I noticed the hard edge of anger creeping in.

"It's nothing," I said dismissively. "Forget I said anything." The last thing I wanted to do was bring up the rumor of us sleeping together. I wasn't sure about Brendan's mental state, but mine sure couldn't handle the topic of us having sex on top of everything.

"Come on," Brendan wheedled, taking my hand as we walked toward Central Park. "We're *finally* past secrets, re-member?" *Damn. He has a point.*

"Fine," I pouted, leaning against the nearest building and taking a deep breath before the words tumbled out. "Ap-parently, everyone at school thinks that I was sleeping with

Anthony. And, um, now they think I'm sleeping with you, too. And that you're embarrassed to be seen with me. Oh, and I also left my last school because I was pregnant. That last bit is all Kristin, whom I'm positive set us up."

"Oh." I could see the muscles in Brendan's jaw tense. "How do you know all of this is going around?"

"I heard them this morning in the girls' bathroom. It was Kristin, Amanda and Kendall, who bragged about hooking up with you, by the way."

"She's *still* talking about that?" Brendan looked taken aback. I just nodded, biting my lip nervously before pushing myself off the building, continuing our walk to the park.

Brendan gave me a sideways look. "Last summer, I was in the Hamptons with some friends, and they wanted to go to a party at Kristin's house. So I went, too. Kendall wouldn't leave me alone all night. I wasn't into her but she didn't exactly play hard-to-get."

"Oh." I gritted my teeth, annoyed that this bothered me just as much as everything else she'd said in the bathroom.

"Please tell me you don't care," Brendan asked, letting go of my hand to slide his arm along my shoulders, pulling me closer. "This happened before I even met you, you know. Please, tell me this isn't bothering you."

"Well, a little," I admitted.

"Emma, I have zero interest in Kendall. I promise you," he swore. "I never gave her a second thought. To be completely honest, I never even gave her a *first* thought. She was just there at the time."

"It probably bugs me because I heard this after I got a nice little note in my locker."

Brendan's head snapped up and he stopped walking. "Someone left something in your locker?"

"Yep."

"What did it say?" Brendan demanded angrily.

"I really don't want to—" I started, embarrassed, but Brendan cut me off.

"Emma, what did it say?"

"It called me a slut."

Brendan stopped walking, and when he faced me his eyes were ice-cold. "I'm going to have a little chat with Kristin," he said, his voice low.

"Brendan, no. Look, we're both in enough trouble right now so there's no sense in confronting her." I tried to keep the panic out of my voice. "Kristin's who she is, there's really not much we can do about it. Besides, Anthony could have left it before leaving school yesterday."

"Still, she has no right to talk about you," he said protectively. "Your name should never even cross her lips."

"Brendan, please. Let it go," I pleaded. "It just made for a hard morning. I'll be fine."

"It's really pissing me off that I'm getting away scot-free in this whole thing, and you're on the hook."

"That's because girls are evil," I muttered. "High school girls are demons, seriously."

"Emma, I don't want things to be harder for you than they already are." His face softened, and he grabbed both of my hands in his.

"They won't be as long as I have you," I promised.

"It's not like we don't have enough to worry about," Brendan whispered, resting his palm on my medallion. "If I could let you go, I would. If I thought it would make things easier."

"It would make everything harder," I said, feeling an ache in my heart when I thought about facing another day like this without him.

"Look, please just don't do anything. Please, let it blow over," I begged.

Brendan eyed me for a moment and bit his lower lip. Then he laughed a low, rumbling laugh and pulled me into his arms.

"Only if you will indulge me with something." I could practically hear the wheels spinning in his head.

"What is it?" I asked cautiously. "I'm not going to break into a pool to go skateboarding with you if that's what you want."

"You might prefer that. But instead, I want you to—" Brendan paused for effect "—go to the stupid winter dance with me."

"What?"

"You heard me," Brendan said, tracing my jawline with his finger. "I want you to go to the winter dance with me."

"You don't want to go at all, I thought," I countered.

"You're right, I don't," he agreed. "But I was thinking about it this morning. I've never really gone to any of these things with a girl I was...involved with."

I raised an eyebrow. "Involved with?"

"Don't make me spell it out, Emma. Look, I want to make a statement with you. I want people to see that I care about you. You're important to me." His tone softened over that last statement.

"Brendan, the last thing I want to do is be trapped in a roomful of those people."

"Then do it for me so I'm not alone with them," he bargained. "And so maybe you can get some peace from the rumors. If people see that we're really together..."

"You have a point," I muttered.

"Look, if they were just talking about me, I wouldn't care," Brendan said. "But I don't want anyone talking about you and if you won't let me tell them off, then let me do this."

"Okay, fine," I conceded begrudgingly. "As long as I'm

allowed to go." *And can somehow get a dress to wear. No helpful woodland creatures or fairy godmothers here. Maybe Ashley will lend me something.*

"I can't believe it, but I'm actually looking forward to it now," Brendan admitted, leaning against a building and pulling me with him.

"Well, I know that I don't get enough of Kristin Thorn's bitch-face during the school day, so an extra dose next Friday night will keep me going through the weekend," I said sarcastically, and Brendan laughed.

"You won't even see her," he promised. "You'll be in the deejay booth with me like a girl in a Jay-Z video."

"I'm not wearing a bikini and a fur coat to this dance, Brendan," I warned.

"Damn." Brendan pouted. "Not even some booty shorts?"

"Isn't this a semiformal?"

"So?"

"And it's November?"

"Oh, I'll keep you warm," he teased, tucking his fingers underneath my chin and raising my lips to meet his. And the minute our lips touched, all my concerns about school faded into nothingness.

I had to hand it to Brendan; his kisses were a better mind eraser than that magic wand thing from *Men in Black*. We both lost track of time, and had to grab hot dogs from a vendor before running back to school. Still, I nearly floated through my afternoon classes, in a decidedly better mood than I was that morning. I didn't even let it get to me—much—when I sat alone in chemistry and heard Kristin's scathing remarks about my hairdo. *Her Oompa Loompa skin is a color not seen in nature and she's making fun of my appearance?* I briefly considered attempting a spell, but figured with my luck, I'd end up turning myself into a chicken burrito. Besides, my last—and only—spell was probably only a success because Angelique, a more experienced witch, was with me. So I bit my tongue and toyed with my necklace, reminding myself that I had bigger things to worry about than Kristin.

After the last bell rang, Brendan was waiting for me when I finally made it down to my dungeon locker room after class.

"What are you doing here?" I asked, happily surprised.

"Just stealing a minute with you before basketball practice." Here I was, worried about myself, when Brendan had more or less gotten one of the best basketball players kicked out of school and had to face his teammates.

"Is that going to be rough?" I asked, embarrassed that I hadn't even thought to ask before.

"Nah, no one liked Anthony," Brendan said with a smile. "They'll probably vote me MVP—you know, when I'm actually allowed to play again."

I grinned, relieved.

"So give me a kiss—I have to get to practice," Brendan playfully demanded, bending down to press his lips against mine. It was hard to remember that we were in school—and to restrain myself from winding myself around him in a very un-scholastic way.

"I'll call you tonight," he whispered, kissing my neck. "Try to stay awake past sunset."

The way I was feeling at that moment, I had no doubt I could stay awake past sunset on Thursday.

Ashley met me in front of the school, impatiently fussing with her blue headband.

"So Emma, did you ask about the cousins?" she asked excitedly.

"I'm sorry, I forgot," I admitted, but vowed to ask Brendan about his cousins next time we were together.

"Good. Holy crap, he's gorgeous up close," she breathed

excitedly. "I can't believe you get to kiss him." I blushed again when she said that.

"I heard he's deejaying the dance, too."

"Word travels fast," I mused.

"It does when it's about Brendan Salinger," Ashley said, adding, "and my friend Vanessa is on the dance committee. She told me."

"Kristin let a freshman on the dance committee?" I was incredulous.

"Well, Vanessa's mom is donating all the refreshments, so that explains it," Ashley said, throwing her hands up in frustration.

"That explains it." Vanessa's mom was a fairly well-known chef at one of the top restaurants in the city.

"Well, I'm going with the deejay if that's what you're wondering," I replied, reminded that I needed to borrow a dress. But before I could ask, Ashley was jumping up and down, excitedly clapping her hands.

"I'm going, too! A bunch of us are going with Vanessa!" She squealed. "Oh, Emma, I don't know why you worry about fitting in! You went on a date with Cisco, now you're dating Brendan Salinger! We have to go shopping for a dress."

"Or I can borrow one?" I wheedled, thinking of Ashley's massive walk-in closet. Even though she was several inches smaller (in every way), I could usually squeeze into her clothing.

"No way, dude, you need something fabulous," she squealed. "We'll go shopping, it'll be great. Besides, I don't think I like the dress I bought. I want another."

"Well, let me make sure Aunt Christine is okay with it," I warned. But it was too late. The minute I turned the key in Aunt Christine's door, Ashley pushed past me, giggling.

"We have to go shopping! Brendan asked Emma to the

winter dance next week!" Ashley called out in her singsong voice to Aunt Christine, who was sitting at the kitchen table reading. Christine removed her glasses and her eyes darted back and forth from me to Ashley, then back to me.

"I mean, if that's okay with you." I rushed to amend Ashley's gleeful proclamation.

"Yes, dear, it's okay," she said with a nod of her head.

"Well, his mother is making him deejay the dance so I'm really just going to keep him company," I explained hastily. "So I don't need to go shopping or anything—I can borrow something of Ash's."

Christine eyed my chest—then Ashley's—and chuckled to herself. "No, dear, I think we can get you something. We'll go to Bendel's this weekend."

"Are you sure?" I asked apprehensively.

"Of course, dear," she said, picking her book back up and turning the page with a rose-painted fingernail.

"Thanks, Aunt Christine," I murmured, a little embarrassed. "I don't deserve all this."

Christine just sighed. "Sweetheart, you *do*. I just want you to realize that. Although, I would like to meet Brendan again under different circumstances."

"He's pretty great," I said dreamily.

"Well, at least I know you'll be safe with the young man. He seems like he'd step in front of a truck for you," she snorted. "Still, I'd like to meet him again."

I nodded, but inwardly cringed. Soul mate or no soul mate, we were still going to have to properly do the "meet the parents" dance, I realized with a silent groan. It wasn't so much that I didn't want Christine to get to know him—I was absolutely terrified of Laura Salinger. Possibly more than I was of an unseen, impending doom.

Chapter 18

By the end of the week, I was amazed that the rumors had died down a teeny bit. Only Kristin was really stoking the fires anymore—but I figured she would be an evergreen thorn in my side, so to speak. I was pretty positive Kristin was my Lady Eleanor, except that she went for character assassination as opposed to actual assassination. The latest rumor? That I cheated on Brendan with a group of guys from Xavier High School. Never mind the fact that Brendan and I had only been public for a week and it would have been physically impossible to accomplish the level of whoring around in five days that I was accused of committing. But Kristin refused to let up. Still, it seemed like Brendan's method of dispelling the rumors—remaining an ever-present figure by my side— was working. If there was one thing he knew, it was how to navigate these shark-infested waters. You know, if the sharks carried Dior purses.

I didn't think it was possible to feel more out of my ele- ment than at Vince A—and then, that Saturday, I went dress shopping with Aunt Christine, Ashley and her mom, my aunt Jess. I self-consciously studied myself in the dressing room at Bendel's, while my family waited on the other side of the dressing room door, where a thick stack of discarded dresses hung on the hook. They were all too…prom-y. And pastel. And poofy. One of them was covered in so many bows, it looked like it belonged at the gift-wrapping counter. And based on the price tag, each bow was a hundred bucks.

I scrutinized the one-shouldered, red-sequined cocktail dress I was wearing in the mirror. "You guys, just because it's November, doesn't mean I have to wear *red*," I protested, opening the door with a frown. "I look like a hooker in this."

"Yeah, but at least it's a high-priced ho." Aunt Jess snickered, and Ashley giggled. Christine gave both of them disapproving looks.

"I know!" Ashley chirped. "Let me go pull a few more dresses. Trust me!" she begged when she saw my face. Visions of sugarplum-colored dresses danced through my head. *Please don't let it be covered in glitter.*

"Here, try this on again," Aunt Jess said, pulling a sparkling white strapless number with a full skirt out of the pile before leaving the room to let me slip into the fluffy frock.

"I look like a snowball," I grumbled once it was on, holding open the door to the dressing room. I stared at my scar with a resigned sigh. They didn't have any long-sleeved dresses that were right for the occasion. I desperately wished I could wear jeans and a black shirt. Why, oh, why was this dance semiformal?

"We can get you gloves," Christine said, noticing me giving my arm the evil eye. "It'll be acceptable." I was relieved. Even though Brendan knew about the accident, he hadn't ever seen the ugly scar. I shut the door to slip out of the dress when there was a stilted banging at the door. I opened it to find Ashley standing there. Or should I say, Ashley's legs, sticking out from underneath a pile of dresses that she had piled in her arms. The stack was taller than she was. All the dresses were black.

"Oh, Ashley, I love you!" I exclaimed.

"Black is something for old women and widows to wear," Christine muttered disapprovingly. "You're young. You should wear something bright and festive."

"Well, you're both, and look at what you're wearing today," Aunt Jess cracked, dissolving into giggles. Christine looked down at her pink leopard-print twinset and frowned.

"I guess you're right," she conceded. "Well, what's important is that Emma feels comfortable, so let's see what you've got here."

We hung up the dresses and my eyes immediately went to a simple strapless dress with a tulle skirt that was artfully shredded. It looked edgy yet classic at the same time. As Ashley pulled up the zipper, I prayed that it looked as good on me as it did on the hanger. I whirled around, completely thrilled.

"If I could wear this every day, I would," I said, holding up the tulle and bowing to my reflection. I couldn't believe that was *me* in the mirror. The most dressed-up I had ever gotten was for my mom's wedding to Henry, and even that was just a pale yellow sundress since they got married at City Hall.

I saw Aunt Christine's reflection smiling in the mirror and dabbing at her eyes with a pink tissue.

"Aunt Christine, are you…crying?" I asked, crestfallen. "Is it really that big of a deal that I'm wearing black?"

"No, honey," she said, a melancholic smile on her face. "You've just come such a long way from how I found you six months ago in June. I'm glad you're getting the chance to be happy."

"Aw, Aunt Christine." I sniffled, stepping over a mint-green lace dress to hug her.

"Okay, okay, no crying on the couture," Ashley said,

alleviating the happy sadness in the tiny dressing room. "By the way, I have shoes that go perfectly with that dress."

That night, I stared at the dress as it hung on the back of my door. I had shoes coming from Ashley (luckily when it came to shoes, we were the same size), a wrap from Aunt Jess, and gloves and earrings from Christine. I hated to admit it to myself, but I was actually excited about getting dressed up and entering a room on Brendan's arm, as his legitimate, bona fide girlfriend. I allowed that thought to remain untarnished, letting it lull me to sleep.

The next morning, I knew Angelique had removed the protection spell.

I only remembered details from this dream because Angelique had suggested I start keeping a dream diary—a way to remember key moments before they faded into the oblivion of my subconscious. I was sitting with Ethan in the kitchen of our old house, playing a board game that I didn't recognize or remember. He was explaining the rules of the game to me, very exasperatedly. It was clear that he'd thought he'd explained them before, and was annoyed that I hadn't gotten the hang of it yet.

"Ladybug, if you go down this path," he said, pointing to dark-colored squares on the board, "it'll be harder to win."

"But I *like* that way," I insisted, sliding my pendant onto one of the black squares. The board kept changing shape—it was stone, then wood, but I still insisted on keeping my pendant on the dark square, holding it in place with my fingertips.

"I don't care if it's harder this way," I told him.

"You could lose the game," he warned. "You could lose everything."

"I don't care."

"It's not safe, Emma. Why can't you stay away from him?"

"I just can't."

"Well, if you insist on going this route, you need a brave teammate," Ethan said, his brown eyes, a mirror image of mine, burning into my face. "Is he strong enough? Do you have enough faith in yourself?"

"I think so." I shrugged.

"Don't *think* so. You need to be stronger," he demanded. "You both do. This isn't really a game."

The board disappeared and we were no longer in the kitchen, but standing in the rose garden from my dreams.

"He has to be strong. You won't even see it coming. He has to be willing to risk it all. Is he strong enough?" Ethan said. He opened his mouth to speak again—only to sing an old Madonna song. The scene before me was slowly replaced by my eyelid-slitted view of my room, and I realized that my alarm clock had gone off, with "Borderline" blaring out of the clock radio. I slammed my hand down on snooze and squeezed my eyes shut, trying hard to return to my dream. But it was gone.

I didn't feel as panicked as I had after all of my other dreams. I felt, oddly enough, encouraged—empowered, almost—like this curse was something I could, most definitely beat. If I could figure out the cryptic warnings.

Brendan had left for his grandfather's house right after school on Friday—he was still checking out his massive library for anything he could find about the legend of Aglaeon—but he wanted to spend Sunday taking me on an official date. Most people have to balance school and dating. We had to balance normal dates with supernatural revelations.

"I want to take you out properly when I'm back on Sunday," Brendan had said, his voice muffled with the static. "I feel like I'm a crappy boyfriend."

No matter how much I argued with him that he was the furthest thing from a crappy boyfriend, Brendan insisted.

"Just let me be good to you," he persisted. "No rumors, no curses, nothing. Just me and you, just us together."

So Sunday, we indulged in a time-honored New York tradition—brunch. My eyes were as big as the fresh-baked bagels piled in the breadbasket when I saw the prices on the menu.

"This place has the best eggs Benedict in the city, Emma," Brendan boasted, slathering a thick layer of cream cheese on a sesame bagel. *For thirty-five bucks, it better come with a new car.*

I did have to admit it, though—they very well may have been the best eggs Benedict in the state. Or on the planet. But as much as I enjoyed them, I enjoyed Brendan more, in a mood I'd never seen him in before. He seemed to relish just being a normal boyfriend—no curses, no rumors, nothing to worry about. As he talked excited about possibly getting a regular deejay gig at a new club opening downtown—as long as he didn't drink, the club didn't care that he was underage—I decided not to tell him about my dream last night. No sense in killing his buzz.

Once we were outside, I impulsively threw my arms around his waist, still reeling that I could touch him whenever I wanted. I had that kind of access to him. It made me a little giddy, I had to admit.

"Thanks for brunch," I said, my voice muffled by his jacket.

"My pleasure. I want to do more things like that with you." Brendan tugged on my coat since I still had my arms wrapped around him. "By the way, I wanted to talk to you about something."

"What's up?" I asked, resting my cheek against his chest

and squeezing him more tightly. I didn't feel like letting go just yet, *thankyouverymuch*.

"My family wants to meet you," he said, tilting my chin up to look at him. "As in, officially meet you. You know, not in the principal's office. Are you okay with that?"

I froze. Doomed soul mates? Yeah, I can handle that. Piece of cake. Battle rumors and evil cliques at school? I could get that done before lunch. Attempting to win over Laura Salinger, however, set off shrill alarm bells.

"Do they know about us?" I asked apprehensively.

"Emma, of course they know that we're together," Brendan said plainly. "Why do you think they want to meet you?" He was avoiding what I *really* meant.

"That's not what I'm getting at." I reluctantly unwound my arms from his waist and faced him. "For all your mom knows, I was just some girl at school that you were defending. What I mean is, do they know about the whole—" I lowered my voice "—curse thing?"

Brendan stopped at the corner and leaned against the frigid brick building behind him.

"Yes, they know what we think. My grandfather called them and told them last night. He thinks we're right, by the way."

I buried my face in my hands. "Why did he do that?" I wailed. "I don't want them to think of me as…curse bait." I looked up. "How did they treat your other girlfriends?"

Brendan snorted and gave me a dirty look. Clearly, I'd offended him. "Emma, be serious. Do you honestly think I've ever brought someone home to meet my parents?" I just shrugged. Even though he dismissed Kendall to me, I wasn't dumb. At some point, some crafty girl had to have finagled an invite to the Salinger home.

"Emma, I would never bring just anyone home to meet my

parents," he said, his tone a little kinder now. "Anyone before you was merely that—just anyone."

"Okay, I believe you," I said, and resumed walking again, hoping he'd forget about the whole meeting-the-parents thing.

"Sweetheart, come on." Still leaning against the building, Brendan managed to catch the hood on my jacket and gently tugged me back. I melted into him, resting my chin on his chest. He encircled me in his arms and kissed the top of my head.

"They're going to treat you like you're my girlfriend, and that's it. Even though—" he tightened his grip "—you know you're so much more.

"And by the way, Emma," he continued, "I want to meet your family, so let's make that happen, okay? I'd like to do *some* things the right way."

"Okay," I agreed, remembering that Aunt Christine had actually requested to re-meet Brendan.

"So I'm going to pick you up Friday night for the dance, and I hope your aunt is there, ready to give me twenty questions." Brendan smiled a toothy smile and I laughed as he reluctantly removed me from his embrace.

"We'd better get going, the movie starts in a half hour." I started walking forward again. The theater was still about twenty blocks away. I stepped off the curb, reaching out for his hand automatically. It wasn't there, and I looked next to me, confused. It was always there.

My eyes danced around, and I finally saw Brendan behind me. He stood about thirty feet away, checking the internet on his phone.

"If we miss it, there's another showing in ninety minutes. That's not too bad," he mused.

"Come on, slowpoke! We can make this one," I called. I

turned my head to look at him as I began crossing the street, and Brendan's green eyes crinkled up with a little smile.

Then his eyes changed—they turned dark, panicked.

"Emma, watch out!"

He shouted my name again as he flung his bag down, running forward and lunging for me. Instinctively, I reached out to him, even though I wasn't quite sure why. I felt Brendan grab at my arm—it felt like it was being pulled out of its socket as he yanked me forward, toward him. My toe caught on the curb and I skidded forward, palms outstretched, onto the sidewalk.

A speeding taxi, racing to beat the light, missed hitting me by inches. It blew through the intersection, horn blaring.

I heard the bleating behind me, and I stayed frozen, sprawled on the sidewalk. Slowly, I was very aware of pain coming from my hands. Brendan was crouched next to me, his arm around my back.

"Emma! Are you okay?"

"Yeah, I'm fine." I moved slightly, disturbing the bits of dirt and concrete lodged in my palms. It made them sting more.

"*Ow!* Well, this isn't awesome."

Brendan smiled a weak smile. "How bad is it?" He tucked his head under my arm and helped me up. Brendan grimaced at my bloody hands. "Sorry."

I looked down and my hands were shredded, fresh blood streaming out of my skinned palms. They looked like I had used a cheese grater on them.

"I may have pulled you back a little too hard," he said regretfully, taking my raw hands in his. "I'm so sorry, Em."

"Why are you apologizing?" He just saved me from being a human speed bump and was asking for forgiveness. Brendan grabbed his bag from where he'd tossed it and pulled out a bottle of water, pouring it on my hands. I flinched at the sting, stepping back—and feeling a sharp stab in my right ankle.

"Ouch! I think it's sprained!" I winced at the pain, hopping back onto my left foot.

"Emma, I'm so, so sorry," Brendan said, his face crest-fallen.

"Please stop apologizing! You saved me from being a hood ornament, you know."

"That's one way of putting it," he said, bitterly. "The other could be that I'm the reason that happened to you in the first place."

"New York is the reason that happened," I said condescendingly. "Or do you think this city is renowned for taxi drivers following the rules all the time?"

Brendan frowned, his handsome face set in an angry mask.

"Oh, come on, Brendan," I said, reaching out to touch his face and wincing when my skinned palms brushed against his faint stubble. It only made him feel worse.

"No guilt trips, please," I begged. "This isn't your fault. This isn't the Salinger curse at work." But Brendan wouldn't look at me and when he did, his green eyes went straight to my raw palms, and he'd blanch.

"I'm a ticking clock for you," he said, keeping his eyes downcast.

"Oh, please, don't be so dramatic," I said, starting to get annoyed. "If a pigeon poops on my head, will you blame that on yourself, too?"

"That won't kill you, Emma."

"It might," I said gravely. "Have you *seen* some of these New York City pigeons?"

Silence, still.

"Look, Brendan, you saved me—again, I might add. I didn't even see that cab coming!"

But something about what I said echoed in my head. *Didn't see it coming…didn't see it coming.*

"Oh. My. God."

"What, Emma?"

"Brendan, um, do you think, just maybe, that was it?" I asked, gesturing to the gutter where I almost became roadkill. Brendan just stared at me.

"What are you talking about?"

"Brendan, what if that was the *it?* The danger? The big bad? And you just saved me from it?"

He remained expressionless, his handsome features like stone.

"It can't be," Brendan whispered. "It couldn't be that easy."

"Okay, don't kill me for not telling you earlier," I said, nervously biting my lip. "But I did have another dream where my brother more or less warned me, and said that I wouldn't see it coming. Those were his exact words. I sure didn't see that coming."

"Emma, what the hell? Why didn't you tell me earlier?" Brendan demanded.

"We were having such a nice time. It was nice to feel normal," I mumbled, looking down.

"Please, please don't keep secrets from me," Brendan whispered, putting both hands on either side of my face. "Anything else?"

I took a deep breath. "There is one."

Brendan shut his eyes and took a deep breath before opening them to stare at me unhappily.

"Spill it, Emma."

"I think I'm a witch," I said plainly. I wasn't expecting his reaction—laughter.

"Emma, you've been hanging out with Angelique too much." He chuckled, kissing the top of my head.

"I have not!" I stamped my foot—then yelped. In my frustration, I'd forgotten all about the sprain. But I was annoyed; curses and doomed soul mates are okay, but me inheriting a little witchy power is oh-so-funny?

Brendan took a steadying breath and eyed me. "I think you're just a little overwhelmed by everything we've learned, and you've been pretty persecuted this week. So of course you'd think that—it does feel like the Salem Witch Trials at Vince A."

"I don't think I'm a witch because of *that*," I retorted. "I think I'm a witch because, well…Angelique sensed it about me. And she's been right about everything else. And I did make the wind blow by doing a spell in her room." I explained as hastily as I could what had transpired at Angelique's house, but Brendan still looked skeptical.

"Something happened when Angelique the mega-witch was in the room. That was probably her, not you," Brendan said with a dismissive wave of his hand.

"No, it was me," I protested.

"Look, Emma, we can talk about this later. How badly does your ankle hurt?" He changed the subject and poured more water on my hands.

"Why will you believe everything else but you won't believe this?"

"Let's just talk about it later." Brendan ignored my question, examining my hands. I pulled them back.

"No, tell me, Brendan!" I snapped, angry. "You're the one who keeps saying, 'No secrets.'"

"Because maybe you were right the first time," he shouted,

and I flinched. "Maybe I do want to believe that, just for a little while, we're normal. I spent every single moment since Friday night reading books about this curse—the same story over and over again."

He ran his fingers through his ink-black locks, his voice getting more agitated with each word. "I read my great-great-grandfather Robert's journals—and what he went through when he lost Constance. I saw a glimpse of what I might go through. What I could lose. So maybe I enjoyed just being with you today, where it wasn't about dooming you to an early grave, or dooming you to be talked about at school, or pulling you back from a crazy cabdriver that almost killed you, or uncovering that you're a witch or I'm a—I don't know, a demon or something. Maybe I am, since I seem to cause you nothing but pain."

I stepped back, the hurt evident all over my face. "Oh, and this isn't hard for me, either?"

"I didn't say it wasn't."

"I didn't ask for any of this, Brendan." I folded my arms bitterly, ignoring the pain in my palms. "It's *my* life that's the one at stake here, not yours."

He was instantly contrite. "Emma, I was wrong. I shouldn't have yelled at you." He reached out to take my hands but I pulled them back.

"Just leave me alone," I mumbled, summoning the resolve to walk away. I didn't know if it was my unwillingness to leave his side—or my lack of desire to walk fifty blocks on a sprained ankle—but I couldn't move just yet.

"I'm really sorry, Emma," Brendan whispered. "I'll be stronger, I promise."

I wanted so badly to hold a grudge, to stay stubborn and remain mad at him. It would have been easier. But his green eyes were sadder than I'd ever seen, and they melted my resolve to stay angry. And this time when he reached out for me, I let him hold me.

"If I'm not jumping in to protect you, I'm apologizing to you," he muttered, stroking my hair as it fell down my back. "I never screw things up this badly."

"You're not screwing anything up." I tried to alleviate his guilt. "Look, this is more complicated than anything either one of us has ever known. It's not like there's a manual for this."

"It's just that I'd never be able to forgive myself if something happened to you." He held me even more tightly, his arms strong around my shoulders. I rested my face against the rough wool of his black peacoat. I swore I could hear his heart beat through the layers.

"It's just that—Emma, I love you," Brendan said, his lips moving softly against my hair. "Can I say that? Is it too soon?"

My heart felt like it was trembling. Although I knew we both felt it, we'd never said it. The impact of what he'd just said colored his face. I touched his cheek with the back of my hand gently, as he had done to me countless times before.

"I love *you*," I whispered. Brendan sighed my name so quietly, I could barely hear him. He leaned down and kissed me softly, a slow, longing kiss that smoldered and burned against my lips. When we broke away, we were both a little flushed.

"Well, I guess I'm going to meet your aunt sooner than I expected," he said with a self-conscious smile. Seeing my confused face, Brendan added, "I'm not sending you back to your aunt with bloody hands and an injured ankle. Not without explaining what happened."

I started to protest but realized that he had a point.

"Fine," I conceded. I began hobbling toward the subway.

"Why don't we take a cab home," he suggested, eyeing my ankle.

"No way, I'm fabulous," I called as I hobbled along. "Check out my pimp walk!"

Brendan laughed, but still hailed a cab and pulled me into it. I hated the idea of springing Brendan on Aunt Christine—or worse, her not being home and coming in to find Brendan in the apartment—but she wasn't answering the phone.

Brendan helped me into the building just as my ankle began to really throb. I put the key in the lock to Christine's apartment and heard the TV inside—so she was home, after all. I got the door open to find my aunt sitting on the couch, watching *World's Wildest Police Videos* on her DVR. Once I showed her how to use the DVR, my proper aunt became addicted to the trashiest kind of reality TV. I thought it was kind of awesome.

"Mrs. Considine," Brendan said, keeping his left arm around me and extending his right hand to greet my aunt. "We tried calling to let you know we were coming. I'm sorry to keep meeting you under these uncomfortable circumstances but um, Emma had a little accident."

"Oh, you make it sound like I wet myself," I complained crabbily as I limped. My ankle was starting to seriously hurt. "I just fell."

I held up my scabbing-over palms and shrugged. Christine's jaw dropped when she saw me, and she flew into the bathroom, pulling out the peroxide and bandages as I hobbled through the living room.

"Honestly, it's not that bad," I called to her as Brendan helped me follow her into the pink-tiled bathroom. "Really, it just looks bad," I said again, but within seconds, my aunt was holding peroxide-saturated cotton balls against my palms.

"I can do it, really," I protested, holding a soaked cotton

ball against my scrapes. "Aunt Christine, *really*. It could have been a lot worse. Brendan pulled me out of the way—a cab came racing down the street and would have hit me if Brendan didn't see it and grab me."

Aunt Christine handed me the bottle of peroxide, and I poured it on my palms, turning my face away from them so they wouldn't see me grimace.

"Those cabs are a menace," Christine huffed. "One almost mowed me down outside of Barneys last Christmas."

I gave Brendan a pointed look, as if to say, "See?" He ignored me.

"I'm just lucky Brendan was there," I said. Reminded we weren't alone, Christine turned to regard Brendan, who was standing in the hallway, peering over Christine's shoulder anxiously.

"Yes, Brendan." Christine stepped out of the bathroom to shake Brendan's hand again. "Nice to meet you under, well, under different circumstances. Thank you for taking good care of my niece here."

"Yes, ma'am. You're very welcome. Thank you for allowing Emma to spend the day with me, and go to the dance on Friday with me," he said with a winsome smile. Brendan was quite charismatic when he turned on the charm. Then he looked at me, and his smile faded into a frown when he noticed I had taken off my boot and sock—and my ankle was blossoming into more shades of indigo than Picasso had used during his blue period.

"Oh, Em, that looks so painful," Brendan said, striding into the bathroom and kneeling next to me as I sat on the fuzzy pink toilet seat. He slid his left arm around my waist, giving me a little squeeze as he pressed his right fingers gingerly against my swollen ankle.

"Try moving it this way," he instructed. I did as he requested, and then after gently making me flex my toes—*thank God I'd given myself a pedicure the night before*—he grinned. "I don't think it's broken." I smiled at his concern, lost in those hypnotic green eyes of his, until we both realized that we were being watched—carefully—by my aunt. Brendan straightened up, and excused himself.

"I broke my ankle playing football a few years ago, and I've seen tons of injuries on the basketball court," he explained to Christine, clearing his throat.

"Not that I'm a doctor, obviously. But it looks okay from what I know. Still, I should probably let you put that ankle on ice. It was lovely meeting you, Mrs. Considine." With another of those angelic smiles, Brendan shook my aunt's hand again and—winking at me—headed for the front door.

After it had closed, Aunt Christine leaned against the doorway and eyed me suspiciously over her bifocals.

"This is all from him pulling you out of the way?"

"Yes, Aunt Christine. Really!" I stressed. "I stepped off the curb and I wasn't paying attention, and a cab raced through the light. Brendan grabbed me and pulled me back on the sidewalk. I tripped on the curb when he pulled me out of the way. *Really.*" I held up my boot, which was freshly cut with a deep scrape on the toe.

"Okay, honey. I just worry about you sometimes. You didn't have the best male role models."

"Aw, Aunt Christine," I mumbled. "All it's done is make me really skilled at spotting the bad guys. My loser radar is *sharp.* That's one thing you don't have to worry about."

She seemed satisfied, and began sticking little plastic bandages haphazardly to my palms. "It's just worrisome, dear. Whenever you're around this boy, there's some kind of trouble or another."

"No trouble that he's caused," I replied, feeling protective of Brendan.

"No, of course not," Aunt Christine amended her statement quickly when she saw the sour look on my face. "I'm just saying it does seem to happen a lot."

"That's…coincidence," I muttered. "And it's only been twice."

"One other thing, dear. The way you are with each other." She sighed. "It concerns me. It looks a little serious for a couple of teenagers who've been dating—what, a week?" *Or, a couple of teenagers who've been waiting for each other for a thousand years.*

"We did meet when we were younger, remember?" I wheedled, reminding her of her earlier story about Brendan and me playing together as kids.

"That doesn't count," Aunt Christine said firmly.

"Well, the first time we hung out was four weeks ago," I countered, thinking of our Met meet-up.

"Still, it seems a little quick for you to give your heart away."

"I've got my emotions in check, Aunt Christine. Really, you don't have to worry about me when it comes to that," I insisted, trying to sound convincing, even though I'd practically gift wrapped my heart for him.

She eyed me suspiciously and said, "Don't go getting pregnant or running off and eloping."

"Aw, come on!" I cried. "Give me a little credit!" I covered my face with my hands and an errant bandage stuck to my chin.

"Well, let's get you off this ankle," Aunt Christine clucked. "With any luck, all you'll need to do is wrap it with an Ace bandage and you can still wear heels to the dance on Friday."

I looked down at the scrapes on my hands, peeking out under the bandages that were randomly stuck all over my palms.

"At least I'm wearing gloves," I groaned, using the towel

bar to pull myself up so I could hobble into my room, peeling the stray bandage off my chin as I limped along.

Later that night, after IMing with Angelique—who was still battling the flu—I was back in my bed, scrolling through celebrity hairstyles on *People* magazine's website, trying to get ideas for the dance. I contemplated wearing it up in a dramatic, ornate style, then thought about copying Anne Hathaway's soft, long waves. She always looked good. But then I realized that my hairdressing toolkit consisted of a hairbrush, a flatiron and a curling iron, so my options were limited, to say the least.

I adjusted the baggie of ice on my ankle—fortunately, the swelling was already starting to subside—and let my mind drift to my afternoon with Brendan. Sure, it was cut short, but—wow, talk about making the most of our time together. We hadn't admitted—in so many words—that we loved each other before. I felt my heart beat a little faster when I thought about how he tucked me into his arms, and how safe I felt there. Even though we'd just had our first fight, the anger disappeared as soon as it had arisen. He was just overwhelmed. He did promise to be stronger....

I sat up like I'd been stabbed with a fork.

"No...." I whispered aloud. I hobbled off the bed, grabbing the dream diary from where I'd stashed it under my bed. I held it next to my laptop, reading it by the dim light of the screen.

There, scrawled in my messy early-morning scribble, were the key things Ethan had warned me about.

Is he strong enough?

"Please, please be strong enough," I whispered into the darkened room. And suddenly, I was afraid.

Chapter 19

The next morning, my ankle looked like one of Seurat's leftovers, with splotches of black and blue dotting their way across my egg-shaped ankle. I wrapped an Ace bandage around my foot and felt even guiltier when Christine slipped me some money to take a cab to school.

"I can't have you walking in that state," she insisted. "You could fall again, or fracture it."

But it turned out that I didn't need to take a cab to school; as soon as I'd polished off my Toaster Strudel Ashley was pounding on the door. Repeatedly.

"Open up!" came the muffled voice on the other side of the door.

"I'm not even running late," I complained to myself, pulling my jacket on and hobbling into the living room, where Christine held the door open while Ashley and Brendan stood in the doorway. Well, Ashley was standing. Brendan was, of course, leaning. Christine looked like she didn't know whether to grimace or laugh. Ashley looked so surprised her eyebrows were practically in her hairline. And Brendan looked—well, he looked hot.

"Look who I found in front of the building!" Ashley giggled, widening her eyes at me.

"I figured you might need a hand this morning, but I should have known your cousin had you covered," Brendan said magnanimously, and Ashley's eyebrows disappeared into her hairline altogether.

"So you're walking me to school?" I asked, confused.

"Not really—one of the perks of being Aaron Salinger's son is access to the company car service. I couldn't think of a better time to use it than now." He flashed a winsome smile at me as Ashley mouthed the word "limo."

"That's very thoughtful of you, Brendan," Christine said a little stiffly, handing me my backpack. "Have a good day, dear. Be good to that ankle."

When the apartment door closed behind me, Brendan grabbed my bag and slung it over his shoulder along with his backpack.

"Not that I don't appreciate it, but—" I pursed my lips and considered whether Ashley was in earshot, since she had run ahead to press the elevator button "—are you babysitting me because of, well, this?" I gestured to my necklace.

"Your chest? Well, Emma, I won't lie, your assets have a way of making even the school uniform shirt look good, but mostly I'm worried about your ankle," Brendan deadpanned, a beatific smile on his face.

"Oh, come on, give me a straight answer." I tugged on his coat sleeve.

"Nope," Brendan said, holding the elevator door for me as we stepped inside for the short ride to the lobby—where out front was parked a shiny, sleek black limousine.

"Thank you, but don't you think the limo is overkill?" I asked as he helped me into the car after Ashley had scrambled in.

"What? I wanted you to be able to stretch out your leg." Brendan shrugged, sliding in after me once I'd gotten comfortable. "Oh, you're getting a ride home from school, too."

"Brendan, really, it's just a sprain, I didn't break it," I protested, but he wouldn't hear of it.

"The last time I sprained my ankle, I kept twisting it because I would walk on it before it had healed. This is something I can do for you. So, please let me do this for you." Brendan just stared at me with those hypnotic, sparkling eyes of his and I nodded dumbly.

So I begrudgingly agreed to door-to-door chauffeur service, provided by Salinger Industries. Brendan's dad's company was responsible for key buildings in the New York City skyline, which explains how Brendan was able to summon a limo with little more than a snap of his fingers. And by Friday, I realized I'd done the right thing by letting my pride take a walk while I took a ride with Brendan; if I'd walked to and from school every day that week, there would have been zero chance that I could have managed the heels I'd borrowed from Ashley.

And there was another little bonus to having a ride home: Friday, we were alone in the back of the limo, which the driver had somehow managed to parallel park on Sixty-seventh Street before taking off for a coffee break.

"I should get going upstairs," I murmured for the four thousandth time, cradled in Brendan's arms as we lay there, stretched out in the enormous backseat of the limo. "I have to get ready...do my hair."

"Your hair looks beautiful as it is." Brendan's fingers twisted in my hair, his breath was warm on my neck. His mouth teased my skin, alternating between gentle nibbles and more demanding kisses.

"I really have to get dressed," I whispered a few minutes later, but contradicted myself by lightly raking my nails down the back of his neck—one of Brendan's more sensitive spots,

I'd come to learn. With a playful growl, he pressed his lips to mine, his urgency flooding my senses.

"I have to, um, I should get upstairs." My thoughts got foggy when he broke away to kiss my neck again. Where did I need to be? Why did I have to be anywhere except in this backseat?

"We have hours," Brendan said persuasively, his mouth moving to my collarbone as his hand traveled up my thigh.

"You might, but it takes me longer," I said, reluctantly pulling myself up and out of his embrace. Getting ready was just my excuse—I felt like if I didn't put the brakes on now, I might not have the strength to stop things if they progressed to a more intimate level. And I was not about to lose my virginity in the back of a limo before a big dance.

"Actually, we don't have hours. I forgot my turntable at home so I couldn't completely set up before school this morning." Brendan gave me an apologetic smile as he propped himself up with one elbow. "We have to get to the dance about a half hour early, if that's okay. I have to set up all the deejay equipment."

"Then I should really go," I exclaimed, grabbing my bag from the wide floor. But Brendan grabbed my hand and pulled me back, reaching into his jacket pocket for something.

"Well, you can't get ready without this, I think," he said, pressing a small box into my hand as he touched his lips to my cheek.

"What— Brendan, what is this?" I stammered as I looked down at the black velvet box, confused. *I already promised Aunt Christine I wouldn't elope….*

"It's just something for you to wear to remind you of how I feel—something *else* for you to wear, I should say," he corrected himself as he ruefully touched his index finger to my pendant.

I opened the box—then gasped. Nestled in the black velvet was a white-gold Claddagh ring—with a sapphire heart-shaped stone in the center.

"Oh, my God, Brendan, this is beautiful," I breathed, touching the glittering face of the ring with featherlight strokes, afraid to smudge the sparkling metal. Two hands gripped the heart, which was adorned with a glimmering diamond crown.

"It's a Clauddagh," he said, taking it out of the box and sliding it onto my ring finger. "You wear with the heart facing *this* way." Brendan tapped the point of the heart, which faced me. "It shows that you're spoken for."

"I know." I smiled, gazing at the ring in awe. "My mom had a Claddaugh." Then a thought occurred to me, and I looked up to meet his intense green gaze.

"Why sapphire? Don't get me wrong—I love it," I said hastily. "But why sapphire?"

A funny look crossed Brendan's perfect features, and he just shook his head.

"I just had a feeling you'd like it," he muttered.

"I do. Thank you, I love it. But I didn't get you anything," I said remorsefully. Brendan just laughed and kissed my lips before kissing my hand.

"You have no idea how much you've given me, Em." Brendan brushed his fingers through my hair, playing with a few strands. "But I should probably let you get out of here and get ready, though."

I glanced at my new ring, then at the clock in the limo's state-of-the-art stereo, and slid my sparkling left hand around his neck.

"I guess we have a *little* time," I whispered, pulling him closer to me for another kiss.

★ ★ ★

A half hour later, I finally made it upstairs, mumbling a lame excuse about traffic before jumping in the shower to start getting ready for the dance. I had about three hours to turn from street urchin to My Fair Lady.

I blew my hair dry in record time, adding a few waves with my curling iron so it looked a little different from my boring straight everyday look. I'd overheard some girls talking about getting their makeup professionally done, but as I surveyed myself in the mirror on the back of my bedroom door, I thought I didn't do too bad of a job—even though the fake eyelashes I'd bought stuck to my fingers more than they did my eyelids. I pulled them off, corrected one smudge on my smoky eye makeup and finished the look with an almost nude lip gloss.

"There. Not too bad," I said, pursing my lips in the mirror.

Christine had just finished helping me zip up my dress when the doorbell rang.

"Of course he's early." I eyed my alarm clock and grumbled, grabbing my gloves in my hand and slipping into Ashley's borrowed Ferragamo heels. I cautiously tested my ankle—not too wobbly, I decided. Still, I threw a pair of thin satin flats into my clutch along with my keys, phone and lip gloss. I pulled Aunt Jess's velvet wrap about me and prepared to make my grand entrance into the living room, where I could hear Brendan and Aunt Christine exchanging pleasantries.

With my chin held high and my shoulders back, I stepped into the living room, hoping to dazzle Brendan. But instead, I was the one spellbound. Seeing him now, it was like the first time I'd laid eyes on him all over again. I was a little struck with how dashing, handsome... Okay, I could think of a billion SAT-worthy words to describe how Brendan looked to me, but truthfully, the only word to describe him at this moment was hot. He looked incredibly, ridiculously, smack-yourself-in-the-face-he-can't-be-real hot.

Brendan's hair was pushed back, this time under a fedora. His green eyes sparkled, and his cheeks were a little flushed from the cold. His peacoat was open, and he wore all black, from his crisp suit to his open-necked black button-down. He looked like he'd just walked off the set of some film about rock stars moonlighting as gangsters. If rock stars held rose corsages, that is. I melted a little against the doorway.

A small smile tugged at the corners of Brendan's mouth, and he crossed the room to me.

"You look gorgeous," he whispered, low enough so my aunt couldn't hear, as he slipped red roses around my wrist. After we obliged Christine with a photo—actually, with several photos—we were soon being whisked away in the limo.

"You are so beautiful tonight, Emma," Brendan said, his arm securely around my waist.

"You look pretty amazing yourself," I whispered, running my hand down his sleek lapel. I doubted there was anyone on the East Coast who looked better than Brendan this night.

"Well, I had to match you," he said. "That's a big challenge."

I fidgeted self-consciously, thinking he'd have to uglify himself a whole lot before we were ever on the same level. Brendan reached for my hand, taking the gloves that I'd been clutching and tossing them on the wide expanse of open seat next to him.

"No, wait, I need those," I cried out, reaching for them a little desperately.

His face searched mine for a moment, my eyes darting between his and the gloves. Slowly, carefully, Brendan picked up my hand and, without his eyes ever leaving mine, kissed my wrist, where the scar began. I bit my lip and looked away, not wanting to see his face when he was eventually repulsed by the scar, and all the ugliness it symbolized.

With his other hand, Brendan touched my cheek and gently tilted my face so it was facing him again. I yearned to look away, but I couldn't break his gaze.

"Would you do me a favor tonight, Emma? It's something that means a lot to me," he said, his mouth warm as it moved against my skin.

I nodded, a little entranced by the way his eyes green eyes burned into mine.

"Remember that nothing else matters to me but you," Brendan said, very softly. He kissed my wrist again, and with his free hand, picked up the gloves and placed them in the hand he was holding.

The intensity of his emotions overwhelmed me for a moment, and I was glad I was sitting down. I dropped the gloves and put my hands on his face, pulling it closer to mine.

I kissed him softly, and with every movement of his lips against mine, I felt myself fall more deeply in love with him, with this strangely perfect person who for some reason, decided to love me back.

After a few minutes in this embrace, I was dimly aware of a tapping sound on the divider between us and the driver. Brendan looked out the window.

"Dun, dun, duuun," he boomed in an impression of the horror movie sound effect. "We're here. Are you ready?"

I gulped and took a deep breath. "As ready as I'll ever be."

After we stepped out into the cold night air, Brendan grabbed a thick black case from the trunk—his turntable—in one hand and my gloved palm in the other. The school looked dark and ominous tonight—and for a second I was reminded of my dream, where I stood in front of the burning house.

I shut my eyes and shook my head, trying to push the creepy thoughts out of my head. *You're going to a school dance, big deal.* I followed Brendan into the main entranceway and down the long hallway to the left until we reached the gym, housed in the annex of the school. Since everything else at Vince A had been over the top, I was expecting a *My Super Sweet 16*-level production for the winter dance. But the gym looked a little like it could have been anywhere: silver and gold helium balloons floated from the ceiling, there were a few tables and chairs set up and decorated with tea lights and the refreshments, but the room was mostly just lined with folding chairs. But it looked like the dance committee wasn't completely done—poor Austin was running around frantically.

"No, I said put the raffle table over *there*," Kristin commanded from her perch in the middle of the dance floor, and a tiny redhead—Vanessa, I recognized—dragged a large folding table across the room with a bitter look on her face. I was reminded of one thing, at least, that set this dance apart from those at other schools. The raffle prize was season tickets to the Yankees. At Keansburg, the biggest raffle ever was for an iPod Shuffle.

"I've changed my mind, put it back where it was," Kristin decreed, picking some imaginary lint off her low-cut red dress before turning her back to the girl and us. Poor Vanessa's updo looked like it was falling apart, and I wondered how many times Kristin had forced her to drag this table back and forth.

If Brendan noticed any of that, he didn't let on. He didn't break his stride, keeping a tight hold on my hand as he marched right past Kristin to the deejay's station in the far left corner to set up his equipment. I just stood there awkwardly, counting down the seconds until Kristin and her legion of lemmings noticed that we had arrived. She left the room shortly after we arrived—to fix her makeup for the billionth time that day, I assumed.

"Emma, do you want me to take that?" I was so preoccupied that I hadn't realized Brendan was standing directly behind me, talking to me.

"I'm sorry, what?" I asked, holding my clutch to my chest.

"Your wrap," he explained, placing his hands on my shoulders and hooking his fingers inside the velvet collar. "I can put it on a shelf down there." Brendan gestured to an empty shelf where he'd already stowed his peacoat under the desk the dance committee had fixed up to look like a deejay booth.

"Oh, yeah, thanks," I mumbled as Brendan slid the soft fabric off my shoulders. I suddenly felt very naked, and looked up. And there it was: Kristin was back—and her lips, freshly painted with a baby-pink gloss, were twisted in a self-satisfied grin as she stared at me. I wanted to look away, but I was kind of amazed. I'd never seen someone look so smug and venomous at the same time before. It was like she'd invented a whole new facial expression to convey just how much she wanted to run me over with a car. *Maybe she was driving that taxi?*

She looked me up and down, then turned to Amanda and whispered something in her ear. They both laughed, staring right at me. *Yeah right, like that wasn't about me.*

I smoothed my skirt self-consciously. "Are you sure I look okay?" I asked Brendan. He barely looked at me before darting his green eyes over to Kristin, who had just linked arms with a blond, goateed guy I didn't recognize. Then he sighed unhappily.

"Emma, don't even compare yourself to them. It's like comparing a diamond to…I don't know…a booger," he said, and I burst out laughing.

"Thanks," I said, feeling some of that you-don't-belong-here uneasiness shed as he kissed my cheek.

"Sorry, I'm going to be distracted for a minute," Brendan apologized, putting on his headphones and fiddling with his laptop. I sat in one of the folding chairs nearest the makeshift deejay booth, pretending to be engrossed in something on my cell phone when the gym was filled with a loud dance track. I looked up and Brendan was adjusting the levels on his equipment, scrutinizing something on his computer screen. After what seemed like an hour—but was really only about three minutes—Brendan put down the headphones, sitting next to me.

"Do you want to dance?"

I eyed the still-sparse crowd in the gym. "Not just yet, thanks."

Brendan nodded his head toward the deejay booth. "Any requests?"

I glanced over at Kristin, who was engrossed in something her blond was saying. "Got any Slayer?" I asked hopefully, and Brendan chuckled.

Within twenty minutes, the gym was packed. I didn't know how many people came with friends or dates or even solo, but Brendan had been right—this was a platform for my classmates to show off. I doubted anyone's glittering earrings or bracelets were rhinestones. But then I'd look down at my own sparkling sapphire ring and smile. The more I looked, the more I started to wonder if the sapphire was bringing out my witch skills.

I decided to test it out, staring at one of the tealights, and willing it to blow out. The flame flickered for a moment before extinguishing. I gasped, then I noticed the brunette standing next to it who had sneezed and blown it out, making a face when she smelled the smoke. *Oops. Guess Angelique really was the key when we made the wind blow in her room.*

I looked around the dance floor, trying to move things and inevitably, I would lock eyes with Kristin for longer than was comfortable. It felt like she was keeping tabs on me.

When the coast was clear—meaning, Kristin had left the gym to apply another coat of her face spackle—I offered to get us some drinks, sticking to the edge of the packed dance floor so I wouldn't spill the nonalcoholic champagnelike cocktails in my hands. On the way back, I stopped to watch Brendan in action. It was an oddly proud moment for me—he was *good*. He switched between MP3s and vinyl effortlessly, his talented hands almost a blur as he ensured that the music never stopped. When I returned to his side, Brendan leaned in and gave me a kiss on the cheek, taking the drink gratefully and downing it in one shot.

"Thanks, it's getting hot back here," he said, shrugging out of his jacket. For the next few songs, he deejayed with one hand, keeping his other on the small of my back. I didn't know what it was like to be prom queen, but I couldn't imagine that it felt better than this. I sighed, happily leaning into Brendan who clicked something on his laptop before turning to encircle me in his arms.

"See, now this isn't so bad, is it?" he teased, giving me a squeeze and I smiled, relaxing into his chest happily.

I should have known my happiness would be short-lived.

"Excuse me, Brendan, you should really be focusing on your duties and not letting yourself get distracted," came the catty comment from the other side of the desk.

I stiffened, feeling every nerve tense up. I didn't even have to look to know who had just interrupted our moment.

"Um, *hello?* I'm talking here." Kristin's voice got more demanding. "All I'm saying, Brendan, is that you're here to provide the music and you're ignoring your job." I turned just in time to see Kristin narrowing her pearlized shadow-covered eyes at me. "Don't forget, you're here as the help."

"I don't hear anyone complaining," Brendan answered, regarding her with a barely perceptible tilt of his head. He didn't even seem to notice her little dig about him being "the help."

"Well, *I'm* complaining." Kristin folded her arms underneath her chest—which had been stuffed and arranged like it was a proud product of the Build-a-Bear Workshop. I noticed she lifted her arms to pump up her shimmer-lotioned cleavage a little more. *Does this girl ever give it a rest?*

"So? Who the hell are you to me? Big deal," Brendan scoffed, keeping his left arm around me as he broke our embrace to put his headphones to his right ear while he changed to a vinyl track.

"The big deal, since you ask, is that I'm in charge of this dance," Kristin sneered, grabbing his wrist with acrylic nails and yanking his arm down. "And I. Am. Complaining!"

My fists clenched. *How dare she touch him!*

As if Brendan could reach my thoughts, he gave me a calming squeeze.

"You're lucky you're a lady," Brendan retorted coolly, pulling his wrist free. "Although it's a loose use of the word 'lady,' I'll admit."

Kristin flinched, a flicker of anger crossing her face. Then she turned her cold gaze to me.

"You." She sniffed, flicking her index finger my way.

"Excuse me?" I asked, incredulous.

"Oh, there's no excuse for you," Kristin jeered, her bow lips turned up in a perfectly pink sneer. "But I want you to come move a box for me."

"I'm not on your little committee." I tried to keep the anger out of my voice.

"Yeah, that's right. You don't do anything for the school except bring its value down." Kristin grinned, baring her teeth.

"Kristin, I swear, if you don't get the hell out of here…" Brendan slammed his hand on the desk and caused the music to skip, the warning tone in his voice bordering on rage.

"Save your stupid insults, Kristin," I said, getting impatient. "What do you want?"

"Just grunt work. I figured you could handle that," she said, regarding me with distaste. "We need another box of raffle tickets brought up from the basement. It's dirty and none of *my* friends should touch something that gross."

"You've wasted our time enough, Kristin," Brendan cut in, stepping between us. "As you pointed out, I have a job to do here. So get one of your little idiots to move whatever it is that you want moved and leave my girlfriend alone."

Kristin scowled when Brendan called me his girlfriend.

"Have it your way," she purred, her voice saturated with saccharine evil. "So on Monday, I'll just go to Principal Casey and tell her that all you did was play some crappy playlist while you made out with—" she pointed at me "—*that* all night. And I'll talk about how upset I am about the terrible way you threatened me and my date when I told you to shape up."

She batted her eyelashes angelically. "I mean, I only wanted what was best for the dance and the school."

"Go ahead," Brendan scoffed. But I stiffened. He was already on probation—one more straw and he was out. The last thing in the world I needed was for him to get into more trouble. His mother already probably hated me.

"Fine, where is this stupid box?" I sighed, resigned.

"Emma, no. You don't answer to her." Brendan glared at Kristin angrily.

"I'll give you two losers a minute to figure it out. Brendan, I have a feeling you'll need to talk extra...slowly...to...her," she drawled dramatically before sashaying away to join her blond date.

"Brendan, you're on probation." I turned my back to the dance floor and kept my voice low, even though I knew no one could hear me over the bass. "You don't need any more issues with Principal Casey."

"If you give in to Kristin now, that's it," he pointed out angrily. "She'll know she can blackmail us, extort us, whatever, to get what she wants."

"Brendan, it's just moving a box," I promised. "It's fine."

"It's not fine, Emma," Brendan argued. "I'll go move it before I let you deal with this."

"Look, she just wants to be bossy and feel superior," I reasoned. "*We* know she's pathetic. Besides, I'm not going to let you get into trouble, again, for me."

"I'll be fine."

"Okay, then how about this? How horrible will things be for me if you get kicked out, huh?" I folded my arms and stared up with him with my best "so there" face.

Brendan began protesting but I ignored him, and turned around to see Kristin striding back across the dance floor. From the smug look on her orange face, you could tell she knew she had won.

"So where the hell is this stupid box?" I asked, my voice dripping with contempt.

Her grimace turned into a smile. "It's in the basement by the lockers. I'll show you the way. Just go get it and bring it up to the raffle table."

I grabbed my clutch from the shelf underneath the desk,

figuring I'd call Ashley and see where she was while I was away from the music.

Brendan slid his hand around the side of my neck. "Emma, you don't have to take care of me."

"Let me do this for you?" I asked, stretching up to kiss him.

"I don't have all night," Kristin yelled, tapping her crystal-encrusted sandal impatiently.

"I know where the basement is," I said scornfully as I fell into step next to Kristin. "You don't have to walk me there."

"Oh, this is my absolute pleasure," she gloated, strutting through the dance floor. I pretended to be oblivious to the confused stares from my classmates who caught us walking together. It would have been less probable to see the Loch Ness Monster do a conga line through the dance floor than it would have been to ever see the two of us peacefully together.

We walked right past Jenn, whose jaw dropped, mouthing "What the eff?" to me when she saw me with my mortal enemy. I just shrugged, figuring I could give her all the gory details on Monday. Then at least I could find out why she was holding Austin's hand.

We passed the raffle table—where a full box of tickets sat at Kendall's feet. When she saw us walking by, Kendall stood up, a disgusted look on her pretty face.

"Kristin, I don't think—" she shouted over the music, but Kristin told her just exactly what she could go do with her thoughts.

So this is just a power play like I thought. Kendall doesn't need the tickets. She doesn't need the box moved. Kristin just wants to let me know who is in charge.

Kristin strutted down the hallway to the basement door.

"After you," she sneered, twisting the doorknob and kicking it open with her strappy sandal.

"So this box is right by the lockers?" I asked.

"I said that already. All the unwanted and unnecessary stuff goes in the basement." I let her dig about my locker location roll off my back and I stepped into the chilly stairwell.

"What, do they turn the heat off after school?" I wondered aloud, wrapping my arms around me as I quickly ran down the stairs, hearing the bass echo in the concrete stairwell. My breath was coming out in smoke. I just wanted this over with.

As soon as I was on the bottom step, I turned to the right to face the row of lockers—and that's it. No boxes. I turned around and looked up the stairs to see Kristin peeking out from the top of the stairs, laughing.

"That's what you get, bitch!" she yelled, and pulled the door shut.

I ran back up the stairs, feeling my ankle starting to throb. I grabbed the doorknob, twisting it and shaking it, but it was no use—she'd locked me in the basement.

I pounded my palms on the thick metal door, calling her name even though I knew it was futile.

"Fine, you made your point, now let me out!"

I pounded again, screaming, "It's freezing in here, let me out!" But I couldn't hear anything on the other side of the door—just the deep bass that pulsated from Brendan's speakers and made the door vibrate underneath my fingers.

"Crap," I moaned, folding my arms and covering my chest with my clutch in a pathetic effort to keep warm.

Then I looked down at my clutch. "Emma, you fool. Remember, you have a phone," I chastised myself. I stepped away from the door and went back down the steps into the quieter basement. I pulled off my gloves to dial the cell phone and texted both Ashley and Brendan.

Kristin locked me in the basement. Pls get me!

The pain in my ankle was now pulsating, so I kicked off the heels and put them in my locker, slipping the flats on as I first called Ashley, whose phone went straight to voice mail.

"Hey, Ash, it's Emma. Are you at the dance yet? Kristin has locked me in the basement. Can you please come get me?"

I tried Brendan next, hoping he had his phone on vibrate. Frustrated, I slammed my locker door shut, hooking my lock back on but leaving it dangling open. I rested my back against the lockers, getting more annoyed with each ring of the phone. Eventually, his voice mail also picked up.

"Brendan, it's Emma. Kristin locked me in the basement. Can you come let me out please? I'm trapped in here and it's freezing and I'm all alone…."

I turned my head—and that's when I saw why it was so cold in the basement. The fire exit door, right next to the entrance to the chemistry lab, was propped open.

"Oh, you're not alone." I spun around when I heard the voice. The only sound I could make was a gasp before the hands closed around my neck, slamming me into the lockers.

Chapter 20

I scratched at the hands that held me pinned against the lockers by my throat, dropping my phone to the floor with a metallic clack.

"Where's your savior now?" Anthony snarled, his bloodshot blue eyes just inches from mine. The alcohol on his hot breath made my stomach churn.

"Hey, tough girl, I asked you a question," he growled, slamming me against the lockers again as his hands tightened around my neck. I felt a blunt pain in the back of my head where I'd hit the raised metal vents on the locker. I let out a choked scream, gasping for air as I tried to pry his meaty hands off my throat.

And then his chapped lips were on mine, invading my mouth as I coughed and grunted out feeble screams, trying to breathe. I twisted my head from side to side, pressing my lips shut as tightly as I could. My aching head was filled with the stale, sour smell of alcohol and body odor. My feet kicked, my hands frantically scratched his face, my nails dug into his cheek as I tried to cause him pain, distract him, something to get him away from me. Blindly, I clawed at his eyes, tearing a gash near his left eye. For a moment, he flinched, releasing my neck as he clutched his bleeding face. I took my chance, raising my knee with a sharp jerk and connecting with Anthony's crotch. He doubled over with a grunt, and I shoved him in the chest, pushing him off me.

"You stupid bitch," he groaned, lunging forward with one thick hand that grabbed a fistful of my hair as I tried to run for the fire exit. My head snapped backward as he sharply yanked on my hair. My ankle wobbled and I fell to the floor, sprawled out at his feet as I gasped for air.

"You ruined my life," he bellowed, towering over me and blocking my path in the hallway, his palms spread out to touch the lockers and the opposite wall. I noticed a smear of blood—my blood—against the metal slots next to his thumb, and my stomach twisted.

"You did it to yourself," I choked out, reaching a hand to the back of my head and feeling a wet spot where my hair was matted with blood. My eyes scanned the narrow, empty hallway for a weapon—any kind of weapon. My gaze fell on my lock, dangling there unlocked. If I could unhook it quickly, maybe I could hit him with it....

"Anthony! What are you doing?" The shrill voice echoed through the small area, sounding more panicked each time it bounced off the walls.

Anthony straightened up and looked at his palm, where he clutched a fistful of my hair. He held his palm out and let the tangled wad of hair drift to the floor before looking at Kristin and laughing. He actually laughed.

"I'm doing what I want, Krissy." He turned his menacing glare on a wide-eyed Kristin, who stood at the base of the staircase, staring at me in horror as I inched out of Anthony's sight and toward the fire exit.

"This isn't what we talked about," she screamed, stamping her crystal-covered feet. "You were just supposed to scare her and make her go to Casey so you'd get allowed back in school."

"That was never going to happen," Anthony growled.

"That's what you told me! It was *your* idea! It was *your* plan!" Kristin cried, her usual composure just a memory as her face twisted with the realization that she'd made a deal with the devil.

"Well, plans change." He scowled at her. Kristin occupied all of his attention so I stifled a cough, pulling myself off the floor.

"No, Ant, this will get me in trouble, too! I can't get kicked out!"

Kristin ran up to him, beating her fists weakly against his broad chest. He didn't even react—it was like hitting a brick building. "I didn't sign up for this," she wailed. "Just forget it, it's over!"

"I'll tell you when it's over!" Anthony punctuated his command with a quick, but powerful, backhand across Kristin's face.

Blood immediately streamed from her nose, dripping on her cleavage and dress, staining it with darker crimson splotches. Kristin whimpered, covering her face with her hand as Anthony backed her up against the wall, his muscles bulging menacingly underneath his long-sleeved black shirt.

"Don't you ever tell me what to do again," he snarled in her face as she began sobbing, her tears mixing with her blood.

"That's right, cry. It's all you're good for." Anthony's voice was chillingly calm as he rested his palms on either side of Kristin's head, trapping her between his massive arms. She cast a terrified glance over his shoulder at me as I steadied myself on my feet, reaching for my phone from where it had fallen. My hands shook as I kept my eyes on Anthony's back, my fingers closing around the small silver case. *Just stay quiet, run outside and call the cops, call Brendan.*

I slowly started backing away from Anthony—when my phone rang. Reminded of my presence, Anthony whirled around, the base madness spreading over his face as he targeted me in his gaze. I saw my lock dangling within inches of my reach; I grabbed it and aimed for his head, chucking it right at his face.

I didn't wait to see if the metal lock connected with him, but I heard him grunt as I whirled around, running for the fire exit. I shoved open the heavy door and raced up the stone stairs, which let me out right near the rear entrance of the school—the entrance that led into the gym. I pulled on the door—locked. Of course it's locked. It's always locked from the outside. I could hear the music—Brendan's music—taunting me through the door, see the lights through the high windows that I could never reach without a ladder.

I started running around the block to the main entrance, but a chilling thought brought me to a halt. *What if he's waiting for you in front of the school? Just run somewhere, just run and hide.*

I raced toward Fifth Avenue, trying to keep my thoughts clear as I ran for my life. Go somewhere with people—go to the Met. There were always people hanging out on the steps of the Met. He wouldn't dare attack me in plain view.

Within minutes I had reached Fifth Avenue. The avenue was flanked on one side by the long stone wall that framed Central Park, and on the other, wealthy East Side homes. I could see the Met in the distance, shining from the spotlights that lit it up at night. I heard two sounds—my own heartbeat, throbbing in my chest, and my own soft footfalls, the rapid but light sound of the satin slippers on pavement as I ran, afraid to look behind me.

And then I heard the third sound—a heavy, thudding, rhythmic sound. I glanced over my shoulder as I ran, and my blood ran cold—a large figure was following me, racing after me.

Even in the darkness I could make him out.

Anthony.

"You better run!" Distant but savage, his warning spurred me on. I ran faster, afraid if I tried to call someone I'd drop the phone, or lose speed. And that's all he'd need to catch up with me. I kept looking at the empty street, hoping to see a taxi or any car that I could flag down. *City that never sleeps my aching butt.*

The phone in my hand vibrated. I opened it and barely had it to my ears when I heard Brendan's frantic voice.

"Where are you? I heard your message, Em, are you okay?"

"Anthony's following me!" I screamed, gasping for air as I ran, feeling a sharp pain slice through my ankle every time my foot hit the sidewalk in the thin slippers.

"Where are you?" Brendan yelled.

"Met," I gasped. "People—there will be people there."

"I called the cops after I heard your message. I'm coming," he shouted. I shut the phone, holding it tightly as I pushed myself faster, seeing the white museum grow closer with each step.

Don't even look behind you. Just keep going. Don't waste any time.

I raced along the empty, dark sidewalk, the streetlights ahead of me flickering as the light inside them stuttered and died. It was as if I were running into a tunnel of darkness. I rounded the corner when I got to the Met, scanning the grass for the sight of anyone—any people, any classmates, even a stray homeless guy. Someone. I needed a witness; I needed someone to see me.

But it was empty. The night was so cold—too cold. But the temperature wasn't what set me shaking. I turned around—he was farther away, but he was still coming for me. And he wasn't going to stop.

In spite of myself, my muscles locked, immobile. Do I continue to run away, up Fifth Avenue? It was a straight shot—nowhere to hide, since the park wall was on one side, practically framing me as prey. Should I try to double back and go to Vince A?

I peered into the park—dark, silent. I could lose him in the park. I knew my way around.

I made my decision, running through the night-chilled grass into Central Park.

I stayed close to the rear of the museum, hoping to find a security guard or someone to help me. I shivered as I rested my back against the museum, trying to quiet my breathing as I listened for his pounding, heavy footsteps. All I heard was the wind rustling the dead leaves along the lawn.

My phone rang again—the tone echoing off the stone of the building as if you were ringing a Church bell. I grabbed it quickly.

"Brendan, no one's here. The Met was empty. I'm afraid," I whispered into the cold metal. "I don't know if I lost him."

"I'm close—where are you?" Brendan's breathing was heavy—it sounded like he was running to meet me.

"I'm behind the Met—I'm trying to lose him in the park." My voice shook as I slinked through the trees. I tried to avoid the lampposts, opting to stay hidden in the dark.

"Emma, don't do that—please, get out of the park. I'll be there in a minute." Brendan's voice was softly pleading, but I could hear the urgency behind it.

I cautiously stepped back on the pathway, looking behind me as I passed the Obelisk behind the Met.

"I think I lost him," I said, relieved.

"Where are you exactly?"

"Not too far from Belvedere Castle," I said, walking backward and watching the empty pathway, which twisted before me.

"I'll be there soon," Brendan vowed. "Just stay on the phone with me until then. Is there anyone there—a security guard, anyone?"

"No. Wait, I only see…" I squinted in the distance at a dark, shadowy form—was that a person? I couldn't tell.

And then the form began moving. It was running. It was coming for me.

"He's here," I choked.

My fight or flight kicked in—because I was flying. I ran along the pathway, berating myself with every throbbing footstep that I rapidly pounded into the dark pavement.

Stupid girl, stupid cliché. Run off into a deserted park. With an injured ankle, too. Find a security guard. Find someone.

And then I remembered my date with Brendan at Belvedere Castle. When security kicked us out.

I changed directions and started running for Belvedere Castle. It sat perched above the park, luminous and bright.

The castle was very close, and in less than a minute I was running up the steps that just two weeks ago, I leisurely climbed with Brendan, blissful in our first date together. And now, I was speeding up the stairs, fearful for my life.

I burst into the stone plaza, flinging myself on the doors of the observatory. I yanked on the doorknob, banging loudly on the embellished windows.

"Help me!" I screamed, pounding on the doors until my already-raw palms split.

An older, gray-mustachioed man rounded the corner, swinging a flashlight and wearing a Parks Department uniform.

"Miss, we're closed," he said sternly. Then he got a good look at me and his face softened.

"Are you okay, miss?" he asked gently. "Did someone hurt you?"

"Yes, please, help me," I croaked, still gripping my phone. "I'm being followed. I was attacked at school—I've been running...."

"Okay, miss, you're safe now," the man said, his voice gentle as he approached me with his palms forward. Only then did I realize how wild I must have looked.

The guard pressed a button on the radio attached to his shoulder.

"Hey, this is Yanek up at Belvedere—"

His kind eyes rolled back in his head as his knees collapsed underneath him, his jaw dropping in an uncontrolled, stomach-twisting way. My eyes followed his fall—and then they looked up.

"You're so predictable, Emma. Running to the fancy lit-up building for help," Anthony mocked me in a high-pitched imitation of a girl's voice, fluttering his hands about excitedly. I noticed he held a bloody rock in his right hand, and he stepped over the man's crumpled-up body, throwing the red-smeared stone to the side.

"You're crazy!" I screamed, backing away from the observatory.

"No, I'm desperate. It's different." Anthony took two steps forward for every one that I took back.

"Because of you, I have to go away. My life is over." He snarled, baring teeth that shone in the shimmering, flickering light of the lampposts.

"No, I can change things. I can go to Principal Casey," I cried, stumbling backward down the steps to the rocks.

Stall, the cops have to be close. Brendan will find me.

"It's too late for that." Anthony scowled, lunging forward and losing his footing on one of the stones that lined the base of the plaza.

"No, it's not," I said hastily, trying to make my voice sound sincere. "My aunt's on the board, Brendan's mom is, too. We'll get you back in the school. We'll do whatever it takes."

"Like I can go back there now," he scoffed. "That part of my life is over."

I looked around me, trying to figure out my options. The guard lay motionless—but his radio sounded like it was going off. Someone had to come up here to look for him. The cops were on their way. And there was no chance I could hop that fence onto the rocks without Brendan's help. Stay out here and let him pound on me until the cops get here? Try to stall?

Stall, stall, stall.

"It doesn't have to be over," I bargained, my pleas getting more creative as he closed the gap between us. "Imagine, you'll look like a hero, finally vindicated. I'll even transfer schools. I can go back home. I don't need to stay here."

"Everyone knows already," he shouted, and I noticed the blood-crusted cut above his eyebrow. I guess I had better aim with that lock than I thought I did.

I tried another tactic. "I think they'll just be impressed with how you stood up for yourself. I mean, I am," I said, trying to make my voice sound flirtatious. Instead, I just warbled shakily.

"Who cares? Everything's over for me—because of you!" Anthony's face turned red with fury—the same look he had when he'd confronted me in the quad. Only Brendan wasn't here to save me.

"I can fix it, I promise!" I begged, letting the tears flow down my cheeks. I didn't have the power to stop them. "Please—"

This time, no one was there to step in. My hands shot up to protect my face, but I was too late. At first, everything went dark—just for a second, a calming, dead blackness. Then the pain exploded across my left cheek like a flashbulb, popping and leaving spots in my vision. The taste of my own blood filled my mouth as my teeth cut into my own cheek.

I pressed my palm against my cheek, but it only made the throbbing worse. And then there was more pain—a familiar agony as Anthony's hands closed around my neck, his fingers twisting the chain that held my pendant. The thin silver links cut into my skin like wire, more effectively choking me than he could do with his hands alone.

I wheezed, my fingers feeble as they searched my throat, trying to pull the chain off me. I could feel my eyes straining as my fingers felt numb against my own skin. Then sudden relief—the chain snapped, my medallion dropping to the floor with a metal plink before rolling away.

My knees crumpled and I fell over on the stone ground, choking for air as the panic began to shake me.

Angelique had said we'd know the threat, the danger, because I'd somehow lose my pendant. The danger was here. The medallion had snapped off, rolling away to wait for my soul when it came to reside in a new body.

Because I was about to be killed.

I screamed as loudly as I could with my rough voice, trying to call anyone's attention.

I pushed myself off the floor, but Anthony grabbed my upper arm, flinging me against the wrought-iron bars effortlessly. My right shoulder took the brunt of the blow, throbbing until it was eclipsed by another strike, a sickening ball of pain in my stomach as Anthony smashed his fist into my torso. I blindly aimed for his throat, throwing all my weight into a punch that only connected with his shoulder. He barely felt it. I fought back, hitting, pulling his hair, scratching his face, punching his nose, his throat—anything I could get—but my weak efforts seemed to just fuel Anthony's rage.

Then another flashbulb blow—everything was dark a little longer this time, and when the explosion flashed before my eyes, it was sharper, more painful. Louder as it reverberated within my head.

"Emma!" I heard the voice, through the bright flashes of pain. It was dim but it was there. And then the bursts of pain stopped as I grabbed onto the metal bars, keeping myself standing.

I forced my eyes to focus. Brendan and Anthony were twisted on the ground, Brendan on top of Anthony, pinning him down like he had in the quad. Only this time, Brendan wasn't hesitating—his knuckles connected to Anthony's face with a quick motion, the brute force behind it evident when I heard a sickening crunch. Blood flowed from Anthony's broken nose as he screamed in pain.

Brendan didn't stop his assault, landing another powerful punch right in Anthony's face. Fueled by his own agony and bloodlust, Anthony kicked wildly, causing Brendan to lose his balance and his grip. The monster's oversize fist sliced through the air, striking Brendan on the right side of his chin. Brendan pitched forward, and Anthony took advantage of his distraction, leaping up and kicking Brendan in the stomach. He groaned, and Anthony raised his leg, ready to stomp on Brendan's head. From his prone position on the floor, Brendan kicked Anthony in the back of the knee, knocking him off balance so he stumbled forward. Brendan heaved himself off the stone floor, this time landing a fast punch in Anthony's stomach. But Anthony took the hit well, slamming his beefy fist into Brendan's chest and causing him to falter.

Frantically, I looked around for a weapon. I wiped the blood out of my eyes as I searched for something, anything, to hit Anthony with, to incapacitate him. He wouldn't be able to hurt Brendan. He *can't* hurt him.

I saw something shiny glisten in the distance—my cell phone. I ran for it, falling on my knees and dialing 911.

"Help, we're up at Belvedere Castle in Central Park, we're being attacked! The guard's unconscious, help us!" I screamed into the phone before dropping it, leaving the call still connected as I grabbed a splintered-off piece of a fallen tree branch. It was no more than a stick, but I raised it like a knife as I approached Anthony from behind.

His shirt was a thick black thermal, so I put all my force into it, plunging the sharpest end of the stick between his shoulder blades. It pierced the fabric, ripping into his skin and twisting itself into his flesh as the rest of the stick broke off in my hand.

Anthony fell forward onto his knees with a bellow, his hand flailing behind him as he tried to remove my crude weapon.

Finally, in the distance, we heard the sirens. Brendan's green eyes found me, and for a minute we thought it was over.

Then Anthony's head snapped up at the sound of the sirens—and a manic look took over his face. He lunged forward, shoving Brendan back and using his massive arms, hoisted himself over the stone wall, around the fence and onto the rocks.

"Emma, just get out of here," Brendan ordered. "I'll take care of him. He's not getting away." Brendan ran after Anthony, pulling himself up over the wall and around the fence.

"No, Brendan, please!" I screamed, trying to follow them and not quite able to get my footing.

They were just a few feet away but they may have as well been wrestling on the other side of the world. I gripped the bars, trying to scale the fence and watching in agony as Brendan and Anthony had a bare-knuckled brawl on the rocks, more than a hundred feet above the Turtle Pond.

Brendan was fast—but Anthony was desperate. He didn't have the precise aim Brendan boasted, but he had an almost feral strength, blindly landing punches with his grapefruit-size fists.

I jumped up again, and this time, I was able to get a grip on the stone wall. I hauled myself over it, and landed on my ankle with a thud.

I gasped at the pain, and Brendan jerked his head my way. Anthony took advantage of the distraction, launching an uppercut that connected right underneath Brendan's chin. He stumbled backward, losing his footing and falling backward mere feet from the edge of the rocks. Anthony towered before him, his fists curled at his side, panting. His silhouette looked more otherworldly, more demonic than I could have ever imagined—this hulking, dark figure that had come straight from Hell for me.

One kick and Anthony could send Brendan over the edge, more than a hundred feet down.

I dashed behind Anthony, farther out on the rocks.

"Emma, no! What are you doing?" Brendan yelled, scrambling to his feet.

"Over here," I screamed. "Hey, jackass! Over here."

Anthony whipped around, his massive chest heaving as he faced me, wiping the blood from his nose.

"Ant, I'm the one you want to fight. Not her. What, can't you fight a man? You have to fight a *girl?*" Brendan taunted, approaching Anthony.

But the monster just moved closer to me, twisting his body to keep us both in his line of sight. Anthony began walking back and forth in between us. Panicked, I looked around me—I was at the end of the rocks—the very end. All he had to do was race toward me and push me.

Anthony coiled, then relaxed his body. Beyond him, I saw Brendan's face twist with a thousand different emotions. Panic. Fear. Fury. Rage. Vengeance.

Anthony's toying with you. He's got you trapped. It's like he's playing with his food.

The lights, the dreams, the belief that I could be the one to break the curse, it was all a lie. All just a game. A game I was going to lose. I wasn't going to survive this. I had all the warning signs—and yet I'd just run into danger's welcoming arms and given it a kiss.

Anthony's blood-soaked blond hair whipped around in the wind as he turned toward me, his eyes gleaming as he picked his target.

He began running straight for me. I tried to get out of the way, but my feet wouldn't move as quickly as I wanted them to. I felt like I was in a dream, where you're trapped in slow motion.

And then I was shoved aside, my ankle collapsing as Brendan pushed me onto the frigid rocks. The tumbling mass of limbs rolled past me, disappearing into the blackness of the drop below.

A guttural shout, then a splash. And then, it was quiet. Nothing but the distant sirens getting louder and the sound of my own ragged breathing as I lay motionless on the frozen rocks where I had fallen. Where I was now alone.

Chapter 21

I felt the ripping in my heart, like whatever stitches had tenuously held it together were slowly being picked apart, one by one, as it dawned on me what had just happened.

Brendan had saved me.

He pushed me out of the way.

And now he was gone.

He was gone. Not me.

Before the final stitch came loose I heard it. The muffled groaning, the strangulated breathing. With raw fingers, I dragged myself to the edge of the cold rocks and saw the hand, the bloodied knuckles clutching frantically to a jagged triangle of rock that jutted out from the cliff.

"Brendan?" I whimpered hopefully, stretching my hands as far down as they could go.

"Take my hand," I yelled, hoping against hope that I was about to help pull Brendan, my savior, to safety—and not the monster.

His other hand clawed at the cliff wall, grabbing hold of a small ridge.

And then I saw them: the glimmering green eyes that peered up from underneath a tangled shock of black hair.

"Brendan," I breathed, relieved.

He only grunted in reply, his feet scraping against the cliff wall as he tried to find some purchase against the rocks. I grabbed for his left hand, while his right still clutched to the triangle of stone that stuck out like a knife.

With my left hand in his and my right hand curled around his wrist, I pulled up as hard as I could. My muscles burned. My arms felt like they were being ripped out of their sockets. But I didn't have the strength to pull him up. I tried to brace myself against the rocks, but my ankle screamed in protest, crumbling when I tried to put any pressure on it.

"Just hold on," I groaned, wincing through the pain. "Help is coming, just hold on."

And then Brendan's hand started to slip.

"No!" I cried, wrapping my hands around his more tightly. I clawed at his sleeve, which just ripped underneath my fingers.

"Emma..." The tone of his voice sounded final as he continued kicking against the cliff, the smooth soles of his dress shoes skidding off the rough surface of the rocks.

"No, Brendan! No! I won't lose you! Help me!" I shouted. I couldn't lose him now. What was the point?

"What good was it to warn me?" I screamed, my voice shaking as I jerked closer to the end, Brendan pulling me down instead of me pulling him up. "Don't warn me if you're not going to help me! Ethan, help me! Where are you? Help me now!"

Brendan's hand slipped another half an inch as his right hand grabbed at the rocks.

"Give me your hand," a youngish male voice next to me commanded. I hadn't even heard the officer arrive. I didn't even look up, I just felt the warmth next to me as another hand shot out, grabbing Brendan's left hand.

We both pulled, hoisting Brendan out of the abyss. I fell back as Brendan lunged forward onto the wintry rocks, his legs still dangling off the edge of the cliff.

Brendan eclipsed everything else. I saw nothing but him, my breathing still heavy as I gazed at the face I loved—cut and bruised, but flush with color, as he braced his palms against the frigid rocks, panting with exertion. He was still alive. He had saved my life.

I wrapped my arms around him, kissing Brendan's face as he pulled his legs under him on the frosty rocks. He slid his arms around my waist, stroking my back as I buried my face into his neck, dampening his collar with tears.

"Thank you, sir," Brendan said over my shoulder, his voice rough as he regarded the officer. And then he pulled back, blinking a few times.

"You— You're— I know you?" Brendan said, his statement coming out like a question. The officer stood up, placing his hand on my shoulder and giving me a squeeze.

"It was my pleasure," the officer said. I turned around to see him but I couldn't make out his face—he was backlit by the flashlights bathing the plaza in swaths of light. A little late, but the cavalry had finally come.

"We're over here," Brendan called, his voice rough with exhaustion. Keeping his arms around me, he rose to a standing position, lifting me with him and helping me limp across the uneven rocks.

"Walk this way and put your hands where we can see them," came a stern voice from behind the glaring light that flooded our faces.

"There's an officer here with us," Brendan said gesturing to his right. But when I looked, there was no one there.

"Hello?" I croaked out, my voice hoarse. "Sir, where did you go?"

"I don't know," Brendan said, his black eyebrows furrowed with confusion.

"I said, put your hands where we can see them!" the officer in the plaza called.

"She hurt her ankle, I have to help her walk," Brendan called.

"Hands in the air *now,*" the voice demanded.

After a short kiss to my temple, Brendan put his hands in the air. I followed suit.

"Miss, are you okay?" the voice continued.

I nodded, my throat too raw and clogged with emotion to talk.

We shuffled closer and I noticed the officer had his gun drawn—and kept it trained on Brendan.

"*He's* not the one who attacked me!" I coughed out, throwing my arm in front of Brendan frantically. "The guy—Anthony—I think he's— He went over the edge of the cliff."

We got to the fence and a burly officer with a moustache helped me climb over. I noticed the security guard, Mr. Yanek, sitting off to the side while a paramedic tended to his head wound.

"Is he going to be okay?" I asked the officer nearest me, who put away his gun. His shiny badge read Lynott.

"He'll have one hell of a headache and need stitches, but he'll be okay," he said briskly, eyeing the two of us. "Why don't we have the medics look the two of you over also? It looks like you've had a rough night."

"That's an understatement," I mumbled, moving my jaw from side to side and feeling the searing pain shoot across my face as another officer led me and Brendan to separate collapsible stretchers. We were examined by medics and interviewed by the officers, but even though he was several yards away, I could hear Brendan asking—okay, demanding might be a better word—when he could see me and make sure I was okay.

I had just finished giving my account of Anthony's assault to a different cop when Officer Lynott approached me after talking to Brendan.

"Sounds like you're quite the strong girl." He looked at me with a hint of admiration in his eyes. "Your boyfriend says you helped lift him up when he was dangling off those rocks."

"There was another officer out there—he's really the one who pulled Brendan up," I said, shaking my head and then wincing when the movement hurt. "Where did he go? I didn't get the chance to thank him."

"Miss, there were no officers on the rocks with you," Officer Lynott said gently.

"No, there was," I protested hoarsely. "But I didn't get to see his face."

"Emma hit her head a few times tonight," Brendan said, hurriedly limping over while clutching his side. His black shirt still bore a dirty footprint from Anthony kicking him. "I think she might be a little confused."

"No, he was there," I insisted as Brendan stood before me, gently tilting my face from side to side, his frown deepening as he surveyed the damage.

Then he brushed my tangled, bloodied hair back off my neck and stared at me in horror.

"Did you see this?" He showed the medic my throbbing neck. "Emma's going to the hospital, right? Is she going to be okay? Can you look at this again?"

"I don't think any permanent damage is done, but I've recommended that she go to the hospital," the medic mused, indulging Brendan with another exam of my aching throat even though she had already thoroughly checked it out. "You both should. We'll know after an X-ray, but I'd say you've definitely got a cracked rib. And, miss, you've got some serious bruising and cuts. I think you may have a concussion."

Then the medic noticed the scar on my arm.

"Whoa, what's that from?" Officer Lynott asked.

"Car accident a few months ago," I mumbled, staring down the ripped tulle of my dress.

"Miss Connor, you have nine lives," he said seriously. "Good for you."

I tried to shrug, but it was too painful. Sitting there, finally safe—the adrenaline rush was over and I felt *everything*. Every cut, every bruise, every last ache reverberated through me, intensifying each time it ricocheted around my body before settling in my increasingly throbbing head.

"Miss, is this yours? I noticed something shiny by the stairs and found this." I looked up to find a female officer jogging over with something in her hand. I couldn't make it out—my vision was getting a little hazy.

It felt like an ice-cold claw was squeezing my heart. *No. Please don't be my necklace.* It wasn't going to end. It would never end. The curse was going to come for me, keep coming, until it killed me. Until it killed us.

Terrified, I looked at Brendan, who just kissed my forehead gently.

"We'll get through this," he promised.

"Is this yours?" the officer asked again. I looked down at her hand to see her holding my badly scratched cell phone.

"Um, yeah," I breathed, my voice and my body trembling with relief. "That's my phone."

Seeing me shake, the medic had me lie down on the gurney

for a moment—but I sat upright again, ready to continue arguing about the officer who helped me pull Brendan up. But as
soon as I sat up, I fell right back down with a searing headache
and pain in my side. I felt every single injury acutely, as if my
senses were hyperaware.

I didn't realize I was moaning until the medic spoke. "See,
it's a good thing we're taking you to the hospital," she said, and
I was dimly aware that I was on the move; the stretcher was
being pushed down the winding pathway toward the waiting
ambulance. Brendan walked—or hobbled, rather—alongside
me, holding my hand. He insisted on going in the ambulance
with me.

"Officer Lynott, what's happening with Anthony?" Brendan asked.

"We have an APB out on him with your description but
that's a pretty big drop. I don't think we'll find him. Well, we
won't find him on land," Officer Lynott said pointedly.

I squeezed my eyes shut and shook my head, which actually
hurt.

"We can give you something for the pain," the medic offered, and I just nodded, keeping my eyes closed; the glare
from the lampposts was like a searing burn into my head.
Once we were loaded in the ambulance, I felt a needle jab at
my arm—and everything went blissfully black.

Narrow slits of light stabbed at a throbbing pain in my head.
That pain intensified as my eyes opened more.

Someone gripped my right hand. I squeezed back, ignoring
the pain. The human contact felt too good.

I tried to force my eyes to adjust to the glaring light in
the room. It was like the light was trying to stab me in the
brain.

"The light…hurts," I mumbled. The hand disappeared, and a moment later, the room was darker. The hand returned.

"Is that better?" It was rough with exhaustion, but I knew that voice. I opened my eyes more easily this time.

"Brendan?" I turned my head toward where the hand was— and he was there, relief and worry fighting for control of his handsome features. From what I could see of it, at least—I was having some trouble focusing.

"You're okay?" I wheezed, reaching out to touch his face, which I now noticed was pretty badly cut up. He had a split lip, the beginnings of a black eye and a few cuts on his cheekbone, chin and forehead. Brendan just turned his head to meet my hand, kissing my raw palm and holding my hand against his cheek.

"Aw, you're all banged up," I said, stroking his face.

"Me?" He snorted, brushing my bangs back off my face. The gesture felt good—normal, even.

"Me? You," I mumbled, a little woozy.

"You got the good painkillers, I see," he observed, chuckling.

"Mmm." I nodded in agreement. "Are you okay?"

"I'm okay, Em," Brendan said gently. "Cracked rib, some cuts and bruises, but nothing permanent."

"It looks like it hurts."

"I've been in fistfights before," Brendan said dismissively. "I'm just worried about you."

"What's the damage?" I asked, vaguely remembering some kind of scan from a few hours ago. The last time I was in a hospital bed, I had a broken wrist and a line of stitches in my arm from Henry's version of driving.

"A concussion, a fractured ankle, and a ton of bruises and

cuts." His dark eyebrows knotted together in worry as Brendan ticked off my maladies darkly, reaching over me to intertwine his fingers with my other hand, as well.

"Concussion," I repeated. "Could that explain why I imagined an officer there? I don't understand...." I let my voice trail off, until I realized that Brendan had a peculiar look on his face.

"Did you see a cop?" I whispered.

Brendan nodded in agreement, his mouth set in a grimace.

"I don't understand," I said again. "Where did he go? Maybe he wasn't a cop and was just a regular person?"

"Emma, honey, it's not important. Let's talk about this after you're feeling better," he said, holding my hand and kissing it.

And then I realized that my ring was gone.

"Brendan, my ring," I cried, then felt a stabbing pain in my head again. "Ow!"

"It's okay, sweetheart. It's just your concussion. It'll get better."

"But my ring," I whispered.

"I have it. The nurse gave it to me," he reassured me. "They had to take it off for the CT scan. The ring—it's safe." He laughed a quiet laugh to himself. "That ring."

In spite of my glorious painkillers I recognized that loaded tone and knew there was no way I was leaving the hospital without the full story. Brendan definitely knew something he wasn't telling me.

"Why are you being weird about my ring?" I mumbled.

"What?" He laughed awkwardly. "I'm not being weird."

"You're not a good liar. You're being weird."

"Um, now's not the right time," Brendan said in a soothing

voice. "You should just rest." He started stroking my bangs back again, a move which could easily lull me to sleep. How sneaky.

"No secrets," I warned, my thoughts getting a little clearer.

Brendan sighed, exhaling a heavy breath that seemed to come from his feet.

"Remember how you asked why I got you sapphire?"

I nodded, and he continued. "I didn't know it at the time, but your brother—" his voice got very soft over that word "—is the reason I bought you that ring."

Brendan pursed his lips, looking down at my arm and stroking the hand-shaped bruises softly with his thumb. "After we had that—I don't want to call it a fight, so I'll say *disagreement*—last Sunday, I felt pretty bad about not wanting to hear about the witch stuff. You didn't deserve that. So I decided to get you a present, just something small that you could wear as a reminder of how much you mean to me."

"A diamond-and-sapphire ring is something little?" I squeaked, shifting uncomfortably in my bed, which set my head to aching and buzzing.

"What? It's not a *big* ring," Brendan shrugged. "Anyway, it was on my mind. So I was going to get you amethyst, your birthstone. And then the night before I went to the jeweler, I had this dream. And this guy was there. He told me to get you sapphire. He said that you would need something to help bring out your power."

"Angelique told me that," I admitted. "Sapphire amplifies a witch's powers. We used it in that spell we did—to give me my natural powers."

Brendan nodded. "The next day, the jeweler showed me the sapphire rings, and I just felt like I should pay attention."

Brendan paused. "The guy in my dream, Emma. Well, he

looked exactly like—no, I'd say he *was* the officer who helped you pull me up. I know it sounds crazy, completely insane, but, Em, I just know it was him. I recognized him, because, well, he looked like you."

I stared at Brendan confused for a moment, before the pieces fell into place.

"Ethan?" I asked, my voice coming out very small.

"I think so," Brendan said, his voice very gentle. "I think the sapphire helped you tap into whatever magic you have when we were out on the cliff. Or at least helped you believe that you could. And you summoned him."

"He tried warning me so many times," I whispered. "It's like he knew I'd need more help…."

I let my voice trail off as I tried to sniff back the tears, which only hurt my head more. I winced, feeling the hot saltwater stream down my cheek.

Brendan grabbed a tissue and tried to wipe my nose, which only made me incredibly embarrassed on top of the pain. It was like pouring hot sauce on a paper cut. It's bad enough I was bruised and bloody—did he need to see me all snotty, too?

"Give me that," I pouted, grabbing the scratchy tissue and blotting at my nose.

"By the way, your aunt went to make a phone call." Brendan changed the subject. "You're just in for observation now, you're going home in a few hours."

"She's here? Is she mad?"

Brendan shook his head, amused. "Mad? No, crazy girl. She's worried about you."

Then he chuckled. "I think she can't decide if she hates me because I'm always somewhere around your troubles, or if she approves of me because I always do what I can to help you."

"She'll approve of you," I promised, coughing and wincing at how it burned my throat. Brendan frowned and gingerly touched my neck, which I had no doubt was a billion shades of purple. "What about you—is your family here?"

"Oh, I'm more or less discharged, I'm just waiting for my parents to get me." Brendan kissed my fingers as he talked. "They're being helicoptered in from some Smithsonian thing in Washington. So I don't know how much time we have right now."

I grabbed his hand, clutching it tightly in spite of the pain that ricocheted through my body.

"I can't believe I almost lost you," I said, reaching out to touch Brendan's cheek. He leaned into my touch as a few more—okay, a lot more—tears escaped. He wiped them away gently before handing me another tissue for my nose.

"Brendan, do you think we broke—" I stopped short, afraid to say the words. Afraid to jinx it.

"Don't think about it right now, Emma," Brendan soothed, his eyes shining with the same hopeful emotion.

"No, tell me!" I pleaded. "Do you think we broke the curse?"

"I hope so," Brendan murmured, his voice shaking. "Emma, when I got there, and you were so scared—I felt my heart break. I thought that was it."

"It was supposed to be. But you saved my life," I whispered, letting the tears come in earnest this time.

"It's my fault you were ever in danger." Brendan shook his head, his green eyes downcast. "I almost killed you."

"No!" I grabbed his hand more tightly. "You saved me."

Brendan pulled my hand up to his lips again. "You're the one who saved me, Emma. In more ways than just pulling me up off the rocks. You've changed my life."

He gently placed my hand next to me in the bed, then

pulled himself out of the chair, wincing a little as he held his hand to his rib cage. Then Brendan leaned over me, touching his lips to mine very softly.

"I love you, Emma. Always."

Chapter 22

Thanks to the concussion and fractured ankle, I was pretty much confined to my bed for a week.

"I feel like I'm on house arrest," I grumbled after a few days. Brendan just told me I was under arrest for being "dangerously sexy." I rolled my eyes at him—which ached like crazy at the time—but I had to admit, hearing Brendan call me "sexy" was worth going a little stir-crazy. Especially when I looked like the loser in a boxing match. Besides, my vision would sporadically get really blurry—and the last thing I needed now was to go walking off into traffic. Especially when a search of the Turtle Pond turned up nothing but turtles. Meaning: Anthony was out there. Somewhere.

The thought terrified me, especially since Brendan was well enough to return to school almost immediately.

"I'm scared he's going to attack you on the subway or something," I fretted on the phone to Brendan, the night before his first day back.

"Emma, I'll be fine." Brendan laughed, like I was worried about him crossing the street and he found my concern endearing.

"We don't know where he is."

"I didn't want to tell you this, Em, but my dad's got some security on retainer. Ex-cops, that sort of thing," Brendan admitted. "It's just for a little while. I have no idea who they are, but they're just supposed to keep an eye out to make sure Anthony doesn't get near either one of us."

"Near…either one of us?"

"Yeah, he's got security for you, too," Brendan confessed. "What can I say, my dad likes you. He thinks you're spunky."

I had met Brendan's parents at the hospital—it was kind of incredible to see Aaron and Laura Salinger together. Talk about opposites attracting. Where Laura was frosty and proper, Aaron was warm and more than a little bawdy. The rubber glove jokes alone…

"So we have security detail," I muttered. "I wish I could say I minded, but I'm glad that you're going to be safe. At least, until they find Anthony."

But according to Brendan, his first day back was exceedingly uneventful—in terms of surprise attacks by sociopathic teenagers, at least. I should have known he was downplaying it. Cisco clued me in to the near social hurricane Brendan's return to school had caused. Not that Brendan would tell me: after his first day back, he brushed it off as "fine" and brought my books over so I could keep up with my studies—especially since midterms were right after Christmas break. Oh, joy. As if Latin didn't make my head already feel like it was cracking open before the concussion…. But tucked into the back of my Latin textbook was a little present—Brendan's old midterm. Cheating, schmeating. Hey, a concussed girl's gotta do what a concussed girl's gotta do.

Ever the charmer, Brendan—who healed ridiculously fast, the show-off—brought some kind of snack and coffee for Aunt Christine every afternoon after school, still trying to work his charisma on her. She had significantly thawed to the idea of me having such a serious relationship—and the fact that Brendan took a dive off a cliff for me helped a lot. I had never realized before how tough Christine was to win over. Ashley's boyfriend would probably have to resolve all third-world debt before Christine would even let him in the door.

I ached from head to toe—literally—but that wasn't even the worst of my problems. New York media *really* liked the story. I'd known the Salingers were rich. And I'd known they were "prominent." But I had no idea what that meant to New York society until Ashley called me, squealing at the top of her lungs to let me know we were the lead item on the *New York Post*'s famed Page Six.

I hobbled up out of bed, grabbing my laptop to check out the story. There it was: *Tycoon's Son Risks Life for Gal Pal.*

"Oh, no," I groaned. The photos they used were our school ID shots. With a rakish smirk and unkempt hair, Brendan looked like he could be staring out from the cover of *Alternative Press*. And I looked like the cover model for *Swamp Thing Weekly*. I scanned through the story—troubled former student attacked me, Brendan saved my life—and then I got to the last line.

> Anthony Caruso is believed to have fled the country. His father, noted defense lawyer Ron "The Piranha" Caruso, is being questioned by police.

I wasn't sure how to feel. I didn't feel comfortable wishing him dead, but only because I knew that was a crummy thing to wish. I should have felt guilty for hoping the police would find him on the bottom of the pond, but I didn't. Anthony was still out there—somewhere. Who knew if or when he'd return? Two weeks? Two years? Would he show up on my doorstep when I was thirty, holding a grudge for years?

I kept hoping for some starlet to be arrested for a DUI to get the attention diverted somewhere else.

The media eventually moved on to another story—some actress's sex tape leaked online, and let's just say she was pretty freaky. And even though I had to put up with stares and whispers from my classmates when I returned to school—especially because I still had a few lingering, nasty cuts on my face—after a few weeks the most dramatic event in my life was me, breaking the laces on my Converse high-tops.

And then, one Saturday around Thanksgiving, about three weeks after the "Rumble on the Rocks" (as one paper called it), Angelique came over.

I was lounging in bed, giving my still-tender ankle a break and pretending to study Latin, when, in fact, I was reading Pink Is the New Blog, when I heard Angelique's voice in the living room. Aunt Christine *adored* Angelique. Mostly, Christine figured her appearance, which was even more witchy when she wasn't wearing the school uniform—or suffering from the flu—meant that she was just dramatic. Aunt Christine loved high drama, and Angelique sure knew how to attract attention.

Angelique poked her head into my room. She had touched up her blond roots, and added a few white and navy-blue streaks to her jet-black hair. It worked on her.

"Hey, Em, how's it going?" she asked, her face brighter and happier than I'd seen it in, well…ever. She wasn't exactly a happy-go-lucky, skipping-down-the-street kind of girl.

"Still headachey from time to time, but okay," I complained, shutting my laptop and placing it on the nightstand.

"So, I haven't had the chance to ask you since you first came home—have you and Brendan talked about the curse at all?" she asked bluntly.

I shook my head. "Not since the little bit we talked about in the hospital," I admitted. "The necklace is gone—and I haven't had any dreams, signs, nada. And I have to be honest though, part of me feels like I lost Ethan all over again."

I scratched patterns into my fleece comforter to distract myself from welling up with tears. Angelique wasn't too big on public displays of affection and since the "Rumble on the Rocks"—I really hated that name—I'd been a highly emotional mess. Poor Brendan had to deal with me tearing up at least once an afternoon.

"So there have been zero signs that the curse is still active?" Angelique asked.

"Like I said, nothing. But what really worries me is this: I lost the medallion during Anthony's attack, but that doesn't mean I'm not still in danger, right?" I threw my hands in the air, frustrated. "I don't know whether to be relieved or ready for war. Was Anthony the big danger?"

Angelique pulled something out of her bag—it was the shiny red *Spells for the New Witch* book.

"I have to tell you something, but first promise me that you'll work on developing your powers."

"I really don't think I'm a witch. I think it was just a one-time thing, Angelique," I mused. "I've been trying to move things around the apartment with my mind for weeks. I got nothing."

"You're a witch, not telekinetic," Angelique corrected me, flipping her Technicolor hair and causing the stacked bangles on her wrist to clang together musically.

"What's the difference?"

"The difference, Emma, is that you can't move things with your mind."

"No way, that's not true," I protested. "I did in your room!"

"No, you did a spell in my room. You demanded your power, then you demanded a sign. And from what you've told me, that's how you conjured your brother's spirit. You performed a spell when you cried out for his help. The sapphire helped amplify your talent, but it was passionate, it was heartfelt—that was a spell."

"So I can't move things?" I asked, thoroughly confused.

"Not without a spell—you need to work on your craft," Angelique advised, laying the book on top of my laptop.

"Promise me you'll read it." She crossed her arms and regarded me solemnly.

"Okay," I agreed, and she smiled, relaxing her posture.

"So what else is new?" I asked, taking a swig of water from the bottle on my nightstand. "What did you want to tell—"

"Oh, just the biggest news ever!" Angelique interrupted. She practically danced over to her heavy black bag, her long black skirt swirling around her feet as she moved. She shoved my feet over so she could sit down, throwing the bag on the bed.

"You're in a good mood," I observed, and she just gave me a toothy smile with her purple-painted lips.

"I think you will be, too," she said, reaching into the bag and pulling out a pristine copy of *Hadrian's Medieval Legends*.

"Just take a look at what I have," Angelique said, bowing her head and holding the book up like Mufasa held up Simba in *The Lion King*. I expected sunbeams to burst forth from the book's cover.

"No way!" I shouted, then winced at the lingering dull thud

in my head. "Is the rest of the legend in there? Please tell me that we're okay."

"Just let me read the rest of the story."

"You're killing me, Angelique," I moaned. "Please, just a yes or no."

"It's better if I read it," she insisted.

I took her good mood as an excellent sign that I would *really* like what I was about to hear. I doubted she'd be this upbeat if the rest of the story said that, oh, a demon was going to kidnap me next, or that the spell could only be broken by Batman.

"By the way, Emma," Angelique said, flipping through the pages of the book as she searched for the tale of Lord Aglaeon. "My mom's friend said Hadrian had a descendant who's apparently a big expert on the supernatural. He lives in New York. I'm thinking of contacting him—I wonder just how many of these legends are actually true. I mean, if *your* story is in here, and is true—I wonder what else is. I bet you Hadrian was a witch, and this is his Book of Shadows." Her voice was getting more excited.

"What's that?" I asked.

"Kind of a cross between a journal and an instruction manual for witches. Every one of us keeps one." She paused, looking thoughtful. "I wonder if this isn't just a really flowery, well-written one." She sat still for a moment, lost in her thoughts.

I poked her with my foot.

"Shadows, schmadows, Angelique," I said, frustrated. "I'm dying here. Quite possibly, literally dying, so please tell me what the book says!"

"Sorry." She smiled apologetically, flipping the pages again. "Here it is."

She cleared her throat and I felt like someone had just

thrown ice water on me. I was terrified, hopeful, curious—but mostly terrified.

Angelique cleared her throat, and began reading the poem from the start.

"If, on your true love a crest is worn
Be cautious, from you that love will be torn
You'll be spellbound, enraptured until your last heartbeat
Which is numbered the moment your eyes meet
If freedom from the curse is your goal
Be warned, it takes a selfless soul
This curse can't be cured with a potion
Since a selfish act set it into motion
Ask yourself, would you perish
To save the life of the one you cherish?
Burden yourself with love's fate so tragic
Sacrificing yourself can break the magic
You'll need the strength of mind, body and heart
Then, true love shall not be torn apart
Break the spell of the evil charmer
If you are strong enough to be her armor
Summon the strength and heed this verse
It holds the key to breaking the curse."

I lay there, stunned.

"Do you get it?" Angelique asked excitedly. "Brendan was the key all along! He had to do what Archer didn't do—he had to be selfless. He had to do what was right for *you*. He had to risk himself. And he did!"

She paused. "I have to admit, I find Brendan slightly more tolerable now."

"So...the curse is...over?" I asked, my voice very small.

I felt like if I shouted it from the rooftops, it might not be true.

Angelique nodded emphatically. "I think so. But this is just the beginning. This book is insane! According to this, you guys are true love. Legit, real, honest true love. And it's magical, because it's so rare. There's one story, let me find it," Angelique mumbled, flipping the pages of the book.

"Wait, just wait. Pause!" I yelled, pulling myself up and sitting on my bed on my knees.

"The. Curse. Is. Broken." I took care to enunciate every word, not wanting to fully embrace this moment just yet. I flashed back to the showdown at Belvedere Castle, when we first thought we'd won—before Anthony made a run for it. I couldn't be sure I was going to be safe just yet.

"Yes, Emma." Angelique grinned. "It is my honest, expert opinion as the smartest witch you know that you are no longer cursed."

I jumped on Angelique, giving her a giant bear hug.

"Thank you so much," I whispered. She stiffly patted me on the back.

"Emma, honey, I don't do hugs." She winced, and I removed her from my enthusiastic embrace.

I held out my hands. "Can I have the book? Please? I need to see Brendan."

"I thought you were seeing him later?"

"I was, but this can't wait."

"Come on, we have a lot of work to do." Angelique shook her head disapprovingly. "I mean, we've got to get you going on your spells and basic herbs...."

"Angelique, this involves him, I have to tell him that we're safe."

"Fine!" Angelique threw her hands in the air dramatically, handing over *Hadrian's Medieval Legends*.

"I'll just leave this here," she said, tapping on the red-covered spell book.

"See you Monday," Angelique said, throwing her bag over her shoulder as I started cramming my feet into my lace-up Converse sneakers, the only shoes that fit over my bulky ankle bandage. Angelique started for the door, then turned around to address me over her shoulder.

"I'll want you to have read the first two chapters of that book by Monday. We'll discuss it at lunch."

"You're giving me homework?" I asked incredulously.

After nodding and bowing with a flourish, Angelique let herself out of my room. I heard her saying goodbye to Aunt Christine as I dialed Brendan's number, cradling the phone in my shoulder as I tried to find a big enough bag to hold the book.

"Hey, sweetheart," came the sexy, deep voice on the other end.

"I need to see you right now." The urgency was clear in my voice. "Everything's okay—it's better than okay—but I need to see you. I can't wait until later."

"Come over now," Brendan offered. "I was actually going to call you after I jumped in the shower—my parents left early so I'm here alone now. I'll send the car."

"No time, I'll grab a cab. I'm on my way," I said, shutting the phone, deciding to just empty my bookbag completely, dumping all the contents on the floor to make room for *Hadrian's Medieval Legends*.

I hobbled to the bathroom to splash some water on my face. *Act natural, Emma.*

"Hey, Aunt Christine?" I called, slinging the bag over my shoulder and pulling my winter coat out of the hall closet.

"Yes, dear?" she asked, looking up from the couch where she was watching a rerun of *Cribs* on one of her billion or so channels. "Look at this, who needs a gold toilet?" she clucked disapprovingly.

"Um, yeah. Wait, what?" I asked, momentarily distracted.

"Nothing, dear." Aunt Christine laughed. "Are you leaving already?"

"Yeah, Angelique reminded me about some stuff that I had to get done, and Brendan's an ace with Latin. Me, not so much."

"Okay, Emma. I know you still have a lot to catch up on," she said, nodding. If only she knew just how much.

I kissed her on the cheek and headed out the door, hailing the first cab I saw. A subway would have been faster—and cheaper—but aside from my still-sore ankle, I was afraid to carry this precious cargo around people. I hugged the bag to my chest, looking down at my sweatpants and sneakers with mismatched laces and realizing that I probably should have thrown on jeans or something a little more presentable.

Brendan was waiting in the street for me, paying the cab driver before I could even protest.

"What's this all about?" Brendan asked with a bemused expression, taking the heavy bag from me and sliding it on his shoulders. His still-damp hair hung in his green eyes, which crinkled at the corners with his smile.

"I'll tell you when we're upstairs," I promised as he scooped me up into his arms, insisting on carrying me up the four flights of stairs. Even though I could have made it on my ankle, I didn't argue with him—much.

I hadn't been to Brendan's house since that first time—so I was at first surprised at how, well, messy his room was.

"Yeah, I was going to clean up before you got here," Brendan admitted sheepishly while he still held me in his arms. After a short kiss, he sat me on the end of his bed and surveyed his room, kicking a pair of video game controllers under the couch. He scratched his hair, sending the damp locks in a million different directions. It looked like his hair was fighting with itself.

"It's not bad." I smiled, looking at the disorganized mess and realizing the first time I'd come over, he'd cleaned up to impress me.

"So what's the emergency? Not that I mind getting extra time with you," Brendan asked, sliding his hands around my waist and leaning into me. I started falling back on his bed, losing my senses as usual whenever he kissed me.

"Wait!" I cried, pushing him back. If we started that I'd never get to the great news. I brushed some magazines off his bed and plunked down my backpack from where he'd set it on the floor, pulling down the copy of *Hadrian's Medieval Legends*.

"Is that book *the* book?" Brendan asked, staring in awe at the intricate, hand-carved leather cover. I nodded, flipping through the pages.

"I have to read you something," I said, launching into the text. I felt like my heart was a metronome, beating in time to the poem's rhythm.

When I was done, I looked up at Brendan triumphantly.

"Can we believe that?" he asked tentatively.

"It was right about everything else," I reasoned.

Brendan took the book from me and reread the poem. When he was finished, he stared at me with a dazed expression on his face.

"Don't you get it?" I asked, placing my hand over his as he held the book in his arms. "You were the key! You saved me—you sacrificed yourself to save me."

"It can't be that simple." Brendan shook his head in disbelief.

"Simple?" I snorted. "Yeah, it was *really* simple to escape a psychopath, battle him nearly to the death, then have you take him out, almost dying yourself, and let's not forgot how I had to conjure a spirit, too. Really simple. And I had to go to a school dance."

A slight smile began to touch Brendan's lips, and soon spread across his face.

"So we're okay, and you're safe?" he asked, placing the book on his bed so he could pull me into his arms again. This time, I didn't fight the embrace.

"I think this is one battle we can put behind us," I said, adding, "As long as you always remember to put me first."

"Little witch," Brendan said affectionately, planting a quick, noisy kiss on my cheek.

"I don't have a problem with putting you first," he admitted. "It's a small price to pay, to keep you safe and with me, always."

"Always. I like the sound of that." I sighed, staring deeply into those green eyes that I loved so much. My heartbeats—now that they were no longer numbered—accelerated.

Brendan gently stroked my cheek, cradling my face with his hand while his other arm wrapped around my hip, holding me against him. Then my soul mate pressed his lips to mine. His hands searched my face, as mine did his. I savored the slow, sweet caress, the way his soft kiss felt against my lips, the safe, secure feeling of his strong hands as they moved up my back. Brendan clutched me to his chest, and I held on to him happily, hearing his heart beat against my cheek.

"So, Brendan, does this mean we live happily ever after?"

He smiled at me and kissed my forehead.

"Happily ever after," he agreed. "Or at least, as happily as we can in high school."

Then he touched his lips back to mine.

★ ★ ★ ★ ★

Acknowledgments

Thanks to my ever-supportive husband, Dave Ciancio, for his love and understanding when I disappear into my laptop for hours on end, getting lost in my own little world.

Thanks to my wonderful agent, Lynn Seligman, for her patience and guidance, and to Dr. Elizabeth Stone, for all her invaluable advice through the years.

Thanks to my editor, Tara Gavin, for her enthusiasm and support—and everyone at Harlequin TEEN for helping me realize my dream.

A big thank you to my first readers, Cyndi Lynott, Catharine McNelly, Dawn Yanek, Maggie Mae Mell, Jennifer Urbealis, Angela Nigro and Sandra Tedt for reading the (sometimes horrifyingly awful) early drafts and giving me invaluable feedback.

Thanks to Jonathan Bernstein, Trent Vanegas, Jason Pettigrew, Rachel Hawkins, Lynn Messina and Nancy Holder for the much-appreciated early support!

A gigantic thanks to Mom for all of her encouragement and faith in me through the years. I love you, Mom. And finally, thanks to the rest of my amazing family—Evelyn, George, Auntie, Connie, Ann Marie, Aunt Babe, Jessica, Jodi, Karen and the Ciancios—for everything. The only way my family could be more awesome is if they had jet packs.

The Things I Deal With for Friends

by

Angelique

I left Emma's fabulous aunt's house, deciding that I'd walk back to my home on the West Side. Maybe I'd walk through Central Park—there was a light dusting of snow on the ground, and the park did look pretty in the winter. Picturesque. It was cold enough that there wouldn't be a ton of people around. I had a lot to mull over, and I hated getting on the subway. Too many people—and often, too many emotions to read. For someone like me, sometimes the subway was like being beaten about the head with a sledgehammer. I'd always been able to read auras. It was like a shimmer, a colorful shimmer that surrounded the person, radiating out. The first one I ever saw was green, surrounding my mother when I was very young as she comforted me over the death of my grandmother.

But being around a witch like Emma, with so much untapped potential, had somehow amplified my own abilities. I don't know how—it just did. I was beginning to wonder if I was an empath, someone who could sense other people's emotions. It would jump out at me out of nowhere, these feelings I picked up from others. The last time I was on the subway, I was assaulted by some guy's guilt over cheating on his wife. I left the train a few stops early, unable to control my tears. And I don't cry.

I headed toward Fifth Avenue, telling myself that I shouldn't be surprised that Emma picked running to Brendan's house over working with me on the craft. I hadn't told Emma about my possible empath abilities yet—she'd had enough on her mind—so I wasn't surprised that she opted to go see Brendan. After all, I wasn't that surprised the first time I saw Emma react to Brendan. Everyone reacted to Brendan like that. Well, everyone except me, of course. I saw the attraction. You had to be blind, deaf and dumb not to see it. He was aloof. He was richer than Midas. And I guess he was handsome in that obvious badass sort of way. I got it. I'd seen it, over and over again.

I headed to the Sixty-seventh Street entrance to the park, thinking about the countless times I've seen girls in our class fawning all over him. The ones who were "fortunate" enough to hook up with him didn't get any repeat business—and they were usually devastated by his dismissal. I'd chalked him up to be nothing more than a big slutty player and never thought he was deeper than a thimble of water. After all, he just wasn't my type. When most girls screamed for the lead singer, I checked out the guy working the lights.

But of course it was just my luck that my best friend at Vince Academy—the only person outside of my family that I could talk to about witchcraft and the supernatural—fell for him. And it got worse: she wasn't just a random hookup for him, like every single girl before her was. Oh, no. He was absolutely head over feet for her. They were supernaturally intertwined with each other—soul mates in the truest sense of the word. So that meant Brendan—the epitome of what I couldn't stand about Vince A—was now a part of my life. Whether I liked it or not.

Sigh. It was a travesty!

I reminded myself that I'd resolved to make an effort, for Emma's sake, as I crossed the threshold into Central Park, enjoying the calm quiet of the day. I promised myself that I would be patient when she got that dreamy little look on her face whenever his name was mentioned. And he did save her life, so he had that big ol' checkmark in the plus column. I didn't doubt he'd do it again, a thousand times over. I didn't doubt his love for her. But generally, just sigh! Travesty! Out of all the guys in the world, couldn't her soul mate have been some video-game programmer? Someone with a friend I at least wanted to meet? Or could tolerate?

So I was trying to be patient. But it was hard. Like when I left Emma with a pristine copy of *Hadrian's Medieval Legends*. There were countless tales in that book—and considering that her own supernatural beginnings were found in that book, I'd venture a guess to say most, if not all, were rooted in some kind of truth. But of course, instead of jumping right in to read these legends—or even flip through the *Spells for the New Witch* book I brought her—she just had to go to Brendan's house.

I got it. Well, I was trying to get it, at least. I knew she and he had this crazy intense bond. That they'd spent a thousand years waiting for each other. And that longing only got more intense every time they were reincarnated. And of course, this time they were in the bodies of horny teenagers. I mean, they spent every free moment they could staring at each other with these big swoony eyes that would have made an anime chick jealous. It would have been entertaining to see big badass Brendan Salinger this devoted to someone if it hadn't had to be my friend.

I was desperately trying to not begrudge her happiness. I just wished Emma would take her natural witch duties seriously! And I wasn't just concerned about how her untapped powers were affecting me—there were some pretty scary stories in *Hadrian's*. Someone with the amount of supernatural mojo she was packing would do well to study up on the craft. Same went for Brendan. If I remembered correctly—and with my photographic memory, I did remember correctly, thank you very much—his wealth, his strength, hell, even his looks, were the direct result of that witch's curse. Archer wanted to be reincarnated into Sex on a Stick, after all. So ol' Brendan had some magical little sparkle about him, as well. Clearly, spells worked on him. Instead of playing kissy-face all afternoon, they should have studied up.

As I walked, I stared at a couple strolling along the rolling white grounds of Central Park, stealing a kiss underneath a bare tree. It reminded me of one tale that just shook me to my core, practically beating into my head how crucial it was to be a responsible witch. If *Hadrian's Medieval Legends* really was a Book of Shadows, then we had barely scratched the surface on just how dark some of the magic out there was.

"Love? How can you define love?" Avelina asked, staring into the looking glass as Elizabeth brushed her daughter's long mahogany tresses one hundred times.

"My dear daughter, what prompts that question? Do you think yourself in love?" Elizabeth asked, placing the brush on the vanity in front of her daughter. Elizabeth tried to keep the trepidation out of her voice; she was no fool, having seen the admiring glances from men whenever she and her daughter ventured into town. Elizabeth had always hoped Avelina would find a match in Colin, their neighbor's gentle, loving son—while her husband, Elias, paraded their fair daughter in front of Gilbert, a mousy merchant who had fallen into fortune after a fire destroyed his competitor's shop.

"I only know I've spent many hours talking with Colin and it barely seems like enough time!" Avelina's shoulders slumped with defeat. "Is that love? I think of him so often."

Elizabeth felt pride swell in her chest, but cautiously picked up the hairbrush again. A union with Colin—a kind, hardworking farmer, who would cherish Avelina—was Elizabeth's greatest wish.

"And what of Gilbert?" Elizabeth gently pulled the silver brush through her daughter's silken strands.

"He's not unlike the rats in the cellar!" Avelina declared in her brazen way. "I should think he eats nothing but cheese and other scraps."

Elizabeth thought about admonishing her bold daughter, but realized she had no recourse against the truth.

"My dear, you must never tell your father that," Elizabeth whispered, trying to conceal her amusement by ducking behind Avelina's head. "Gilbert is his dear friend."

"Gilbert steals eggs from the chickens!" Avelina cried, and Elizabeth joined her daughter in laughter.

"So what of Colin, then?" Elizabeth set her hands on Avelina's shoulders, and peered at daughter's reflection in the looking glass, a younger version of Elizabeth's own beauty.

"I do hope he calls on me tomorrow," Avelina replied, her soft hands twisting together wistfully. "He did mention calling on me when he returned from town. I should think I'll wear my blue dress. He has yet to see the blue dress. Perhaps we could go for a walk along the brook."

"That sounds lovely, my dear," Elizabeth said, her joy stretching across her peaceful face in a smile. Elizabeth had married Elias for a comfortable life, and were it not for Avelina, Elizabeth would have regretted the union every moment of her existence. She had hoped Avelina would choose love over wealth, and Colin's mother had clucked that she believed Colin's intentions were to ask Avelina to be his bride.

Elias exhaled slowly, keeping his presence hidden from his wife and daughter as he skulked in the hallway outside of Avelina's room.

This won't do! he thought, angry. His daughter's beauty was his greatest asset; the men in town craved Avelina for their own bride. And his foolish wife was willing to let Avelina go willingly into the arms of Colin, whose means were less than Elias's own!

"What is the purpose of having a fair daughter if I cannot profit?" Elias fumed. Gilbert had offered him a handsome price for his daughter, but Avelina continued to spurn his advances, politely conversing with him but offering him no encouragement. Yet she went for countless walks in the garden with Colin. Oh, that dullard Colin, who only recently found his horse after it broke free during a trip into town. Simple Colin couldn't even manage to secure his steed properly.

"My dear Avelina, your life will be one of ease with Gilbert," Elias argued later that evening. "Do you wish to struggle to stay warm in the winter?"

"If I am cold, I wish my husband be someone I'd want by my side for warmth!" Avelina replied, her insolence earning a swift strike from her father's angry hand. Elias's hands were quite skilled in administering punishment for impertinence, having practiced the art for all of Avelina's young life. Tears in her eyes, Avelina ran from the parlor.

"Husband, why must you force our daughter's hand?" Elizabeth begged, falling to her knees before her husband to plead for her daughter. "Colin is a kind man. I do think she would be happy!"

"Does her happiness make my purse heavy?" Elias sneered, shoving his wife away.

"You cannot force her to marry Gilbert!" Elizabeth got to her feet and faced her husband, fire flashing in her blue eyes. "She'd rather live as a spinster."

After giving Elizabeth a handprint on her cheek to match the red one on their daughter's face, Elias stormed out of their house. He simmered in his rage, bothered that Elizabeth did indeed tell the truth. Elias could no more force Avelina to marry Gilbert than he could force the sun to crash into the moon.

Gilbert had spoken of turning Avelina's heart against Colin. "There are ways," Gilbert had promised her father. "Dark ways, for which you will be handsomely rewarded."

The time has come for desperate tactics, Elias thought, beginning the long walk to Gilbert's manor. He arrived at Gilbert's doorstep in the dead of night. Elias knew the wealthy merchant would be so grateful for the advance notice of Colin's intentions that he'd likely give Elias one of the horses from his own stable to ride back to his house—and keep as his own!

"What is this, are you mad?" Gilbert asked, twitching his long nose and thin, whispery moustache at Elias when he rang the door.

"My dear Gilbert, the time is running short for you to own my Avelina," Elias said, pushing open Gilbert's door. "She will say yes to Colin tomorrow unless we act tonight."

Gilbert peered at Elias, wrinkling his nose again and rubbing his little pink hands together. "Yes, Elias, do come in. We, ah, have much to discuss. Of course, you will be handsomely rewarded for the hand of Avelina."

The scheming men sat in Gilbert's parlor, the flickering light from the fire illuminating the fine drapes and rich furnishings.

This could all be mine, Elias thought, greedily running his hands over the satin couch.

"I've thought that it may come to this," Gilbert squeaked in his high voice, walking to a brass-embellished wooden box. Slipping a small key out of his pocket, Gilbert opened the box, pulling out a thin leather strap and a velvet satchel.

"So shall we threaten Colin? Steal him away from town?" Elias asked, excited by the intrigue of a rich plan.

Gilbert scoffed, wrinkling his long nose in disgust. "My dear Elias, do you think I would meddle with such physical affairs?"

"We shall hire a mercenary then!" Elias cried—but Gilbert, again, just laughed at Elias as he knelt in front of a low table.

"Have you ever pondered my fortune in business?" Gilbert asked, taking a black candle out of the satchel and lighting it. The flames reflected in his dark eyes as his thin lips stretched over his teeth in a smile.

"You're quite intelligent, dear Gilbert," Elias replied, unsure of Gilbert's point.

"That may be true," Gilbert said, grinning that same eerie smile, "but Mr. Fitzpatrick had to shutter his shop when it burned—and I inherited his customers."

Elias spread his hands graciously. "Fortune stepped in, sir."

"Fortune?" Gilbert spat out, taking out a black bowl and a small scrap of paper. "I believe you make your own fortune in this world, sir. I desired his clientele, just as I desire your daughter, so I took the necessary steps."

"Did you pray for God to strike Fitzpatrick's shop with the lightning that set it to burn?" Elias asked.

"Not God." A little giggle escaped Gilbert's lips as he wrote the name "Colin" on the scrap of paper and placed it in the black bowl along with the leather strap.

"What are you doing there, Gilbert?" Elias asked, peering into the bowl.

"Making my own fortune," he answered, holding up the end of the strap. "This is part of that fool Colin's bridle—I stole it! It's why his horse ran off. I wondered if I'd need something of his to prove to Avelina that I'm her match."

Gilbert lowered his head, staring at Elias through his thin lashes. "By tomorrow's eve, Avelina will not desire Colin—and you will no longer want for any mortal delights."

He held out his shiny pink hand and Elias greedily grabbed it.

"Now, repeat after me," Gilbert said, licking his thin lips and holding his other palm outstretched. Elias mirrored his pose.

"Become what your heart fears
Bring anguish upon one you hold dear
Bring her pain! Bring her tears!
Become what she fears!"

A bitter smell reached Elias's nose, and he opened his eyes to see smoke rising from the paper and bridle in the black bowl. The candle's flame grew longer, slithering through the air like a snake.

"I give you vision inside her heart
What will break your bond apart

Destroy her love, release your hold
To you Avelina will turn cold!"

The flame twisted and coiled through the smoke, shooting up through the air with a sudden, violent spike before plummeting into the bowl, which erupted in flames.

Gilbert let go of Elias's hand and raised his palms in triumph over the inferno, throwing his head back and laughing.

"What is this?" Elias demanded, scrambling to his feet to back away from the fire, which exploded in a burst of black-and-blue flames before shrinking into ash with a hiss.

"This is me, deciding my own fate." Gilbert cackled. He again stood at the curious wooden box and pulled out a small bag, the contents of which jangled musically. He casually tossed the bag to Elias.

"The first payment for Avelina," Gilbert said. "By this time tomorrow, she will have no love in her heart for Colin. Bring my bride to me and you'll receive another handsome payment."

Gilbert rubbed his small hands together again. "I'm anxious to begin my honeymoon."

Elias pocketed the bag of coins and, with a brief nod to Gilbert, attempted a hasty exit.

"Elias," Gilbert called, his black eyes glimmering like the dying embers in the fireplace, "you walked here, yes? Take one of my horses…dear Father."

Elias nodded a thank-you and went to Gilbert's stable, his fears over the merchant's penchant for black magic forgotten when he found a prize steed to take as his own. Elias galloped home, his mind clouded with thoughts of rich meals, fine garments and faraway lands.

The next day, Avelina sat in her family's parlor, anxiously

smoothing wrinkles from her best blue dress. Her thoughts turned to Colin, to his intentions. She dreamed of sitting in Colin's parlor, welcoming him home.

"She doesn't seem vexed by Colin," Elias fretted, staring at his daughter. She inspected her slightly red cheek in the looking glass and offered her father a venomous stare.

She does, however, seem vexed by me, Elias thought, pondering if Gilbert's dark machinations had soured.

Colin called on her early, wearing his finest garments. Elias sneered at the rough fabric—*This is not fit to warm my new horse!* he thought—but allowed Avelina to depart with Colin for a walk along the brook.

"I do hope your travels weren't troubled at all," Avelina said when they had reached the banks of the lovely brook babbling below them. They watched the water kiss the stones that lined the bank, and she smiled at how Colin's warm brown eyes appeared almost honey-colored in the sunlight.

"My dear Avelina, I did encounter one unpleasant man—a man I admit to wishing you could meet, only to hear what wonderful commentary you would have offered me," Colin said, smiling. "And my dear, I would endure a thousand more troubles if you were at the end of every journey."

Avelina gasped, realizing Colin was declaring his intentions to her. He took her hands, and she marveled at the tenderness underneath his strong, work-hardened skin. So unlike her father, so unlike Gilbert. Colin was a kind man—just and honest. He was often amused by her brazen statements. He found humor in her impolite comments. He loved all that was Avelina.

So this is love, she thought, smiling at Colin's gentle nature. *This is how you define it.*

"Avelina, I would—" Colin paused, and violently shook, his body trembling and twisting like a small leaf.

"Colin!" Avelina cried as he fell onto the lawn.

She collapsed on her knees next to him, her hands fluttering about him as his face contorted in pain.

Then—calm. Silence. Colin opened his eyes, and Avelina gasped. It was as if the black center of his eyes had overflowed, spilling over the honey-colored and white banks, overtaking his vision.

Colin sprang to his feet with catlike precision and grabbed Avelina's tender jaw.

"Colin! What has come over you?" she cried through her teeth, clenched underneath his strong grasp.

"You will obey me!" Colin ordered in a rough voice—a voice not his own. A voice not the same as the one who had found humor in her statements. A voice not the same as the one who had often asked to call on her. It was a voice that sounded otherworldly…demonic.

"You will mind what you say! You will cater to my desires!" Colin demanded, shaking Avelina again.

She protested, tears overflowing her eyes and spilling down her fair cheeks, until they touched Colin's hand.

"How dare you defile my skin with your worthless tears?" he snarled, and Avelina stepped back, fearing the once-gentle farmer.

"Colin, I beg of you—"

"You will beg! You will beg and plead, you worthless cow!" Colin growled, and Avelina took another step back.

"You will submit to me!" With a final roar, Colin stepped forward, and Avelina retreated again. Her footing faltered on the slick banks, and she fell down—

★ ★ ★

There was indeed a blessing and a curse to my photographic memory. The blessing was, well, studying was a breeze. But the curse…I would never, as long as I live, forget that story. I would never forget the horribly graphic way Hadrian described Avelina's fall, how she crushed her head on the rocks and died. How Colin snapped out of the curse at her death, and later killed himself, sure that he had somehow caused Avelina's demise.

And I would never forget the foolishness of Gilbert, the epitome of magical carelessness. Casual magic was dangerous. It was lethal. Of course Avelina died—just look at the wording he used in his spell. Avelina was, indeed, cold to Colin. She was cold to everyone.

Because she was dead.

I stepped out of the park, glad to be on my side—the West Side—of Manhattan. I fit in less on the Upper East Side than Emma did. I stared back into the park, seeing shadows of people crossing the white grounds. Just a short time ago, Emma was hunted in this park, running, fearing for her life.

"Okay, Emma's been through a lot. Give her a break, Angelique," I told myself. "Give her the weekend to be with—" *Sigh! Travesty!* "—Brendan."

I vowed that we would start working on her own witchy ways on Monday—for her and for me. After all, the girl may have turned me into an empath and summoned a spirit without meaning to—who knew what else she could do?

What's on Brendan & Emma's iPods?

Brendan and Emma are both devoted music fans—Brendan likes to tease Emma that she's a musicologist—and they often retreat into their iPods to find solace. Here are just a few of the songs they've been addicted to.

"Runaway" **Linkin Park**
Emma listens to this song back in Keansburg High, when, ostracized by her classmates and friends, she eats alone in the library.

"Sounds of the City" **Bouncing Souls**
The summer before junior year, Brendan often listens to this song, not aware how prophetic is.

"Carousel" **Blink-182**
When Emma struggles with her attraction to Brendan, she listens to this song on repeat while jogging in Central Park.

"Hurricane" **Something Corporate**
They've never admitted it to each other, but both Brendan and Emma listen to this song after hanging out for the first time at the Met. It captures the thrill—and terror—of being on the precipice of falling hard for someone.

"Stand Inside Your Love" **Smashing Pumpkins**
After Brendan snubs her at school, Emma plays this while running along the East River—before the lights begin exploding.

"My Life Inside Your Heart" **Rise Against**
Brendan is listening to this song when he walks into the quad and sees Anthony threatening Emma.

"Six Feet Under the Stars" **All Time Low**
This song is playing when Brendan decides to take Emma to Belvedere Castle for their first date.

"Miracle" **Paramore**
Emma listens to this song while walking to school alone after she and Brendan spend the afternoon at his house.

"Just Like Heaven" **The Cure**
After they're officially a couple, Brendan listens to this classic while waiting for Emma outside school. He's always liked the song but never quite relates to it until now.

"What It Is to Burn" **Finch**
After visiting his grandfather's house and reading Robert's journals, Brendan is in emotional hell, having a hard time reconciling the curse's inevitable outcome with his pull to Emma.

"Church on Sunday" **Green Day**
When Emma recuperates at home, Brendan finds himself listening to this song every time he visits her.

"The Adventure" **Angels & Airwaves**
After Emma brings *Hadrian's Medieval Legends* to Brendan's house—and they realize they've broken the curse and this adventure, at least, is over—Brendan put his iPod on shuffle and this song appropriately comes on. Another bit of magic?

Download this playlist on iTunes at http://bit.ly/spellbound_playlist

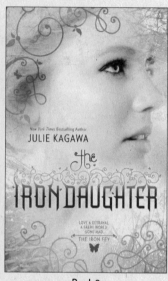

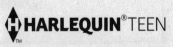

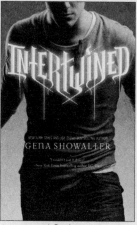
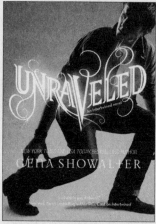
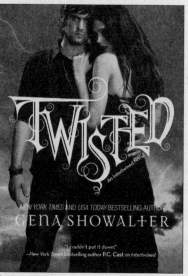
HTGS2010REVTRR

Facebook.com/HarlequinTEEN

Be first to find out about new releases, exciting sweepstakes and special events from Harlequin TEEN.

Get access to exclusive content, excerpts and videos.

Connect with your favorite Harlequin TEEN authors and fellow fans.

All in one place.

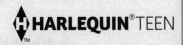

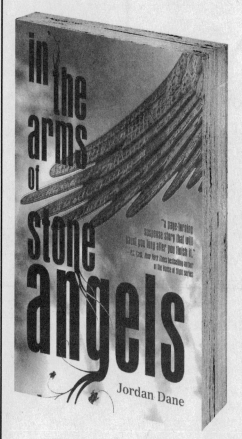